*On the shores of Loch na Keal,
they pledged a dangerous troth . . .*

Taking off her soft doeskin shoes, Brianna let the water splash over her feet. She felt safe here, in her secret haven . . . so she was doubly surprised to see a stranger silhouetted in the trees.

"Don't be afraid." His voice was a low, husky rumble. "I'm no ogre, lass, though I think you must be a water sprite."

He was tall, muscular, handsome. A shiver danced up and down her spine.

The way he spoke proclaimed that he was not from her isle. "Who are ye?" Brianna asked.

"A man who relishes beauty."

For one timeless moment they stared at each other. Without a word, he reached out and traced the shape of her mouth with the tips of his fingers. Brianna held her breath in expectation. His face hovered only inches from her own.

Then all at once it was too late . . .

Most Pocket Books are available at special quantity discounts for bulk purchases for sales promotions, premiums or fund raising. Special books or book excerpts can also be created to fit specific needs.

For details write the office of the Vice President of Special Markets, Pocket Books, 1230 Avenue of the Americas, New York, New York 10020.

Flame Across the Highlands

KATHERINE VICKERY

POCKET BOOKS
New York   London   Toronto   Sydney   Tokyo   Singapore

This book is a work of historical fiction. Names, characters, places and incidents relating to non-historical figures are either the product of the author's imagination or are used fictitiously. Any resemblance of such non-historical incidents, places or figures to actual events or locales or persons, living or dead, is entirely coincidental.

An *Original* Publication of POCKET BOOKS

POCKET BOOKS, a division of Simon & Schuster Inc.
1230 Avenue of the Americas, New York, NY 10020

Copyright © 1990 by Kathryn Kramer
Cover art copyright © 1990 Roger Kastel

All rights reserved, including the right to reproduce this book or portions thereof in any form whatsoever. For information address Pocket Books, 1230 Avenue of the Americas, New York, NY 10020

ISBN: 0-671-67000-X

First Pocket Books printing February 1990

10 9 8 7 6 5 4 3 2 1

POCKET and colophon are registered trademarks of Simon & Schuster Inc.

Printed in the U.S.A.

This story is dedicated to my twin uncles—James Douglas Vickery and John Donald Vickery—one is a scholar, teacher of astronomy and inventor, the other a well-traveled, war-decorated military man and professor of air science. They epitomize not only the kind of men who have added so much to our own century but the bold and daring men of previous centuries as well. This story is for them in token of the MacQuarie blood we share and the many evenings we spent together when I was a child, telling stories and listening to tales of those who came before us.

As always, I thank my mother, Marcia Vickery Hockett for her help on this manuscript. I wish her success in her own writing career as Kathryn Hockett.

A thank-you to Lois Canaday, who has been so generous in loaning me books and magazines from her interesting library of Scottish books, particularly the one on the clans which has been invaluable.

A special thank-you to Alan M. MacQuarrie for sharing his extensive information on Clan MacQuarrie.

And last, but not least, I must mention a woman who, although I never knew her, gave me inspiration for this story. Mary Margaret MacQuarry, my great-grandmother who came from Scotland to the hills of Kentucky and even farther westward to Colorado. Her courage touched my heart.

"Still the blood is strong, the heart is Highland,
And we, in dreams, behold the Hebrides."

A CANADIAN BOAT SONG—COMPOSER ANONYMOUS

Author's Note

Scotland. Land of Robert the Bruce, Robert Burns, Rob Roy, Bonnie Prince Charlie, and Mary, Queen of Scots. Known for tartans, bagpipes and Highland clans. It is a majestic land of islands, mountains, meadowed plains, narrow valleys, and wild moorlands; a land where sea lochs gouge deeply into the shoreline, icy streams tumble through green and wooded glens, and the ever-changing blue of the sky unfolds above like a banner.

During the Dark Ages Scotland, like the rest of Britain, was a melting pot for the roving peoples of Europe—Angles, Picts, and Celts who had sailed from Ireland in the fifth century to settle in the Highlands. They had little in common except the newly learned Christianity and the fear of Norse raids. This fear united Picts and Scots under a single King—Alpin. The clans MacQuarie, MacDonald, MacKinnon, and MacGregor were among the branches of clan Alpin. MacQuarie (Guarai) was second son of Gregor, son of Alpin. Priding themselves in their nobility, they ignored the authority of the English and French-inspired feudal system and continued to fight for their lands and chieftains as their Celtic tradition dictated.

Until 1297, after Alexander III's death and a fight between various claimants to the Scottish throne tore Scotland asunder (culminating in Robert the Bruce coming to power), the MacQuaries were among seven families that held one-third of Scotland. They were in possession of the northwestern mainland and offshore northwestern isles. After that time they were pushed farther west by the Campbells who

Author's Note

claimed the land by charters given to them by Robert the Bruce. The Campbells were granted their lands along with the titles of barons. The MacDonalds and MacQuaries, considering themselves true Scottish lairds, continued to fight the clan Campbell, more often than not ignoring the authority of the newly crowned king, Robert the Bruce.

The clan system was the basis of life in the Highlands. All too frequent among men of untamed independence were clan feuds whose consequences were often tragic. Jealousies, atrocities, and endless raiding of goods, cattle, and women were commonplace. Complete loyalty to the clan chieftain was absolute. A man driven out of his clan lost his identity. Indeed, clan members claimed kinship from a common ancestor whose name they bore. The word *clan* comes from the Gaelic word *clann* which means "children." Clans were first known by the badges worn in their bonnets and in later years by the tartans they wore. People today still wear the tartan of their clan to proclaim their pride in a world and time now past.

The clans lived by the sword and perished by the sword. Warriors were summoned into battle by messengers, carrying a cross of fire-blackened wood, who ran through the territory shouting the clan war cry. Fierce. Frightening. Yet they also had their times of peace and family tranquillity. Each clan chief had his poet or bard to praise him and tell him stories on a long winter night. Gathering together, the men, women, and children would listen to tales of long ago and relish the music of pipes, fiddles, and traditional songs, until the children fell asleep and were carried off to be tucked in their beds.

Sentiment and the primitive virtues of courage, loyalty, and strength mingled in the Highland character. The clansmen considered themselves to be of more noble birth than any Lowlander. It was their great pride which never died, even though in the eighteenth century the clan system was at last rendered powerless. The last embers of the fire-blackened crosses flickered and were extinguished on the field of Culloden in 1746 where the loyal clansmen fought for the return of the Stuart dynasty and the kingship of Bonnie Prince Charlie. The glens which were emptied of

Author's Note

these brave men, however, were filled with the legends, myths, and stories of days long ago. Such a story I would like to tell, one of two lovers who would ne'er be parted. Their unquenchable passion became part of the beauty of the Highlands.

Note: The island of Staffa, later to become known for the strange rock formation of Fingal's Cave which inspired Mendelssohn to write the music for his immortal overture, was at this time owned by the MacQuarie clan. The original name for Fingal's Cave was Gaelic—*An Uamh Ehinn,* or "the musical cave"—and was derived from the sounds of the sea echoing through its depths.

Note: Surnames are the mark of modern clans, but were not in general use in the Highlands before the seventeenth century. For the convenience of the reader and to clarify, however, I have given my characters a surname—Brianna of clan MacQuarie and Ian of clan Campbell. Brianna Nic Lachlan (*Nic* meant "daughter of" Lachlan) and Ian Mac Niall (*Mac* meant "son of" Niall) is how each would have been commonly referred to.

PROLOGUE

Fog, thick and heavy, lay over the horizon. A Highland mist veiled the lochs and glens below like an unearthly shroud, hiding the men who slowly and stealthfully made their way over the land. Only the faint glint of moonlight penetrated the eerie, smokelike veil, dancing on the shields and swords as if to give a warning, a warning that was not detected. Thus unobserved, the armed band pressed on relentlessly, guided by their chieftain.

"We will take them unaware," whispered one husky voice, "we can kill them in their beds."

"Nae, Perth!" A deep rumbling voice was adament. "That is no' my way. When we are upon them I will gi' them fair warning. Duncan Campbell is no coward to cut down unarmed men, no matter what they might hae done. I willna avenge my son in such a manner, by a bloody slaughter. I will meet the MacQuarie clansmen face to face. I will gi' them a chance to arm themselves, though they didna gi' the same to my son Morgan."

The awesome man who answered was a black-bearded, shaggy-haired Scotsman warrior of immense strength and girth, leader of the Campbell clan. His skill in fighting was not to be equaled in all of the Highlands, thus he was feared all the way from the Hebrides to London. The right arm of *the Bruce*. Such a fighter too had been his son, Morgan Campbell. Perhaps that was why a coward had struck him from behind and left him on the hillside to die. His attacker had not been man enough to fight, Duncan Campbell reasoned. There could be no other explanation. Duncan had found his son upon the snowy crags and rocks, his blood seeping into the ground. Though he had taken him back and had his wife and daughters carefully tend the lad, the wound had festered. Slowly it had poisoned the once strong, youthful warrior, stealing his strength as each torturous day passed by.

"Who did this to ye?" Duncan had asked the question over and over but only one mumbled word had passed the young man's lips. *MacQuarie!* A name that had long harried the clansman's soul. MacQuarie. Now they would pay for their treachery.

The MacQuaries had long been Duncan's adversaries. Traitorous curs that they were, they refused to bow their heads to the king. They had the effrontery to claim themselves as royal descendants from a long-ago king. A quarrel over land had started the feuding, land granted to the Campbells in reward for fealty but claimed by the MacQuaries. The MacQuaries insisted the land granted to Duncan's clan as being *their* land, though Duncan angrily disputed such reasoning. It was true that the MacQuarie clansmen had settled on the land for hundreds of years, but they held no written parchment from the king to assert their right. And they were yet to harken to the Bruce's banner to reap reward. Thus the last five years had been particularly volatile. But that was not why the Campbells were marching now. Indeed, it was because of Morgan's death. The MacQuaries would pay dearly, Duncan vowed.

Hatred scorched Duncan's heart, corroding his mind, his soul, making him blind to reason or mercy. He had summoned the clan to the rallying ground with the fiery cross, shouting his hostile war cry. Now, like a swarm of raging ants, the Campbells climbed the hill and marched across the boggy meadow, crossing to the MacQuarie land which bordered their own. In their bonnets they wore a sprig of fur club moss to tell any who might wonder that they were a mighty clan, the Campbells!

"Now. Gi' them a sound to strike terror into their hearts.

The bagpipes, mon! The drums!" His voice was like thunder. Hurriedly the warriors harkened to obey his order.

It was a droning, pounding, fiercesome sound, making no secret of the marchers' intent. Had there been any misunderstanding, the bloodcurdling war cry that sliced through the night soon announced what was to come.

The sound of pipes and drums did indeed carry across the glen, as it was meant to do. It alerted a small group of men that their land was being invaded. Scrutinizing eyes stared through the fog at the threatening band, examining the garments they wore—the *leine-chroich,* the green tint of the *breacan,* and light woolen coverings worn up to the knee. Friend or foe? As the army marched closer the fluttering banners of black and tan proclaimed the identity of the approaching men.

"The Campbells!" cried out a voice. "They've crossed Loch Tuath. They're coming this way!"

"How many?" Lachlan MacQuarie, a ruddy-faced, red-haired man shouted out the question, knowing well the seriousness of the matter. It was a disaster to be taken unaware. On such short notice the MacQuaries could only assemble a small group of clansmen, and he felt a sudden certainty that they would be outnumbered. The Campbells always swarmed in large numbers. "How many?" he bellowed again.

Cautiously, the man at his side surveyed the scene from the parapet. "From here I count at least *forty!*"

Forty warriors it was indeed. They came in a grumbling, growling wave of ferocity that had yet to be equaled. Swarming across the land, swords slashing, axes swinging, shields clanking, dirks striking out, they quickly swept any obstacle from their path in a vicious carnage of destruction. The MacQuarie men came bravely to meet them for it could not be said that Lachlan MacQuarie was a coward, nor any of his brethren. Desperately they stood in defense of their lands, their homes.

The battle was bloodily brief. The Campbells waged a

relentless battle. Having substantially outnumbered their opponents, the outcome was one-sided and predetermined against the MacQuarie men, though they made a most noble attempt that even Duncan had to respect. When at last the long blue shadows lay across the land and the fight had ended, however, the MacQuarie fighters were thoroughly conquered. The glen was strewn with wounded and those who would never rise again.

"And so we have won, Duncan. Ye canna ask for more!" whispered a raspy-voiced man beside the chieftain.

"I can, Cameron, and I will!" Pulling at his dark beard, Duncan Campbell smiled triumphantly, a menacing grin that sent shivers up the other man's spine. "My revenge is not yet complete. The desire for it sours my belly and canna be quenched!" So saying, he gestured for Cameron to follow him to the now defenseless castle. There he braced his muscled arm against the door, shoving with all his might until the wood shattered in a splintering crash. Explosively the barrier was cast aside.

Emboldened by his victory he brazenly entered the hall, wandering from room to room, coming upon a chamber filled with the clan's women. There seemed to be no men about to guard them. The men were all on the battlefield.

Seeing Duncan enter, the women reacted with the wailing, piercing shrieks of a banshee as they dispersed. Scattering, they ran to and fro, fleeing the chamber in panic for their lives. When at last the room was in silence, Duncan and Cameron cautiously looked around, lest they be taken unaware. They had no desire to be ambushed by a swordsman hiding in a corner.

"Hmmmph. I see no men. Proceed, Cameron."

The only light came from the embers of the hearth, but the reflection was bright enough to illuminate the tortured expression of the woman who lay on the bed. MacQuarie's wife? Duncan did not know for certain, but made that assumption from the grandeur of the room. The chamber was large, but cluttered with all manner of objects—tables, stools, chests, benches, and a large bed. One basket held the freshly unswaddled form of two female babies, crying now that their reverie had been disturbed. Duncan Campbell moved forward for a closer view.

"Go away! Ye dinna hae reason to be here. How dare ye enter the laird's chamber." An old toothless woman, dressed in dark brown, stood at the bedside. Coming out of the shadows, she blocked the woman who lay upon the blankets from view with fierce protectiveness. "Lachlan MacQuarie will hae yer heads for this!"

"As he did my son's life?" Duncan's voice trembled with fury. He took another step. "Is this then *his* wife?"

"Aye!" Speaking hastily, the old woman regretted her outburst as she saw the wicked gleam in the dark-haired man's eyes.

"Then stand aside, ye old harridan!" With a mumbled growl he flung her out of his way, intending to take with him the woman who lay upon the bed. He would take MacQuarie's wife. Abduct her! Crouching down, he touched that woman, but the contorted expression on her face halted him.

"A baby! Another bairn! It is coming, Cara!" Mac-Quarie's wife gasped her pain as the baby's head forced its way through the already traveled passage.

In anger and awe Duncan and Cameron witnessed the birth of a third child. Triplets! An unsettling omen. Watching as the midwife cut and tied the chord, Duncan pushed forward to see the sex of the child. A *son!* MacQuarie's heir. In that moment he knew well what he would do. He would take MacQuarie's son in payment for his own. Was it not written, an eye for an eye, a tooth for a tooth? Was it not right that he be repaid? Was it not fair? A child for a child. A son for a son.

"Gi' me the babe, old woman!" Before she could deny his request he swooped the newly birthed child from her hands.

"Och! No! Ye canna touch him. Filthy Campbell hands will foul this wee bairn!" With gnarled hands she tried most valiantly to retrieve the babe, but when she could not she yelled, "Curses! Curses on ye! Ye will be damned for all eternity if ye do this thing! I swear that ye will!" Her shrieking epithets only sealed her doom. Duncan Campbell moved forward, angered by her shouting.

"Silence, witch!" In anger he brutally lashed out.

Mouth agape, eyes staring, hands and arms in a position to ward off his blows, she engaged in a scuffle, but was easily subdued. Even so, she fought on like a wild animal to protect the child. Once again Duncan pushed her aside. She fell to the ground, striking her head on the stone of the hearth and spoke no more. Her outrage was quieted.

"What hae ye done? Ye've killed her, Duncan. A woman. 'Tis no' our way." Bending down beside the old woman, Cameron soon found his words to be true. The midwife would breathe no more the air of mortal life. She *was* dead!

Duncan reacted quickly. "Take the bairn, wrap it in swaddling and come with me! Hurry! Before it is known what we hae done and we are intercepted. I hae plans for the babe."

Cameron shook his head. "Nae, ye canna think to take the bairn! Ye canna, Duncan. Ye canna! The child has done ye no wrong. We hae never waged war on children before. Ye canna take him from his mother."

"I can and I *will!*" Ignoring Cameron's outcries, Duncan Campbell did indeed steal Lachlan MacQuarie's heir, saving his ultimate vengeance for another day to come. Through the mists that had spawned them, the men left the MacQuarie land to return to their own.

"My child! My bairn!" Opening her eyes, Iona MacQuarie realized what had happened but was too weak to follow in pursuit, though she tried. All she could do was cry, a heart-rending wail that echoed across the rolling hills, reverberating through the night like the keening of a bagpipe. The sound of a broken heart.

PART I

THE HIGHLAND TWINS

The Isle of Ulva
Fourteenth-century Scotland

All who joy would win
Must share it,—happiness was born a twin.
—LORD BYRON
    DON JUAN, CANTO 1, STANZA 22

CHAPTER ONE

The first flowers of spring covered the Highland meadow, filling the cool morning air with their fragrance as the wind blew across the glen. The harsh winter fog which always covered the land like a low-flying cloud had now faded, leaving the sky clear and blue. Overhead the early morning sun spread its warmth, shining down upon the two seventeen-year-old girls who lay upon their backs, squinting their eyes against its glare. Such a perfect spring day was rare, and they both were of the mind to take advantage of it.

"'Tis strange to think of how many MacQuaries have looked up at the sky from this same spot upon the heather, is it not, Glenna?"

"How many do ye suppose?" Glenna asked, stretching, then settling herself more comfortably upon the thick, purplish pink carpet of flowers.

"I dinna ken exactly. Hundreds, I would say, and all at odds with the Campbells, I would imagine. How bothersome. Men and their constant warfare. When will it all stop?" Rolling over on her stomach, Brianna, the more adventuresome of the twins, looked toward the wild sea lochs that gouged deeply into the land and breathed a sigh. This land, Mull and the island of Staffa that she could see in the distance, had been inhabited by the MacQuarie clan for hundreds of years, or so it seemed from the tales the *seanachaidh* revealed. To the east were the lands of the MacLeods who marauded the countryside with their savage bands, to the south were the Campbells, seemingly encroaching closer and closer. MacQuaries and Campbells had been at odds over land possession and other things for as long as the girls could remember.

They had been told often enough of the fiercesome battle the night they had been born. That same night their mother had lost touch with reality. Now that poor tortured woman was dead and resting in peace in her grave but the story and memory of her ravings haunted Brianna still. Rantings of a child being stolen from her arms by the very devil.

Perhaps it was their father's determination to have a male heir that had caused her mother's insanity. The poor woman had always insisted until her dying day that there had been another child born the night of Glenna's and Brianna's birth. A male child, a *son*. Lachlan had questioned the women about the birth and they had insisted two children and two alone had been birthed. Thus, he had humored his wife's outbursts, certain that childbed fever had brought about her mumblings. There had been a stillborn child, then two more daughters, Morgana and Orianna, had been born to her father and mother, but never a son. At last Iona MacQuarie had dwindled into ill health and died when the twins were seven years old, leaving Lachlan a lonely and heartbroken man. Was it any wonder that Brianna had tried to soothe his pain, had tried to make him proud of her? He needed no male child, he had her, and she was as bold, as spirited, and as daring as any son Lachlan MacQuarie might have had.

"Aye, I'll agree that men can be troublesome, but they can be wonderful too!" Glenna's voice had such a strange, whispery tone that Brianna looked at her twin with a start, staring into wide brown eyes so like her own. The two young women were in fact identical to each other. So much alike that even their father could not tell them apart, that is, when he saw them alone. When they stood side by side it was a far different matter, for Brianna's eyes were a bit larger, her nose a wee mite shorter, her fiery tresses just a half-shade darker than Glenna's. Glenna was the gentle one, the shy one who had always relied upon her sister for guidance. Brianna, her feisty twin, was the brave sister who had always taken the lead in everything.

"Men can be wonderful, ye say?" Brianna cocked a well-arched brow. "What is it, Glenna? Ye sound so . . ."

"I'm in love." Glenna smiled sheepishly. It seemed she had been the first to fall in love. "And it is a wondrous feeling!"

"Love?" The very thought disgusted Brianna. Love was nonsense! A woman's wishful prattling. Still she asked, "With who?"

"With Alastair. But ye must not breathe a word."

"Alastair. The bard?" Though she thought men to be a quarrelsome lot, oversure of their cunning and prowess, she had to agree that Glenna had picked a handsome young man to moon about. Tall, blond, and well-formed of feature the bard was pleasing to the eyes, though a bit too poetic for Brianna's taste. His long-fingered hands had not a trace of a swordsman's callus and his baritone voice was soothing but did not stir any feelings in Brianna's heart. She was glad of that now for in all ways she thought the union of her sister and the bard to be a perfect match. Both were gentle, both held a love for music and laughter. Both Alastair and her sister flitted too often into their fantasy worlds. Brianna was a realist.

"Aye, the bard." Glenna blushed, the dark pink covering her cheeks and nose. "And I hope he has set his eyes upon me too. Oh, he is such a handsome laddie." Hugging her arms about her knees, she sat up and looked at Brianna. The faraway look in her eyes told her sister that she had taken flight once again to the land of dreams. Reaching down Glenna plucked a flower from the ground and tucked it behind her ear, then gathered more of them as if for a wedding bouquet. "Aye, Alastair. Alastair, I will take thee unto my husband."

Standing stark still as if in the midst of a trance she smiled as the wild wind whipped the long tresses about her shoulders. Only the sharp prick of her sister's well-aimed pebble brought her back down to earth. With a shy smile she turned her head to look at Brianna, who flashed her a mischievous grin.

"I didna want ye soaring away lest ye become a prisoner of the sea-fairies. They come upon wee lassies when they do not pay attention to their sisters and instead look like lovesick goslings."

Glenna looked contrite. "I'm sorry, Brianna, but he is on my mind all the time. I canna even sleep without seeing his face. I wish ye could find a man to love, then ye would know how grand it feels."

"Love? *Gorach!* I have no need for such foolishness. Men. Ha, they are all the same." She snorted in derision.

"But someday Father will want ye to wed. We must carry on the MacQuarie line. Ye must find a man to take on our proud clan name. Would ye not rather it be someone ye love?" Glenna was shocked by her sister's attitude and greatly saddened. She wanted Brianna to be happy, too. "Is there no one special?"

Brianna tossed her head, sending her hair flying in a whirl of dark-tinted flame. "No. One man would be as good as another, providing he be pleasant to look upon and swears he willna beat me. I could well be a match for any of the men around here."

"But dinna ye long for moonlit kisses that set ye to tingling all over?" Thinly arched brows shot up in question.

"Nae!" Brianna was certain of the answer. She'd ne'er make a fool of herself over any man. Malcolm, Erskin, Jamie, they were interesting to talk with, to spar with, but she had learned to keep an arm's length away from them. When they were in their cups they too often set their hands to wandering. "I dinna care for kisses. The magic wears off soon enough, I would wager. Marriage is but a settlement, to impoverish the lassie's father and make of the groom a wealthy man." Her grim-faced statement was met by giggles of laughter. For a moment all thought of weddings and midnight trysts was forgotten as both young women gloried in the beauty of the day.

The early morning chirping of the birds filled the meadows with music. Brianna contented herself with listening to the sound. Truly it was more beautiful than Alastair's plucking and tooting, though she dared not reveal her opinion to Glenna. Instead she allowed her thoughts to ponder if peace would ever come to the Highlands. She thought not, for surely men seemed stubborn in their pride and driven to quarreling and fighting.

It had been thus since ancient days when the greater part of Scotland had been divided into large tribal districts, seven in number, corresponding to the territorial divisions of the country in ancient Pictish times. Ambition had fueled quarrels that had not ended even with the lands uniting under one Scottish king. Indeed, it had only added to the confusion. That the *Lowlanders* took control of the crown and bowed to English ways only added to the turmoil.

Brianna had heard the story from her father of how King Malcolm Ceanmore had changed Alba over two hundred years ago, moving his capital to Dunfermline. The Celtic system of tanistry was discarded in favor of Saxon feudalism, all because of the influence of his second wife, a granddaughter of the King of England. The King had even encouraged the coming into Alba of a large number of Saxon and Norman nobles from England to whom he made feudal grants. At court the discontinuance of Gaelic as the court language and the substitution of Roman Catholic practices for those practiced by the Celtic church only widened the gap.

Since that time her clan had sworn its allegiance to the MacQuarie laird instead of the King, and to Angus MacDonald and the Lords of the Isles. The only exception having been when her great-grandfather, Cormac Mor, joined Alexander II in chasing the Norsemen from the isles. Since then a series of rebellions had kept Alba from being united into the Kingdom of Scotland the people desired.

When the Lord of the Isles was defeated at Renfrew, bringing Galloway under control of the Crown, it was a loss her father mourned. Now Lachlan mocked Robert the Bruce, saying he was not a man worthy of the honor of king. Still, he and Eachuin, his brother, had fought in the army at Bannockburn on the side of the Bruce, just to insure Scotland would not become England's vassal again. Her father had fought for pride in the ancient independence of Alba and for his king.

Now, however, Lachlan resisted the Bruce's authority, yet again, clinging to the old ways. His only hope was that someday a man would come along who was worthy and who would unite all of Scotland, leading them totally away from English influence. Certainly such had not been the case since the death of Alexander III. John Balliol, who proceeded the Bruce, had turned out to be a puppet to England, a lamb among wolves. Bruce, on the other hand, had proved himself capable of being ruthless. Her father wanted the Highlands to remain strong and free of the Bruce's influence and he wanted eventual peace. That was her hope too. Until then there would be war, war, and more war. It made her head swim just to contemplate it. And the feud with the Campbells only made life all the more miserable.

"Certainly those Campbells are bothersome," she exclaimed. They'd been a constant source of trouble for her father. It seemed they instigated one argument after another. As leader, *ceann-cinnidh,* of the MacQuaries he led the fighting, causing Brianna to worry lest something happen to him. Under the ancient patriarchal system the land belonged to the clan. They worked and fought together, giving allegiance to the laird in time of peace as well as war. Sometimes a sept or a branch of another clan, too small to protect itself against surrounding clans, entered into a treaty with a neighboring clan for protection, thus there was always fighting.

Indeed the clan was perhaps the most important thing in their lives. A man's very being, his identity, was permanently bound to the clan. To be driven out, to face exile was to lose all sense of self-worth. A man alone was as isolated as the island Brianna looked upon again—*Staffa*. Turning her eyes toward the sea, she watched as the foaming waves hit its rocky shore and basalt cliffs with noisy fury. Only the din of bagpipes jarred her from her thinking. The pipes, summoning everyone to gather. The sound was unnerving. Shattering.

"What is it? What can have happened?" Glenna voiced her fear. She could not help but wonder if another clash of shields and swords was about to ensue. How many men would be killed or wounded this time? It was a sobering thought and one which filled her with apprehension for Alastair. During any battle he walked beside the pipers and there was always the danger of a wayward dirk or sword harming him. "Oh, Brianna!" Glenna clutched at her sister's hand.

"It willna do us any good to be afraid." Putting her arm protectively about her sister's shoulder, Brianna pretended a bravery she did not really feel. She was just as worried by the sound as Glenna only she would not allow herself to show it. Instead she whispered sternly, "Come back with me to the hall!" Pulling Glenna by the hand, she led the way over the well-worn pathway.

Total pandemonium greeted the twins as they pushed through the heavy wooden door of the large stone hall. Ominously, the MacQuarie clan were preparing themselves for the imminent danger they thought was to come. Brandishing their weapons, which reflected the flames ablaze in the hearth, they grumbled in anger as they waited for their chief, Lachlan MacQuarie, to enter the hall.

Brianna's eyes darted back and forth, searching for the familiar form of her father. Where was he? As if her anxiety conjured him up, he soon pushed through the door of the adjoining room he used as a council chamber. His face was contorted in puzzlement but not outrage. Pulling at his beard he strode back and forth before the fire, muttering beneath his breath.

Her heart went out to him for she realized the responsibility he bore, to govern the clan territory for the benefit of the clan. He administered justice in times of peace and led the warriors in time of war. As chief he was responsible for the good of his people who on their part gave every assistance to him for the mutual good of all members of the clan.

Pridefully, Brianna looked at this tall, big-boned giant of a man with flaming red hair. Despite his forty-five years he was ruggedly handsome. Only one scar along the right side of his face marred his facial features. Now that scar twitched as he furled his craggy brows. She gazed upon her father's face trying to discern his thoughts.

"What is it, Father?" Only Brianna dared ask the question that all within the room wondered.

"I've just received a message from Black Duncan. He calls for a truce between the clans. I dinna ken what to make of it!"

"A truce?" A ripple of uneasiness swept throughout the hall. It had long been proved that the Campbells were not to be trusted. What wickedness had they planned this time? The mood of the assembled men changed swiftly from apprehension to suspicion.

"The lookouts warned of approaching horsemen but when I rode out with Malcolm and Erskin to see wi' me own eyes, I found it to be but a lone rider. A messenger with a most surprising missive. 'Tis a most unusual proposition and one that I canna think upon lightly." Lachlan paused and in that moment he met Brianna eye to eye. "The Campbell has suggested that his heir, Robbie, should marry one of my daughters!"

"Och!" All watching eyes widened in startled surprise.

"Nae!" The men were unanimous in their shout.

"Ye musna even think of it!" The women echoed each other.

Anger buzzed around from man to man like an enraged bee as the clansmen savored this bit of information. "The *Campbell* heir. Ha! He isna good enough for a MacQuarie! We are descended from kings, not English vassals."

"For all we ken, it's a trick and they be plannin' to attack us again. I lost two sons seventeen years ago and a nephew last December." The boldest of the men stood up as he spoke, venting his anger.

"The word of a Campbell is worthless!" Another followed, then another. Total turmoil raged.

Lachlan MacQuarie silenced the protestations by raising his hand. Though in truth he was but a few inches taller than most of the men, he seemed to tower over them as he pulled back his shoulders and held up his hand. "I've told myself all the things ye are sayin' now. I've scorned the Campbells and damned them with my every breath. I've even told myself that Black Duncan was but jesting. But now I think not. There comes a time in every mon's life when he longs for peace." He had come to that time.

"Peace with the Campbells? Never!" cried out a voice.

"They started the feuding and we canna just forget it. Too many men hae been killed!" Another man would not be silenced.

"Aye, too many men. That is my thought exactly." Through the years there had been times when the MacQuaries had won, times when the Campbells had been victors in the battles, but at the cost of many lives. Both clans had been losers in the toll taken on their families. Warfare between the rival clans had brought forth a torrent of heartache. Lachlan knew it was in their best interest to contemplate this offer of peace. And yet what a price he would have to pay! To give up one of his daughters. "We canna go on fighting forever. If a matter of such a marriage can stop the bloodshed, then I am prepared to make the sacrifice."

"What?" Brianna was aghast at the thought and made her view known by her audible, "no!" A MacQuarie married to a Campbell was unthinkable.

"Aye!" Lachlan looked at his two eldest daughters with an appraising eye. Both possessed a beauty no man could resist. Their finely chiseled noses, high cheekbones and enormous dark-fringed brown eyes of a copper hue were beyond description. Their slender waists and long legs were no doubt the envy of all the women, their well-formed breasts and slim hips were a poet's dream.

They were dressed in identical *arasaids,* a long garment that reached from the head or neck, to the ankles, fastened at the breast with a large brooch and at the waist by a belt. Beneath this colorful length of material they wore gowns of thin wool which clung to their gentle curves. They were so alike, very lovely, and made him very proud. Heaven help any men if they dared to mistreat his daughters.

"Bonnie! Bonnie daughters that I hae. No doubt the Campbells hae heard and that's why they seek to make such a bargain." He strode round and round the two young women.

"But ye didna! Ye willna!" Once again Brianna voiced her thoughts aloud.

"I must!" Lachlan looked from one to the other, noting that while Glenna's *arasaid* was carefully belted, Brianna's was haphazardly tied. A smudge of dirt at the tip of her nose made her discernible from her twin. Brianna was the least manageable one and yet even so, it was Brianna that had always been his favorite because of her spirit. He could not even think of sending her away. Glenna then. He would send the gentle twin. She would do as he bid without argument and make the young Campbell a docile wife.

The matter was discussed among the clansmen, for Lachlan was not a man to make such a weighty decision alone. Though it was to be his daughter that sealed the bargain, what was decided today would affect all the members of the clan. Though there were quite a few mumblings, voiced words of disquiet, the others at last approved of the marriage, convinced by Lachlan's arguments.

"But which one?" Malcolm raised the question.

"I hae decided on Glenna." Lachlan's answer thundered through the room. All eyes looked that young woman's way as she paled.

"No! No!" Glenna's breathless protestation was accompanied by her tears. She loved Alastair. Her father could not even think to send her away! She felt cold, couldn't breathe. It was as if a forceful blow had winded her.

"Aye, daughter. It will be as *I* say." Lachlan had not expected argument from Glenna. "A daughter has been asked for and a daughter I will offer up this day." Folding his arms across his chest he gave proof that he would brook no defiance.

"No! No!" The trembling girl collapsed in a flood of tears.

Brianna's heart ached for her and she knew in that moment she could not allow her sister's unhappiness. Having heard from Glenna's own lips of her love for the blond bard, Brianna stepped forward to shield her sister from their father's wrath, standing in between them.

"Then 'tis a daughter the Campbells shall have, but her name will be Brianna and not Glenna!" It was an act of protectiveness, just as she had always instigated when there was trouble to be dealt with. "Glenna is gentle. She will never fare well amongst a fiercesome clan that is not her own. She needs love and security." She tried hard to smile though her hands trembled and a large lump had suddenly arisen in her throat.

"*Ye?*" Lachlan was astounded, never expecting such a development.

She tried to make light of the situation. "I'll give the Campbells more than they bargained for!"

"Aye, that ye will, lassie." From across the room Erskin was quick to agree, grinning wickedly. He remembered the punch to the ribs she had granted him when he had wanted naught but a kiss. "Much more."

"Dinna be hasty now . . ." Lachlan's expression pleaded with her silently to change her mind. "If ye say that ye'll marry the laddie, there will be no turning back!"

"I know."

"Think, daughter . . ."

Brianna cast a sideways glance at Glenna, saw the frightened look that was still in her sister's eyes and in that moment made an unwavering decision. "I'll marry Robbie Campbell. I hae no other choice." She had acted on impulse because of her love for Glenna and now she would have to keep her word.

CHAPTER TWO

Glittering beams of sunlight streaked through the gray of early morning, giving light to the hall where Brianna prowled about. She had spent a sleepless night tossing and turning, going over in her mind the impulsive, impetuous thing that she had done. In but a moment, with only a few words, she had consigned herself to marriage, had made the bargain which would take her from this hall and the people she so dearly loved. In but a few weeks time she would leave family, friends, and this beloved Island of Ulva to live among a clan that had been an enemy to her own people since long before she was born. Dear God, what could have possessed her? What bewitchment had caused her to be so foolishly bold?

Her eyes flitted about the room as if to brand a permanent image in her mind for the days ahead when she would be far away from here. Memories. So many memories. Down the center of the hall was a long hearth over which big pots from the evening's meal were still placed. How many stories of fairies, water beasts, witches, and ghosts had she listened to in front of the evening fire? Though her family was Christian they knew that their lives would always be ruled by older beliefs too, knew that other beings occupied Ulva and Mull as surely as did those of flesh and blood. As a child she had listened in awe to such stories and tales of long ago.

Before this same hearth she had blissfully enjoyed the music from fiddle, harp and pipes, riotous songs or soothing songs of reverie that had at last lulled her to sleep. Somehow she had always awakened to find herself in her bed, thinking perhaps the fairies had bewitched her and brought her to her room. Now in her adult years she knew it had been her father who had carried her off to bed, holding her tenderly and lovingly within the strength of his arms. Now she would be leaving the protection of those arms for a husband's embrace. A husband. How strange that sounded. Just yesterday she had laughingly talked with Glenna about such a thing, had voiced her adamant opposition to any suggestion of marriage. How quickly one's fate could change.

A loom and several spindle whorls for spinning wool stood against the farthest wall and Brianna curled her mouth in a bittersweet smile as she recalled how often she had rebelled at joining the women for their daily chores. Cooking, weaving, and sewing bored her. Washing with the harsh lye soap seemed a thankless task. Waulking, or hand shrinking woolen cloth, was a long and laborious process which she had no fondness for. In truth, she had scorned woman's work, finding a dozen reasons for avoiding tasks anytime she could. But now, oh, what she wouldn't give to be able to stay among these women instead of women she would not even know. And Glenna, sweet Glenna. They had shared such closeness, had been like the two halves of a whole. Now they would be parted, never more to enjoy maidenly prattle.

"And yet I dinna believe I could hae done any less than I did," she whispered aloud. As difficult as it would be to face this new life that beckoned, it would have been all the more impossible to live with herself knowing of Glenna's pain. Knowing of the love Glenna would have had to sacrifice.

"No, ye couldna done anything else. Not my braw lassie."
Hearing her father's voice from out of the shadows, Brianna

turned around, knowing by the tortured look in his eye that Lachlan MacQuarie was suffering even more than she. "Oh, lassie! Lassie!"

As if she were but a child again, Brianna flew to his arms, furiously dashing tears away with her hand as quickly as they filled her eyes. Lachlan's eyes were misted too, yet he held his emotions under control. He would not let his daughter see him shed unmanly tears.

"I hae half a mind to tell Cambell *no.*"

"Father, ye can't. Ye canna go against yer word nor can I go against mine. What was said was said, what was done has been done. Let us hope that some good will come of it. If there will be peace then it is worth the price." Pulling away she feigned a bravery she most certainly did not feel. "Besides, 'tis adventure I hae always craved. To see a side of Mull I've never seen before, the Campbell's territory. Perhaps I'll even be fortunate enough to see Duart Castle, at least from afar." Once owned by the MacDonalds, that massive fortress was now in MacLean hands since they had taken supremacy of the region. It was far grander than Aros Castle which belonged to the MacQuarie clan. Duart Castle had inspired more than a story or two. "And as to this Robbie Campbell, how ferocious can he really be? Am I not a match for any man?"

"Aye, lass, that you are! You've always been close to my heart because of your spirit and daring. You've soothed my longing to have a male heir, for no son could please me any better than ye!" Holding her at arm's length, he looked into her eyes.

"I wish . . . that I could stay here forever," she breathed.

"As do I." Taking her hand, he led her toward one of the large wooden benches lined against the wall and sat her down beside him. "It's just selfish that I am, Brianna. I've always hoped to keep ye near me. Ye are the one who always makes me smile." He sighed, for just a moment letting down all his defenses, all semblance to his puffed-up, manly pride. Only Brianna was ever allowed to look into his heart, to share his joy, to feel his sadness. "So many of those dear to me have been taken in one manner or another. Two of my womenfolk . . ."

"You're thinking of Mother and Aunt Mary." Resting her head against his shoulder she closed her eyes, remembering.

"Aye. Your Aunt Mary, my youngest and favorite sister, vanished without a trace. Though we searched both islands, looked high and low, not even a hair of her head was to be found. Bewitched, some said. Carried off by those spirits who lay in wait to capture unsuspecting souls." Brianna had heard the story several times before. It had long been supposed that her aunt Mary had drowned. Two fishermen had seen her walking along the shore, looking out to the sea as if it somehow drew her. They were the last living mortals to look upon the young woman. She had never been seen or heard from again. Had she jumped into the ocean's depths or had an unseen hand reached out to take her captive? An unsettling thought. "And your mother's death . . ."

"It was not your fault."

"Aye, but it was. I hounded that poor woman like a savage beastie, always with the thought in mind of having a son. Is it any wonder that the poor woman lost her mind? Always chattering about her other child, she was. Always insisting she had born me a male bairn. My fault for going on and on about bringing forth a son to pass on my chieftain's feathers to. Poor tortured soul. She wanted a boy bairn so badly to please me that it confused her reasoning."

"It wasna yer fault, but our ways which make a son so important," Brianna said with a slight curl of her lower lip. To the clan a successor or tanist was of utmost importance. That successor was always a male. Her father had been his grandfather's tanist and had succeeded as chief when the elder MacQuarie had died. The clan organization consisted of the chief, the tanist, the chieftains, the captain, the *daoin'-uaisle* and the general body of the clan. So far, being without a male heir, her father had not chosen a successor, which made the matter of *all* his daughters' marriages of utmost importance. Oh, if only she had been a son, Brianna thought, perhaps her mother would not have succumbed to he madness.

"Our ways and my all-consuming pride. I didna gi' her the understanding that she deserved and so God at last took her away. Ten long years I've lived without her. But you've soothed my heartache, lass. You and yer sisters. Now I'm going to lose *ye*."

"You'll never lose me, Father." Reaching for his hand, she squeezed it reassuringly. "Wherever I may be ye will be in my heart and in my thoughts. And I willna hae ye worry. The Campbells dinna intend to harm me."

"They dare not!" He clenched his fists in anger. "If a one of them causes ye pain, they will rue it." He might have said more but for the intrusion of the other men and women entering the hall, rustling about as they made ready for the morning meal. So many people.

The clan consisted of *native men* and *broken men*. The native men being those related to the chief and to each other by blood ties. This blood relationship was an important fundamental in the clan system, all being bound together in a common interest. The clan also contained branches composed of clansmen who had become powerful or prominent in some way and who had founded families almost as important as that of the chief. The broken men were individuals or groups from other clans who had sought and obtained the protection of the clan. That the clan kept increasing in size was a testimony to her father's fairness and good name. Aye, how very proud she was that her father was the man who led the MacQuaries.

The smell of the bubbling cauldrons of oats and barley filled the air. The clan system recognized that land, the basis of life, was not an individual possession, but belonged to the people in common, and that every clansman was duty bound to assist other members of the clan in time of necessity of any kind, irrespective of his rank. Thus, though Lachlan's daughters were related to the chief they still were required to do their part in the work. Brianna took her place beside Glenna to stir the steaming pots.

"I've not had time to thank ye for what ye did." Glenna's eyes held appreciation and more than a hint of respect. "You're much braver than I. Had it been ye who had been requested to go, ye who were already in love, I wouldna have had the courage to take yer place, Brianna. Can ye forgive me?"

"There is nothing to forgive. It was my choice to take your place. No one forced me to speak as I did." Seeing Alastair's heated gaze upon her sister she felt assured that what she had done was right. He was as drawn to Glenna as she was to him, though just as shy. Looking at him searchingly, Brianna sensed he would make her sister happy. Catching his eye, she smiled her approval, but seeing that he had attracted Brianna's attention, Alastair hastily looked away. No doubt he was fearful that she had seen his smoldering look. "The decision has been made. We'll speak no more about it."

"But Brianna . . ."

"Nae, not a word. Besides, there's a young yellow-haired laddie a giving ye the eye. It's my thought that ye should favor him wi' a smile, before he dies from longing. I wouldna wish to have ye a widow before you're a bride." Brianna watched as her sister took her advice, noting how the mutual attraction between the two was like two rays of sunshine lighting the room with warmth. Once again the wisdom of what she had done was reinforced by the knowledge that her sister would find happiness with this man. Playfully, she gave her sister a push in Alastair's direction. "Ye dinna need to flatter me by making me think it's my company ye seek. Go to yer laddie's side."

Glenna scurried away, taking Alastair a steaming bowl of the cereal as an excuse to approach him. Soon they were engaged in conversation but not so much so that she forgot to flash Brianna a grateful smile.

The hall buzzed with voices as those assembled filled their

plates and bowls, then stood aside to eat or talk. With so much to do at day's beginning, the breaking of fast was always eaten while standing. Brianna did the same, yet when it came time to eat she found despite her hunger she could not force even one spoonful past her lips. The company of the others, which she usually welcomed, now made her feel the necessity for privacy. Now more than at any other time in her life she wanted to be alone. There were thoughts and emotions rattling about inside her and she needed to sort them out. She needed to be away from the stifling air and close walls surrounding her.

Making her way across the room, Brianna stepped out into the cool morning air, feeling soothed by the soft breeze which caressed her face ever so gently. How many days she had left to roam the MacQuarie lands in freedom she did not know. All too soon the arrangements for her betrothal would be made. Until that day, however, she was unrestricted, unrestrained, bondless, and she would enjoy life to the fullest.

CHAPTER THREE

Across the loch in Argyll, another hall was dimly lit. Only the dying embers of the fire shed illumination on the two figures sitting side by side, intent in conversation. They were two men in the autumn of their years whose bond of friendship had weathered the march of time. Two bold men, Duncan Campbell and his comrade in arms, Cameron.

"Ye canna do this, Duncan! Ye canna do this, I say," Cameron was mumbling.

"And who is there to stop me?" Duncan was defiant as he stood up, facing the other man squarely. The years had threaded both men's hair with gray, but he was still an imposing man. One who knew his word was law.

"You! Your conscience!" Reaching out, Cameron gripped the other man's shoulder, digging his fingers into the firm-muscled flesh with bruising strength. "What ye plan is vile, a sin against both man and God. To marry the laddie to his own sister!" Like Duncan his hair was silvered, though not as noticeably so, for the tawny strands blended well, making it almost invisible to the eye. "'Twill be the ruination of Lachlan MacQuarie when he finds out, and perhaps of ourselves as well." Only Cameron dared say what was on his mind. Unlike the others he did not fear the great clan leader.

"Do ye think I care about Lachlan MacQuarie? Do ye not know I *want* to cause him pain? The same pain he caused me the day he struck down my son!" The blue eyes beneath the thick brows were slits of anger, an anger that had never dimmed throughout the years. "Seventeen years ago I foresaw this moment when I took MacQuarie's bairn, his son. I wilna let any man's chattering cheat me of my rightful due!"

Duncan Campbell had indeed stolen the MacQuarie's heir, though up to this moment Cameron had never really understood the reason for the heartless deed. He had thought the matter put to rest. A son for a son, that was what Duncan had said. Had he known to what ends the Campbell would go, he would never have involved himself in the deed, never promised to keep the secret. Had he known the devilishness of Duncan's thoughts he would have put the child back in his mother's arms. But it was too late now to have regrets. What was done was done. When the proposal had been made with an offer of peace he had hoped that perhaps Lachlan MacQuarie would not accept and all would be well. If that had happened, Duncan's thirst for vengeance would have been thwarted. Such a hope was shattered with the return of the messenger. Lachlan MacQuarie had said yes.

"Nae! Nae!" Cameron shook his shaggy-haired head, trying once more to reason Duncan's fearful obsession away. There were more people involved in this scheme than the leader of the MacQuaries. There was a young girl whose only offense was her clan name. There was also a young man who looked upon his foster father with a worshipful eye, a youth whose trust was most shamefully being betrayed. Robbie. What would happen to the lad when he found out what treachery had been planned? It could well destroy him. "Nae!" Cameron said again.

"Ye hae naught to say on the matter!" Striking his palm upon the trestle table Duncan caused all the goblets to bobble about as if an earthquake had just struck the area. "It will be done, or my name is not Duncan Campbell!"

"And hae ye no care for the laddie? Think ye not what it will do to him? Poor Robbie." Cameron had watched the boy grow up, had watched him exchange toys for a man's skill with weapons. Robbie had become an integral part of the Campbell clan. He thought himself to be the child of Duncan's sister who lived far to the south. He and the others of the clan had been told the story that Robbie had been sent to his uncle to be fostered out and raised as a possible heir since there was no man child. Duncan had craftily weaved his tale so that not one of the Campbells doubted the story. No one knew the truth except Cameron. A heavy cross to bear. Especially now. "Poor Robbie," he repeated. "He is a good and brave lad. Do ye have no sympathy for him?"

Duncan spat the answer. "He is a MacQuarie!" He might have said more, the quarrel might have continued well into the morning if not for the entrance of another man into the hall. The black hair on the young man's head declared him kin to Duncan. He was Duncan's nephew, his dead brother's son. Ian was the young man's given name.

Tall and lean but well-muscled, he had a strength about him that was almost overpowering. Even his manner of dress proclaimed his self-esteem. He was dressed now in a breacon, a length of cloth wrapped round the waist and belted, a length of which was draped over his shoulder and pinned with a jeweled brooch; a light-colored *leine* or shirt and a pouchlike sporran made from the head and skin of a badger. Unlike some of the others who often went barefooted or wore *moggins,* stockings without feet, his *curans* reached almost to the knee and were made of cowhide and held in position with thin thongs to cling to the shape of his leg.

Duncan looked upon Ian with pride. Ian had been born at midnight, the "wee sma' 'oors," and thus had been regarded as one who would manifest in later life some peculiar brilliance of intellect or prowess, though allied to a little wildness. As he had grown to manhood it had been proven true. His particular distinction was on the battlefield and he had done the Campbells proud.

It had been whispered that when Duncan laid up his sword Ian would take his place as leader of the clan. Surely it seemed an honor he could well fulfill for he had proven himself in battle time and time again. When he was still but a lad he had distinguished himself fighting at Robert the Bruce's side, defeating the English.

"You sent for me?" There was a hint of an English accent to his brogue from years spent at the Anglicized court in Edinburgh. Ian had been sent there after his resounding show of bravery, to secure a place for the Campbells in the future being molded for Scotland. It had been whispered that Duncan hoped for a noble, nae even a royal bride for his favored nephew, and it was true, though Ian had balked at the mere mention of marriage. He was a bold rogue to be sure, with all of the courage and stubbornness Duncan possessed. He walked forward now with a slight swagger which said that he was sure of himself, used to being in a position of importance and leadership. Even Duncan did not make him cower.

"Aye, that I did. I sent for ye." Giving Cameron a look of warning, cautioning him to hold his tongue, The Campbell grabbed an empty flagon and filled it to the brim with whiskey, a brew of scotch he had saved for the occasion. "I'm sending ye on a most important mission."

"A mission?" Ian took the goblet, looking questioningly at his uncle.

"A pleasant one." Duncan looked at the handsome youth over the rim of his own flagon, suppressing his smile.

"Tell me what it is and it shall be done."

"I want you to help me bring about peace."

"Peace?" It seemed the last word the bold young man expected to hear. "Peace you say?" Holding the goblet to his lips he drank deeply of the contents then wiped his mouth with the back of his hand.

"I've had enough of fighting, I want to bring about peace. I've proposed that Robbie marry one of MacQuarie's four daughters." The mouth surrounded by the peppered mustache and beard at last gave in to a grin. "Ye are to be my emissary, to arrange the betrothal and ceremony. A sort of cupid, if ye will."

"Cupid?" Ian Campbell filled the room with the sound of his laughter. "If it's Cupid you are wanting then I fear I'm not your man. Any arrows that I may aim will be for myself. I do not like to share my spoils." By his own admission he was a ladies' man, one who had left many a broken heart behind. Ladies and milkmaids alike had fallen under his spell. In truth Ian had lost count of all the women he had wooed and won. "But if it's a sword arm you need to keep the MacQuaries in line, then I'm your man!" Holding out his flagon he watched as Duncan filled it again to the brim, then drained it dry. By his manner and smile it was obvious that he thought his uncle to be jesting. "A Campbell marry a MacQuarie, indeed."

"It's deadly serious that I am. The glen has rumbled with our warfare but now I offer peace. Dare ye to refute me on this?" Standing up, Duncan crossed his massive arms across his chest, looking as menacing as he had intended. He would not take argument from this young pup no matter how skilled at arms Ian might be.

"Refute you? Nae. It is your place to decide. I'll not be quarreling. But it's glad that I am I'm not the intended groom. I would not want to settle down with any maiden. With the whole meadow abloom with flowers who would want to choose only one?"

"Spoken like a true Campbell." Cameron could not hide his own mirth. He liked young Ian's spunk. Duncan was too used to being treated with deference.

"Robbie doesna feel that way. He will do as I bid him." Duncan knew well how hard the younger man always tried to win his approval, as if somehow Robbie could sense his so-called uncle had no true fondness for him. Ian, however, was a different matter. He was a constant source of irritation and had the effrontery to disagree now and then. "Robbie will marry who I choose."

Shrugging his shoulders, Ian Campbell threw the end of his *breacan feille* over his shoulders with a jaunty air. "Then I wish him well in his marriage and hope his bride will not be too homely." He made a face. "Let us hope MacQuarie's lassie does not look like her sire. I would wish for Robbie a bonnie bride."

"Bonnie or not, *MacQuarie's* daughter is the one that I hae chosen. By first light of morning ye will travel to the MacQuarie's hall and make the necessary arrangements."

"And will young Robbie go with me to meet the lass?" Ian cocked his brow in question, puzzled by Duncan's icy stare.

"Nae!" Duncan knew he could not take the chance of the MacQuaries coming to know the lad, lest they suspect his kinship. Though his hair was a deep brown it was touched with the MacQuarie red. "Robbie willna meet his bride until his wedding day." Sensing Ian's scrutiny he added, "I willna place him in the hands of the MacQuaries lest something go awry. Robbie is not as skilled in weaponry as ye are." Seeing Ian's puzzled frown he added, "Nor as glib of tongue and as agile as ye are."

"You will have him stay behind?"

"'Tis common enough to proceed with the arrangements this way. Ye will sign the contract and see to the banns." Quickly he added, "I would protect him."

"I see." Ian did not envy young Robbie Campbell. The thought of having a woman forced upon him was distasteful. He would never submit so docilely. "Then it is up to me to woo the lassie. I hope 'twill not be too unpleasant a task."

"Woo her if ye like if it will insure a wedding. But hae a care . . ."

Ian feigned innocence. "Uncle, you chide me unnecessarily. I'll give her up to Robbie's arms when the time comes." He smiled. "Indeed I can see that I am your man, for I've had my share of practice in matters of the heart. I'll win

33

Robbie his bride. You'll have your fine wedding. I will not disappoint you. But I make a request of you. That I be allowed to take Aulay with me. In case I meet with treachery I would welcome his sword arm." Though the man he spoke of was a dwarf, Ian knew there was no finer fighter among the clans. The little man had fought right by his side at the battle of Bannockburn. Aulay was fierce and cunning, more than a match for those twice his size. He'd sent many an Englishman straight to hell during warfare between England and Scotland. "He has been my boon companion for many years."

"Aye. Agreed. Though let us hope ye hae no need of him. The MacQuaries must be at least half-civilized as obstinate as they are. Let us assume that all will go well." Once again Duncan smiled. "Let us hope that all will go exactly as I planned."

A brisk breeze whipped through Ian's hair as he leaned against the stout stone wall of the castle allure, the wall-walk behind the west parapet. So, Robbie was going to be used as a peace offering, he thought. He had sympathy for the lad though there was not much to be done about it. When Duncan had made up his mind there was little hope of changing it, though Saint Michael himself declare it a wrongful conclusion. He'd do as Duncan said and hope he would not rue it, but MacQuaries indeed! All he'd heard since he was a lad was a list of their sins; now seemingly all was to be forgiven with a snap of Duncan's fingers. Strange. And he to be the ambassador to this official act, he who had once been shunned as a lad by his own clan.

Gazing out past the rocky crags to the meadows and burns beyond, his mind pondered what the future held in store, and wandered over the events of the past when he had been brought to Dunstaffnage Castle as a small boy after the death of his mother.

"What is this?" Those were the first words he'd heard Duncan's wife, Fionnghuala, utter as she'd appraised him with her perpetual scowl. From that moment on they'd been at odds over the years, her attitude toward him as cold as her ice blue eyes. Indeed she'd treated him more as a stable boy than her husband's brother's son, keeping him busy with lowly chores. His father, deeply mourning the death of his wife, enshrouded in his own sorrow, had seemingly been oblivious to the handling of his son. Taking refuge in his ale, he had granted Ian less and less of his time and did not even seem very interested in anything the lad did whether it be for good or ill. Thus, Fionnghuala had raised him, never ceasing to remind Ian that his mother had been naught but a tinker's daughter with whom his father had run off.

Ian had worked hard at all duties he was assigned, always finding time to watch the menfolk at their mock battles, admiring his cousin Morgan's skills as much as Robbie admired him now. Ian had adored Duncan's son for his kindness to him as much as his prowess. Morgan had taught the lonely boy how to use a sword, and in the obsessive determination to please the elder lad, Ian had practiced hard with both *claymore*, a Scottish two-handed sword, and the English broadsword. He would be ready if the need arose.

Because Ian was the son of a woman of lesser rank, he had to be twice as good at everything he did. He was not as arrogant as some would imagine. It was just that he had had to prove himself double the worth of anyone else. A hard shell had been erected around himself in his boyhood, for he was more sensitive than he would ever have cared to admit and loathed it as a weakness. His father's death, Morgan's death, and the devastation he had felt had only hardened that shell. He built an aura around himself that made him appear invincible as he hid at times behind a silent, mockingly arrogant mask.

The turmoil for the Scottish crown and a fight to free Alba from Edward I's English had given young Ian a chance to prove himself. Amidst a clattering, clamoring, weapon thrusting, shouting throng he had at last come to full manhood. It was then he had been fully accepted into the clan, his tainted "peasant" blood at last forgotten in the glory of his heroism. It had been a turning point in his life. The men of clan Campbell, including his uncle, had admired him for his strength and leadership, and the lassies had granted him their smiles and much, much more. Falling under the spell of his striking male comeliness, they had given him their all-consuming passion and aye, their love. It was a reward Ian accepted as his due.

Now I add one more duty, wooing Robbie his bride, Ian thought. Well, he liked the lad. Right from the first when he'd seen the wee babe he had formed a bond with the boy. Now he would do him proud and hope all would be well. So thinking, he turned away from the wall and headed back to his chambers. He would try to keep this mission in perspective. He'd seen so much blood and killing that he fully intended to live to the fullest! It was a brutal world but he could survive if he kept the right attitude. Appreciate each day of life, that was his motto. If he was of the right frame of mind it could well be an adventure, a chance for merriment. That was another reason he had asked that Aulay accompany him, for the little man was never boring and seemed to understand Ian's moods as no one else could.

Aye, Aulay, he thought with a smile. The dwarf was the son of a half-French, half-Scottish court jester who had once been trained in that humorous skill until Edward's declaration of fire and sword had nearly taken his life. They had been friends for so long he could hardly think of a time when the dwarf had not been at his side. And perhaps the reason Ian had befriended the little man quite so stoutly was that he knew what it felt like to be an outcast. Under his tutelage, his stern defense, Aulay had at last been fully accepted.

"Uillean, summon Aulay. Tell him to make ready for a journey," Ian instructed as he passed one of the castle manservants. Ah yes, the more he thought about it the more determined he was to enjoy this journey.

CHAPTER FOUR

The changing colors of the morning sky lit up the rocky shoreline and cast a glow upon the small fishing boat, a *curach,* that skimmed through the waters of Loch na Keal. Two men sat aboard the skiff, one pulling relentlessly at the oars.

"We must be daft, Ian, to come by boat and no' by land. I've fought at yer side for many years now but I hae no intention of being some water beastie's meal." Aulay, a tawny-haired man nearly half Ian's lofty height, though just as muscular, voiced his misgivings with a deep-throated rumble. "I'm a warrior no' a fishermon like the MacQuaries."

The sea water whipped and churned around the boat. Grabbing tightly to the oars, Aulay cast his companion a surly frown. So intent was he in his grumbling that he paid little heed to a large rock looming in their path until it was nearly too late. Only at the last moment was the dwarf able to steer the craft to safety. The boat just barely cleared the obstacle, brushing the granite with a scratching sound.

"Aye, I can see that you are no mariner." Anxious to avoid another near collision, Ian quickly took the oars, guiding the boat toward the land. Only when the boat was back on course did he speak again, answering his friend's unspoken question. "I thought it safer to travel by boat. This so-called peace is too new for me to be too trustful of traveling MacQuarie lands. Remember what happened to Morgan eighteen long years ago. I would not want to be taken unaware. I have no liking for a claymore to be piercing my back."

"Och! Ye hae been wise." Aulay massaged his tired, aching muscles. "I can see that now when I think on it."

Both men squinted their eyes toward the shore as they approached with caution. The western coastline of the island appeared to be of solid rock, its cream- and gray-colored granite walls rose vertically from the sea. Such sea cliff scenery was awe inspiring, Ian had to admit. Duncan no doubt had his eye on claiming it, thus this matter of the marriage, he thought.

Ian remembered Eachuin, a chief of the MacQuaries, talking about this area of Scotland when Robert the Bruce's Highland troups were awaiting battle. The land was said to teem with wild beasts that outnumbered men and hunted with a ferocity and joy seldom found elsewhere. The sea was silver with fish. Noisy clouds of wildfowl hung above the coastal waters. Boar rooted in the forest lands. There were even said to be wild herds of cattle with flowing manes like lions, and red deer that roamed in thick herds.

In the distance a stone fortress was visible, high on a hill rising somberly above the rock walls. Ian knew it must be both an observation point and in times of peril a place for clansmen to congregate. It looked stern and solemn as the sun rose behind its massive structure, reflecting off the stones. A reminder of the warfare that had raged for years.

"It looks quiet enough. No boats. No sign o' any MacQuaries guarding the beaches." If they proceeded much farther, however, they might be seen by some of the inhabitants of the stone and thatched-roof huts further down the shore. Aulay looked questioningly at Ian.

"We'll move on. You're right, it is quiet." Ian touched his dirk nonetheless to be prepared if need be. "No sentries. Could it be that Lachlan MacQuarie is as daft as Duncan?"

"Och! To say such a thing!" Aulay was taken aback by such a comment. It was unlike Ian to show such disrespect.

"It's true. 'Tis not only the MacQuaries that make me uneasy but Duncan as well. He has been acting so strange of late. There is a faraway look in his eye. And this sudden talk of peace when all he has held in his heart up to now has been hatred for our enemies. It makes me wonder."

"He is growing old. He and Cameron and a few of the others will be throwing down their claymores afore too many more years hae passed. Then ye can be clan chief."

"Or Robbie! The law of tanistry makes him as much a successor as am I." Tanistry, or succession by cousinage, meant there was always more than one claimant. It was up to Duncan to decide and to name his successor.

Aulay shook his head. "That young laddie has none o' Duncan's mettle. He looks to me as unlike a Campbell as a changeling. There are many who are uneasy because of the mystery surrounding the laddie. I've heard the talk. It was as if he came out of the mists. All of a sudden he was in Duncan's hall being nurtured wi'out much explanation."

"Duncan explained the story to my satisfaction." Ian was quick to defend the young man. "He took Robbie in when his parents died, to keep him safe from those who are jealous of the power we Campbells now wield."

"Perhaps, but I dinna think the others will choose to follow such as he, an untried youth who is little more than a bairn. Nae, it will be you!"

Ian tensed his jaw. "We should not even think of choosing another chief until Duncan lays his sword and shield aside. He has not yet chosen me as tanist. Until that day I'll do as he bids. Even take myself to Lachlan MacQuarie's hall."

No more was spoken on the subject as both men concentrated on guiding the boat toward the shore. There were places along the island that were less rocky, flatter. Ian made his decision to disembark on one of the white sand-strewn beaches near a fjordlike inlet far below the fortress. Maneuvering the small craft into the inlet, they were soon out of range of view of anyone down shore. It was here they beached the skiff.

On the shore, shells, driftwood, logs and seaweed littered the rock-strewn sand. They made their way through the tangled seaweed until they came to several pathways leading in or out of the valley. Which one should they take? Ian made the choice, walking briskly along. The smaller man tried to keep up, taking two footsteps to one of Ian's long strides.

As they moved farther inland they could view the moss and lichen-covered rocks more closely. The scenery was quite wild. They found the rocks and sand gave rise to an oasis of fertile soil further inland, however. There was greenery—hazel shrub and flora—and widespread heaths. The woodland gave way to broad valleys and rich green land crisscrossed by rivers and streams. Aside from the fact that there was not as much arable land and pasture, it was not vastly different from their own territory, Ian reflected.

Reaching the summit of a hill, Ian could see a group of men and women working the fields with the *cas-chrom*, or foot plough. The patches of land appeared to be too small for horses to be of use. Beyond, a small herd of shaggy cattle grazed peacefully on the hillside. Wishing to maintain at least a semblance of secrecy about their presence, Ian paused in mid-stride, retracing his steps to go in the opposite direction, toward the forest lands. It seemed a convenient point from which to investigate this island whose chief paid but scant attention to the Crown. There would be time for explanation of their being on the island as soon as they found out where the MacQuarie castle keep was located.

Suddenly a sound behind Aulay startled him. Remembering Ian's concern he drew his sword, fully prepared to defend himself, but it was only a whimbrel, disturbed in the midst of eating its dinner. Voicing a squawking protest, the sea bird took flight, joined by others of his kind.

"Now is no time to go hunting, Aulay." A grin teased the corner of Ian's mouth.

"I wasn't . . ." Seeing he was being teased, Aulay relaxed his own mouth in a smile. "Well, let's hurry on then and be done wi' it."

"Aye. I'll settle the matter of Robbie's bride and perhaps find a lassie for myself."

"And one for me as well?" The hopeful expression on Aulay's face was comical as it was meant to be, yet Ian's smile faltered.

"Perhaps . . ." Despite his tone of merriment, Ian sensed a loneliness in Aulay and he could only hope the dwarf's longing would soon be fulfilled. If men were judged by heart instead of size he knew that Aulay would tower over everyone.

A hush of quiet had settled over the land as Ian and Aulay hurried along, yet years of constant warring had made them both overly cautious. Though the only voices they heard were from a flock of gulls circling overhead, they attuned their ears to hear every sound. Being in another clan's territory made them very vulnerable and most certainly unwelcome until they had made themselves known and explained their mission.

Focusing their eyes on the mottled golds, browns, and greens of the land that rolled before them, they kept a lookout for any sign of danger. Even so, Ian was startled as a white and saffron-garbed figure darted out of the foliage several feet away. The well-proportioned figure and long flowing red hair told him instantly that it was a woman.

"A lassie!" Aulay's whisper gave voice to the obvious. Two pairs of eyes watched as the woman walked slowly over to the edge of a small lake gouged into the land. She was unaware of their stares. Silently the two men crept closer, close enough to see that she was beautiful. At that very moment Ian was bewitched.

"Look at that hair! 'Tis like a fire, like a raging flame." As the woman threw her head back, the long tresses whipped about her shoulders, catching the rays of the sun, setting her hair ablaze with magenta highlights.

"Now, Ian. Ye canna be thinking. Not so soon. I thought what ye said was all in jest, about finding a lassie. Ye shouldna . . ." Aulay had seen that look in Ian's eye before and knew his protestations were in vain. Still he continued, "She might be one o' the fairies. A kelpie. I've heard they roam here about."

"She looks real enough for me. Beautiful." Ian craned his neck for a better view.

"Och, then she might hae kin who would not look favorably on a man of Campbell blood." Aulay threw his hands up in exasperation. He knew Ian as well as he knew the freckles on the back of his hand. There would be no reasoning with him once he'd set his mind. "Ye could start the feuding up again just for a kiss."

Ian didn't hear, he was too involved in watching the young lass. "I have to see her eyes, to know if they're blue or green." Leaving Aulay behind, Ian moved closer, his eyes caressing the mounds of the woman's breasts, moving to the narrow waist which he knew he could span with his hands. The gentle swell of her hips and long legs were outlined by her gown, completing the enchanting image.

"Ian, ye are daft! I know it for a certainty now!" Aulay followed Ian, voicing his declaration, only to be silenced by Ian's hand upon his mouth.

"Hush, you'll chase her away before I have time to speak with her." Ian flashed Aulay a challenging smile. "You go on ahead. I'll catch up with you somehow." As Aulay hesitated he said, "On with you now. But be careful. I'll be along soon."

"I'll be along soon!" Aulay echoed. Mumbling beneath his breath, he walked on ahead, narrowly missing a tree trunk as he turned back to look at Ian. With a cluck of his tongue he shook his head again in warning. Ian ignored his friend's chastisement. Easing out of the shadows he moved toward the girl, seduction most definitely upon his mind.

CHAPTER FIVE

A soft whispering breeze caressed Brianna's face as she stood by the loch. Glancing about her, she viewed the untamed woodland of tall, slender silver birch trees. It was a natural wonderland, a haven with a mossy floor hidden from view by a drapery woven of hundreds of leaves. It was so achingly lovely here in the fairy glen. The mountains and moorlands sparkled like jewels. Tranquil. Each stone, each tree, every inlet of water that gouged deep into the glens was precious to her. How she would hate to leave.

The Island of Ulva was a happy, smiling place, whose mood was that of its upland meadows, bright with wild flowers, waterfalls, and lush green bracken. There were reminders of ancient cataclysms in the gigantic lava terraces of the island and basalt columns of its neighbor, Staffa. Yet there was a loneliness about the land that seemed to touch Brianna's heart. Today she looked at it as if viewing it for the very first time, each leaf and rock becoming precious to her.

More than at any time in her life Brianna regretted the passing of her mother. Had her mother felt as uncertain as she did now at her betrothal? She needed her mother's advice, wanted to ask so many questions, but there was nowhere to turn. Her sisters were too young and didn't know any more than she, and her father just didn't understand a woman's ways. To him it was all so simple, just like playing a chess game. He wasn't being hardhearted about the matter, to the contrary. It was just that he couldn't share her inner turmoil. Belonging to someone else for the rest of your life was an unnerving thought.

Flocks of gulls and terns glided overhead. The wild, beautiful music of the inland birds serenaded her as they flew from bough to bough, a melancholy song which fit the mood of her reverie. Staring into the azure depths of the loch, her eyes focused on the water as if somehow she might read her fate there. Would she be happy? Would she grow to love her young husband? Would this joining of the clans truly bring about peace?

Unaware that she was being watched, she slowly lowered her body in a graceful motion to sit upon a large rock by the lake's edge. This was a spot she had not even shared with Glenna, a place that she felt somehow belonged to her. Soon, like the other things she held so dear, this secluded haven would be but a reflection in her mind. A memory.

Taking off her soft doeskin shoes, she let the water splash over her feet as she closed her eyes. She remembered childhood days when she had come to this hideaway to escape from her mother's ravings or her father's moody frowns. Somehow she felt safe here, assured that no one knew of this secret haven. That was why she was doubly surprised to look up and discover that she was not alone. A man stood silhouetted in the trees, looking in her direction. Was he friend or foe? Warily she watched him.

"Don't be afraid, I won't harm you." His voice was low, a husky rumble. "All I want to do is appreciate the beauty you offer, soothing and stimulating to a man's eyes."

"I'm not afraid!" For an instant her eyes betrayed the truth of her boast as she searched for any sign that he had been accompanied by other men. It seemed that he had come alone and that thought comforted her. Still she said, "But I do not wish ye to come any closer."

Ian paused for a moment in an effort to reassure her.

"Then I won't." At least for the moment, he thought. Ian was mesmerized by the beautiful vision, though he saw at once she had an air of sadness about her. The urge to carry her with him into the cool water, to frolic there and wipe away all trace of her frown, teased his thoughts. He wanted to see her smile, hear her laugh. Instead, however, he contented himself with looking at her. She reminded him of a butterfly and he had no wish for her to elude him. If he moved closer, she might fly away.

Satisfied that his presence did not mean immediate danger, Brianna turned to him. "Who are ye?" He spoke so strangely. The way he said his words proclaimed that he was not from the isle.

"A man who relishes beauty!" She had asked him who he was but he had no wish to blurt out the Campbell name just yet.

Slowly he moved again through the bracken and trees, not wanting to frighten her, yet unable to resist getting a closer look at the young red-haired beauty. He supposed her to be one of the fisherman's daughters, whose huts he had seen dotting the gently sloping hills. Or perhaps Aulay was right. Perhaps she was not real at all but just a figment of his dreams.

"What are you doing here?" Her voice had a sharp edge to it as she asked the question. As he took another step forward she took one step back, her hands stretched out as if to push him away were he to come too close.

"I'm no ogre, lass, though I think ye must be a kelpie, a lovely water sprite sent to tempt me. Are you?"

"No." She was trapped. There was nowhere to go except to hurl herself in the depths of the water.

He moved with all the caution of a predatory animal, slow and sinuous in his grace, coming at last to the water's edge. Poised just a few feet from where she stood he gave his eyes full reign. She was even lovelier up close than she had been from afar. Ian felt his heartbeat quickening as she met him eye to eye. "Why, they're brown. A bonnie, bonnie brown."

"What?"

"Your eyes." Not blue or green, nor even gray. They were the loveliest shade he'd ever seen, a copper-colored hue, fringed by dark brown lashes. Her face was now clearly revealed to him, the sunlight caressing her forehead and cheeks where he would have liked to place his hand.

There was an ethereal beauty about her, yet he knew her to be real. His gaze touched upon her well-formed nose, a nose with just a slight tilt at the end that gave her a haughty air. There was something enticing about her wide, sensuous mouth. Her cheekbones were high and prominent, adding to her beauty. A necklace strung with small seashells emphasized the slimness of her neck.

Wordlessly, Brianna regarded this man, this stranger, just as he was scrutinizing her. She knew immediately that she had never seen him before on her travels with her father, for she would have remembered a man like this if she had. This tall, muscular, handsome man was not the kind a woman would ever forget. He had a bold look about him, an impression heightened by the curve of his brows. Brows that shadowed piercing blue eyes. Ah, those eyes haunted her. They were as unfathomable as the sea. He was not of the MacQuarie clan to be sure. Which clan, then? He wore the strange hoselike trews, a combination of breeches and stockings that none of her clansman would wear. His dress, the way he talked, all puzzled her. Who was he, then? He had come from the direction of the coast which led her to believe he might well be one of the MacLeans. Was he one of them? She soothed herself in judging it must be so. Just as well. Her clan had no quarrel with them.

Forgotten for the moment was her contemplative mood, her sadness. The air crackled with anticipation. A shiver danced up and down her spine, though she refused to let this man know the effect his presence had on her. She told herself that it was the sense of surprise and danger that so activated her senses. She asked again, "Who are ye?" He remained silent, which was puzzling.

The blue black of his hair glistened in the sunlight. For one timeless moment they stared at each other across the short distance that separated them. Strange how just a look could be so exciting.

"You charm me, lass." He had a roguish grin, his teeth straight and even. "By Saint Michael you do!" His eyes caressed her with a boldness few had dared, held her, forced her to acknowledge that something was going on between them. An undefinable fascination.

At last Brianna had to admit to herself that she was attracted to him. She held her breath in expectation as he reached out. Without a word he caught a fistful of her long silken hair and wrapped it around his hand, drawing her closer. With the tips of his fingers he traced the line of her cheekbones, the shape of her mouth, the line of her brows. He seemed motivated by curiosity, as if to prove beyond a doubt that she was not a dream.

"I like you well. You have lips I long to kiss, curves that beckon my hands . . ." His face hovered only inches from her own.

"No!" She would not listen to such honeyed words. Fiercely, Brianna drew away. She was soon to be betrothed. Her father had given his word. She must not let this man touch her with such familiarity. He had no right.

"Haven't you heard such words before?" He was puzzled by her reaction. "I would think there would be dozens of laddies wanting a kiss." Ian misunderstood her reaction, telling himself that it was but maidenly shyness. So much the better. Far more of a challenge to be the first. "If you be afraid, I'll take it a bit slower, though I'm a man used to taking what I want."

"Oh? Well, ye'll not be havin' me." She was adamant. Even so, she did not recoil again when he reached out to stroke her cheek.

"You are a most bonnie lass. Most bonnie." His appraising gaze seemed to cherish her, his words mesmerized her and though Brianna knew all the reasons she should run away, she somehow did not. Then all at once it was too late.

At first he simply held her, his hands exerting a gentle pressure to draw her into the warmth of his embrace. Then before Brianna could make a sound his mouth claimed hers in a gentle kiss, one completely devastating to her senses. She was engulfed in a whirlpool of sensations. Breathless, her head whirling, she allowed herself to be drawn up into the mists of the spell. New sensations clamored within her. All she could think about was that Glenna was right. A kiss could be most enjoyable.

Leaning against the man who held her, Brianna savored the feel of his strength. Dreamily she gave herself up to the fierce sweetness of his mouth, her lips opening under his as exciting new sensations flooded through her. She was aware of her body as she had never been before, relished the emotions churning within her.

Ian's lips parted the soft yielding flesh beneath his, searching out the honey of her mouth. With a low moan he thrust his fingers within the soft, silken waterfall of her hair, drawing her ever closer. Desire choked him, all the hungry promptings of his fantasies warring with his reason. His lips grew demanding, changing from gentleness to passion as his hands moved down her shoulders and began to roam at will with increasing familiarity. More than anything in the world he wanted to make love to this young woman. Here. Now. Upon the grassy bank of the lake he wanted to blend with her, give her pleasure.

"Your skin is as smooth as a newly birthed babe's," he whispered, as he drew his mouth away. The words tickled her ear, making her vibrantly alive and atuned to her senses. The song of the birds seemed even more melodious suddenly, the colors of the meadow more intense, the perfume of the blossoming flowers stronger and more fragrant. Every instinct within her intensified as she stared at this stranger.

Never had Brianna thought a kiss could be so overpowering. Like a spark, it ignited a fire in her blood. Her heart skipped a beat as he brought his head down and traced the bare curve of her shoulder with his lips. A near madness seized her, and she found herself thinking the most dangerous thoughts. She wanted him to keep on touching her this way, wanted to touch him back.

"Ah, yes, darlin'. You feel it too, this magic between us," he was saying. "I want to see your body unclothed, to swim naked with you in yonder pool, to make love with you until we both . . ."

His words brought her back to reality with a thud. *Naked?* The word reverberated in her ear. How dare he! Not one of her own clan's rogues had ever talked to her in such a way or even dared to suggest such a thing. Who did he think he was to be so bold? And her, what was she doing, foolish girl, to let this stranger touch her as he did? What had come over her? She tried to shake the confusing feelings from her body. She was soon to be betrothed and even though Robbie be a man she had never seen before, a Campbell, she would not allow dishonor to besmirch their betrothal. What this man wanted, and it was obvious what that was, she would not give. So thinking, she jerked back her head, pushed at the hard strength of his chest with her hands.

"What is it, lassie? Come, do not pull away. I want to love you, my lovely kelpie, for I am drowning in the sweet depths of your nearness."

For a moment she had forgotten everything in the grasp of his embrace but now it all came flooding back. She was soon to be wedded, was to be an instrument of bringing peace to the clans. She could not, would not allow herself to bring dishonor on her father or clan. The man was a stranger! Perhaps that most of all made her feel shame.

"Lassie?"

"Ye canna . . ."

"Ah, but I will. Come, do not be coy with me, lassie." No woman had ever said no to Ian. They clamored about him in fact, vying with each other for his eye. Was it any wonder he did not take Brianna's denial seriously? One well-curved brow quirked upward as he drew her into his arms again, before she could say another word. "Love you I want to, and love you I will, and you will not be sorry. I'll bring you to cooing like a dove."

This time the kiss he gave her was far from gentle and Brianna was mutely aware of the firm muscles of his body as he moved against her. Before she could protest he had pulled her down with him to the soft woodland grass. This time she was not mesmerized by his touch, however. Indignant fury surged through her. She would let no man take her against her will! That he was a man used to women and therefore potentially dangerous for that knowledge, she sensed now. This was no shy Jaimie whom she could frighten away with a scowl or an angry word. He had said that he was a man used to taking what he wanted and what he wanted right now was her. Well, she would soon burst his bubble. Arrogant oaf, she thought, he would not cajole her.

Locked against him as she was, there was no mistaking his male arousal. Oh, she'd heard the women talk, knew what was to follow if she did not keep her head. Conceited toady. Who did he think he was to fall upon her? She was The MacQuarie's daughter, not some village trollop he could take because he so chose.

"Let me go." she commanded. He did not heed. Even now he was smiling, so smug in his self-assurance. Well, she'd given him fair warning but he had not heeded it. Now there was but one course of action. She would soon wipe the smile off his face with a well-aimed blow, right to that area of him that he seemed to prize so highly. So determining, Brianna aimed her knee, putting an end to his lustful thoughts. She watched as he doubled over in agony.

"I say ye willna take me, and by the saints ye shall not!" Disentangling herself from his arms, she stood with hands upon hips as she assessed him. He was not so sure of himself now. He did in fact look most miserable. She should have felt triumphant and yet somehow she did not. Fool that she was, she felt nearly regretful, though she did not know why. In truth, he had it coming, did he not? And yet he had made her feel beautiful, at least for a moment. She had enjoyed his kiss, there was no lying about that. To her mortification she had to admit to herself that despite his boldness she was attracted to him. Even now.

"You're a spirited lass," Ian managed to say at last. An echo of pain shadowed his face yet he regarded her with open and somewhat mocking admiration as he lay in a heap upon the ground. Ian Campbell had never been so fiercely upbraided in his life, especially by a woman. He took a deep breath, gratified when the pain at last was gone. "But could you not just have said no?"

"I did and ye didna listen." She glared at him defiantly, hiding behind a veil of anger.

"Aye, that you did. That you did. But I didn't think you really meant it, lass. You responded to me, you can not say otherwise." He met her gaze for a long moment, unable to look away. "And in spite of what you did I'm still drawn to you. It is my wish that you'll have second thoughts." As he spoke his eyes swept over her suggestively.

Smooth talking rogue, she thought. Oh, he was clever—and dangerous. Doubly so because of his charm.

"I'll not be changing my mind." Shielding her eyes she scanned the undulating landscape, looking toward that road from where the Campbells would be coming. It was a well-traveled horse trail, clearly visible from the hillside. Not a sign of anyone coming. What then if he abducted her, kept her from fulfilling her promises? A flush of guilt stained her cheeks for just a moment, knowing that such a thing crossed her mind. Appraising this dark-haired, terribly handsome man, she wondered if she would be very anxious to be rescued. The answer quite honestly was that she would not. Oh, if only he were Robbie Campbell.

Robbie Campbell. What was Robbie Campbell like? She could not help but wonder. Would he be anywhere near as much a rogue as this man? Would his kisses be just as potent? She scolded herself for such musing. Few women married for love or sweet kisses. She had spoken that fact quite truthfully to Glenna. Why then should she be the exception? Be he handsome or plain, Robbie was to be her bridegroom. She would push away any other thoughts. She was soon to be the instrument of bringing peace. What greater gift was there than that?

"You say you'll not be changing your mind? I wouldna be too sure of that." He startled her with another smile. His blue eyes were disarmingly frank. He looked bemused with the situation. Slowly Ian stood up, feasting his eyes on her for several moments longer.

"Och!" His arrogance was not to be borne. "You'd best be sure of it. Yer boldness will bring nothing. I tell ye now to go away." That he had charmed her she refused to allow him to see. "Now, leave me once again to my tranquillity. It's much I've got on my mind."

"Leave? And never see you again? Is that really what you want?" Disappointment rankled him as he realized she meant exactly what she said. Strange how her denial only seemed to make him more determined. He hated to lose. There were hundreds of pretty young women in the Highlands, yet somehow at this moment she was the only one he wanted. He laughed at such a predicament. He, Ian Campbell, had been shunned. How Aulay would laugh at that.

"Aye. It is my wish ne'er to see ye again." The finality of her tone stung him. So she was not just being coy. Remembering the pain she had dealt him, the physical comeuppance, he was reminded that she was not.

"Well, then so be it. I wish you good day." His last look was a wistful one before he turned to walk away. He knew the image of her would be etched in his memory for a very long time. At least until he came upon another winsome beauty, he thought with a grin.

A tidal wave of silence consumed them. For the first time in his life Ian did not know quite what to say. Thus he stole away silently, not sensing the eyes that followed him, watching as he moved through the trees. Nor did he know that for just a moment the woman he had briefly treasured was looking at him with regret, wondering what might have sparked between them if the fire had not been extinguished before it came to full flame. They might never meet again, that was all Ian knew and perhaps, he thought, it was just as well.

But what was her name? He did not even know that. He suddenly realized that she had not told him. Fool that he was, he had left without even a hint as to her identity. The thought crossed his mind that he had admitted defeat far too easily. If he ever beheld her again he would not let her go. Not again. With a shrug of his shoulders he set off to find Aulay.

CHAPTER SIX

The strum of harp strings echoed throughout the hall. Glenna smiled as she went about her woman's work. She relished every plink and plunk brought about by Alastair's adroit fingers. From time to time she cast a longing glance at him over her shoulder as she cut up the vegetables for the stovies. A hundred times she had imagined what it would be like to find herself in his arms. He was handsome, so undeniably handsome. Surely no warrior could have had arms as strong, a face so wonderfully chiseled, or hair that shone like gold in the sun. Now while he practiced his singing for the evening's feasting, his hair gleamed in the firelight, taking on a dark hue.

Only when his gaze met her eyes did she realize how poignantly she was staring. Hastily she looked away, but not before she witnessed the smile that curved his lips. A tantalizing grin that gave her hope that he was thinking about her too. Oh how she wanted to wed him. With Brianna promised to the Campbell heir it was entirely possible.

Ah, please let him ask for me soon, she thought. "I will take no other but Alastair," she swore beneath her breath. No other man had touched her heart as he had. He was the man she wanted. She could feel it with every beat of her heart. Even his very name deeply stirred her, filled her senses as deeply as a draught of her father's ale. And yet though he talked with her, walked with her, sang soft flowery verses that she sensed were meant for her, he had avoided telling her in words what his intentions might be. He would ask for her, would he not? Surely he was not just teasing her, toying with her affections?

Glenna gasped as she accidentally nicked her thumb with the knife. Resigning herself to keeping her mind on what she was doing, she nonetheless found it to be an impossible vow. She just couldn't keep her eyes from roaming to where Alastair sat slumped on his bench, the harp propped against his knee.

"Ah, the finest voice in all the Highlands, that he has." The young, dark-haired woman who spoke licked her lips, daring a much bolder smile at the *seanachaidh* than Glenna might have dared. "His hands are gentle on the strings. I dare to think they might stroke a woman's body with as much magic."

"Och! Ye be brazen to say such a thing!" Just the thought of Alastair holding any other woman in his arms wounded Glenna to the quick, nor could she hide her emotions. "Fie, Jeanne!"

"Brazen because ye have set yer sights on him? Ye be not alone. There must be at least half a dozen wi' the same thought in mind. Ha, I'd even say there are some o' the married ones who would shove their husbands aside to have the bard in their bed." She giggled suggestively. "Ye know what they say aboot a tall mon wi' long fingers."

Glenna did, and she blushed to the roots of her hair. She had heard the women talking, espousing what went on between a woman and a man. They had even been so bold as to talk about marital secrets, comparing their husbands' lovemaking. Some had been said to be ample, others found wanting. Whisperings about the bard had been bandied about. His looks, his voice, his gentleness made him a romantic figure about the hall. Though Glenna was an untried maiden, all the twittering had sparked her curiosity, beset her with fantasies. Wild primitive desires invaded her young body, flamed with a fever that ofttimes shocked her. It was her greatest longing to be wed. It was a yearning that sparked her impatience. Now Jeanne's whisperings made her even more anxious to marry Alastair before another claimed him.

"Och, I can read yer thoughts as clearly as the bard can his scribbled words, but little good it will do ye, lass. Yer The MacQuarie's daughter. Love is no' for the likes o' ye. Ye'll marry to further the interests of the clan. Yer sister is marrying a Campbell. Perhaps a MacLeod will be in yer stars." Glancing sideways through her cloak of dark hair, Jeanne giggled. "But I'll make certain Alastair doesna pine long. Aye, that I will." She sauntered off with a toss of her head and a swish of her long woolen skirts.

"Marry a MacLeod?" Glenna worriedly tossed her head. Brianna had made a sacrifice, had given up her own freedom so that Glenna could follow her heart. She would not allow her sister to have made such a gesture in vain. She would marry Alastair or be damned for a coward. "It will be Alastair," she murmured, feeling a sense of urgency rise like a tide within her. Oh where was Brianna? How she needed her wisdom, her advice. Looking around for her, she saw to her dismay that her sister was nowhere to be found. Indeed it seemed the pattern of the day lately that Brianna was spending a good deal of time by herself. She would have to use her own intuition then.

Glenna would have liked to wait until Alastair made the first move in the matter of arranging a marriage, but now Jeanne's words sparked a recklessness in her heart that she had never felt before. Laughing softly, she thought that perhaps when it came to important matters, she might not be so very different from Brianna after all. Her hands began to tremble at the thought that she must be the one to initiate the wooing. She must encourage the bard to ask her father for her hand now, before another decision was made as to her mating. Lachlan would be preoccupied with matters of Brianna's nuptials and might very well be manageable. Hopefully she would find that to be so, for though Brianna withstood his rages with a smile, Glenna always trembled.

Crossing her fingers for luck, Glenna crossed the hall in silent strides, coming up behind Alastair before caution could take hold of her mind. With a nod of her head and a quirk of her brow she artfully spelled out her message so that none in the hall was any the wiser, that she wanted to meet him by the old, gnarled oak tree. Would he? Could he? The smile that he gave her answered yes.

Wind whipped at Glenna's hair, sending the strands flying about her shoulders as she stepped out the door. Carefully she adjusted her arasaid, a long length of material draped around the waist, and covering her head like a shawl. Making her way to the appointed place of the rendezvous, she tried to calm the rapid beat of her heart. A tight stirring in the pit of her stomach coiled at the very thought of what she was about. How should she bring up the subject? What should she say? How should she act? Just how did a woman instigate a proposal of marriage? Oh, if only for just one moment in time she could become Brianna. Brianna would have little trouble. She would merely say bluntly what was on her mind, come right to the point. Why then shouldn't she? Over and over again she rehearsed in her mind just what words she would utter.

"Glenna!" His voice startled her, for she had not seen nor heard his footsteps as he approached. Now that he was here she wondered if she had been foolish in supposing that matters of the heart could be so simple. What if she was wrong? What if he did not feel for her what she felt for him? Her fears were dispelled as he took her hand.

"Alastair . . ." Despite her heart's prodding, words failed her and all she could do was to look into the depths of his sea-blue eyes. Nervously she tugged at the fabric of her blue *arasaid*. Alastair pulled it down leaving her hair to blow wildly in the wind.

"I like yer hair flying free as it is, unplaited." The warmth of his fingers gently caressed her hand. "Ye look bonnie wi' the fury of the breeze stirrin' the flame. It makes me wish . . ." His voice was low and held the same rippling baritone as when he sang. "It makes me long for things I canna have."

"What things, Alastair?" Somehow she found her voice, but it came out in a croaked whisper.

"You." He shook his head, pulling his hand away as he took a step back from her. "Though to even contemplate loving you is madness. I've let my dreams lead me on to treacherous ground."

"Nae, ye haven't." She hurried to reassure him. "I've only been too shy to tell ye verbally that I feel the same about you." Glenna's heart hammered so loudly in her breast that she could barely hear her own words. Reaching out she clasped his hand, but Alastair pulled away.

"It is a thing that canna be. The bard and The MacQuarie's daughter? If I would but kiss ye The MacQuarie would hae my head. Lachlan would ne'er approve of me." Slumping his shoulders he started to turn away, but Glenna pulled at his cloak to stop him.

"Being the *seanachaidh* is a noble calling, passed down from father to son as surely as my father's own honor. How can ye then walk away?" Tears of frustrated longing stung her eyes and she blinked them away.

"Had yer father many sons he might grant a joining between us, but think, Glenna. He has no heir. He'll be wanting warriors, fighting men to wed his daughters. He'll be wantin' his grandsons to be wielding claymores, no' plucking harp strings. The MacQuaries are a noble lineage. Lachlan will no' be wantin' them to die out. He'll be tyin' ye up wi' a MacDonald, MacKinnon, or MacGregor, distant members o' his own clan wi' the blood of kings in their veins. No' a minstrel."

"But ye are a MacKinnon. Ye've blood ties to ours."

"Aye, but my father was born on the wrong side o' the

blanket. The stain of bastard's blood taints my sire. 'Tis but another reason yer father will no' gi' his permission for anything to pass between us." He shrugged his shoulders, passing his hand through his hair to tame its unruliness in the wind.

"And so ye'll gi' me up just like that? Drench the fire before it's kindled?" Glenna clucked her tongue in a rare gesture of aggravation. "Do I mean so little to ye then? Perhaps I should tell Brianna that *I* will go to The Campbell. I had thought . . . I had hoped . . ." She tried to blink back her tears, but this time they overwhelmed her, washing away her anger as they rolled down her cheeks in a torrent. Sobbing, she covered her face with her hands. He didn't care. Not really. He couldn't and act so resigned to their fate. A caring man would fight to win her, not give up so easily.

"Glenna, sweetling, dinna cry! Please. I canna stand to hear it. I didna want to hurt ye, just to talk common sense. *Hinny!*" Grasping her shoulders he pulled her toward him, drying her tears with his fingers. "Come, cry no more." With a mumbled imprecation he cupped her chin in his hand, bent his head and claimed her mouth in a hungry kiss.

What a strange sensation it was to feel his lips on hers, Glenna thought, but she found it pleasingly stirring. She was giddy, conscious only of the warmth emanating from his male body. Closing her eyes, she gave herself up to the titillating sensations that swept through her. Reaching up, she wound her arms around his neck, holding him closer, never wanting to let go. At last, however, Alastair pulled away.

"Och, it was heaven." The look in his eyes made her feel the depth of his desire, a desire that made her flush a brilliant shade of pink that clashed with her hair. "Ye hae made me the envy of every man in the hall," he whispered in her ear.

"And I the envy of every woman." Jeanne's words came back to taunt her, but even so she smiled. That bold miss would get little enough chance to claim the golden bard if she had her way. "Come wi' me, Alastair. We'll speak to my father now." She tried to hide her own fear of her father, hoping he would not be as fiercesome as she supposed. "It will be all right. Ye'll see." She crossed her fingers. "He has other daughters to wed wi' his warriors. Orianna is nearly of age and Morgana holds promise of being lovely when she is grown. And we'll hae Brianna on our side." Shyness came back to claim her and she lowered her eyes. She was brazenly pushing the matter despite what he'd said, all his declarations, but she wanted him so.

"I can't! Not yet. I . . ."

His reluctance deflated her new-found courage. Disappointment surged through her. "Ye canna? Or you willna? Are ye then so faint of heart, Alastair MacKinnon? Go then! If ye be so afraid, I'll no' goad ye longer." Though he reached for her hand she tore it away as if scalded, taking to her heels, fleeing through the undergrowth. She felt humiliated. Devastated. Felt heartache engulf her. Hardly even caring where she was going, she ran back toward the hall, stumbling along. Suddenly it was as if she ran right into a stone wall. Almost toppling to the ground from the force of the collision, Glenna looked up in stunned surprise at the grinning personage that stared down at her.

"So we meet again. I'd be lying if I pretended I'm not delighted, lass." One dark eyebrow shot upward as the deep blue eyes traveled over her slender body. His gaze was bold, tracing every valley, every curve as if to memorize the sight. "But how did ye get here before me? 'Tis a puzzlement, lass. Ye must be as fleet of foot as a deer or have magical powers. You are a kelpie. I know it now." His eyes lingered on the provocative fullness of her breasts. "But I do think I liked the other gown much better. Made ye look like one of the angels."

"Angels? Meet again?" Glenna was understandably baffled, but being preoccupied with thoughts of Alastair's lackluster wooing, gave it little contemplation.

"There was magic between us back there at the water's edge. Ye knew it and so did I. It would be to my liking if we conjured up such enchantment again but *continued* it this time." He winked.

"Ye must be daft!"

Before she could protest he embraced her, holding her tightly against him as his lips brushed against hers in the preliminary of a kiss.

"Unhand her!"

Ian felt the chill of cold, hard metal pressed against his neck. Was it any wonder he was quick to obey, disentangling himself from the red-haired woman's arms as hurriedly as he could. Turning around, he was seared by the eyes glaring at him. "I ought to kill ye! I ought . . ."

"Gruesome punishment for naught but a kiss." So the lovely kelpie had a keeper. "I know not who you be, friend, but as for me I have no desire to greet God's angels prematurely." Ian stuck out his hand in a gesture of peace but it was ignored.

"Who is this overbold churl, Glenna?" Though he pulled back his dirk, the bard still posed an obvious threat.

"I've no' seen him before."

"Och, 'tis not becoming to tell such a lie, lassie." Ian crossed his arms across his chest, piqued at the falsehood.

"It's not a lie. I don't know who you are, nor have I seen you before."

So that was the game she was playing, Ian thought. He stared hard at the blond man who had for a moment lusted for his blood. "She is your woman?"

"Aye. Mine." Alastair eyed the stranger suspiciously. "And if ye ever come near her again I'll . . ."

"Ye'll have no need." Ian watched as the other man sheathed his dagger. "She should have told me she was already taken and I would not have been so bold." His eyes were reproachful. "Next time I come upon a maiden perched like a mermaid by the water's edge I'll keep walking." Squaring his shoulders, he stalked off.

"By the water's edge?" Glenna threw back her head and gave vent to bubbling laughter as the truth of the situation dawned over her. "Brianna! 'Twas my sister that he saw and not I." Oh, but how glad she was for the mistake this day. Never would she forget the look on Alastair's face as he came thundering up behind that bold rogue. She thrilled at the thought that her gentle bard would have fought for her honor. He did care after all.

"Brianna? Of course." Alastair joined in the merriment, then just as quickly his mood sobered. "He means naught to ye. I'm glad," he said softly. "For a moment . . ."

"I should hae let ye think that, my fine bard. I should hae let ye be jealous for at least a day or two, but I love only ye, my own brave laddie. Now doubly so."

"And I do love ye, lassie." Alastair's words were muffled by Glenna's lips as she welded her mouth to his. They made a charming sight as Ian looked back. In spite of his vow he felt disappointment and anger surge through him. She scorned him but granted her kisses freely to another. It was the first time in his life that he had lost a lady love to another man. That it was a bard tweeked him. A man who wielded a harp and not a sword. Well, let him have her. He turned his back on the lovers, granting them privacy, then following a pathway through the outer bailey, made his way to the castle courtyard.

CHAPTER SEVEN

The castle of The MacQuarie stood on the hillside overlooking the entire valley, a roughly-hewn stronghold of weathered stone yet impressive in its own way, Ian thought, as he viewed it from afar. Standing strong and defiant amidst woods of beech and oak, the tower looked much like a guardian. Two protruding stones jutted out like furled eyebrows, and he could nearly imagine huge eyes staring at him as he walked.

The motte on which the castle stood was a steep sided, flattened cone formed by nature from hard packed earth and rock, a perilous climb which Ian had maneuvered quite well. At the base of the mound was a trench, hacked out of the hard dirt, the stone being used to form the high wall that enclosed the entire area. Buildings below the motte and dun were also of stone with thatched roofs and lay within the safety of the wall, a guard gate limiting access. It had been easy to find his way and Ian supposed Aulay would be somewhere within the bailey awaiting him, ready to offer up chastisement for Ian's wenching, as it was called by the English.

"Wenching, ha!" He was in a foul mood, still chafing from the realization that his manly charm had been scorned. He'd made a fool of himself, chasing after some red-haired woodland nymph like a stag after a doe in season, while all the time the object of his pursuit was already spoken for. To a man, who by the hue of his long flowing breacan, was a bard. A singer of songs, no less.

A bard! She prefers some golden-curled, effeminate warbler of tales to a man of strength, he thought sourly. Well, perhaps it served him right. He had gone about the matter with as much finesse as a bull in a potter's shed. And yet he'd sensed a fire in her kisses, had for one moment known it to be a mutual attraction. How then was he to explain her sudden coldness, as if summer had given way to winter frost? She had said naught about her brightly-beclad harpist. Would it have made any difference if she had? Ian drew in his breath and exhaled in a long, husky sigh. The answer was no. It was as if for just a moment he had abandoned all reason. He had been drawn to her as fiercely as the tide to the shore.

Frustration surged through him. By all the saints, why should her face and form have had such an effect on him? He'd known a hundred women who were by all measures beautiful and yet when he'd looked into those copper-colored eyes he'd been lost, caught up in a fascination more potent than a witch's spell. It was totally unusual for him to feel such a sudden, compelling, explosive physical attraction, and yet he had.

Ah well, he would keep his thoughts on more important matters from now on. Fie on flame-haired maidens, he preferred dark hair anyhow. She had been too skinny, too long in the leg, he tried to tell himself. Much too slender. He preferred his women buxom. Her chin had been a little too strong, clearly showing her to be a lass who would not easily be managed. Clearly a young woman like that would be trouble. Even the fiery hair gave proof to that. He would forget her. It would be easy to push this lass out of his mind, would it not? He convinced himself that it would be if he determined it to be so.

Why then did her face hover in his mind's eye? How was it

that he could still remember her firm breasts pressed against his chest? The sweeping arch to her hips and waist? Those enormous eyes haunted him. "By Saint Michael, what did the lass do to so bewitch me?" Aulay had always laughingly prophesied that one day Ian would meet his match. It seemed to have come to pass much sooner than he had expected. A woman who had scorned him. He, Ian Campbell.

As he walked he thought of just what he would say to Aulay to explain and soothe his sagging ego. He'd changed his mind. He'd tell the little man. That was it. When he'd gotten up close to the lassie he'd found an imperfection in her smile, her eyes. He'd sensed something strange about the girl and passed her by. Lassies were as plentiful as heather blossoms in the spring. He'd expound on the timeliness of their mission, the need for immediate settlement of the marriage contract. There were a great many things to consider, for Duncan would expect the bond to be profitable. Hopefully, the MacQuarie lass would have a rich dowry. It was a must to find out. He'd make Aulay see the wisdom in resolving the details of the betrothal as soon as possible. So determining, he moved forward to look cautiously at the stones that loomed in his path.

The castle was of rugged gray granite, a three-storied structure with a semicircular tower on the west side overlooking Loch Tuath. It obviously had been built to withstand seaborne invading forces and looked sturdy enough to frustrate any intruder. Square and oblong cut windows high above ground level gave proof that it could be amply protected with swords and arrows. Its size and strength made it appear impressive, nearly impenetrable, though as Ian came closer, he could see that it was much smaller than he had supposed. Not nearly as imposing as Duncan's castle. Even so, as he viewed the structure he envisioned the possibilities for expansion that existed here. With a few additions and some reconstruction, this castle would fit into the Campbell plan quite nicely. It would give them a stronghold for raiding the MacDonalds and MacLeods. No doubt that was what Duncan had planned, why he had suggested the joining by marriage to this enemy clan.

The air whistled as an arrow flew by his ear. From out of the shadows a large, hulking figure appeared above the guard gate. Ian came cautiously closer. "Dinna be coming any nearer." The voice was gruff, as if the sentry had sensed Ian's thoughts. "Strangers are no' welcome."

Careful to avoid touching his weapons, Ian raised both his hands, holding them palms up. A gesture of peace. "I've come a long distance to see The MacQuarie. I've come in peace."

"Peace? Ye're armed to the teeth." Ian could sense the guard's eyes scrutinizing him, moving from his flat soft cap and the wild myrtle worn there, to the sword and dirk hanging from his belt.

"For protection only. Do you think any man would come unarmed?"

"Ye come alone?" This time the voice did not sound as harsh.

"I was accompanied by a man just half my size. A dwarf. You might have already seen him." Ian hoped Aulay had been met with more hospitality.

"Aye! He's inside the walls. Then ye must be . . ."

"Ian Campbell, mon. Come to make arrangements for a wedding. I did not think I'd be met with arrows!" He took a step closer to the portcullis. "Am I to understand that Lachlan MacQuarie has changed his mind?" A rattling of chains and groan of wood was his answer as the gate was raised. "Ah, that's more like it."

Beyond the wall, within the enclosure, were storage facilities, cattle corrals, small garden plots, and a variety of stone buildings. The smoke rising from one told him clearly that a blacksmith lived within the encircling stones. A weapon maker, fashioning shields, swords, and other metal items used against his clan. The thought made him bristle, for his own father had been felled by a MacQuarie sword, a fact that still rankled. It was in the clan fighting over nine years ago that Ian had watched the man who had sired him, killed. A man, who until he had taken to drinking excessively, had been his hero. There upon the battlefield Niall Campbell had poured out his life's blood upon MacQuarie ground, bidding his son a final farewell and a plea of forgiveness for so many wasted years.

Lachlan MacQuarie and his clan robbed me of my father, he thought. Or had his father truly died long before that battle, the day Ian's mother died from childbed fever after giving birth to a stillborn daughter? Had he not lost both parents that day? Now he was standing within a stone's throw of that old man's castle. Turmoil raged in his breast and only by the greatest determination was he able to quell it. Duncan was clan chief and if peace was what he ordered then it was up to Ian to do all he could to bring it about.

That his arrival was greeted with suspicion and hostility did not make it any easier. It was obvious to see that the guard had quickly spread the word that a Campbell was within the walls of the bailey. Unfriendly glances challenged Ian, though not one threat was spoken. Did these damn MacQuaries then adhere to the laws of hospitality? Just in case they did not he touched his dirk reassuringly. He'd heard nasty tales about them in Edinburgh, of what uncouth heathens they were, of how they refused to obey the feudal laws like civilized men. They called themselves "free"; the king called them disobedient. Ian would judge for himself.

Broodingly, he surveyed the interior of the upper bailey, searching for Aulay. If any harm had come to his small friend he'd see to severe retribution, that he vowed. He wandered in agitation until he found him near the castle buttery, surrounded by a group of chattering, twittering women. "They think I'm one of the fairyfolk, the wee people."

"It seems they've never seen a dwarf before," Ian said, trying to smile. Aulay was clearly enjoying the attention. He wouldn't spoil the little man's fun with his own ill humor.

"Och, no. 'Tis just that they've ne'er seen a mon so handsome, isn't that so, lassie?" Aulay took off his cap in a gesture fitting of the finest courtly English gentleman and was rewarded by a joyous lilt of cooing laughter. The women made no secret of the fact that they found him enchanting. "But tell me, just how did yer tryst come about?"

Ian's jaw tensed. "Let me just say that I remembered my duty to Duncan in time."

"Ah?" Aulay raised his brow quizzically. "Then ye didn't . . . ?"

"Nae. A few kisses, that is all." Not wanting to talk about the matter, Ian pretended interest in a tall, blushing beauty.

"Are ye wantin' to sup?" the tall, slim woman was quick to ask, displaying far more courtesy than any of the men. "It must hae been a long, hard journey."

"Or a dram of liquid refreshment?" suggested another, hovering over Aulay like a mother tending her child. Both men were led to the tiny kitchen, a small room adjoining the castle's hall. Ian accepted a small glass of whiskey, for by custom that was the first thing offered on crossing the threshold of another's dwelling. To refuse would have been tantamount to spurning MacQuarie's hospitality. Aulay's mind, however, was on his stomach. He'd sniffed a pot of stew bubbling in a cauldron over the hearth and was determined to have a taste. The kitchen rang with sound—pots clanking, spoons rattling, as the dwarf's bowl was filled. Ian viewed the scene stoically, troubled by how very much this scene reminded him of similar moments spent in the Campbell kitchen. Women at least did not differ greatly from clan to clan.

"These lassies know how to make a mon feel welcome, even if their menfolk don't," Aulay said behind his hand. "It makes me sorry to bring about peace. I've half a mind to abduct the lot of them and take them back to our own stronghold. What do ye say?"

Ian started to answer when an indignant sniff alerted him to another presence in the small room. "What's going on here?" A woman's voice asked the question. As he turned around he was totally surprised to see the red-haired "kelpie" standing in the entranceway, dressed this time in the same garments she'd worn by the lake. "You!" Her eyes widened in total surprise.

"Aye, me," he answered, still smarting from his disappointment. "You saw me outside the bailey's walls. It should be no surprise just where I was headed, or is it that ye were too intent on 'other things' that ye did not even notice?" He lifted an eyebrow at her, remembering well the sight of her in the golden-haired bard's arms.

"Outside the walls? I did of a certainty *not* see ye there." Brianna held her chin high, her eyes flashing as she remembered his boldness at the lake. "Had I done so I would hae given strict instructions to the guards to send ye away." She scowled at him, hoping he would not notice the tremor in her voice. Seeing him again had shaken her to the core. Inside she was a mixture of emotions. He'd come into her life with the sudden jolt of a lightning bolt and now here he was again. "Just what are ye doing here anyway?"

Her hostility made her eyes glow like amber and he was startled again by her loveliness. Still, he hid behind a veil of anger. "I'm here to arrange a wedding, if it's any of your concern." Ian matched her tone with one of like gruffness.

"A wedding?" Was he imagining it or had she gone quite pale? "It canna be! Ye canna be . . ." She'd heard the tongues wagging about a Campbell being within the bailey's walls and had hoped to get a look at the man for herself, but she hadn't expected to come face to face with this one.

"A Campbell? Ah, but I am."

A Campbell, that explained his brashness. An English-loving Campbell! It gave her yet one more reason to espouse her defiance of him. "I shouldna be surprised. Ye do act like one." Brianna's back stiffened.

"I'll take that as a compliment. Now, if ye'll only see to it that Lachlan MacQuarie knows that I'm here. I've come from the Campbell stronghold to seek him out. I've no time to talk with lassies, pretty though they be. There's a marriage to be planned."

Robbie Campbell, she thought. By the blessed King's bones on Iona it must be he. Come to seal the bargaining for her hand with her father. She didn't know whether to be elated or appalled. In truth a myriad of emotions flooded over her at the very thought. She'd hoped this Robbie Campbell would be a man easily managed, who would give in to her whims, a man she could wrap around her finger as easily as she had her father. Clearly this was not such a man.

"Fie, but it seems he's not in any hurry to be talking with me, else he'd have come to meet with me by now. Surely all the other men of the castle are aware that I'm here. Just where is your noble chief?"

For the first time in her life Brianna was totally speechless. Though she tried to answer, all that came out was a gasp. This was her bridegroom, this same man who had set such a fire in her blood. This was the man her father had decided would wed her and bed her. The idea should have been repugnant to her and yet she felt a strange flush of excitement take hold of her. "I'll . . . take ye to him," she somehow managed to say, but the young Campbell did not seem to hear her. He was staring in the direction of the doorway.

It was Ian's turn to be surprised. There beyond the archway was a startling sight, a duplication of this fiery-haired lassie. His eyes moved from one to the other in fascination. The same height, soft curves, and beauty was mirrored in two young women. Throwing back his head, he gave full vent to his mirth, laughing uproariously.

Aulay joined in the laughter, then paused. "What are we laughing at?"

"Twins."

"Twins?" The little man's eyes followed in the direction of his friend's. "Aye." For the life of him he didn't see why that was cause for merriment.

"Twins!" Ian exclaimed again. His lovely kelpie had an

identical sister and it had been *she* who had embraced the bard. She whose heart was already taken. All was not lost after all.

"Aye." Brianna looked at him in puzzlement, she too wondering at his joviality and not liking it one bit. She didn't like to be laughed at no matter what the reason. "She's Glenna and I'm Brianna," she said haughtily.

"Brianna . . ." The name tripped lovingly over his tongue. "A fine name for a lovely lassie. Brianna." His heart soared on a wondrous flight. When this matter of Robbie's marriage was at an end, he intended to woo and win the red-haired young woman he had spied by the pool. So thinking, he flashed her a warm grin, but the appearance of a young, burly clansman put an end to any chance of furthering the acquaintance for the moment.

"The MacQuarie wants ye brought to him. Ye are to follow me."

"Then I would not want to keep him waiting." With a last parting glance over his shoulder, Ian Campbell followed the breacan-beclad man to Lachlan MacQuarie's hall.

CHAPTER EIGHT

The sun slanted down in a curtain of fiery rays, outlining the tall, proud figure that strode away in search of Lachlan MacQuarie. Brianna couldn't avert her gaze no matter how hard she tried. He was a man who held the eye, she had to give him that. Though he wore the same saffron-dyed shirt as the men of her clan and a similarly flattened round cap—sported, however, with a rakish air—he looked infinitely more dashing than the others. *Was* he Robbie Campbell? She had not had time to ask, and yet who else could he be? He'd come to arrange a wedding he had proclaimed so arrogantly. *Her* wedding! That startling declaration had thrown her momentarily off guard but now she wished she'd had her say, told him just what she thought of overbold lads.

Marry him? A man who took liberties with the first girl he met? She had no desire for a husband who would wander. She'd entered into this matter in good faith and expected like consideration. If that meant keeping her handsome bridegroom on a leash, like her father's hounds, then she would do it. Ah, she'd soon prove to him that she was no timid lass. She'd give him more of a battle than he bargained for. Indeed, perhaps she already had, she thought, stifling a giggle with her hand. She remembered their encounter and how she'd put a quick end to his lustful intent. Let him think on that and reflect seriously before he cornered another young maiden.

Brianna put her hands on her hips as she watched the dark-haired man disappear through the thick front portal of the castle's hall to meet with her father. Just what did she think of her bridegroom to be? Her emotions were hard to define and were certainly confusing. She loathed the man, thought him a strutting rooster, did she not? No. If she were totally honest with herself she would have to admit she had enjoyed their kisses. His warm lips on hers had kindled a host of sensations she'd never thought she would feel. Desire? From what she had heard the women chattering about she knew it to be so. Some talked of their husbands with awe, some in rapture, and there were others who spoke of hating the "duties" they were called upon to enact. Men could be tender, it seemed, or brutes. This Campbell had been strangely gentle, despite his passion. The hard length of him pressed against her soft form had given her firsthand proof that he was also virile. At least in the marriage bed she would not find her mate repugnant. But out of it? That was a thought to cause worry for she most definitely would not be dominated. She'd heard the English treated their women like simpletons, nothing better than brood mares. Hopefully, the Campbells did not emulate their allies completely, for Brianna was used to speaking her mind when the need arose.

"Ye're going to scorch yer eyes, sister dear, if ye dinna stop staring that way." Glenna's soft, melodious chuckles accompanied the statement. "Aye, but he is a fine sight to behold."

Brianna flushed at Glenna's comment, for in truth, had she known her sister had come up behind her, she would never have been quite so open in her gawking. Whirling around, she hastily sought an excuse. "I was but having a look at the strange hose he was wearing. Ye know Father

FLAME ACROSS THE HIGHLANDS

canna stand to hae his legs covered with cloth. Nor can the others. But I guess that's what happens when a mon keeps company with the English. Ha!" She curled her lips scornfully.

"Looking at his hose, were ye?" Glenna's giggle broke into full-fledged laughter. "Ah, shame on ye, Brianna, thinkin' I'd be believing that story."

"I . . . I *was* . . . looking at . . ."

"The fine shape to his calves and thighs, I'd be thinkin.'" Tilting her head to the side, she studied her sister. "Ye like what ye see."

"Nae!" Brianna's soft mouth tightened, and she was slightly indignant in trying to explain herself. "I was but studying him, wondering if he is Robbie Campbell."

"He *is!* I heard the men talking about it." She nodded toward the stables where a small group had gathered. "He's Duncan Campbell's nephew and heir to be sure, they said. The dark hair is proof enough of that. Jamie says he's fought him on the battlefield. They speak of him with respect even though they nearly met their death at his hands."

"Our enemy! I wonder how many MacQuaries he's sent to their graves?" Brianna frowned darkly.

"It doesna matter." Glenna seemed determined to defend him. "There was a war going on. Campbell men met their deaths as well. That's the way of battle, Brianna. He might not be a saint, but he canna be said to be a devil, either. No more so than Father."

"Hold yer tongue!" Throwing Glenna a stern look of disapproval, she turned away.

"It's true." Placing a tentative hand on her sister's shoulder, Glenna's voice was gentle. "But now there's a promise of peace and for that ye should be grateful."

"Aye, peace." Stoically, she considered that fact and its implications. She was an offering in this matter. Quite a load on her slim shoulders. "Perhaps then I should hae looked at this Campbell laddie in more detail. We've ne'er seen one up close, ye know. And as to his legs, they seem a bit bowed to me. Perhaps he spends a bit too much time on his horse."

"I think he's a fine-looking laddie and so do you."

Brianna sputtered in protest, then, throwing up her hands, gave up all pretense. She could not be anything but honest with Glenna. Since they were children they could read each other's minds. "Och, I suppose he is pleasant to the eye, but he is far too aware of it."

"Were my heart not already taken by Alastair I'd be changing my mind about marrying The Campbell." Coming closer, Glenna threw her arms around Brianna's neck. "Ah, when I heard that's who he was I felt all flushed with happiness for ye. I'd feared Robbie Campbell might hae a wart on his nose or be as unsightly as the MacKinnon heir is said to be. I feared at first that he was the tiny man, accompanying him, but he is bonnie. Robbie Campbell is as fine a looking man as there is. More importantly, ye're taken wi' him. Don't tell me differently. I looked at Alastair the same way when he first came back from his training in the *seanachaidh* school to reside in Father's hall."

"Taken wi' him am I?" Brianna pulled away. "Ye're daft, if ye think that. I was merely recalling to mind our first meeting." Briefly she related their encounter by the lake, absently brushing the soil from her thin woolen dress. "He is an overbold rascal!"

"Nae, he is merely a mon who sees what he wants and seeks to claim it. Were only Alastair of that inclination." She sighed, telling her own story of Alastair's reluctance to seek out their father. "Yon Campbell did me the greatest of favors, though he knew it not. When your bold lad mistook me for ye, he tried to begin where ye'd left off at the lake. Alastair came upon us and vented his jealousy." She clapped her hands with glee. "Ah, ye should hae seen it. He was going to fight for me."

"Alastair fight?" Brianna's brows arched in surprise. She'd always viewed the bard as a bit of a coward, but perhaps even a lamb would turn lion for the woman he loved.

"He claimed me as his own and said he *would* speak with Father."

"Oh, Glenna!" Now it was Brianna's turn to show affection, protectively putting an arm about her sister's waist. "I know he will."

"But Father . . ." Her brow puckered in concentration.

"Will say yes. I know he will when he's made to see reason." She smiled mischievously. "Just leave him to me."

"You'd charm the devil of his very horns and ask for his tail as well."

"Aye." The courtyard rang with their laughter. "That Campbell laddie is lucky he doesn't hae to deal with me on the marriage terms." As quickly as her laughter started, Brianna sobered. A clan chief's daughter was a pawn in the game of politics played by men. Most of a woman's life was spent under the guardianship of first her father then the man she married. Once she was married, her husband was responsible for her until she was widowed. Her father wanted peace, but she knew he would want the marriage to be profitable as well. A groom would be expected to give a large sum of gifts for her. What would be her bridal price? She couldn't help wondering just what the men were saying to each other right now. What she wouldn't give to hear the conversation going on in her father's chambers.

Brianna would have been surprised to find there was no talk at all. Indeed, all was silent except for the growling of the russet-hued wolfhounds that guarded the door. They seemed to be Ian's greatest hazard as he entered the chamber. Bristling and baring their teeth, they gave warning of what they would do if he made a wrong move.

"Easy. Easy. I'm here as a gesture of peace." Ian slowly, carefully moved past the two animals. "It seems no one has informed the dogs that the MacQuaries and Campbells are no longer at war," he whispered to Aulay, who clung behind him as closely as a shadow.

"Perhaps they haven't been *fed*," Aulay whispered back, following as Ian walked toward the far end of the large chamber. There Lachlan MacQuarie sat in a carved chair, gazing intently ahead as if Ian and Aulay were not even there. At last he spoke.

"Come closer. I would look upon yer faces. The only time I've looked upon a Campbell has been wi' a shield standing between us."

"As you wish." Ian thought of a glib answer but instead decided on a more diplomatic approach, bowing humbly before this man, who until now had been his fiercest enemy. They looked upon each other, each judging the other as a determined man.

"I wasna expectin' ye so soon. Ye sent no word." His eyes took on a look of coldness, aloofness, that warned of danger if Ian did not respond quickly. He seemed to perceive treachery, showed it by every furl of his brow, the tenseness in his jaw. "Ye sneaked up on us. It's lucky for ye that ye didn't get an arrow for yer daring."

"Duncan was anxious to have the matter settled. He thought to send me as both messenger and emissary. Some of our men are difficult to contain and he is having a trying time keeping them under control," he said truthfully. He did not add that he had been just such a man.

"As have I. There is a river of bad blood between us."

Ian nodded. "I hope that together we can build a bridge to span that river, if not with friendship, then at least with some measure of understanding."

"Aye. There's been enough blood spilling to last my lifetime." Boldly he assessed Ian. "So ye are the Campbell that's to take my favorite daughter away? Ye are Robbie Campbell?"

Ian shook his head. "No. I have come in his stead."

Lachlan MacQuarie swore beneath his breath. "Why?"

Ian himself wasn't satisfied with Duncan's explanation, was himself confused as to why Duncan had sent him, but he thought of a hasty excuse. "Robbie was needed at the castle. Thus I was sent to make the arrangements. As I mentioned before, time is of the utmost importance."

"Ha! Ye expect me to believe that? Either this nephew of Duncan's is a weakling or he is deformed in some way. Why else would he not reveal the lad to me? Eh?" His eyes were accusing. "I smell a fish and it's not in the kitchen."

For just a moment Ian was at a loss for words. He'd gotten the impression from Duncan that one of the reasons Robbie had been left behind was because Lachlan MacQuarie was not fully to be trusted, but he could not tell the clan leader that. Nor did he want to give the impression that the Campbells were trying to foist some sickly or homely young man upon his daughter. Damn Duncan, he thought, to put me in such a position. For just a moment his mind went blank as he sought anxiously for an explanation.

"Ha, just as I thought." Lachlan MacQuarie's eyes narrowed to slits.

Ian cleared his throat. "The matter Robbie is attending to is rebuilding the castle to suit his bride as befits her rank. He seeks to make the daughter of The MacQuarie comfortable in all ways as befits the daughter of such a powerful chief. He sent me to pave the road to good will. As you yourself know, moreover, it is not unusual for the *toiseach* to make such arrangements. I am that man." Folding his arms across his chest he held the older man's eyes without wavering. "You have my word that Robbie is a young laddie that would make any man proud. He will be a good husband to yer daughter."

Aulay, who had up until now kept silent, now spoke out. "Robbie Campbell is a comely young man. No' weak. No' ugly. He would cause no lassie shame."

"But if you have changed your mind then we will talk no more about it," Ian added, turning his back as if to walk away.

"Dinna leave just yet. I've not finished wi' my say." At his gesture two guards came as if from out of nowhere to block the portal. "I'll take it on yer word that Duncan's kin will be suitable." Once again he scrutinized Ian with his piercing eyes, his expression of suspicion diminishing. "Ha! I'll take ye at yer word!" Plucking a sword from its resting place on the wall, he threw it at Ian and seemed pleased by Ian's quick reflex action in being poised for a fight. "A born warrior. Allow me to say that I hope the laddie is much like you. I hae need of strength in my clan."

"He is every bit as brave," Ian warily handed the broadsword back to its owner wondering what to expect next, "and has always been most loyal."

"Bravery. Loyalty. Good qualities in a mon. So, let us begin with this *peace* your kinsman proposes." He looked toward the door and nodded. The soldiers who had been waiting there vanished and a small-boned, tawny-haired girl entered with three glasses of ale. "One of my daughters," Lachlan MacQuarie said in answer to Ian's unanswered question. "Orianna is her name."

The girl nodded politely as she placed the goblet in Ian's hand. He eyed her with interest, wondering if she was the one who had been chosen to be Robbie's bride, though nothing had been said verbally. She was fragile looking, pretty, and obviously shy, seemingly a fit bride for Robbie, though very young.

"She's very pretty."

"Aye, all my daughters are bonnie lassies. All four." With a flick of his wrist he sent her from the room in a swish of skirts. "But no sons, which brings us to the matter that's been weighing on my mind." He stared deep into the depths of the tankard as if to find a solution there. "I hae no sons. My only hope of carrying out my line is through grandsons." His thick fingers clenched and unclenched on the wooden armrests. "I'll put it to ye bluntly. One of the terms of the marriage contract is that Robbie Campbell take on the MacQuarie name and that any children of the union will take same."

Ian bolted up from his chair. He was incredulous. "Robbie Campbell take on the *MacQuarie* name?"

"That's what I said." His fingers curled into aggressive fists. "It is not an unusual request in this instance."

Ian paced up and down the chamber in agitation. No, it wasn't unusual. He knew that what The MacQuarie was requesting had been done before. But surely Duncan would never agree. A Campbell to take upon himself his enemies' name, to sire children that would belong to a hated clan? Be tanist to The MacQuarie! Ian slammed his fist into the palm of his hand to vent his tortured anger. He wanted to scream out *no* to decry it as an outrage, but fought to retain his composure. "The name MacQuarie is poison to our tongue," he breathed.

"As is Campbell to mine. Still it is a thing I ask. I will not agree to a marriage wi'out it." Lachlan MacQuarie sat upright in his chair with all the regal bearing of a king. The stubborn tilt to his jaw gave proof of his determination.

"Agree, mon. Agree!" Aulay was adamant as he buzzed in Ian's ear. "Wi' Robbie a MacQuarie, the way will be open for ye to claim the chiefship when Duncan dies."

That much was true, but that was not the reason Ian finally agreed to the terms. Duncan had been adamant about this joining of clans. He had revealed to Ian the importance he placed on this marriage. If it was that necessary, then he would do the agile diplomatic dance and pay the piper later. "Agreed. But as per Duncan's request, the lassie must live among the Campbell kin, at the Campbell stronghold until the firstborn child is of age to be named tanist."

Lachlan MacQuarie nodded. "It is agreed as first spoken." The usual haggling followed, and the cleric sent in to draw up the contract. It specified the bride's dowry, several rich acres of pasture land between the two strongholds. Land made fertile with the blood of both clans. If Robbie Campbell died, his bride would inherit one third of everything he owned. Lachlan in turn asked for several head of cattle, three loads of oats, and some hunting dogs to match the ones he already owned.

A further stipulation was enacted which forbade any future heirs from granting land to foreigners. The English dogs, as Lachlan called them. It was specifically forbidden that any form of feudalism be enacted, for The MacQuarie was against it and fought to protect his people. The two systems had existed side by side albeit at serious odds with each other. Under the Celtic patriarchal system the land belonged to the tribe, but feudalism meant that the land passed into the possession of the king, to be parceled out according to his whim or necessity. If the reason for this sudden show of friendship was to wrest his land away, Lachlan thought, he would insure its protection by written word.

"The terms are acceptable," Ian said, affixing his mark.

"All is agreed." Lachlan MacQuarie's frown had vanished, to be replaced by the grimace of a smile. "The banns will be posted on the next three successive Sundays. In the meantime relax and enjoy yer stay. Tonight there will be a celebration. Feasting. Dancing. Drinking."

"I will look forward to such hospitality." Indeed he would, Ian thought. It would be a perfect time to woo his flame-haired kelpie, and that was exactly what he had planned. And who could say. Perhaps when this was all over he would find a way to take her back to the Campbell hall with him.

CHAPTER NINE

Like a flash of lightning, Brianna fairly flew up the circular stone staircase, taking the steps two at a time in her hurry to prepare for the night's feasting. As she passed her father's chambers she couldn't resist pausing, however, putting her ear briefly to the door. In disappointment at hearing no voices beyond, she continued up to the second floor bedchamber that she shared with her sister. Once inside, she plundered her large wooden trunk and pulled several items of clothing from the pegs on the wall, determined to find just the right garments to wear tonight. Indeed, she would clothe herself with as much care as if she were going into battle. Perhaps in a way she was, she mused.

"The russet undertunic," she decided aloud and a dun-colored arasaid striped with a rainbow of colors, the one Glenna had woven for her on the large loom in the ladies' hall. The large gold brooch with a simple chain around her neck. Carefully, she laid the items on the large bed that stood in the middle of the room. Perhaps a wreath of flowers in her hair for the occasion.

She thought how Glenna would be amused to see her take such time in choosing her garments, she who was usually haphazard in her dress, taking little care what she wore.

Well, it is to make Father proud of me before The Campbell, she determined, defending herself. It was to make the MacQuaries proud and for no other reason.

A small packet of flowers and herbs that Glenna always used in her bath taunted her now. Oh, she knew what the Lowlanders and those of the royal Scottish court said about the Highlanders and Islanders. That they were uncouth barbarians who smelled of horses, hay, and worse. The King of Scotland, that upstart Robert de Brus, prided himself on being of French descent, affected their manner, speech, and culture while reducing the true Celtic Scots to virtual slavery. Why, he even bore a Frenchified name. He called the true Scots *bruti* and contained them in the hills as much as possible. He seemed to forget that those were the "bruti" who had helped him secure his throne, including those bearing the MacQuarie name. And no doubt her betrothed, this Campbell, was much the same. Well, she would show him!

Brianna had always scoffed at Glenna's frivolity before, but now had second thoughts. Since it was the third day of the week, it was the women's turn to bathe. In truth, perhaps she would feel much better once she had the warm cocoon of water surrounding her. It would relax her and give her time to think things out, to get used to the idea of having a husband. So thinking, she grabbed an old woolen tartan and made her way to the bathhouse.

Pushing open the thick wooden portal, Brianna was grateful to see that all of the six large wooden tubs that studded the rush-strewn floor were empty. She would have the seldom granted opportunity of privacy. A well for washing or drinking water was available at the central drawing point, thus she busied herself with procuring a plentiful supply, filling the buckets and heating the water in the large iron pots that were perched over an open fire. Struggling under the heavy burden of the large cauldrons, she nonetheless managed to carry them to one of the tubs, completing the job of filling her bath. Turning around, lifting the skirts of her undertunic up to her knees in preparation of disrobing, she heard the door creak. The sudden unwelcome feeling that someone was staring at her crept over her. Whirling around she was startled to find herself face to face with *him* again.

"What a welcome surprise," he said pleasantly, shutting the door behind him. "It seems I'm always finding you perched by water. That must mean you *are* a kelpie."

"I'm no such thing and I'm tired of ye taunting me wi' it," she snapped, holding the tartan protectively up to her bosom to hide the outline of her breasts beneath the thin linen.

The soft, orange yellow glow of flickering torchlight illuminated the room and gave her a clear view of his manly form. He was naked to the waist, wearing only a breacan. Her eyes took in his broad shoulders, muscled arms, and the thick wisp of dark hair covering his chest. "And just what are ye doing here anyway? 'Tis the women's turn to bathe."

"It is?" Ian had felt so grimy and dirty from the journey that the very first thing upon his mind, after his meeting with Lachlan MacQuarie, had been a bath. "How was I to know?"

Brianna conceded the point. "Ye wouldna." He was a guest to her father's hall, he would have no way of knowing their particular customs. "But . . ." From the corner of her eye she took in every detail of his appearance. This time he wore no trews, and she noted his legs were finely shaped and muscled. He was not knobby of knees like some of the men, nor were his legs battle-scarred. As he took a step forward, she backed away and looked toward the door. The only way out was to go past him, and this she did not want to do. She wanted to maintain as great a distance as possible between them.

In the silence that pervaded the room each one was conscious of the other but somehow afraid to move or speak. Brianna was aware of him in every nerve, pore, and bone in her body.

"Ah, lassie, I do not blame you for being apprehensive after the way I acted at the lake."

"Ye were a bold rogue and well ye know it." Haughtily she pointed her nose toward the ceiling.

"Aye, I was a bold buffoon, but I promise, lass, I will not ravish you." He grinned, his strong teeth a glow of white in the torchlight, contrasting sharply to the bronze of his face.

Ravish her? By his tone he was making light of their encounter, angering her anew. She did not like his mocking, teasing manner. Her volatile temper started to boil as furiously as the water in the pots.

"Indeed ye shan't." Picking up a large wooden stool from beside the tub, she wielded it like a weapon, threatening him if he made a move.

"Whoa, lassie! I thought there was to be peace between the Campbells and MacQuaries." He held up his hands, palm up in a gesture of surrender. "I apologize for my boldness at the lake, but I was 'struck' by your beauty. I do not need to be 'struck' again." A wide grin etched across his face. "If I acted in a manner to alarm you, I am truly sorry. But isn't it time to call a truce?"

"A truce?" Why was it she always felt compelled to fight with him and yet at the same time longed for . . . By all the saints, he unnerved her most definitely, confused her with contradicting emotions. Even so, she put down the stool. It wouldn't do for her father to find her future husband lying senseless on the bathhouse floor.

"Aye, a truce." He could not keep his eyes from the cleft between her breasts that showed just slightly when she bent over, nor could he keep from watching the sway of her hips as she moved. In a flickering glance he took in everything about her. He'd been an impatient lout, but this time all would be different. He would woo her with finesse.

Truce indeed, she thought. It seemed the Campbells always furthered themselves by marrying daughters of chiefs who owned lands. This Campbell was no exception. She must remember that he was her enemy, at least for the moment. Still she said, "Agreed!" struggling to appear poised. She betrayed herself as she lowered her eyes from his gaze.

"Good!" Oh, how he wanted to kiss her, but he held himself back.

"Now, ye may leave." She pressed her lips together tightly as she pointed toward the door. If he thought there was going to be any dallying, just because he'd flattered her, she would let him know he was wrong.

"I'll leave, but first I do want to soothe the ill will between us. It's still there despite your words." His eyes focused on hers, his gaze intent as he walked the short distance that separated them. "Let us have peace."

Brianna started to turn away but just at that moment he reached out and captured her hand. Bending low over it, he pressed his warm mouth into the palm in a gesture he'd learned from courtly knights who used such chivalry to charm a lady. It always worked, he thought with a smile.

"Dinna ye ever think of anything but kissing?" Her voice was a whisper. His mouth had seemed to sear her flesh, awakening that same flutter in her stomach she'd felt at the lake. She found herself remembering the pressure of those warm, knowing lips against hers. Though it was her hand he touched, her heart pulsated as rapidly as the wings of a trapped bird.

"You bring such thoughts to my mind." Seeing that his words caused her to stiffen he added, "I mean that as a compliment."

"Ha, I know yer kind. Chasing after every woman ye meet. Ye nearly said as much." She tried to ignore the sensations running down her arm as he caressed each finger with his lips. In a gesture of defiance she pulled her hand away. "Enough!" Holding out her slim, long-fingered hand she looked at the calluses that marred her palm and fingers. What had he thought when he'd kissed her hand? Had he felt the same stirring she had?

"I'm a warrior, not a poet. I know not any words that will

make you see into my heart." The soft material of her undertunic tightened across her firm breasts. Ian fought against the urge to take her in his arms. Tearing his gaze away he said merely, "All I can say is that you are the first woman who has affected me so strongly. It's magic, lassie. I know it and you know it, too. Don't let my foolishness break the spell."

"Spell?" Her eyes widened in apprehension. Indeed, she had felt as if a power beyond herself was drawing her to him.

"You know very well what I mean, lassie. Come, give me a grin from your heart. If there is to be peace between the Campbells and MacQuaries, how can we do any less between ourselves?" There was a sincerity in his tone that soothed her, softened her resolve. "I promise to behave myself if only you will grant me one smile."

"A smile and then ye will leave?" She had to admit that he was a man who interested her, drew her. He did stir a feeling deep inside, but more than that the union between them would bring peace to their clans. How then could she let personal feelings gnaw at her and destroy any chance of contentment between them. She couldn't, at least that's what she told herself. If they were to be married it was time they got acquainted, she thought. Hostility would not get her very far. "Agreed." How could she refuse? Slowly she curved her lips up, let down her defenses, and responded unguardedly to his natural charm. He had it aplenty.

"There. More potent than a hundred words. You are bonnie, lassie." He seemed to have banished the bold, aggressive behavior, showing her a more restrained side to his nature. Perhaps he really was sorry, she thought.

Brianna capitulated to a strange, unexplained burst of happiness. The peace between them was fragile, but it was enough for the moment. They continued to talk for a few moments longer. The wavering torchlight danced on his strong cheekbones and Brianna stared, fascinated at the way the flames played across his boldly carved nose and hard jawline. Just as she had first supposed, he would be a difficult man to best, but at least now she felt more comfortable in his presence. It was a beginning.

"Now, I promised to leave, and I will show you I am a man of my word." Ian moved slowly toward the door, tempted to turn around and cast his better intentions aside, but a promise was a promise. Opening the portal he eyed her with regret. "Good night, sweet Brianna. At least until I see you again."

She followed him, gently but firmly pushing him with the weight of the door until he was outside the room. "Good night, Robbie Campbell."

Ian heard the door slam behind him, heard the grate of the bolt as she slid it in place. *Robbie Campbell,* she'd called him. "No, wait. I'm not. . . ." He tried to open the door but she had securely locked it. It just wouldn't do for her to think he was the man spoken for. It was no wonder she shunned him. He didn't want her to think he was to marry someone else. Banging on the thick wood, he found it was to no avail. At last, throwing up his hands, he stalked away. He'd soon let her know just who he was. The matter would be straightened out at the first opportunity.

CHAPTER TEN

The large hall was bathed in firelight and candle glow, from the planked floor to the lofty ceiling. Flames in the vast hearth danced about spewing tongues of red and yellow, illuminating the clan banner hanging proudly for all to see. Rushes and herbs—basil, balm, camomile, costmary, and cowslip had been freshly strewn on the floor for the occasion. The walls of the castle were ornamented with hanging objects and artifacts—shields, swords, dirks, and claymores—which told of the MacQuarie bravery.

Tables covered with platters and bowls were nearly sagging under the weight of the food piled high—wild duck with wine sauce, smoked haddock, roast grouse with sprigs of heather, roast venison, pickled herring, boiled goose eggs, beet root salad, curds, wild carrots, honey cakes, and wild raspberries. Barley broth bubbled noisily in a cauldron over the fire, its steam giving off an aroma which heightened appetites. Lachlan MacQuarie would show the Campbells how the MacQuaries gave a feast, the clansman thought. It seemed that nearly every edible creature God had created was on the table. The aroma of roasting meat permeated the air. Platters were artfully arrayed with fruits and vegetables in great variety. Red heather and ropes of laurel hung from wall and ceiling alike and combined their fragrance with the tantalizing aroma of the betrothal feast. A celebration Lachlan had promised and indeed that's what it was.

A raised dais of stone ran the full length of the hall, across from the fireplace upon which many of the guests sat. Lachlan MacQuarie sat in one of the massive chairs at a table placed across from the others. Raised to a lofty height by means of a platform, he looked awesome as he peered down at the assemblage. Extra trestle tables and several benches had been assembled to accommodate the overflow of clansmen. Ian sat to the left of The MacQuarie and the vacant chair to his right was unquestionably for the bride-to-be. Was it the tawny-haired maiden he'd seen in The MacQuarie's chamber who would share Robbie's bed or one of his other daughters? The MacQuarie had mentioned he had four. Which would be Robbie's lassie? When the blond-haired lass took a seat at another table, he knew he had made a wrong assumption.

He sat pensively sipping his ale, bemused by the doings. He had to admit that it promised to be a fine feast. No man or woman here would go away hungry. Obviously, The MacQuarie was anxious for word to get to Duncan that all the raiding had done naught to diminish the MacQuarie wealth. Perhaps then Duncan had been right in this matter of peace.

Ian watched as Lachlan MacQuarie was served the hero's portion, the first cut of meat, a gesture to show him to be the bravest of the clansmen and to assure that his status was noted by all present. As Ian drank and supped he looked at the door from time to time, hoping for sight of the red-haired maiden. He caught sight of her sister, sitting near the bard, but where was *she*? A lassie as pretty as the fair Brianna should be seen.

Brianna was at the moment taking plenty of time in readying herself for the night's celebration, daydreaming of charming Robbie Campbell into being her adoring slave.

Oh, how she would relish that. And why not? She had even luxuriated in washing her bright red hair with a special foaming root Glenna had given her. Now it glowed like fire.

She stood gazing into a small decorative chest, taking an inordinate amount of interest in choosing just the right jewelry. Indeed, she took care with every detail of her appearance. Robbie Campbell would not regret taking her for a bride, she vowed, carefully donning her undertunic. She was expert in draping the saffron- and blue-striped arasaid around her slim body, tucking it around her hips, fitting it snugly around her waist with a brown leather belt. Yards and yards of cloth fell in graceful folds just below her ankles, then looped up to cover her shoulders like a shawl. She secured it with a brooch, a handworked gold circle with intricate scrollwork.

Observing herself in a long steel mirror, she smiled as she stared back at her reflection with a certain amount of gratification. Humming to herself, she slipped through the doorway and down the circular staircase that led to the second floor, feeling proud to have taken great care to preserve her father's honor.

Boisterous laughter and mumbled voices stilled as the crowd caught sight of her. When Brianna entered everyone turned their head, just as she had hoped. The whispered gasps of awe sounded like the rustling wind. Artfully, she made the most of her entrance, slowly walking the length of the vast room, her head held high. All eyes were on her, but it was only one pair of eyes she wanted to look upon her with favor. He did. Raising his head from his full trencher, he sat upright in his chair, blinking as if he perceived the vision of loveliness to be a creation of the whiskey and wine of which he had partaken. There was a sense of anxiety that consumed him, a certainty that she was no common maid. Dressed as she was, she looked as glorious as a Scottish princess.

Cups were filled to the brim with fiery whiskey. Tankards were passed among the revelers again and again. As Brianna stood next to Lachlan MacQuarie, Ian nearly spilled the entire contents of his cup. No! He didn't want to even consider the possibility. And yet what was it about Lachlan's face that troubled him? There was something familiar about the eyes, the hair. She had to be his daughter. Why hadn't he noticed the similarity before? Because he was too besotted. He had heard that Lachlan MacQuarie had twins. Why hadn't he remembered when he'd seen the two young women?

Dogs snapped at the table scraps tossed to them, fighting now and again over a tasty morsel. Ian barely noticed the noise. In truth, all he could seem to hear was her voice talking in cheerful tones to Lachlan MacQuarie as she took a seat beside him. She was his daughter and the bride. Laughing and smiling, she was enchanting. Ian felt a stab of physical pain as all the pieces of the puzzle fit together. How could she be so happy when suddenly he was so miserable?

The aroma of fruit-decorated *bannocks,* baked especially for the occasion, wafted in the air as they were passed around, but Ian had lost his appetite. He wished the evening would end, that he could take her by the hand and lead her away from this melee. There were many questions he wanted to ask, many truths to be unveiled.

"Aren't you hungry?" Brianna's tone was teasing as she smiled at him.

"I've already eaten too much." The truth was he was starved for much more than food. She was so lovely in the candlelight. He wanted to touch her again as he had in the bathhouse and was afforded that opportunity when she picked up a scone and handed it to him. He took her small gift, their fingers brushing in a gentle caress, one that sparked a flame deep within him.

Brianna's sparkling eyes met his over the rim of her cup as she sipped her wine. She stared into the deep blue eyes that regarded her so intently, wishing she could read his mind. The wounded look upon his face nearly made her feel sorry for him. Nervously, she tugged at her brooch, wondering if he had changed his mind about marrying her. She had given him quite a time. And yet now she looked ahead to their life together with anticipation. Smiling again, she tried to purvey her feelings to him. He'd said there was a special magic between them, and he was right. So very, very right. Even now she felt it. A potent current that hovered in the very air when he was near.

Amidst the candle glow and firelight, Alastair stood and began strumming the strings of his harp. He sang a droning, seemingly endless account of the MacQuarie ancestry and a lavish praise of the clan, which usually held Brianna in rapt attention, but now caused her to be anxious for its end. She had other things on her mind. Like getting to know her bridegroom for one thing.

Guarai was a second son of Kenneth MacAlpin, he recounted, one of the ancient chiefs of Ulva which was why the MacQuaries held a place of honor as an ancient tribe in the councils of the Lords of the Isles. Alastair told a tale of ancient days, of the clans' voyages across the sea, and migration to the Isles. He talked of the heroes of Caledonia, the favorite of these being Cormac, surnamed *Mor* or "the great," who lived in the time of Alexander II. He joined with his followers and three *biorlins* or galleys of sixteen oars each in the great expedition against the inhabitants of the Isles under Norwegian rule. It seemed in those days the Scots and Vikings were always fighting. The king's death in the Island of Kerera rendered the attack abortive. Cormac, by appearing with armament, brought on himself a severe retaliation. He was attacked, his forces overthrown, and he was slain. His sons, Allan and Gregor, were compelled to take refuge in Ireland. Brianna had heard the story so many times that she fought against a yawn. The wine she sipped relaxed her, but when she looked in her groom's direction she felt a mild anxiety. What did she really know about this man who was to become her husband? As if sensing her searching eyes, he looked again in her direction, and she could tell that he was troubled.

What will it be like to share my life with this man? she wondered. Would she enjoy his lovemaking and moan with pleasure at his touch? What would she experience in the years that lay ahead? With a sigh, she turned her attention back to Alastair, closing her eyes, her mind gently drifting with thoughts of what was to come. At last the bard's song ended and the men clapped and roared their approval.

The room became silent as Lachlan MacQuarie stood up. "As ye know, we're gathered tonight to make celebration and begin upon a period of tranquillity." He took Brianna's hand, gently pulling her to her feet. "My daughter will gi' her hand in marriage to Robbie Campbell. Brianna will help to bring about peace by joining her hand to Duncan Campbell's nephew. The contract is signed and the banns will be posted." A cheer broke out but Ian did not respond. Instead he sat in a trance. No. He didn't want to hear it. Robbie's bride? Brianna? His lovely flame-haired kelpie? There must be something he could do. Fate could never be that cruel. But it was. The eldest daughter, and Robbie's bride, and the lassie who had won his heart were one and the same. Oh, that she were to be his own.

Brianna looked at the dark-haired Campbell, expecting him to smile, but was met by a cold stare and could only wonder why. Her question was answered as her father nodded in the young man's direction. "Duncan has sent an emissary to prepare the way for the nuptials. His other nephew, Ian, has acted most faithfully in the negotiations."

Ian, Brianna thought. What was this? Her eyes darted to her father's face, expecting him to correct his mistake. "Father. *Robbie* Campbell."

"Is arranging a welcoming for you. *He* isn't Robbie Campbell!" Lachlan looked at his daughter's pale face and suddenly understood her confusion. "Ye thought that he . . . Och, girl. It's my foolishness. I should hae made it clear, should hae introduced ye before now. But I didn't . . ." In that moment Lachlan MacQuarie read into his daughter's heart and felt her heartbreak. "Ah, lassie. Poor, poor lassie."

The empty goblets, tankards, and platters were cleared away. Benches were pushed back, the trestle tables folded and placed against the wall in preparation for dancing. The pipes began their keening, a familiar tune Brianna recognized at once. First, the men danced alone, a rousing dance of high-kicking feet. Then the women joined in, choosing partners for a spirited reel which set every foot tapping. The Great Hall was a din of laughing, talking, accompanied by the drone of skirling pipes and the thumping feet of dancers. But Brianna had no heart for the revelry. The man who drew her heart was not her intended husband after all. Not Robbie Campbell. For the first time in her life she sincerely wished she could make herself invisible—flee the hall before her expressions gave her true feelings away. Though she loved to dance, she longed for an end to the feasting so that she might sneak away to her bed.

Ian Campbell was his name. What a liar he was! Making her think he was the man she was to marry! Anger coiled within her, and she turned her rage outward, scowling furiously. But no. She wanted to feel anger at him, but knew him innocent of any blame. He had never told her he was her groom-to-be. She and Glenna had merely assumed it. Nor had he any way of knowing who *she* was. She had never told him she was Lachlan's daughter. Tears erupted in her eyes, threatening a storm. She had already bartered her maidenhead away. But how was she to know she'd meet a man who would so ensnare her heart? Now she would have to pay the price in heartache.

CHAPTER ELEVEN

The flames engulfing the huge logs in the hearth sputtered and burned low. One by one the smoking candles and torches that had once brightened the hall flickered, hissed, and then died out. Darkness was gathering under the high ceiling, shadows hovered in the corners and behind the massive pillars of the room like eerie spirits waiting to pounce. The women had retired with the small children, leaving the men alone at their drinking.

The hour was growing late. Very few guests lingered at the trestle tables. Why then did he? Ian wondered. Perhaps because he dreaded the solitude of his thoughts, he chose to remain in the huge room moodily drinking cups of whiskey and tankard after tankard of ale. This lethal combination promised to give him a raging headache come morn. Somehow he didn't care. The soothing beverage numbed his senses and that's what he wanted right now.

Robbie Campbell's bride. The thought kept whirling about in his mind. Lachlan MacQuarie's daughter would be Robbie's wife, not his. Never his. He remembered guffawing lightheartedly, espousing the hope that the MacQuarie daughter would not be overly homely. The fact was she was exceedingly bonnie. The joke was on him, for he'd made the promise to woo and win MacQuarie's daughter for another laddie.

"One without even the first stubs of a beard," he scoffed, though in truth he was overly fond of the lad. He knew how much Robbie always admired him and tried to emulate him in all things, but that didn't soothe his irritation at the situation.

Ian's vision blurred, his head buzzed, as he continued raising the cup to his lips. He'd never let his drinking get so out of hand, but then he'd never lost a woman before, he thought sourly. "Lost her 'fore I ever set foot on this soil," he grumbled aloud.

"Lost who?" Aulay came to sit beside him, eyeing him worriedly, obviously disturbed by his mumbling.

"Her!" Ian nodded in the direction of the dais. The chair now stood vacant.

"There's no one there now." The little man's eyes bulged with shock as he looked from Ian to the empty chair and then back again. Teasingly, he put his index finger to his temple and moved it in a circle. "She was there. Brenna . . ." He rolled her name over his tongue as if relishing a rare wine. "Brenna . . . Sooooooo pretty." Ian's eyes gazed in rapt attention, envisioning her in his mind as if she still sat there, her nose at that lofty angle, her flaming hair tumbling down her back in thick waves. "Should have been mine."

"Ye are daft!" Grabbing the half-full cup from Ian's hand, Aulay poured it on the floor causing little rivulets to flow through the rushes. "What's ailing ye? Never mind. I dinna need to ask. The lassie. That's as plain as the nose on yer face. She made more of an impression on ye than ye would admit to me." Aulay repressed a smile, forcing his features to remain expressionless. Only his eyes gave any hint as to his mirth.

"Aye." Even now he could see her, sitting by her father's side as regally as a queen.

"Put her out of yer mind. Ye've said yerself that women

are as plentiful as waves in the sea." Aulay shrugged his shoulders. "Find yerself another."

Ian shook his head stubbornly. "Nae. I want *her*."

"Because she canna be yours. The forbidden fruit is always sweeter." The air was disturbed by Aulay's hiccup, a noise soon replaced by his gurgling laughter. He laughed so hard that tears shimmered in his eyes. "After all the lassies' hearts ye've broken at last ye meet yer match."

Ian pounded the table. "What're you laughing at, you buffoon?" With one well-aimed kick from his foot he sent Aulay's chair flying across the room.

Aulay just barely regained his balance. "Just thinking Cupid must hae a sense of humor."

"Sense of humor, is it?" Snorting in derision, Ian turned away. "Well, I wish he'd take his laugh and have done with it."

"He will." Pounding him on the back, he tried to lighten his spirits. "Ye've been repaid in kind. If ye notched each conquest ye hae made on yer sword ye would hae whittled it away by now! Think on it."

Ian did, but it didn't improve his mood. Instead it made him even more surly, determined that one slim, haughty red-haired lass was not going to get the best of him. Oh, how she must be laughing right now, knowing of the mistake he had made in trying to seduce the very woman he'd come to marry to his kin. Well, he'd prove to her just how little he cared. He'd avoid that often-frowning miss, pretend she was as invisible as a ghost whenever he was forced to be in her company. Aye, that he would. He'd bite his tongue before he gave her one kind word. He would be damned before he'd look her way. He'd hurry and be done with this business of the wedding and scurry back to the Campbell Hall without another thought about her.

"Och, Ian. Such a face. Ye didna even look so tragic when we faced the English at Bannockburn!"

Closing his eyes, Aulay thought back to that time of turmoil and the perils it had brought. Scottish civil war was well in progress then, a time without a king, but only those fighting to become king. After Alexander III's death the Campbells had supported Robert the Bruce's grandfather, that other Robert de Brus, of Annondale. Other Highlanders had supported John Balliol of Galloway. At first Robert de Brus and the Campbells had sought the English King's aid only to find that he sought to take advantage of the situation. When the Scots balked and tried to throw off the English yoke, Edward I had taken Berwick and slaughtered the townspeople to show he was master of the Lowlands. Prisoners had been taken, the Stone of Destiny stolen as a symbol of conquest.

Aulay and Ian had been but lads, playing with toy swords, and yet they had been immersed in the catastrophe. Aulay would have become a victim if not for Ian's quick thinking. Even then he had shown prowess, wielding that wooden sword as if it were real. Miraculously, he had knocked the broadsword out of Aulay's attacker's hand and tugged him to safety. They had been boon companions ever since. Then at the battle of Bannockburn Ian had saved his life once again, pushing him out of the aim of an English arrow.

"Bannockburn!" Ian sighed. "Better to face an army than one haughty woman. Ha! Brianna MacQuarie is a spoiled, willful lassie, who is in great need of a strong hand, aimed at her well-shaped backside."

Resting his head on his arms, Ian closed his eyes too. Suddenly he was very tired. Sleep was what he needed. He had best catch at least a few winks for he'd heard Lachlan MacQuarie had two full days of festivities awaiting them as part of the betrothal ceremony. Games. Hunting. Usually, Ian would have been elated at the prospect of preening his skills before the large assemblage, but now all he wished was to be far away from here. By Saint Michael, even now she haunted his thoughts.

"Robbie is not man enough for her. He's naught but a boy! A wee laddie not much older than she. Not a skilled warrior," he murmured miserably. "He knows nothing of women or how to please them."

"He's a comely young lad and ye know it. There is no dishonor in being young! Wi' a lovely young bride like MacQuarie's daughter in his bed he'll soon learn what to do." Again Aulay laughed, trying to steer Ian's thoughts away from the situation. "Ye learned quickly enough the first time a fair Highland flower passed yer way. Tomorrow ye'll see another lassie that catches yer eye. There are several I hae seen. Leave the bedding of the MacQuarie lass to Robbie as ye should."

Ian flinched, imagining for a moment Brianna MacQuarie lying naked in her bridal bed. To await another. Suddenly he wished it were he marrying the lassie. Strange how he'd never even contemplated marrying before, had always thought marriage a curse. He must be bewitched. Opening his eyes, he sat up with a start. Rising to his feet he strode up and down the hall like a restless, prowling wolf until he was so exhausted he could hardly see. "She's a witch." He sat back down, slumping in his chair. "A flame-haired witch."

"Or an avenging angel."

"Aye. Och, I'm so tired, Aulay. I don't even want to think about her anymore." The whiskey and ale had combined in a most potent manner.

"Then come to bed. Ye've had enough ale to pickle a herring." Aulay helped Ian to his feet, tending him as carefully as Ian always did him when he was in his cups. Struggling under Ian's height and strength, he nonetheless managed to push and pull him up the stairs and to the door of the third floor guest chamber they'd been given. "Time to sleep." Aulay slammed the door to the chamber, causing the thick stone walls to vibrate. "Ye'll see things differently ere morning comes. Ye'll see." He clucked his tongue. "Besides, I've heard it said, and rightly so, that a mon should stay clear of a red-haired lassie. They're cursed wi' a bad temper. Go up like kindling if a mon says a wrong thing."

"Aye. And she's much too skinny. Not nearly plump enough." The chamber had two beds with heavy wooden frames interlaced with rope. Ian stumbled toward the one nearest the door and fell backward upon its thick feather mattress. "Too skinny," he repeated, though he knew that to be a lie. She was just right. Entwining his arms around a thick quilt, he burrowed his head in its softness and warmth, as if embracing her. Murmuring her name again and again, he fell into a peaceful slumber as Aulay watched over him.

"Aye, perhaps ye are bewitched." Throwing the edge of his breacan over his shoulder, Aulay sprawled his small frame in a wooden chair near the bed. Suddenly he was not as amused at the situation. Ian Campbell was a man with a fiery nature, be it for fighting or loving. Perhaps this matter of the lass was not so unimportant after all. Ian had never displayed such longing for a woman before, and yet truly he could not seem to get his mind off of this one. He knew Ian was a man of passionate emotions who always took what he wanted. Would he be easily swayed in this matter? Aulay was troubled, for he knew well what problems could be created when a man was obsessed with a woman. Closing the door, he tugged a fur coverlet over Ian's sleeping form, then sat back, determined to watch over his friend lest his desire for the MacQuarie lass lead them all into trouble.

CHAPTER TWELVE

Summer storm clouds and sunlight competed over the green valley. Opening the shutter of her small bedchamber window, Brianna peered out through the slits, gazing at the sky, thinking how the day matched the confusion of her mood. Laugh or cry, which was it to be? Of a certainty she hadn't slept a wink last night. She'd tossed and turned until she was certain she'd made so much noise that poor Glenna's slumber had been disturbed. All because some arrogant laddie, whom she should scorn anyway for his boldness, was not to be her husband. Robbie Campbell had allowed someone else to be sent in his place. Her assumption had been a terrible mistake.

Ian, not Robbie, of clan Campbell was the man who had taken such liberties with her. The bold rogue was merely a proxy! Why was that so disturbing? She should be relieved, not unhappy. Certainly, she'd have to be daft to even think one moment longer about it. Ian Campbell was a devilish rogue. She had to believe that Robbie Campbell would be a far better man than *he*. Even so, she was acutely conscious of the fact that Ian was situated just down the hall from her own chamber. That knowledge was strangely stirring.

"Get a hold on yerself, lassie," she scolded quietly. "Stop wondering what might hae happened *if.*" It would only bring her more frustration. Her mind screamed at her to cease fretting over something not in her control to manipulate. She was promised to another. What's more, she had offered herself into the bargaining. Aye, what was to be, would be. And yet . . .

The more she thought about *him*, the more confused she became, at herself, her feelings. The burning memory of his kiss drove all else from her mind. He'd called her a "kelpie" but surely he was *Old Nick*, the devil, himself. He had tried to steal her heart, her soul, and had come perilously close to succeeding! But never again.

In anger she stripped off her sleeping tunic and flung it across the room. A comb and the pillow followed. She'd not think one more moment about him. Her self-respect, her pride was at stake. She must act as if nothing had happened, bite her tongue before she ever gave him even an inkling that she was drawn to him.

"Fie, sister, ye would hae the room in a shambles. I dinna ken what is the matter wi' ye. Canna ye no' even let us hae order for just a few wee hours this morn?" Glenna's voice held a tone of scolding as she bounced from the bed to retrieve Brianna's things. Glenna was the tidier of the two and could not stand a mess.

"I'm sorry."

"Och, so he's gotten under yer skin more than I realized. I should hae known." Glenna clucked her tongue in sympathy.

Brianna sighed, turning her back on her sister as she dressed in a long saffron-hued shirt and a loin cloth. "I dinna ken what ye mean," she said defensively.

"Aye, ye do. I know what's wrong, Brie."

"Ye canna." Brianna kept her eyes averted from her sister. Her mind rebelled against the ache in her heart.

"I do. Ye're disappointed that he's not Robbie Campbell and I canna blame ye." Gently touching her shoulder, Glenna turned Brianna around to face her, looking deeply into her eyes. "Confess!"

"Nae, it was the mattress, that's all. It's lumpy and needs to be restuffed, and I . . . didna get a wink of sleep all night."

"I dinna imagine ye did." Playfully she tugged at Brianna's hair in rebuke, stifling a giggle.

"Glenna! Dinna think that I . . ." Brianna sighed. It was no use lying to Glenna. "Aye, I was thinking about my mistake in thinking he was to be my groom. I was such a muddle-brained nanny goat to think such a thing wi' no proof. But his being here . . ."

"Was deceptive. Och, and I'm sorry I jumped to such a conclusion. I wouldna hae wanted ye to be unhappy. It was I who made mention of it first. If only I hadna thought . . . and said . . ."

"It doesna matter. One husband or the other is all the same to me." Tossing her flaming red hair, she returned to the window trying to make light of the subject. Looking at the crags and hills, she tried to focus her thoughts on other things, but Ian Campbell hovered in the room like a ghost. "It doesna matter. Really." Why then did her voice sound so shaky? "We willna talk about it any more."

Wrapping a plaid similar to the kind the men wore, about her waist and shoulders, braiding her hair, she convinced herself to put it far from her mind. She quickly changed the subject, bringing the conversation to the matter of Alastair, listening to Glenna's enraptured cooing. Glenna was determined to approach their father during the evening's supper and relate to him her desire to marry Alastair.

"I hope he will no' shout at me."

"If he does then just shout back!" Brianna put an arm about her sister's shoulder. "Father's bark is far worse than his bite, as ye will one day find out."

"I dinna ken . . ."

"Be braw!" Brianna pursed her lips in mock severity. "I'll stand behind ye, hinny."

Brianna spent the better part of an hour trying to bolster her sister's courage while convincing herself that she cared not a wit for the dark-haired stranger in their midst. For the moment Ian of the clan Campbell was forgotten. As a matter of fact, by the time she had joined the others in the hall, she had talked herself into believing that all had worked out for the best. Glenna would marry Alastair and be secure living with her own clan. Brianna meanwhile would join with Robbie Campbell and find excitement in giving the entire clan a challenge. And that was the end of *that!*

A long time had passed since there had been much to celebrate, what with feuds and so forth. Now with the promise of peace, the drone of bagpipes, the trill of harps, and the sound of happy chatter filled the air. A dozen or more smiling faces greeted Brianna as she walked through the door. Though she was not in a particularly good mood, everyone else was, and the gaiety was infectious, soon wiping away her frown.

It was not a feudal society here, there were no serfs to do the work. All were of the same kin and willingly did whatever chores necessary. Even a clan chief's daughter. Everyone was busily working at some task or other, thus Brianna took her place beside the women preparing the food. Breakfast was to be simple—porridge and fruit and fish—for the men were eager to be about the day's activities. Filling a cauldron with water from a wooden bucket, Brianna was anxious for her chore to be done so that she could hurry out to the field.

Thoughts whirled in her head as she brought the water to a boil and let the oatmeal trickle into it. From the corner of her eye she scanned the room as the men filed in. Ian Campbell stood out like a bull amidst rams. He wore a white shirt instead of the more usual saffron and a colored breacan of bright green and blue plaid, the long ends draped over his left shoulder and pinned in place with a brooch. A leather sporran hanging over his breacan from a belt emphasized his maleness. Even in the crowded room she was aware of *him*.

With a chill she remembered their first meeting, as if even

then she'd known he would be a ripple in her mood of content. Stirring the pot constantly with a spurtle—a wooden stick about a foot long—she glanced his way. He looked grumpy, surly, and she heard him mention more than once to the tiny man who walked at his side that he had a horrible headache. No doubt he'd stayed long into the night with the other men, drinking and celebrating, she thought with a frown. While she was feeling miserable, he had been enjoying himself. Fie on him! On all men. They were ever the source of a woman's lament.

But oh, how the women flocked around *him*, like gulls to a fishing boat, she thought sourly. She could hear Jeanne's prattle from clear across the room as she flirted with him. Overbold wench. She was a perfect match for him. Ha, he'd soon have his hands full with that one. She convinced herself she didn't care. Aye, lucky she was not to have been betrothed to such as this Ian!

Casting him a haughty look, she was irritated that her snub went unnoticed. His eyes focused over the top of her head as if she were invisible. How could she prove how little she cared about the situation if he did not even look her way? She was of a mind to show him. Ha! She would ignore him too.

She let the porridge cook steadily for a half-hour, stirring to watch for lumps, determined to avoid looking at *him*. Once or twice, however, though she was careful in her cooking duties, her attention was diverted when she cast a glance at his manly presence. She nearly scorched the porridge, only emphasizing to her what trouble he could be.

Breakfast was eaten standing. Brianna ate her oatmeal with fresh milk and salt, choosing wild berries and curds to appease her voracious appetite. When Glenna teased her about it she retorted that she needed her strength for what was planned for the day. Her brow puckered in concentration. Today there would be further celebrating. Games. Horse racing. Such competition would surely make her forget her foolishness.

"Do the women weave in Edinburgh?" Jeanne's voice pierced the air.

"They weave but not as well as they work their needles. Their tapestries breathe with life," Ian Campbell answered.

Brianna attuned her ears to Ian's talk of the skills of the courtly women at stitchery and turned up her nose. He claimed they sat on stools before the fire, sewing all day. Those women were addle-brained pudding heads if that's how they spent all their time. How boring they must be. Ha! She'd show him what a MacQuarie lass was made of. She'd match him skill for skill. So thinking, she merged with the crowd as they left the Great Hall.

Banners flew, bagpipes played on, tents were placed haphazardly about. There was the same enthusiasm and joviality as when appreciating a fair. A field just outside the castle's walls was used for the popular game of shinnie, a simple game using curved sticks and a ball. It was a dangerous sport, one said to be the fastest ball game in the world. To play it a man needed to possess extraordinary athletic abilities—a quick eye, ready hand, a strong arm, and be an excellent runner and wrestler as well. Brianna was not one to sit idle like the other women and watch the event. She elbowed her way among the crowd to join in. Plucking up a stick she aligned herself with the players as a shocked Ian Campbell looked on.

The field had the appearance of a battle scene. That she found herself on the same side as the Campbell rogue was the only thing that marred her exhilaration at the event. Even so, she plainly showed him how to play the game, throwing herself into the fracas. She was pleased when at last she caught sight of a look of surprise merged with admiration on Ian Campbell's face.

"Ye fight as furiously as the Scots' Army," he said, meaning it as a compliment. Pursing her lips, Brianna did not answer, merely turned her back on him, but she was pleased nonetheless.

Despite his aching head, Ian made a good show of it. He

couldn't let a woman show him up. He was quick and strong, ran with easy grace, cutting back and forth across the pasture with his stick. Fighting the others for the ball with a reckless ferocity, he strove to impress the red-haired MacQuarie lassie. He reminded Brianna of a fighting cock. Grudgingly, she had to admire him. Though she was more than a match for Erskin, Malcolm, and even Jamie, this Ian Campbell swung his stick as powerfully as her father wielded his sword.

"You played a good game." Huffing and puffing, Ian tried to catch his breath. By Saint Michael this woman was full of surprises. Who ever would have imagined that such a lass of beauty could also possess skill and strength. It was impossible to ignore her though he'd made such a vow. She reminded him of the wild cats that roamed about in the Highlands. Oh, that he could be the one to tame her.

"I'm thankful we were on the same side." Brianna saw no reason to withhold her praise. "Ye played a good game too." For the first time that morning she smiled, issuing him a challenge. "But let's see how ye measure up with a bow." She nodded her head toward a far area of the field where a target was being set up for the archery contest, then sauntered off, Ian following her.

Archers' equipment—flint-tipped arrows, arm bracers to withstand the rebound of the bow strings, and bows—littered the field. Ian chose the lightest bow he could, favoring the English method of archery which shot from the area of the chin. He looked in astonishment as Brianna took time to choose one for herself, running her hands over the wood, testing the tension of the cord. Surely a woman couldn't wield such a weapon, he thought. His expression told his thoughts.

"Aye, I'm skilled with a longbow," Brianna exclaimed. "My father has taught all his daughters to shoot. The night I was born the castle was undefended while the men were away. That will no' happen again." Her words held a warning.

Again Brianna made a good account of herself proving her skill. She hit the target squarely again and again, shooting in the Scottish manner, aiming from the chest. There wasn't anything she couldn't do and do *well*, it seemed. As the morning unfolded Ian's admiration grew.

Horse racing, road bowling, and rounders took up much of the morning. The men took part in feats of strength and mock sword fights. All the while guests arrived intermittently from villages and castles nearby. Some of the guests were distant kin who Brianna and her family rarely saw. The MacDonalds and MacKinnons made their presence known. Soon the field was fairly bursting at the seams with drinking, merrymaking and laughing. Only the fading sun put an end to the revelry, and it was then the throng returned to the castle, Ian Campbell in their wake. His blue eyes were riveted on the breacon-clad figure of Brianna MacQuarie and in that moment he was fully aware that no matter how vehemently he might swear otherwise, she'd won more than the archery tournament today. That wee, braw slip of a girl had won his heart.

"By Saint Michael, give me the strength to stay away from her." He couldn't hurt Robbie, would never cuckold a cousin, a member of his own clan, and yet heaven help him, the longer he was here the more dangerous the situation became.

CHAPTER THIRTEEN

The Great Hall was warmly lit, the roaring fire inviting. Retreating to her own chamber, Brianna did what she could with her wind-tousled hair and bedraggled appearance. Choosing a kirtle of plain beige wool and a brightly colored arasaid of yellow and green, she again became a lady. Reentering the hall with her head held high, she took the honorary seat beside her father which would be hers throughout the period of preparation for her wedding.

The hall fluttered with frenzied activity as large kegs of whiskey and ale were tapped, and venison was prepared for cooking. The Highlanders would boil a quarter of flesh, whether mutton, veal, goat, or deer. The animal's skin was turned inside out, cleaned, and fixed to hang on a hoop over the fire. Now the meat sizzled and gave off a tantalizing aroma. Brianna could not argue her hunger.

"Something for your appetite, Brie." Orianna grinned as she offered her older sister an oatcake from a large wooden tray.

"My thanks."

"I made them myself just for you." Orianna waited expectantly as Brianna dipped it in honey, cherishing its sweetness. As the future bride, she was to have the honor of taking the first bite of all the delicacies tonight.

"Very tasty!" Tears of deep emotion stung Brianna's eyes at the gesture. Over the years she and Glenna had been so close that they had neglected forging a strong bond with their younger sister. She felt a flush of guilt as she realized how they had unwittingly shut the younger girl out. Now she regretted the lost opportunity. She would be going away and would miss the chance of seeing Orianna likewise honored when she came of age.

"Brie?" The girl's long, slim fingers grasped Brianna's hand.

"Aye?"

"I hate for you to go away." The blue eyes mirrored a deep sadness.

"And I hate to go, Orianna." Both blinked back their tears. "I . . ."

"Och, this is a time for merriment, not for cryin'!" Lachlan's voice was gruff, but Brianna thought she detected a mist of moisture in his own eyes. "A daughter is born for the use of bringing the strongest clans together." Indeed, Lachlan's youngest daughter had been the first to go, fostered out to the MacGregors to strengthen friendship between the clans when she was but five years old. In turn, the MacGregors' small son was growing up at the MacQuarie hearth.

The custom of fosterage did much to bind members of clans together, or so Lachlan insisted. Fosterage consisted in the mutual exchange of the infant members of clans, the children of the chief being included. Since Morgana was the youngest without a mother, it had seemed significantly appropriate for her to be the one chosen for fosterage.

"Kindred to forty degrees, fosterage to a hundred, as they say," Lachlan said. The custom had the advantage of enabling one-half of the clan world to know the other half and how they lived.

"But ye'll miss us just the same." She'd never forget how he'd cried when his youngest daughter had been bundled off by the leader of the MacGregor clan. She knew how much he would miss her too. He'd already told her.

"Aye." Lachlan let out his breath in a deep rumbling sigh. "I'm afraid I'll be naught but a lonely old mon when my lovely chicks leave the nest." Oh, how he loathed the thought of Brianna going away, but even so, he knew the sooner this matter of the marriage was completed the better. Tears did not make him blind. He saw the heated glances Ian Campbell was granting his daughter when he thought no one was looking. It boded of trouble.

"An old man? You? Never." Giving in to an impulse, Brianna kissed his cheek and Orianna followed.

The hall rang with raucous laughter, a babble of voices and the underlying accompaniment of music. A parade of trays and bowls passed Brianna's way. Strangely enough, though she had thought herself to be famished, she only nibbled at the fare, trying to quiet the unusual feelings stirring in the pit of her stomach. Was it all the talk of her leaving that was upsetting her or was there another reason? Certainly her head ached. As if a wee brownie was inside, pounding with a hammer. Ignoring the pain that throbbed in her head, she looked in Ian's direction. The look that passed between them had the potency of a kiss. Looking hastily away, Brianna joined in the revelry that rioted in the room.

Get hold of yourself, Brianna Nic Lachlan! she scolded silently but it was no use. Brianna knew she could deny it no longer. She was drawn to Ian Campbell devastatingly, beyond thought, beyond reason. Indeed, she did not have to look his way to know where he stood, how he moved. She sensed it. Every time he turned his heated gaze her way the hair at the back of her neck prickled in anticipation. It was a feeling that unnerved her, she who had always had complete control over her emotions. Had she no pride, no loyalty? She was to wed with another and yet he drew her eyes despite all her avowals to the contrary.

A myriad of fantasies whirled about in her head, thoughts of what might have happened between them if she hadn't been spoken for. A vision flashed before her eyes of a man pressed close against her body beneath the quilts, lulling her to blissful sleep by the steady rhythm of his heartbeat. Closing her eyes, she allowed herself the luxury of dreaming until her father's elbow nudged her in the ribs.

"The dancing, daughter, the dancing. It's up to you to lead it."

Lachlan MacQuarie rose from the table and signaled for the dancing to begin. Within a matter of moments the room was transformed, tables pushed back, chairs and benches pushed against the wall. Brianna chose her father as her first partner as the clansmen hooted their approval.

"Let's see Brianna dance. It's her betrothal we're celebrating," cried out Jaimie.

"Aye, let's see her kick her feet." Erskin boldly winked. "Everybody must dance."

Three pipers appeared, accompanied by Alastair on his lute, and a small boy banging on a tambour. Lachlan MacQuarie danced with the agility of a young lad, laughing all the while.

"Ye remind me of yer mother, lassie. It's as if the years hae been wiped away. We danced together, she and I, at our own marriage feast. And now my wee bonnie daughter has grown up. Where hae all the years gone, hinny?"

"Perhaps the fairies hae stole them."

"Perhaps." He reflected on that notion.

Laughing young women chose partners and one by one other pairs of dancers took to the floor as Brianna and her father returned to their seats. Stepping gracefully, quickly, toes pointed with precision, hands thrown upward in exuberation or warmly extended to smiling partners, the revelers frolicked. The couples met and parted, moving their feet in spirited abandonment. Her father told her that long ago this type of dancing was part of a magic ritual. Surely there is a primitive aura about it, she thought.

Patterns of dancers formed, then just as quickly dissolved to form new patterns. Breacons swayed jauntily, skirts rippled as the tunes from the fiddler and bagpipes filled the Great Hall. Ian Campbell threw himself into the celebrating, dancing first with Brianna's sister, Orianna, then with the promiscuous Jeanne. Brianna seethed with a strange anger. Seeing him in the arms of any other woman was strangely painful. With a toss of her head, she thought to put him out of her mind. Everyone was dancing a spirited reel which set her toes tapping as she watched the gaiety. For the moment he was forgotten, but not for long.

"Let's see Brianna dance wi' The Campbell!"

"Aye. Just because her husband isna here doesna mean she should be idle. The Campbell! The Campbell!" echoed a chorus of laughing girls.

"Let's see how a Campbell dances wi' the elder daughter of our chief."

Brianna was unable to ignore the round of shouts which echoed all around the hall, and in truth perhaps she didn't really want to. Drawing in a deep breath, she watched as Ian walked with lionlike grace across the wooden floor, then she was in his arms. "You have been ordered to dance with me."

"Aye, so ye hae."

"Come." He whispered, "If only for the moment, you belong to me."

Brianna's breath stilled at the touch of his warm hand. She stepped down from the dais, back onto the floor. Her blood quickened as his arms encircled her waist. There was a glow in his eyes she'd seen that first time by the pool, and she reveled in the knowledge that in spite of her rudeness to him, in spite of her betrothal to another, he still wanted her. It was as heady a feeling as drinking too much ale.

The pipes began keening, and she moved her feet dreamily as smoke from the hearth fires swirled about the hall. It was like a dream, and she was caught up in the spell. All around them her clansmen were clapping and cheering, stamping their feet in time to the music, watching as a member of a rival clan swirled her around the room.

Brianna had never felt so passionately alive! Her whole being was filled with conflicting emotions. He was swinging her around on his arm, whirling her about to a jaunty tune. Her bright red hair flew about her shoulders in a fiery web as laughter bubbled from her throat. She felt immensely happy, danced with complete abandon. Kicking up her heels, bending her slim waist, her eyes fused with his as for just a moment their faces were mere inches apart, close enough for a kiss. They were too breathless to speak, but their expressions conveyed a mutual attraction.

"Let me show you a dance we did in Edinburgh," he said at last, longing to fit her soft curves against him. He explained, hurriedly showing the others how to do the steps. It was a different kind of dance—one in which the women executed the intricate steps of a dance as they moved in a circle, men on the outside, women on the inside.

Unlike the Scottish way of dancing, keeping an arm's length away, Brianna was shocked to find that there was a great deal of touching and brushing against each other. She could not help but relive the moment they had been together at the lake, and a strange quivering took hold of her, wanting him but knowing she must put such longing from her mind.

"You're as graceful as a bird. Is there nothing you can't do, little kelpie?" The sound of Ian Campbell's low, husky voice teased her ears. His mocking smile appeared to taunt her, yet scold her at every turn. His hard muscular body seemed to press against her own and burn where it touched. His gaze seemed to strip her naked, and with a blush she remembered his caress.

She made no effort to pull away as he grasped her by the waist and lifted her high in the air as the pipes keened on. Indeed, she sought the firm strength of his arms. Their hearts pounded in unison. For a moment it was as if the two of them were all alone in the vast room. Och, if only he were not so handsome, and yet it was much more than that. He had revealed a strength, a determination today on the field that she could not help but admire. He was in every way a most masculine man.

It was more clear to her than ever that she longed for Ian Campbell, not some boy she'd never even met. Not some laddie who let another stand in for him. A feeling deep inside told her Ian Campbell would never let another man woo his bride.

"Ian!"

"Brianna. Ye must mingle wi' yer other guests!" Only her father's booming voice brought her back to reality. With slight embarrassment she realized the music had ended and deeply regretted that fact. Even so, turmoil raged in her heart. Long after the fires dimmed, as she settled in her bed, Brianna's mind danced with memories of the all too brief time she'd shared with Ian Campbell in the forest and in his arms tonight. It pushed all thought of her impending wedding away. She wanted Ian Campbell. By Saint Michael she could deny it no longer. The question that haunted her was what to do about it.

Glenna viewed the stairs with trepidation, knowing she must somehow find the courage to talk with her father. Even so, it was very difficult to force her legs to take the necessary steps. She was a coward, terrified of the blustery anger her father was capable of. Was it any wonder then that she stood as still as a statue, hesitating to make the first move to his chamber? She'd tried to bolster her bravery by drinking several draughts of ale but all it had done was make her a bit dizzy. There was just no potion that could give her courage that did not exist or put into her brain the right words to make her father understand her feelings.

"But still ye must ask him or take the risk of losing Alastair," she scolded herself breathlessly. That prodding seemed to work, for somehow she found herself walking upward.

Though it was a short distance to her father's room, it

seemed like a mile of plodding, one foot in front of the other. Up, up, up the stone stairs. Force herself to continue. Oh, where was Brie when she needed her? The last time she remembered seeing her twin sister was when she was whirling about on the floor with the Campbell laddie. More than likely Brianna was already abed just as *she* would be if she had gotten this matter over much sooner. She lamented the fact that she had not sought Lachlan out earlier, for surely she had meant to broach the subject at dinner when Brianna could be of help. The dancing had been a distraction. Somehow the moment of self-confidence had dwindled and her courage had left. Now she would have to face her father all alone.

The chamber door loomed in her path like the most awesome portcullis. Raising a trembling hand to the wood, however, she knocked, hesitantly, a gesture which reflected her apprehension. Even so, the sound was heard, for his bellowed *"Who is it"* thundered in the silence. It nearly sent Glenna scrambling back down the stairs. Only her love for Alastair urged her to stand her ground. Then there was no more chance for flight when the door was yanked open.

"Who disturbs a mon's sleep!" The furled brows darted up in surprise as he eyed the intruder in the soft torchlight of the hall. "Ah, it's you, daughter. But Glenna? Brianna? Which one?" The timidity with which she entered the room told him. "Ah, my gentle dove. What brings you here after the candles hae been snuffed?"

Though she tried to speak, her words came out in a strangled gasp. "To . . . talk with ye!"

"At this time o' the eve? By God, lass, what could be so important?" Taking her hand he squeezed her cold fingers with his own, pulling her inside. Lighting a taper he lowered his bulk into a wooden chair and gestured for her to do the same. Instead, Glenna remained standing. "Well, speak up, child."

Glenna's words came out in an excited rush. "Alastair is . . . is going to ask to take me to wife and I love him,

Father. I want to marry him. Please. Ye canna tell him no." She fidgeted with the tie of her belt, averting her eyes.

"I canna? I *can* and I will!" The words exploded from his lips. "I will no' hae a slip of a lassie telling me what I can say. I am the chief of the MacQuarie. My word is law!"

"But . . ." Glenna could not keep from quaking, and she cautiously positioned her arasaid to hide her knocking knees. Dear God, she'd done just what she'd feared. Angered him. "I . . . I only meant that I want to be his wife and . . . I . . ."

"Nae! No' the daughter o' The MacQuarie. Ye'll no' be tyin' yerself wi' a harpist." His face turned red as he ranted, he balled his hands into fists. "There's no advantage in that. Nae, by God!"

Blessed Saint Michael, she'd made a mess of it, just as she'd known she would. "Please! I love him!" She wrestled with the dilemma of her fate, at last saying stubbornly, "I willna marry anyone else."

"Ye will if I say!" His eyes glittered in the candlelight, simmering with rage.

"Nae! Nae!" There was such a fiercesome pressure pushing at her chest that she feared she couldn't breathe.

"Ye'll do as I say! My daughters will mate wi' warriors and make of clan MacQuarie a mighty clan. We're a small clan no' as big as the MacDonalds or MacLeans but we're noble. One of the branches of the great clan Alpin. Be proud of that, lass. The blood of kings runs in your veins, remember that."

"I am proud and I do remember, Father."

He lapsed into a story she'd heard a hundred times or more about a faraway ancestor being the second son of the first Scottish King. "And my grandfather Cormac Mor, chief of the MacQuaries in the time of the second Alexander, was a hero. He was." He sighed. "Aye, when at first I had no male MacQuaries I lamented the succession of the chiefhood, but now I realize how precious daughters really are. Brianna, Orianna, your wee lassie sister and *you*, all four daughters. Ye are my hope for the clan. To increase our territory and power. Aye, I'll find ye all noble men."

Glenna shook her head. "Warriors. Bullies all." Her deep affection for her handsome bard gave her a surge of courage to defend him. "Alastair is worth ten of your fine Highland lairds. He's kind and gentle and . . ."

"Bah! He's useless to me in battle except for the marching rhythm he brings with his plucking. I need a buffer from my enemies. That's the way o' men o' the Highlands. To unite and form a stronger clan to offset the common enemy. Bah, the bard is already one of the clan. I repeat, there is no advantage in marrying you to him." Striking his fist on a wooden table near his chair, he startled Glenna. "Besides, 'tis not a woman's place to make a fuss over such things. It is for you to wait for me to find a husband for you, not for you to go sniffing after a man like a bitch in heat."

"I'm not!"

"I've seen ye making cow eyes at him, but I'd hoped it would pass. Now I see I hae made an error in judgment. Ye hae no sense, daughter. No more than a titmouse."

Without warning Glenna burst into a storm of tears. Though Brianna could emerge unscathed by Lachlan's temper, she could not. She had a softer heart.

"It isn't fair." Men and their constant warring, their lopsided code of honor. When all was said and done she didn't mean any more to her father than his horses, fie, his cattle. "You're cruel, Father. Cruel. I never . . ." Dashing the degrading moisture from her cheeks, she sniffled.

Lachlan was unnerved by her tears and regretted his outburst. Touching her shoulder, his eyes softened. "I dinna want to sadden ye, lass. I agreed to let ye stay here among yer own. I willna send ye away. What more can I do than that? Surely 'tis more than some fathers could do. Yer sister is the one chosen to go away. The bargain is sealed. You'll stay among yer own clan."

"Ye promise."

"Aye, lass. I'm thinking to contract ye to Jamie MacDonald. He's grown up at our hearth. He's made his home *here*, so ye don't need go away from yer home. Ye've known the laddie since he was a bairn and fostered him wi' us. He'll make ye a good husband and will unite us to clan MacDonald."

"Jamie? Jamie? An ambitious laddie who follows ye about like a shadow. Fie, I dinna want such as him." Her lower lip curled under in a pout.

"Then Colin. He's a distant cousin and a MacKinnon."

"No!" A swift emotion made her foolishly brave, though her voice quivered as violently as a leaf in the wind. "Alastair's blood is every bit as good as his. He's of clan MacKinnon blood too."

"Aye, but touched wi' the stigma of a bastard in his family tree."

"I don't care." Her shoulders heaved as she wept. "Oh, please. I don't want to marry any man but my bard. I canna."

Lachlan glowered into eyes so like his own. "Aye. Ye will. One or the other. I am The MacQuarie and yer father. Were I to choose him you would marry the very devil himself at my command. I would soon be rocking the next generation of MacQuaries on my knee, taking them up to their beds when they fall asleep before the warm fire."

"And that's all I'm to be, a breeder for your grandsons and granddaughters?" Her voice came out in a hopeless whisper as she asked the question. "Hae I no say in the matter of who shares my bed?" His stubbornness threatened to keep her from the one man her heart cried out for. Again she lamented that she had not the feisty, able tongue of Brianna.

"That's what I'm saying, though it's not as harsh a reality as ye make it sound, lass. I married yer mother to forge a bond wi' my clansmen. It's the way of the Highlands."

"But it's not *fair,*" she whispered again. Men were never understanding of a woman's woes, she thought unhappily. Girls didn't fight and kill, and because of that they had no voice in their lives. Even Brianna was unhappy, wanting one man, betrothed to another.

"It is the way o' things," he exclaimed, letting his breath out in a long, deep sigh. He was weary to the bone. It had been a long, exhausting day and he little relished this confrontation.

Glenna was a gentle, shy soul who reminded him a great deal of Mary. Somehow he had to make her understand that some things in life were of necessity. "Let me tell ye that it is not the first time I've had to so loudly deny such a request. I hae told few people but I will tell ye now that yer aunt Mary wanted to marry a mon I did no' approve of many, many years ago."

"Aunt Mary?" All Glenna had heard of her aunt was that she had disappeared.

"Aye." In the dim light she looked much like his sister. For a moment the years were swept away as he remembered. Mary's plea had been just as tearful, and he could not help but wonder what might have happened if he'd been more lenient with her. Had she been so unhappy that she had willingly drowned herself? It had been a thought that had weighed on his mind all these years. And yet he could not have done other than he did. " 'Tis a story I hae never told."

"Tell me!" The castle was so silent that she could hear his breathing. Clutching her hands tightly, cocking her head to one side, she listened intently.

"Yer aunt wanted to marry one of the hated Campbells! Her effrontery was much greater than yers, lass." Deep lines engraved a path around his mouth as he stared at the candle's flame, remembering. "A Campbell! They who hae cheated us of Mull." For a moment he seemed to be talking to himself. "Whenever MacDonald, MacQuarie, MacGregor, or MacDougall lands are lost by forfeiture there is always a Campbell or a member of his family to claim a large share of the redistribution. Och, the greedy Campbells."

"And yet ye hae promised Brianna to one."

He wore such a pained look that Glenna wished she hadn't been so bold as to say such a thing. "I did. I hae sacrificed my own flesh and blood for the good of the clan. But it was different way back then when yer aunt asked my permission to marry one of *them*. I tell ye this just so ye will know that I loved my sister and denied her. Likewise I love ye and must make a similar denial." The stern timbre returned to his tone. "Ye willna marry the bard!"

"And that's the last ye'll say on the matter."

"Aye!"

Glenna wanted to rage at him, plead with him, get down on her knees if it would do any good, but the stubborn, bearded jaw of her father was held so rigidly that she knew he'd not change his mind. Not tonight. In dejection she walked toward the door, not even bothering to say good night. Her last thought was that she and Brianna had made a fine mess of things. Now there were two unhappy lassies, neither one allowed to follow their heart.

CHAPTER FOURTEEN

The soft sound of weeping woke Brianna from a fitful sleep. "Glenna?" She propped herself up on one elbow, squinting across the room at her sister's tiny bed. "Glenna, what's wrong, hinny?"

"F . . . F . . . Father!" She gasped the story between sobs. "I talked with him late last night, told him about Alastair but he said he wouldna let me marry him!"

"I was afraid he might be a stubborn old goat." Brianna scurried from her bed, crawling between the covers and hugging Glenna tight. "Hush now! Dry yer tears. It will be all right."

"Not if I hae to marry Colin or Jamie. I might as well hae married Robbie Campbell if I can't hae the man I love," Glenna wailed. "And then at least maybe you could be happy."

"Don't talk foolishness! Ye'll marry your laddie if I hae any say about it. I promised ye I'd talk to Father and I will." Plopping back on the pillows, she crossed her arms behind her head and gave the matter considerable thought. "It won't do to fuss, he'll be expecting that. He will only stand his ground all the more firmly. Ye know how he can be. If ye refuse he'll only lock ye in yer room and ye'll be the one to suffer. Ah, I think I hae it." She stifled a giggle with the back of her hand. "Father thinks he rules this roost, but he can be outmatched, or so I've found."

Glenna blinked through her tears. "Then ye think there is hope?"

"Are ye willing to gamble? Is Alastair in truth a strong mon despite his calling? Ye told me once he was."

"Aye! He's tall and slim but sinewy. I think he might hae been a good warrior if he'd needed to be but . . ."

"Then that's yer answer." Taking the edge of the coverlet, she dried her sister's tears.

"What is?"

"I'll find a way to persuade Father to let Alastair fight for ye!" Ignoring Glenna's shocked look of awe, she detailed a plan as they dressed and combed their hair. Lachlan would be so certain that Alastair would lose any kind of combat that he would surely agree to her idea. Anything to keep Glenna from moping about like a wounded rabbit. "But we'll make certain that he doesna lose."

"But how can we do that? Brie . . ." Glenna started to protest but Brianna silenced her.

"Alastair is nimble in his fingers, is he not? And he's not totally unskilled in weaponry, though perhaps a bit out of practice. Leave it up to me. And hae trust. Remember how it was when we were little?"

Arm in arm the two sisters sauntered down the stairs, Glenna dressed femininely in a hunter-green gown with dun-colored arasaid, Brianna once again in her mannish shirt and breacon. They were late. The morning meal had already been eaten, thus they had to content themselves with the scraps that were left, but even so, both lassies wore a smile.

"Ye look as mischievous as two wee brownies!" Lachlan eyed his daughters suspiciously, fully expecting Glenna's tears again. "What hae ye been plannin'?"

"A bit o' strategy, Father, to make an old bear see reason."

"She told ye about our confrontation." He scowled warningly, causing Glenna to take a step back. Brianna merely smiled.

"I silenced her crying by reminding her that our father is *always* a most fair man. I told her ye'd not let her go without allowing her man at least one chance to claim her."

"Nae, there'll be no changing my mind!"

Brianna pulled his beard. "Och, stop yer growling and let me explain." She looped her arm through her father's. "We need excitement around here! It's been a long time since we've had a lad fight for his lassie. But I've been thinkin' it to be just about time."

"Yer daft if ye think I'd . . ."

Brianna rambled on, undaunted. "Glenna in turn promised to abide by the outcome. No more tears. If Alastair loses she'll give in to her fate without even a whimper."

"Brie!" The terrible thought that Alastair might lose tempered Glenna's forced smile. She tugged at Brianna's sleeve but was ignored.

"What more can ye ask for than that, Father?" Before he could utter a word of protest, Brianna quickly proposed a show of skill, the winner becoming Glenna's bridegroom and son-by-law of the MacQuarie chief. She winked. "And would ye be wanting to wager on the outcome?"

"There'll be no wager and no fight!" Unwittingly, he was playing into her hands and he knew it.

"Because yer afraid Alastair might *win?*"

"Och, sometimes ye can be a trial, daughter, but I can tell ye one thing. Ye're wrong if ye think the bard *can* win. I'm a fighting mon and I know. He'll lose."

"Ha! I say yer wrong! If we're to believe the tales he sings, then love can bring a powerful magic. But just give the word and we'll see firsthand how potent love can truly be. Agree to the combat."

"Glenna must marry a fighting mon! A mon to bring strength to the clan. And honor. We'll talk no more about it." He grumbled beneath his breath. Bending down, he laced his curans, fur side out. "Time for the hunt." His announcement seemed to cool his ire. Brianna knew it to be his favorite pastime.

"Would ye care to wager on who can fell the largest deer?" Following her father as he tromped out of the hall and to the area of the castle grounds where the horses were tethered, Brianna caught sight of Ian Campbell. Strange how he always caused her heart to flutter so, she thought.

For the hunt, men would use bows and arrows, though some took their swords and dirks with them. Usually Brianna went barefoot in summer, but today she wore *cuarans*—laced shoes with deerskin worn with hairy side outward just like the men. Out of the corner of her eye she could see Ian Campbell, and was surprised to see that he was dressed in like manner. Had he been as mesmerized by the contact between them last night? She could not help but wonder. As their eyes met and held, she was given her answer. He had been.

The horses were equipped with *keisans,* woven baskets slung over a horse's back to hang on both sides and carry back any small game or birds. The horse's harnesses were of twisted withies, rods of hazel, the saddle was a piece of goatskin. Brianna heard Ian mention more than once that he was used to English leather saddles and bridles, but it appeared he soon mastered the more simplified version. He seemed surprised to see Brianna mount a horse, armed with a bow.

"A woman going hunting?" he asked. Some of the English women went falconing, but he'd seldom been in the company of a woman skilled in bringing down animals. Ian shook his head as he rode up to take his place beside Brianna. After meeting her his impression of women sitting docilely at their sewing had been shattered forever. Yesterday she had shown her skill at the games; today it seemed he was to learn she accompanied the men on their hunts as well.

"I've been hunting since I was no higher than my father's knee," she answered tartly, misunderstanding his words to be criticism. Joining a small party of hunters, she sat on her mount proudly. "We'll see if ye can keep up with me." So challenging, she nudged her horse's flanks and quickly outdistanced him. Teasing him, taunting him by her very aloofness. She hoped to embarrass him, but like a shadow he seemed always just a horse's length behind or in front of her.

The island of Ulva was much like a flat, terraced cone, composed of mountain tops and stark naked volcanic rock. The ground was porous and bracken grew rampant. Trees of many kinds grew well in the sheltered parts on this base-rich soil from the volcanic rock. There were green, even terraces with occasional gullies. Truly a beautiful landscape, Ian thought as he rode along.

"The hunting here will be a mite different," Lachlan MacQuarie declared proudly, riding up beside him. "Our animals include the rhum mouse, brown rat, pygmy shrew, pipistrelle bat, gray seal, common seal, and otter. Besides the red deer there are feral goats, lizards, and palmate newts. Make yer choice. Ulva is a wonderland of fish and wildlife." He explained that salmon was rare, brown and sea trout abundant, and eels common. Edible crab was fished off the rocky coasts. "Oysters are present in the Outer Hebrides."

"Oysters! A welcome delicacy."

"We'll hae some at tonight's feast." Lachlan pointed toward the Island of Staffa, its hexagonal columns rising up abruptly from the sea. MacQuarie territory too, though no one had visited the island in a long while. "It's said to be haunted by a ghost. A frightening woman who sings a wailing song," he announced, pausing briefly as he pointed in the direction of the sea.

"Staffa? I've heard of it." He wondered if it was really haunted.

Above them a dark shroud of ominous clouds were gathering. Ian wondered how long it would be before there would be a storm. Strange how thunder and lightning always seemed a portent of evil. Ah, well, he'd put it from his mind.

He was far more interested in the world of the living than in any "other world" beings. Nudging his horse, he tried to keep pace with the MacQuarie clan leader but was soon outdistanced, unfamiliar as he was with riding on such rough terrain. Glancing out of the corner of his eye he was embarrassed to see Brianna again guide her horse past him. As she looked at him he smiled, but it was not returned and her aloofness stung him after the smiles she had given him last night at the dancing. He had just begun to hope that any enmity between them had been soothed.

"Ye had best hurry," she called sharply over her shoulder.

Seeking a firm grip on the reins, Ian guided his horse in the direction that she had taken, trying to catch up with her at the top of the hill. "Brianna, wait!" Hearing his frantic shout of her name she slowed her mount and waited for him. Truly she did not want him to get lost or come to harm.

By Saint Michael what a lovely sight she made, he thought. Wearing that short garment similar to a man's, her shapely long legs were plainly visible beneath the hem of the plaid, drawing his stare again and again. If it was disloyal to Robbie to ogle her, he couldn't help it. Surely it did no harm to appreciate beauty.

"You ride well, lassie," he breathed. Despite his resolve, a tightness constricted his breathing whenever he caught sight of her. She had proved beyond a doubt that she was an amazing woman who could not be ignored.

They thundered through the forest amid a tangle of horsemen, Lachlan's huge russet wolfhounds leading the way, hot on the scent. Their voices mingled in an eager racket of barking which echoed through the lonely forest as they sighted their prey across a large burn. Bows were raised as the clan chief gave the signal. A whirr of arrows stung the air, bringing down the quarry of a large red deer.

"He's down!" Lachlan MacQuarie gave a triumphant cry, accompanied by a thunder of hooves and a splash as the hunters forded the water. Ian, however, did not follow. He'd sighted his own target, a deer larger than this one. To his surprise, he saw that Brianna had spotted it too, for she managed to beat him in reacting to the prize. In a flash of red and green she rode by him.

They rode long and hard. It was a predominantly oak forest, Ian noticed. Some pine and birch. Much of the ground was high with a lot of bare rock and scrub, difficult to travel through. On such ground there was no animal better adapted than the red deer.

"Ye'er laggin' behind again."

Oh, how she was enjoying her victory, he thought. "I'm not used to such rocky ground!" he shouted out. "But even so, I'll give you a contest if that's what ye're after."

"I dinna want ye to get lost. The others are way up ahead."

Once again, Ian tried hard to smile as he nudged his horse closer to hers. He had intended to ignore her, but now gave up that idea. Truly he wanted her to at least like him. "Can we make a truce?" he asked at last, more than a little unnerved by her apparent hostility toward him. Ignoring the attraction he felt for her was not going to work, but why not at least try to have some semblance of peace between them.

Her red hair came loose of its plaits and long strands blew into her eyes. Reaching up, she brushed the silken, flaming strands away. "A truce?" Her mouth was set in a grim line but it relaxed. "All right." This time she didn't barge away but rode with him into the meadows and beyond, coming to the spreading trees of the forest. Brianna seemed to be intent upon filling her eyes with the beauty of the woodland, but Ian kept his eyes upon her.

"You are a surprising woman, Brianna; as well as being beautiful, you're as skilled as anyone I've ever seen."

She didn't answer him, taking refuge in silence as they rode. Ian knew he'd been too bold in praising her looks. Perhaps she would never be able to forget how brazen he had been in kissing her. It condemned him in her eyes. And yet he did not regret for one moment what had passed between them.

"Brianna. I meant no offense. If calling you beautiful has angered you . . ."

"Dinna fash yerself. I was no' offended." Clutching her bow, Brianna took off in search of the red deer that disappeared into the forest, at last dismounting and stealthfully following the trail on foot. The tracks led down a steep embankment. Ian dismounted to walk down a narrow trail. Once again, Ian felt the allurement of being in her company. Leading the horses down the hill, being careful to duck their heads to avoid being struck in the face by the low-hanging branches, they were nonetheless enticingly aware of each other.

"What a beautiful world it is. Your father should be proud of his land, Brianna."

"He is." She was all too aware that she was devastatingly drawn to him. It was a feeling that unnerved her. She'd always had complete control over her emotions before, but now it seemed whenever he was near her heart fluttered like a bird's wing. That knowledge prompted her to be curt with him, to avert her eyes whenever he looked her way.

"Whew, I'm tired. It was a long evening yesterday." Pausing by the bank of a small pool, he sat down, nodding for her to sit down beside him on a large, smooth rock. "Brianna, you act as if you were a doe and I a fox in pursuit. Please, if we are going to be kin, we should get to know each other better." His voice was low and husky, sending shivers dancing up her spine. She sensed his presence with every fiber of her being. How could she think or breathe when he was so close to her? His very masculinity gave her cause for foreboding, particularly when she remembered the other times they'd been alone together.

"Know each other better?" She was wary. What a fool she was to let the others ride on ahead, knowing the kind of man he was.

"You are a woman to admire. I want you to think well of me." In a gesture of gentleness, Ian reached out to touch her face, to brush away the red hair that tumbled into her eyes. She mistook his gesture, however, remembering the touch of those warm soft fingers against her flesh. Stiffening, she bolted to her feet in indignation.

"Dinna touch me!"

"I was merely . . ."

"I know well what ye were doin'!"

"I'm a man of honor, Brianna, I wasn't . . ." As she turned away he sought to stop her. He didn't want her to leave. He meant to touch her arm but his fingers brushed against her breast instead. He felt her shudder. "Brianna."

"So much for honor," she spat, putting as much distance between them as she could. Ignoring Ian's apology, his avowal that he had meant no offense, she hurriedly mounted her horse. She'd ride back to the castle, and if this bold Campbell got lost it would be his folly. Clouds announced a storm, the one that had threatened this morning. The sky was quickly becoming overcast with ominous, gloomy clouds and held the stillness that precedes a serious storm. Usually Brianna would have been cautious, but riding the path at a furious pace, she ignored his cries. A low-hanging branch nearly unseated her, but she was oblivious to all else but the sound of the thundering hooves pursuing her, clattering loudly over the rocky terrain. She didn't want him to catch her.

The wind slapped her face as she guided her horse furiously up the mountain. Suddenly, a sliver of lightning sliced through the air, startling both horse and rider. Her horse whinnied, rearing and snorting in fear. Another flash of lightning lit up the sky, followed by a loud crack of thunder. Gusts of wind sent leaves and dirt hurling around in the air, pummeling her horse's legs. To her dismay she knew her uncontrollable mount was headed toward a cliff's edge. She strained desperately for the reins, but found they had been pulled just beyond her reach. The horse shied, then bucked and reared.

Ian shouted out Brianna's name as he urged his horse on.

He had offended her and not even meant to do so, yet he understood her response. "Brianna, please wait!" Though he tried, he was unable to catch up. In frustration he watched from afar as she was thrown violently from the saddle.

"Brianna!" he screamed. His voice echoed in her ear before she hit the ground and was engulfed in total darkness.

CHAPTER FIFTEEN

Huge gray clouds hovered above the hillside, pouring rain, drenching Ian Campbell as he ran frantically toward the crumpled figure lying on the ground. "Brianna!" Her eyes were closed. She looked frighteningly still. Bending over her unconscious form, he whispered a fervent prayer. Please let her be alive! Seemingly, his plea was answered, for as he put his head to her breast he could hear her heartbeat. "Brianna!"

Her breathing was even, though her face looked ashen. Apparently, she'd struck her head when she was thrown from the horse. The cut on her forehead attested to that. Ian gently wiped the blood away with his fingertips. Cautiously, he examined her, probing her arms and legs to determine if there were any broken bones. There did not seem to be, but still he was careful. He'd seen men unhorsed in battle, knew it could be dangerous to move someone if they were hurt internally or had injured their spine. Even so, he could not leave her unsheltered out in the storm. Already her tunic and breacan were soaked from the torrent pouring from the sky.

Where could he take her? Looking hastily about him, Ian tried to get his bearings. He seemed to recall passing a small cottage a few yards back. At the time he'd only glanced at it, his thoughts intent on Brianna and her coldness toward him. He did remember now approximately where it was located. It would be a haven from the sudden storm that had engulfed them.

By all the saints, how he wanted her to awaken, he thought as he stripped off his breacan and used it to shield her from the rain. Carefully, he picked Brianna up in his arms, cradling her head against his chest. For a long moment he stared down, mesmerized by how vulnerable she appeared. An all-consuming sense of protectiveness surged through him, an emotion he'd never felt for a woman before. Now the urge to safeguard her, to shield her, consumed him. Holding her close, he slushed through the wet foliage, hoping he could find his way to the cottage. Somehow he did.

It was a tiny dwelling of thatched wattle and daub, probably going back a hundred years or so. An interesting legacy of stone, thatch, and slate. A lookout point perhaps? The question flitted through Ian's mind as he kicked open the partially closed door. Whatever its purpose before, it was a blessing now. It would keep them dry.

The walls of the cottage were cracked in several places. It had been left in a ruinous state. Broken pottery, pieces of wood, and straw littered the earthen floor. The interior was covered with a thick coating of dust which caused Ian to cough as he pushed his way inside. As he scanned the small one-roomed dwelling, he caught sight of a straw mattress in the corner. Gently, he placed Brianna upon it.

Oh, how he longed for her to open her eyes, to speak to him, even if her tone was scolding. Turning away for just a moment, he hurriedly gathered the discarded, broken wood and bavins scattered upon the floor. Using a primitive method of rubbing two twigs together, he was at last able to build a fire in the fire pit in the middle of the floor. The thing of utmost importance was to keep Brianna warm. The flickering yellow and orange flames soon radiated a welcoming glow, the smoke rising through a hole cut for that purpose high on the south wall away from the wind.

Returning to her side, he noticed her shivering. Doing his best to make her comfortable, he stripped off her soaked garments, then hung the clothes on a pole by the fire to dry. Standing over her, he studied her quietly in the glow of the hearth fire. His breath was trapped somewhere in the area of his heart as he stared at the loveliness presented to him. She looked so fragile, so young, so desirable. She did look like a kelpie, as beautiful as some unearthly being. Bundling her up in a faded quilt he found in a corner of the room, he tried to ignore the desire that stirred within him at the sight of her tiny waist, firm breasts, and long, perfectly shaped legs. She was even more beautiful than he had supposed. Och, how fortunate was Robbie!

Ian brushed her fiery hair aside to examine her head. "A knot the size of a goose egg!" No wonder she was still deeply asleep, he thought. He'd had experience tending the wounded, knew a cold damp cloth would bring some relief. Tearing off a strip of his breacan, he dipped it in a rain barrel outside the door, laid it on Brianna's forehead, and sat back to wait, all the while ignoring his own discomfort. His clothes were soaked but the warm fire would soon make him dry. For the moment, only she was important. The small pole might break if any more weight was added to it.

"Brianna!" Bending down beside her, he called her name over and over again, his pulse quickening as he saw her eyelids flutter. "Brianna."

She was so lovely, he mused, from the tip of her toes to the top of her red-haired head. He let his eyes move tenderly over her in a caress, lingering on the rise and fall of her breasts. For just a moment he gave in to temptation and kissed her soft warm mouth. A parting kiss, he thought. A sad tribute to what might have been. With a regretful sigh he moved away from her, keeping an arm's length away, to return to his vigil. She was the kind of woman he had been searching for, but a woman he could never hope to obtain. The longing that he felt would forever remain unfulfilled. And yet, if she would only awaken perhaps he could accept that. He would try.

Ian sat unflinchingly by Brianna's bedside, leaving only to light the small torch he had made of straw or to change the cold cloth on her head. He stared at her, entranced by the way the golden torchlight played across the curves of her body beneath the coverlet, creating tantalizing shadows and reminding him of her beautiful body. The thoughts rambling through his head were dangerous, and he shook his head furiously to clear such musings. No doubt Lachlan MacQuarie was scouring the whole countryside for his daughter, he thought with a grimace. He would have been accused of all sorts of villainy by now if they were seen riding together. Feuds had been started for less than this. It was a worrisome thought, one he must contemplate. How ironic that for once he was innocent.

"Ohhhhh!"

"Brianna?"

She was moaning, moving her head from side to side. It was the first hopeful sign she'd given of returning to consciousness. Reaching out, he touched her face, relishing the softness of her skin, but grimaced as he remembered that it was just such a gesture that caused her mishap in the first place. For a moment his mouth tightened. She'd thought he was going to try to seduce her, that's why she'd run away. And why wouldn't she have thought that? Certainly he had given her reason to think the worst of him. But this time he'd only wanted to offer friendship. Ironic wasn't it.

"Brianna." Seeing her eyelashes flutter again, he took her hand, willing her to open her eyes. "Brianna. Wake up, lassie."

She stirred, putting her hand to her temple. "Mmmmm. My head," she moaned. Instinctively, she reached out feeling disoriented, clinging to him, needing stability in a turbulent, whirling world. The closeness of her softly curving flesh was nearly his undoing. The brush of their bodies wove a cocoon of warm intimacy that he relished. He was flesh and blood and not a saint, yet his passion was tempered with a more tender feeling. He swallowed with difficulty, longing to clasp her in his arms in a closer embrace.

Light flickered before Brianna's eyelids as she struggled to open her eyes. Where was she? She was confused. "What happened?" she asked softly.

"Your horse threw you, lass." Pushing her fiery-hued hair aside, he examined her injury yet again. His fingers were strokes of softness, making her feel warm and tingly inside. She nestled closer, her face buried against his chest.

"Ohhhhh."

"You hit your head on a rock."

Suddenly recognizing *his* voice, Brianna's eyes flew open to find him sitting on the edge of the mattress, his fingers entwined in her hair. His dark, unsmiling visage illuminated by firelight was the first thing her eyes focused on. "Ian Campbell!" She remembered now that she had dreamed that he had kissed her. Had he? Her thoughts were hazy, her head throbbed painfully as she sat up.

"Aye, I brought you here," he murmured huskily, remembering their brief embrace.

They stared at each other, two silent, shadowy figures in the dimly lit cottage, each achingly aware of the other. The very air pulsated with expectancy. Brianna could not help but wonder what he was going to say, what he was going to do. Sitting like a stone figure, her eyes never once left him as he moved forward.

"Ah, lassie. When I saw you fall, my heart stopped beating. I thought . . . I feared! By the saints I never realized until that moment how very special you are to me." The tone of sincerity in his voice deeply touched her.

"Am I?"

"Aye, that you are." He knelt on the edge of the bed,

causing the mattress to sag under his muscular weight. This time when he reached out to touch her face she didn't pull away as she had when they were alone in the forest. "Very special."

Slowly Ian bent his head, cherishing her lips in a kiss. Gentle. A much different kind of kiss than he had given her before. Her lips parted in an invitation for him to drink more deeply of her mouth. He did, igniting a warmth that engulfed her from head to toe. Breathlessly she returned his kisses, tingling with pleasure when he began to hungrily probe the inner warmth. Following his lead she returned his caress, tentatively at first, then passionately, tangling her fingers in the thick dark bristle of his hair.

"Brianna!" Their kiss was his undoing. All he could think about was the pounding of his heart as he relished the warmth of her body. She'd haunted his dreams no matter how fiercely he'd tried to put her from his mind. And now she was here. How could he let her go? Even though a voice inside his head shouted out that he was playing with fire, that it was sheer insanity to tease himself so, he couldn't pull away. He wanted her too badly, was tempted at last beyond his endurance.

Capturing her slender shoulders he pulled her up against him as his mouth moved hungrily against hers. Her head was thrown back, the masses of her fiery hair tumbling in a thick cascade over his arm. "Ah, lassie. Lassie!" With hands and mouth he sought to bring her pleasure.

A hot ache of desire coiled within Brianna. Fear warred with excitement in her veins. Fighting against her own desire was more difficult than she could ever have anticipated. How could she push him away? How could she ignore the heated insistence in her blood? There was a weakening readiness at his kiss, a longing she couldn't explain but which prompted her to push closer to him, relishing the warmth of his hands as he outlined the swell of her breasts beneath the blanket. When he drew his mouth away she tugged his head down, seeking his lips eagerly.

Brianna didn't understand this all-consuming need to be near him, she only knew that Ian alone aroused an urgent need within her, a longing to embrace him. She craved his kisses, his touch, and wanted to be in his arms forever.

"Ian." She moaned his name into his hair as his lips left her mouth. Soft sobs of pleasure echoed through the cottage's silence, and she was surprised to find that they came from her own throat. Her senses were filled with a languid heat that made her head spin. She closed her eyes, giving herself up to the dream of his nearness.

Agonizingly, he gently traced a path from her jaw to her ear to the slim line of her throat until his lips found her breasts, touching their rosy peaks. Dear God, she tasted so sweet. He was mesmerized by her, by how right it felt to hold her in his arms, his hip touching her stomach, his chest cradling the softness of her breasts. The longing to make furious love to her overpowered him. Kissing was not enough to satisfy the blazing hunger that raged through him. She was too tempting, and the delicious fact that she was responding to him made him cast all caution aside. Compulsively, his fingers savored the softness of her breasts as he bent his mouth to kiss her again, gently lowering her onto her back.

She stared up at him, watching as he studied her, and the look of desire she saw branded on his face alarmed her. Her woman's body craved the maleness of him, but her logical mind screamed at her to make him stop.

She arched up against him. Through the haze of her pleasure she felt his hands roaming more intimately and struggled to push him away. What was she doing? The question replayed itself over and over. Her body warred with her mind. She could not surrender her body to him. No! Biting down on her lower lip she fought to come back to her senses.

He shifted his position, reaching out to smooth the tangled strands of hair away from her face. It was the chance that she needed. She jerked violently away, forcing herself to say, "Leave me be! Take yer hands away," even though she didn't mean it.

"What?" He frowned, looking down at her.

"I said get yer hands off me, Ian Campbell!"

He rolled away from her, coming to his feet, standing with his legs sprawled apart, his arms crossed over his chest. His breathing was deep as he struggled to get control of himself, his emotions. He swore a violent oath. "You took a long time to tell me no." Clenching and unclenching his hands, he sought to put his thoughts in order. By all the blessed saints, why was she glaring at him as if he and he alone was responsible for what happened between them? He had meant to pull away but she had clung to him.

"I . . . I wasn't thinking clearly. Ye took advantage of me." An unfair censure.

She tried to get up, shivering as the cold, damp air brushed her bare arms. Pulling the quilt up, she looked at him in outrage as she realized she was completely naked beneath the blanket. So much for her dream. How dare he put her at his mercy? She stiffened, looking at him accusingly. "Ye be the devil himself! What kind of a man . . . ?"

"It was pouring out. Your clothes were drenched." He pointed to where they hung before the roaring fire. "You were out like a snuffed candle, lassie. I was only trying to make certain you didn't catch a chill."

"Ha! A likely story!" She flushed a deep red as she realized he'd viewed her unclothed body. In truth, she was angry at herself, not him, for capitulating so thoroughly to his lovemaking. By Saint Michael, she had wanted him, and that thought shamed her.

"I did what had to be done."

"Take my clothes?" She licked her lips, then met his gaze with a bitter stare. Her only refuge was in anger. "What else should I expect from a Campbell?" She spat the name like a curse. She nearly jumped from the bed in all her natural glory, then remembered that she had not a stitch on. Instead, she pulled the quilt up to her chin.

"What else should I expect from a MacQuarie? You're ungrateful. I should have left you lying there with heaven's tears pouring over you. And as to our lovemaking, I didn't try to ravish you this time. You kissed me back, if I remember." He clenched his teeth to keep from uttering the curses that came to his mind. He was wet and tired and hungry and not in a mood to quarrel.

Rain drummed on the roof, corroborating his story. Slowly, Brianna's eyes moved about the room, to the fire and her garments. She could see that he was wet, the shirt he wore clinging to his broad-shouldered form gave truth to his words. She remembered the lightning and thunder that had frightened her horse, the pain as she fell. She also knew deep down that she *had* given him her kisses freely, but her pride would not let her admit it.

"Ye are a blackhearted scoundrel who thinks he can trifle with a lassie's heart. Ye had it in mind to seduce me. That's why ye brought me here."

"I've been as circumspect as a priest, lass. I swear by my father's name I had no ulterior motive in bringing you here." Wordlessly, they regarded each other again for a long, long time until Brianna looked away. The pulse at the base of her throat fluttered wildly, her heart beat so frantically she thought it would burst.

"Ye shouldna hae . . . Even a Campbell should hae some honor." She regretted her outburst. She should have held her tongue, not made such a hostile statement.

"Your virtue was safe."

"No thanks to you." Her flashing eyes made further accusations.

"I tell you I would not have touched you if you'd told me nae, and my word is true." Clearly she'd angered him, she could see it in his face. "I did not do anything you didn't freely tempt me to!"

He leaned so close that she could feel his breath stirring her hair. It thrilled her, yet frightened her, too. The effect this man had over her was unnerving. She wanted to melt into his arms, give herself up to the strange feelings he always inspired. Instead, she again sought haven in sharp words.

"I hae much to be thankful for, then. That I did come to my senses in time to know what ye were about." Eyes wide in her pale face, she stared at him, following his movements as he strode away from her and paced the length of the cottage until his temper had cooled. At last he returned to her side. His anger was tempered with regret.

"Ah, Brianna. Brianna, I can not blame you I suppose for thinking the worst. But it is unwarranted." He shook his head. "I would not *take* that which belonged to another man. If you had spoken one word of reproach I never would have tried to make love to you." Burying his face in his hands, he sighed deeply. "You belong to Robbie. How could I have forgotten that fact. *Robbie.*" His whole body tensed as he spoke the name. Tearing his gaze away from her, he stared grimly at the torch, watching its flickering flame.

"Ohhhh." Robbie. The name came up like a wall between them. She had put him out of her mind too. She swallowed the lump that rose in her throat, certain it matched the one on her head for size. How could she have forgotten her betrothed. "Aye, my husband-to-be."

"I have a great deal of respect for that lad. He's a gentle and a *trusting* . . . "

"Ha! Unlike me, he has no reason to doubt the sincerity of what ye say." The bitter scathing words were deafening to her ears.

"Why, you ungrateful! . . ." He seethed inwardly. "I should have left you lying there, Brianna MacQuarie!" A muscle in his jaw ticked warningly, but she took no heed. All she knew was that she felt safer, from herself, her own emotions, when they were arguing.

"Aye, that ye should hae, I be thinking." She regretted her ingratitude the moment it passed her lips. She wanted to tell him she was sorry, to thank him, but the words were stuck in her throat.

"Then perhaps it's not too late to make amends." Angrily moving toward the fire, he tore at her garments and threw them on the bed. "Here. Get dressed. I'll leave you be."

That exclamation should have relieved her mind, but strangely, it did not. She felt bereft the moment he left her side. She wanted to reach out to him, to beg him not to go away, to tell him she had wanted him, but pride and stubbornness kept her from speaking. How strange that this man she hardly knew could so complicate her feelings. "Aye. Go," she somehow managed to answer instead. "Before ye shame me." Or I shame myself, she thought.

"I'll go. If you're feisty enough to be disagreeable, I won't worry about you."

"Disagreeable?" How quickly the fire of their passion had turned to heated words, utterances she wanted to take back. To see that look of desire upon his face again, not that cold look of vexation.

Ian's eyes flashed fire. "I thought Robbie was to be envied, but I can see that he has been granted a shrew for a wife." Rejection and unfulfilled passion merged in a potent rage within his veins. Without even a backward look, he kicked open the door and blended with the rainy night, leaving her all alone to stare at his retreating figure in stunned silence and regret.

CHAPTER SIXTEEN

Ian Campbell's anger bubbled like a cauldron as he strode the rocky pathway in search of his horse. He'd never met such a stubborn, irritating lassie in all his born days. Accuse him of being dishonorable, would she? Well, let her hurl her insults at the cottage walls, he'd not stay around to listen. Mumbling out loud a string of curses, he put as much distance between himself and the cottage as he could. The fact that he could not find the horses did not improve his humor. Kicking at rocks and clods of dirt, he trudged along.

Walking the pathway, lost in his own tumultuous thoughts, he was frustrated by his body's response to the young woman. Every time she was near him he lost his head, he who was always so calm and levelheaded when it came to battle and other lassies. What an infuriating dilemma, for by his every glance at *her* he was condemned in his own heart and mind as well as others'. Brianna Nic Lachlan was forbidden, as well he knew, out of reach unless of course he was willing to throw away all he had worked for these long years. His clan, his position, his honor. Even then, it would do him no good, for from the first, Brianna had scorned him as the boldest of rogues, albeit with good reason. Perhaps that piqued him most of all. And yet he had felt her respond to him, for just a moment in time.

Bell heather grew in tufts among cairns and rocks, sparkling now like jewels as the moisture from the rain caught the glow of the slowly fading sun. Somehow the lush beauty soothed Ian's mood, and he paused to watch a plump reddish-brown grouse feed upon the leaves of the purplish-pink flowers. Though most of the low ground was covered with willow scrub, heather grew so well and so thick here that he supposed regular burning was necessary if a good crop of young heather was to be kept going for sheep and wildfowl.

Another grouse joined the first bird, then another. They seemed to be plentiful and for a moment Ian regretted not having his bow. In the frenzy of Brianna's accident he had dropped it to the ground and just left it. Now it would be to his humiliation that he would return to the castle hall empty handed. Once again he cursed her beneath his breath. He was tired, in a surly mood, yet his former anger faded away as he walked up a hill and viewed the scenic splendor. The fading sun splashed its pink, gold, and lavender rays through the canopy of the forest. In view of such beauty, who could fail to be touched? This was the land that Brianna loved thus he could not help but love it too.

His temper cooled, he viewed things differently. Looking over his shoulder, he swallowed, now feeling a sense of shame. She had been right. He had tried to seduce her. His wounded pride in the face of her accusations was foolish. No matter how honorable his intentions had been at first, once he had kissed and caressed her, he had gone beyond the point of self-control. In truth, he was angry with himself and not her at all, were he to admit it. Even so, he had stormed off like a wounded bear, leaving her behind. Damn his pride! He should not have left her behind no matter what she had said. She'd fallen and hit her head. What if she was more gravely injured than he had realized? And even if she had completely recovered there were other dangers. He'd heard that wildcats lived in the remote Highland hills. What if that fierce and dangerous little beast came upon her? Like Ian, she was weaponless too.

Ian debated his actions and called himself a fool and worse. Overcome now with anxiety, he took to his heels, tracing his steps back to the cottage through the thick undergrowth. Before he'd gone halfway, however, he was intercepted by three of the MacQuarie clansmen. Their arrows were pointed his way.

"Are ye lost, Campbell?" One of the most fiercesome of the clansmen bared his teeth, showing his animosity.

"Of course not!" Ian took a step forward but decided against too much show of bravado. "I'm returning . . ."

"He looks lost to me, Erskin." The second clansman quickly cut in, snickering openly. "And as helpless as a bairn. He is not armed."

"He willna get a stag wi' his bare hands, Jamie," another taunted.

"Unless he's trying a new method of hunting. One he learned from the English? The Campbells hae some strange ways . . ." The three men guffawed.

"There's been an accident." He didn't have time to stand here and jaw with them, Ian thought. Brianna might at this moment be in danger. "Lachlan's daughter fell from her horse. I was going back to . . ."

"Brianna? Fall? She was practically born on a *garron*. She's a braw lassie." The third clansman confronted Ian with suspicion.

"Her horse bolted during the storm."

"And ye left her?"

"What kind o' mon are ye?" All three pairs of eyes stared at him, revealing their malice.

"I don't have time to explain." There was nothing they could say to him, no retribution that could make him feel worse than he did at that moment. There was no excuse for his actions. "Follow me; I'll show you were she is."

Ian led the three men back to the cottage, his heart

thundering like a hammer as he pushed open the door. A lone candle sputtered, sending a soft glow throughout the small room, clearly revealing the cottage to be empty. Brianna MacQuarie was *gone*.

"I dinna see her!" The man named Erskin gave Ian a sharp poke in the ribs with his bow. "It seems ye hae some explaining to do."

"If ye hae harmed her . . ." another growled, brandishing his dirk.

"She was here!" Ian's eyes searched frantically around the room but her garments were gone. All that remained was his plaid breacon and the crumpled quilt.

"And just disappeared into the mists." The tallest of the clansmen nodded his head and the others surrounded Ian. "Something doesna seem right. The last time I saw the lass she was riding beside *him.*"

"What if he has harmed the lassie!" All the years of anger and hostility bubbled forth as Erskin forced Ian's arm behind his back. "Where is she? Where is she, Campbell?"

"I don't know, but she was here and now she's gone!" Ian's own fury matched his captors'. It enraged him to be treated like this, to be manhandled, he, The Campbell's nephew. A muscle twitched in his jaw as he said, "But I can tell you one thing. Lachlan MacQuarie will hear of this."

"Aye, sooner than ye think." The three men marched him back up the hill to where the other hunters were encamped at the edge of the wood. A tally was being made of the fare—six rabbits, four red deer, a roebuck, and several birds. The MacQuaries' *keisan* was filled to the brim with game. Lachlan had felled a buck at a hundred and seventy yards and was being heartily congratulated. Bending down, he joined the others in dividing up the meat. The scent of blood drove the two russet wolfhounds into a frenzy of barking. Lachlan quieted them by throwing them the animal's entrails.

"We'll hae a splendid feast tonight!" Looking up, he eyed

the men who held Ian in their grasp with surprise. "What is this? Erskin?"

"Brianna! No one can find her. She was last seen wi' this mon." The mood of the huntsmen swiftly changed from gaiety to surliness. All eyes turned toward their chief.

"Och!" Lachlan stood motionless, his eyes like two glowing coals as he gazed intently at Ian. The unwavering stare seemed to scorch the Campbell. "Where is she?" Stepping closer, he lowered his voice so that only Ian could hear. "I hae seen the way ye eyed my daughter." He'd noticed the way Brianna hovered about this man as well, and he liked it not one bit. Like the others, he succumbed to the ill feelings that had brewed between the clans in the past. It would not be the first time that a rival clansman had perpetrated evil. "What hae ye to say? Where is my daughter?" The scar on Lachlan's face turned pale, deep lines furled his brow as he awaited an answer.

Heavy mists clung to the hillocks and craigs, but the rain had stopped as Brianna walked back toward the castle. The air smelled fresh, clean, of grasses, flowers, and leaves, but for once she didn't notice. Her head ached, but it was her conscience that pained her even more severely. Ian Campbell had only done what was necessary to see to her well-being, but instead of being grateful she had shown him her scorn. Aye, and she had kissed him back. So much for her protestations! If she were honest with herself, she would admit that she didn't regret what had passed between them.

For the first time in her life she regretted her volatile temper and her cursed quick tongue. She had ranted, she had raved, because she had been afraid. Not of him so much as of herself and the way her body had so hotly betrayed her common sense. She couldn't lay the blame for what had passed between them at Ian's feet alone. Not if she were honest. And Ian? He was a man of fiercesome pride. She had the feeling that he would long remember her careless words.

It was a long walk over rocks, through foliage, up a steep hill, stumbling in the semidarkness. Brianna cursed herself over and over for a fool, knowing that if she had treated Ian Campbell differently, she would've ridden, not walked, this distance. Feeling dizzy, she put her hand to her head from time to time, wishing fervently that he would be more forgiving than she and come back for her.

Coming to the top of the hill she looked down the sloping side and saw for herself the reason that he had not. A circle of men told the story. Bonfires tore at the black sky, flames licking up toward the stars. Brianna could see several of her clansmen tearing at the logs with their swords to feed its hunger. In the light of the fire she could see her father and his staunchest clansman holding Ian at bay like one of their quarry. Even from far away she could hear Ian shouting out his innocence in the matter of her disappearance. Quickly, she ran down the hill, hoping in some way to make amends.

"Father!" In a huffing, puffing heap she stumbled to his side. "What's going on here?"

"Daughter?" Lachlan MacQuarie moved forward, welcoming her with a bearhug. "Are ye? . . . Are ye? . . ."

"My head hurts a bit but that is all. Banshee threw me and I hit my . . . my head." She looked in Ian Campbell's direction with an unwavering stare as he bowed to her in mock politeness.

"It seems your clansmen think the worst of me, just as you did."

Brianna realized the jeopardy of the situation, for one look at Erskin's, Jamie's, and her father's face gave proof of the tenseness of the situation. "Leave him be! He has done nothing to censor. 'Twas my own fault I fell. If not for yon laddie I might hae fared worse," she hastened to say. "He . . . he took me to the old abandoned cottage in the woods and tended me, keeping me out of the rain."

"Tended ye?" Lachlan's voice was gruff. "What do ye mean?"

Briefly she explained, leaving out, of course, the embarrassingly intimate part, expounding only on his care for her head wound.

"Then he was telling the truth." Lachlan turned on Erskin. "Unhand him, mon." Folding his arms across his massive chest, he faced Ian squarely. "I owe ye an apology. I hope ye will take it."

"I will." Though he spoke to Lachlan, his gaze was focused in Brianna's direction, his outrage softened by the look of good will he read there. A far different glow than he'd seen there before.

"And I owe him a debt of gratitude," Brianna whispered, flushing under the potency of Ian's stare.

"Do ye now . . . ?" Lachlan MacQuarie's thick red brows drew together questioningly. He looked from one to the other. No, he did not like what was happening between them, it would only bring his daughter heartache. She was already promised to the other Campbell. "When ye up and disappeared Erskin was certain he'd harmed ye, but my first thought was that he had abducted ye, that he had ye hidden somewhere and had taken ye for himself."

"As you can see, he did not." Why was there disappointment in her tone? Because the idea of Ian Campbell carrying her off was not such an unpleasant one.

"Aye! And it's glad I am. 'Twill save me from wearing out my horses in chase." His tone of voice left little question of his meaning. Were Ian to even think of such a thing, there would be repercussions. Beneath his breath, Lachlan cursed Robbie Campbell silently. A man should come himself to claim his bride, not leave it to another. That the Campbell lad had not was complicating this delicate matter. "But come, daughter, let's go back to the hall. There's a lot o' venison to be savored."

"Aye, and I'm as hungry as a wolf." It took a great deal of concentration to tear her eyes away from Ian Campbell. Her father's impatient tug gave warning.

"Come, Brie!" His lips curled up slightly. "The women-folk hae been busy preparing another feast while we've been gone." Scooping Brianna up in his arms as he had when she was just a child, he placed her on his own horse, then climbed up behind her. The clansmen followed suit, Erskin making amends for his rough handling of Ian Campbell by allowing him to ride double with him. The ground thundered with hoofbeats as they all rode back to the castle.

CHAPTER SEVENTEEN

Rain pelted through the window as Brianna reached out to close the shutters. One of the borrowing days, she thought, a spell of unseasonably cold weather. How bleak and lonely it appeared. The heavy mists eclipsed the hillocks and enshrouded the castle as if it were separate from the rest of the world. If it were, would she care? At the moment she had to admit she would not, for then she would not have to marry Robbie Campbell.

The pattering raindrops increased their frantic rhythm. Such a storm! It seemed to rend the very heavens. Brushing several strands of her damp dark-red hair from her eyes, she stepped back as a pulsating ribbon of lightning shivered through the sky. A crack of thunder followed, echoing in the room like a shout. Just as it had when she'd been thrown from her horse, she thought, closing her eyes. The memory of yesterday flashed back in a maelstrom of visual and sensual remembrances that stirred her blood. Wicked thoughts bandied about in her mind, and she put a hand to her temple as she conjured up what might have happened had she not pulled away from Ian's embrace.

"Brie! Brie!" Glenna's voice sounded worried. "Is yer head aching again, hinny? Perhaps then ye had better go back to bed."

"I'm fine. Fine!" Oh how she wished there was somewhere she could go to be alone with her thoughts, her imaginings. Shivering, she turned back to the leaping fire.

The storm was doubly unnerving because of the crowded conditions of the castle. With so many guests Aros's few chambers were full to bursting, many of the clansmen sharing beds, others wrapped in their plaids sleeping on the floor in the very same spot where the trestle tables were set up for the meals. On a clear spring day these same kinsmen would have slept outside, but the law of hospitality could not deny them shelter from the rain. Even Lachlan's favored hunting hounds which usually shared a warm spot before the hearth fire had been relegated to the storage rooms on the first floor of the castle. Their whining protests could even now be heard.

Glenna and Brianna too had been forced to share their room. Orianna, who had given up her own room, shared Brianna's narrow bed, and a cousin sprawled her long length in Glenna's. Jeanne and Anne slept on a pallet on the floor. Thus there was little chance for privacy. In such crowded conditions it was hardly surprising that she could little avoid Ian Campbell. In truth, perhaps she didn't really want to. Everywhere she looked he was there, his eyes showing a strange look of tenderness when they came into contact with hers. In those moments she wanted to reach out to him, and only the fierce sense of honor she'd been taught gave her the strength to turn her back instead. Quickly, she pushed such tantalizing dreams to the back of her mind for she was a realist, a practical lassie.

"Look, Brie! Ian's friend. What is he doing?"

In apparent understanding of the boredom staying cooped up inside initiated, Aulay did his best to keep those gathered entertained. With a smile he showed them tricks he had learned at court, standing on his head, leaping and rolling about. Brianna held her breath, certain he would fall and harm himself, but he managed with grace. Turning somersaults and handsprings with arms and legs extended, like the turning of a wheel he soon had a cluster of children settled around him, as well as those of more mature years. Brianna laughed to see her father caught up in the spell, watching intently from his wooden chair on the dais.

"Surely he *is* brownie or fairyfolk," Jeanne giggled. Always one to have eyes for any man, she asked behind her hand if the little man would be as agile and skilled in bed.

"Fie! Ye are brazen to even ponder!" Glenna said, blushing a deep red.

Brianna took another approach. "Why don't ye find out?" Her challenge silenced the bold-talking lass.

"Och, ye should hush, Brie," Glenna chided. "I wouldna wish her on that little mon. He's a dearie and deserves a fine lass to love. Like Seana perhaps." Both Glenna and Brianna delighted in the fact that the petite young woman did show interest in the dwarf.

Aulay tossed a few eggs up into the air, one, two, three, and four, keeping them all suspended, juggling them with such deftness that even the most sullen clansman applauded. Brianna waited for the little man to drop them, but he managed quite skillfully to collect them all, turning them over to Seana to cook for the evening's meal.

"Everyone needs someone to love," Glenna whispered, watching the two small people casting longing gazes at each other. It was a statement said quite innocently yet it caused an ache in Brianna's heart. Somehow she had to find a way to be alone, to give vent to the thoughts whirling inside her head. Seeking some manner of privacy, she left the hall with the thought in mind of taking refuge in the storage area. In her mood perhaps the hounds were the best companions after all.

It was dimly lit and she shuddered in the chill as she made her way down the stairs. Her fingers fumbled at the walls to give her aid. A low, warning growl sounded from the unlighted room as she stepped inside. "Hush! Farquhar. Iomhar." Suddenly an arm slipped around her shoulders and she gasped. "Who? . . ."

155

"By Saint Michael!? You!" Ian's voice enveloped her like a welcome cloak.

"Ian Campbell." She would never have wanted to let him know how glad she was that it was him, yet her voice betrayed her. "What are ye doing here? I didna even hear ye."

"I must have taken the other route."

"Oh?" There was only one stairway that led below, but she had not heard him following her. Had he preceded her here? Or had he purposefully stalked her? The thought sent a quiver up her spine.

"I must have had the same idea as you. I'm a man fond of company, but the buzzing of the bees can soon get on the nerves. I sought solitude as you obviously did." Reaching up, he grasped a flickering torch from a sconce outside the door and held it aloft as they explored the small room filled with casks, barrels, and boxes. "No, that is an untruth! I followed you down here." He came to stand beside her; the flaring torch cast strange flickering shadows over his face and burnished his blue eyes with fire.

"I supposed as much, unless ye can walk through solid walls like a ghostie, Ian Campbell." In spite of herself she laughed, joyful that he had sought out her company after the way she'd scolded him the previous day.

"I wanted to talk with you." His arm slipped around her shoulders as he steered her around a sharp corner and down a short flight of steps. There was a crazy leap in her pulse as she felt the firm pressure of his hand. "Be careful. Watch the stairs. They're steep and slippery."

"Talk with me?" He was standing so close to her that the toe of his curan rested against her foot. Even such a casual gesture moved her deeply. Her body always responded to him. "About yesterday?"

"Aye!"

"There is nothing for ye to say. Let's just forget about it." She was uncomfortable even thinking about the embraces they had shared.

"I wish I could." Cupping her face in his hand, he tipped her chin up and looked deep into her eyes. "I'm sorry for what happened." Ian stared at her for a long, aching moment, wishing she weren't quite so bonnie or that he weren't quite so conscious of her. He had meant to stay away from her and yet here he was.

"Sorry?" Now that she had had time to think it over she wasn't really certain that *she* was. Not if she was really honest with herself.

"I know there are no words that can undo what I've done, that can make you feel more kindly toward me, so I won't even try."

"Oh, but there is. I hae forgiven ye." But not quite forgotten. At that moment she realized that perhaps she had far less control over her emotions than he did. She was mesmerized by him, very aware of his nearness.

"You have bewitched me, lassie. I vowed I'd stay away from you, but God help me . . ."

"And God help me, I dinna wish ye to . . ." A sudden crash of thunder sent her tumbling into his embrace. Brianna felt his arms around her as he crushed her tight against him and her blood screamed with delight. Somehow it seemed that it was with him that she belonged.

"I promised myself I would not touch you, only talk. How quickly I break my word." With a sigh of regret he pushed her way. "You see I am not the rogue that you have supposed. Not really."

"What are ye then, Ian?" What was this man really like?

"A man loyal to his clan and his kin. Since I was just a lad I've known one thing and that has been warfare. I thought that's all there was in the world that really mattered to me, but now I see I've been wrong. There is a different kind of belonging that has nothing to do with kin."

She knew what he meant, for despite all the times she'd scoffed at love when talking to Glenna, she felt it now, the sudden longing to belong to him. Why did he draw her so? "And do ye then want to belong to someone?"

"Aye." He turned away before she could read his eyes, taking refuge by staring at the torch's flame. "My father felt a deep bond with my mother. She was his whole world." There was a sudden easy relationship between them as he told her about his boyhood, his memories of a gentle, smiling woman. It was the first time he'd ever told her anything at all about himself and the glimpse into his heart and mind made her feel close to him. Despite his manly courage and pride, she sensed a loneliness about him that gripped her heart. Stepping closer to him, she put a hand on his shoulder, listening as he revealed more about his life, coming at last to his meeting with Aulay.

For just a few endearing moments Ian seemed to have banished the bold, taunting, mocking manner in which she had cast him in her mind of late. As they continued to talk for some moments longer, she was struck by the thought that sometimes people were not at all what one thought. Oh, he had an infuriatingly arrogant way at times, but now she understood why. Right from the first he had had to prove himself. Hadn't it been much the same with her? Trying to make up to her father for his lack of a son? It was as if she sensed in him a kindred spirit.

"Ian." He turned around as she spoke his name, and as their eyes met she read a glitter of raw desire in the blue depths gazing back at her. She reached out to him, closing her fingers against his as he took her hand.

"Ah, lassie, what ye do to me." His breath was warm against her face, his voice husky. With a soft groan he bent his head, captured her shoulders, and brought her closer as he crushed his mouth demandingly against hers. So much for good intentions, he thought. Compulsively, his hand closed over her breast, his thumb moving back and forth over the peak as he slid his mouth down her throat. Oh, why was it this particular lassie that stirred him so? Desire alone or much, much more?

Ian kissed her over and over, but kisses alone did not quell the blazing hunger that raged through him. His hand trembled as he pushed her away as suddenly as he had sought the embrace. She was too tempting, too soft and yielding in his arms. A moment longer and he would do something he could never forgive himself for.

"Nae! Nae!" He'd followed her to tell her he was sorry for yesterday and had ended up committing the same folly.

Brianna stared at him in muted disappointment, her eyes wide with confusion. He was as unfathomable as the tide, pursuing her one moment, pushing her away the next. She watched the expressions that took control of his face, the wanting, the passion, the regret, and felt the same, though there was no help for it. Robbie! Like a ghost he stood between them and any happiness they might have had.

"I will prove to you that I am a man of honor!" Without saying another word he gripped her shoulders, and in a seemingly angry mood, propelled her through the door. "Back to your father, lass." He pushed her ahead of him, up the narrow steps. They went the next two turns of the spiral staircase in silence, each one exceedingly conscious of the other, but neither willing to voice what they knew must be said. *Goodbye.* It was the only word that could be said, yet the very thought left Brianna with an unquenchable yearning and a deep sadness.

CHAPTER EIGHTEEN

The storm had passed but its moisture had left the castle damp. A slow drizzle still fell. An early morning mist hovered over the land, shrouding the hills in a thick, white cloud. Gazing out the window, Ian thought how the weather matched his mood. But it didn't matter how foggy it was beyond the castle walls. Last night he'd made his decision to leave, and he would carry it out no matter what! After what happened in the cottage, the passion that had flamed within him for Brianna MacQuarie, and then what might have happened in the storeroom, he knew he had to get away from here. Leave or take the chance of betraying young Robbie Campbell and besmirching his honor forever.

No, I cannot risk the temptation of being near the lassie, he mused. With that thought uppermost in his mind, he dressed in shirt and trews, wrapping his plaid to drape over his shoulder, and busied himself gathering the few belongings he had brought with him. He put the smaller items in the sporran hanging from the belt at his waist, then striding across the small chamber, bent down and nudged Aulay's snoring form.

"Wake up! Aulay, get out of bed, we've got a long ways to go."

"Mmmmmm. Go away!" In protestation of awakening, Aulay nestled deeper in the bed, pulling the quilt up over his head.

Grasping the dwarf by the shoulders, Ian shook him gently but firmly. "I hate to intrude on your dreams, but I want to get an early start."

"Grhph! Let me sleep. It's not morning yet." Aulay tried to brush the insistent hands away.

"It *is* morning, and I can't let you snore the whole day away. Get up!" The authoritative tone in Ian's voice could not be ignored. Opening one eye, Aulay groaned. "Too much ale? I'm sorry, my friend, but that's the way of things. Come on. Get your *bahookie* out of bed. Now!" Taking the end of his wool plaid, he snapped the dwarf on the backside.

"Och! You are a cruel mon, Ian!" Dangling one bare leg over the edge of the mattress, he swore beneath his breath.

"Get up."

"I am getting out of bed. See. I hae my foot upon the floor." Stifling a yawn with the back of his hand, he slowly maneuvered the other foot to touch the floor. "Now, by all the blessed saints, what's sparked yer fire this mornin'?"

"The marriage negotiations have been completed. There is no reason to stay here an hour longer. We're leaving this morning to go back to our own hall."

"Go back!" Aulay was clearly disappointed. "When I've just decided I like it here? I've got a lassie nearly as small as I fighting wi' the others over the privilege of my company. And ye tell me we're going back! Why?" Ian's face held the answer. "Och, The MacQuarie's daughter. Dinna tell me that what ye feel for her is more serious than even I supposed."

"I think I love her! If so, then I'm a damned fool." Sitting on the edge of the bed while Aulay dressed, Ian related the incident of the cottage to him. "I would have made love to her. I wanted to. Without even one thought of Robbie. What kind of a man am I? He's my own kin. He's been like a little brother to me. How could I have been so tempted as to nearly betray him that way? With his betrothed bride! And then again, I followed her with the innocent intent of but talking to her, making amends, and I could not keep my hands off her."

"A man can lose his head when he wants a woman. Ye'd not be the first. Adam lost his boon in paradise because of Eve. Dinna be too harsh on yerself, laddie."

"How can I not be? For whatever reason that motivated him, Duncan sent me here in good faith. He trusted me. Right from the first I proved what an ass I can be. You said so yourself. Oh, I thought I was so braw approaching the lass by the pool, but she bested me." Ian grimaced. "You laughed to think I'd finally met my match. But it isn't funny, Aulay. It hurts. More than I could ever have known."

Aulay clucked his tongue. "Then it's sorry that I am for ye, Ian. I never would hae laughed if I had known. Matters of the heart can cause a wound as deep as any sword." He spoke as if he knew by experience.

"Aye, and now that I have felt its prick myself, I'm sorry for any pain I might have caused in the past. From this moment on I am a changed man." Standing up, Ian shrugged his shoulders as if hoping to cast off his unhappiness. "But what is done is done. All I can do is hurry away from here and wish Robbie happiness with his new bride."

"Ye'll no try to claim her for yerself?" Aulay seemed surprised. "Will ye no' try to sway The MacQuarie?"

"Nae! I made a promise that I will keep, to give her into Robbie's hands. There is little else but to put her from my mind." If I can, he thought sadly. He planned out exactly what he would say to Lachlan MacQuarie when he told him goodbye. He'd thank him for his hospitality, assure him that the wedding plans would go smoothly, then make up a reason why he was returning to his own castle so soon. Lachlan was a fighting man, a clan chief, who understood responsibility. He would tell him there were duties pressing on his mind. It sounded reasonable.

"Just like that ye'll go away. And will ye no' tell the lassie goodbye?"

"Nae! No doubt she'll be glad to see me go. Enough thunder has passed between us to wake the dead on the Isle of Iona! Nae." He remembered the way she had looked at him when he had kissed her. If he pursued the matter any more he would end up hurting her, and he didn't want that. There would be little joy for him in stealing her heart and breaking it. She was too fine a lassie for that. He repeated again. "Nae!"

"Ye're so afraid of the lassie, then?"

"Afraid? I'm not afraid. I just don't think it is very wise for me to put temptation in my path . . . and in hers. I've been rogue enough already." Even now her words still stung him. More so, because they were partly true. He was a rogue to have ever let his feelings get so out of hand for any reason. "She'll be glad to see me go."

Stamping his foot, Aulay shook his head, sending his long, tawny hair flying. "If ye think that, then ye're a fool, Ian Campbell. A fool. I've seen the way she looks at ye, particularly last night. She is drawn to ye, mon. Like a bee to honey, I might say." Throwing his breacan over his left shoulder, he stood as tall as he could, about four feet in height. "She'll be disappointed if ye don't say goodbye."

"It's better if I don't." Ian's voice was a choked whisper.

"For her or for you?" Aulay clucked his tongue again. "Shame, shame, shame, Ian Campbell. I never thought I'd see the day ye'd show yerself a coward, and yet ye're afraid of one wee lassie. Aye, ye are."

"I'm no coward!" Ian bristled, stiffening his body from ankle to neck, tensing his jaw.

"Then seek her out, mon. Dinna sneak off wi' yer tail between yer legs like a wounded wildcat. Tell the lassie goodbye. It may well be all that ye'll hae to remember each other by."

Ian argued furiously against Aulay's suggestion, but in the end reneged. He did want to see her again. Just one more time. One last look at her, that's all he would take. And then he would say a final goodbye. One last farewell before he gave her into Robbie's arms forever.

Intent upon talking with her, he sought her out in her chamber, only to feel the sting of disappointment when her sister said she was not there. That might have been the end of the matter had not fate taken a hand. After seeking Lachlan MacQuarie out, Ian's next stop was the kitchen to stock up on food supplies for his return journey. He needed oats for the small cakes he would bake in the small iron griddle that he carried with him, fresh water, and dried fruit. It was here he found Brianna, sharpening the knives that hung from hooks on the kitchen wall. She was beautiful in the early morning sunlight, her hair hanging down her back like thick dark-red threads. Ian feasted his eyes, finding himself suddenly tongue-tied.

Brianna sensed his presence, turning around to meet his stare. "Ian?" Her eyes questioned him silently, hopefully.

Though the very sight of her sent his heart pumping, he maintained a cool aloofness. "I only came to say goodbye and to wish you every happiness, Brianna."

"Goodbye?" He was going away so soon? She had been expecting it, but even so, it was strange how that made her feel utterly devastated.

"Aye."

"But there are three more days of feasting and . . ."

"I *must* go, Brianna. Especially after yesterday. I . . . know there are no words that can say what is in my heart. All I will do is to wish you every happiness. I want that, Brianna. With all my heart." He pulled the whole soft, supple length of her against him, breathing in the fragrance of her hair, whispering her name as he kissed her with sweet wild desire. His hands caught in her hair, stroking it with a tenderness that belied the passion that raged within him. Then he pulled away and strode through the door, taking Brianna's heart with him.

CHAPTER NINETEEN

It was stifling in the hall. A muggy heat permeated the stone walls, making it a truly miserable day. Smoke from the cooking fires stung Brianna's eyes as she worked diligently at the loom trying to forget Ian Campbell. It was difficult if not impossible. Oh, how she missed him! He filled her thoughts by day and her dreams by night, haunting her like a ghostie. She'd never realized she would be so miserable not seeing him. Over and over again she conjured him up, reliving that last moment when he had kissed her and said goodbye.

"All I will do is wish you every happiness," he had said. "I want that, Brianna. With all my heart." Then he had walked away and out of her life.

"Brianna! Be careful. You're tangling the threads." Jeanne's high-pitched voice sounded a warning.

Brianna drew in a deep breath and let it out slowly in a sigh. "I'm sorry. I wasna paying much attention to what I was doing." Plucking at the wool, she hastily rectified the situation, untwisting the thread, then passing it more cautiously back and forth, interlacing the *weft* through the warp threads with her shuttle.

"Och, so we've noticed." Orianna's smile expressed her

sympathy though she did not pry into what was wrong with her sister. If Brianna wanted to tell her, she would.

Brianna focused her attention on the loom, a simple rectangular frame made of wood, watching as the other women rolled up an end of the finished cloth to make way for a new length of weaving. They unwound the spindle and measured off the vertical threads in roughly equal lengths. The threads would be the warp of the extended length of cloth. Setting the loom upright again, tilted against the wall, they let the warp threads go taut, hanging down vertically across the wooden frame. Blessed Saint Michael, Brianna thought, rubbing at her eyes. It somehow reminded her of the small mattress at the cottage. She could imagine herself lying upon its softness, could feel Ian's strong body pressed against hers. What might have happened if? . . .

"Careful tipping the loom or we'll be done for it!" Jeanne's irritated shriek at Mary startled Brianna out of her daydreaming and she jumped. Her nerves were unreasonably on edge.

"What is it that has ye so jittery, Brie?" Orianna shook her tawny-haired head. "Ye nearly jumped out o' yer skin just now." In sisterly concern she touched Brianna's arm. "If ye need an ear, mine are always available."

Brianna shrugged. "Wedding nerves, that's all."

"Aye, but yer wedding is not for many, many days yet. Ye'll be wi' us a time longer." Orianna eyed her sister quizzically. Certainly, both Glenna and Brianna were acting strange lately, both seemingly in a secret place where the others could not trespass.

"Aye, but there's much to do," Brianna answered. That was true enough. There was her wedding gown to finish, her father's breacon to weave, and a hundred other things to do before the ceremony. The days were passing with unsettling quickness.

"No doubt she's just anxious to leave." Jeanne's smile was all-knowing. "Sleeping alone in a bed can be tedious. Perhaps her mind is on that bridegroom o' hers that's awaitin'." Throwing back her head, she giggled. "If he's anything at all like the *other* Campbell then I'd say our Brianna will hae little woe in leaving us. Maybe she hopes this Robbie is likewise endowed."

Brianna's cheeks colored. "'Tis none of yer concern what's on my mind, Jeanne," she answered tartly. She'd been thinking of a Campbell all right, albeit a different one. *Ian*. She was remembering the gentle way his hands had stroked her face, belying his strength. Just the thought made her tingle all the way down to her toes.

"Och, you've embarrassed her. She's as red as the cloth we've been weaving." Mary, the oldest of the women, shook her finger at Jeanne. "Ye should hold yer tongue, ye overbold lassie."

Jeanne quirked a well-arched brow. "Fie! If she's blushing, it must be that I hae spoken the truth. Hae I, Brianna?"

Brianna ignored the question, keeping to her silence, pretending unwavering interest in the *maide dalbh*, the pattern sticks that served as a guide for the weaving.

"Ha! Hold the pose of an angel, ye'll no' be fooling me. No lassie is so pure that she does no' crave a man's arms and *other* things." In answer to her bold comment, two of the women twittered and looked Brianna's way. Brianna pretended not to notice, calling Jeanne a silly goose beneath her breath as she riveted her concentration on the loom before her.

Brianna and the other women were working on a plaid for Lachlan MacQuarie to wear to the wedding ceremony. He'd go to the Campbell hall in pride, Brianna had vowed with determination. With that thought in mind, she had suggested that the cloth be made with his favorite colors—red wool, colored by a dye made of dark lichen, a plant that grew on the face of a rock, and black wool, colored with alder tree bark for the darkest hue. It was a tedious undertaking, for the breacon was to be made from twelve ells of plaid, a long piece of cloth to be certain. They had to work carefully. Anything with more than one color increased the complexity of the weaving, necessitating more than one shuttle and a careful counting of threads to match the established pattern.

"And while we're talking, I never thought I'd see the day when you would seek out our company for longer than a few wee minutes, Brianna." Seeing she'd already flustered Brianna, Jeanne continued her prattling, watching as Brianna shifted in her seat and grasped her shuttle more tightly. In and out, in and out, she worked with her spindle. "She usually shuns us in favor of more adventurous pursuits."

It was true. Brianna couldn't deny it. The fact was that she avoided the women and their weaving every time she could. Usually one to seek the outdoor air, Brianna had been strangely reflective these last three days. Doing women's chores was her only escape from the thoughts and memories which taunted her. Still, she fired back a scathing answer. "'Tis none of yer concern where I spend my time, I'd be thinking, Jeanne," she answered again.

"Perhaps. And yet it does make a lass wonder."

"She's to be a new bride, ye foolish girl." Again Mary came to Brianna's defense. "Of course she'd be turning to women's work."

"Mmmmmm . . . maybe."

Brianna ignored Jeanne's teasing smile. The best way to avoid the whole matter was to concentrate on her work. Ah yes, the plaid would be perfect for her father. It was his favorite pattern, one her mother had woven for him so long ago. As soon as the cloth was finished it would be tread on in water to fill the weave and then fluffed with dried, prickly flowers called *teazels* to raise the fiber. The last step to the process would be to dry the fabric and stretch it on poles to block it. Indeed, her father would look grand in the new tartan, and yet every time she tried to imagine Lachlan wearing it, she was haunted by the memory of the way Ian Campbell threw his breacan so jauntily over his shoulder.

"I must be daft!" Brianna gasped aloud, causing the others to stare. Quickly she covered her lips with her fingers, regretting the outburst. Why oh why couldn't she get the laddie out of her mind? Why? The answer screamed at her. She was trying to run away from her heart by working so diligently, but she couldn't escape her desire. She could not flee from her feelings.

Somewhere to the southeast was Ian's clan's castle. Was he, even at this moment, gazing into the fire somewhere, talking man talk, planning a hunt or engaging himself in battle strategy? Did he ever think of her or remember the kisses they had shared? He'd caused turmoil in her life. Had she done like to him? She could only wonder.

"But don't ye ever wonder just what yer Robbie is like. Dark of hair or light. If he is a short or a tall mon. If he's muscled or thin?" Anne was asking.

"What?" Once again to her dismay, Brianna dropped her spindle tangling the thread.

Jeanne clucked her tongue. "Our Brianna takes often to flights into her own musing." Clearing her throat, she loudly announced, "Anne was asking if ye aren't a wee mite curious about yer bridegroom-to-be, considering that ye've ne'er seen him." Jeanne giggled again. "Ye must hae curiosity about the man ye'll be making babies wi'. Just what kind o' mon is yer Robbie?"

"I dinna ken." Didn't that foolish girl realize she'd asked herself the same question? All she had heard of him was that he was just about her age, seventeen or eighteen years. She was to marry some beardless boy who had not even insisted on seeing his bride before he claimed her. He knew no more of her than she did of him. Would he be pleased? Was he looking forward to claiming his bride or did he even care?

Anne sighed. "I suppose it doesna matter. Were he as homely as a toad and as foul tempered as an ogre, Brianna would still hae to marry him. That's the way it is."

Aye, Anne was right. Women had no say. It was a galling fact. She wanted to blame Robbie, but knew he was just as much of a pawn as she. Marriages were not for love but for binding together property. An angering fact but true. And yet the more Brianna thought about it, the more it aggravated her. Why hadn't this Robbie shown enough interest in their marriage to come to meet his bride? Why would he agree to send someone else, no matter what the reason? It would serve him right if she changed her mind, she thought. And yet to do such a thing could cause the quarreling all over again. She'd agreed to marry The Campbell heir and that was a thing she must live up to no matter her trepidation. There was no going around it.

Brianna carefully counted the threads she was weaving, determined to put the matter out of her mind. Ten black threads. Time to change to the red-threaded spindle. And when her father's plaid was done she'd begin on the cloth for her own gown. Perhaps she'd use the wool that had just been dyed blue with elderberry. Or then again, the yellow. Fie! It really didn't matter. Her heart was just not in it. In truth, she didn't want to marry.

"As for me, I'm glad I'm not of close kin so I can be handfasted." Jeanne winked. "I be thinkin' that way to try out a mon before I say any solid vows." Indeed, handfasting was a custom within the clan that was used on occasion whereby a man and woman contracted to live together for a year and a day, and if there was no issue within that period they were at liberty to dissolve the contract. In Brianna's case, however, where property was involved, there would be no such option, much to her woe. At least Jeanne could cast her husband off if he did not suit her and vice versa.

"Who do ye suppose will take Duncan Campbell's place when he lays down his sword, Brianna? My Gregor is no' so certain it will be yer husband-to-be. He thinks Ian Campbell is the strongest of the two heirs." Anne prattled all that she had heard about Ian Campbell's prowess.

"Aye, there are those who wonder if Lachlan should no' hae held out for the older o' the two nephews. They say having Ian Campbell on our side would be a great advantage." Jeanne closed her eyes. "Aye, to see Ian Campbell arrayed in chieftain's finery would be a sight." The way

Jeanne spoke the name with such a familiar tone irritated Brianna yet it set her to thinking too.

Ian Campbell was Duncan Campbell's nephew, the older of the two. Why then was it Robbie who was marrying first? It set an odd precedent that made her wonder. Why had she not been betrothed to Ian? For that matter, what difference did it make if it was Robbie or Ian that she married? Both were nephews of Duncan, the laird of the clan. Why could she not have her pick? That thought made her grumble silently.

"If it were me who was The MacQuarie's daughter, I would hae insisted on choosing between the handsomest and lustiest o' the two." Jeanne grinned suggestively. "No doubt our fine comely Ian will go to the MacLeod lassie, but oh, how I'd love to hae that braw, handsome laddie in my bed."

"Well, ye willna!" The thought irked Brianna. As for the MacLeod miss, she'd seen her at a fair once, a pie-faced girl who giggled all the time with hair as pale as the snow. The very idea of Ian Campbell being married to such a lass rankled her. "As for the MacLeod lassie, it's little ye know, Jeanne, to be suggesting that. She's no' right for him!"

Jeanne grinned, at last having made her mark. "And of course ye would know. I saw ye making eyes at him."

"I didna! I barely noticed him in fact." Oh, what a lie! Reaching up she touched her nose. When she was just a little girl she'd heard it told that the fairies punished those who whispered falsehoods by making their noses grow long. Thankfully, they had not heard her words.

"Ha! I say ha again. But it is yer life, Brianna. I would go to The Campbell and ask for a chance to choose."

"Well, I willna." Or would she? Why not? Why not have some say in who she married? Was she to let herself be mated like her father's prime cattle or sheep? Was she to tie herself up with a man she'd never even met? Robbie Campbell indeed. An elusive man at best. One more interested in decorating his castle than meeting his bride. Was she to go meekly to her wedding bed like a docile little lamb without even having a choice in the matter? Was she to be as spineless as he appeared to be? No! Suddenly, she was determined that this was not going to be the case with her.

An idea took fruition in her brain, one she could not dispel. Why not go to the Campbell castle and talk with Duncan Campbell himself about the matter? She'd face the fiercesome laird and voice her misgivings. Perhaps he'd be impressed with her fortitude and daring and reward her by allowing her to choose the man she preferred. Aye, she liked that idea. She'd show Duncan Campbell she was a lassie with spunk. She would marry a Campbell, on that she'd keep her word, only there was every possibility that his name would be Ian.

CHAPTER TWENTY

The castle was shrouded in darkness. Everyone was abed except the two red-haired lassies who faced each other squarely across the narrow bed. "I've thought it out and there canna be any other way."

"Brie, ye must be daft! Touched in the head if ye think ye can get away wi' this. Father will hae yer head and mine as well! And it will all be for naught." Glenna clutched at the folds of her dress, frightened for her sister and for herself. Surely, Brianna could not be serious about what she proposed, to boldly travel to Campbell territory and take matters into her own hands. "Father will . . ."

"Be an old goat! I dinna ken what is wrong wi' him of late. Look how stubborn he has been on the matter of Alastair. When I was so certain I could make him listen to reason." Her father's unrelenting attitude piqued Brianna.

"He has yet to agree to let Alastair fight for me, but . . ."

"But he willna get the chance to tell *me* nae." Coming to Glenna's side in three quick strides, Brianna grasped her by the shoulders. "Please, Glenna! I must get this matter settled. I canna dawdle, I hae to hurry. Once assured of the marriage settlement, once Father hands me over to The Campbell, thereafter the contract is unbreakable and I'll hae to take Robbie as my groom."

"But to travel by boat! Ye might be taken by the *cailleach uisge* and I'd ne'er see ye again."

"Och, I'm no' afraid of the water hag and besides, I won't be alone. I'm taking one of the fishermen's sons wi' me. Darach. He's the only one I can trust not to tell Father what I'm planning." Proving her determination, Brianna moved about the room, gathering up a few necessary items to take with her on the journey, wrapping them in a bundle. A comb, her *curans* to wear along the rocky path, a brooch, a *curraichd* to tie around her head if it was windy.

"Oh, Brie! Don't go! Ye'll disappear just like aunt Mary and I willna see ye again." Yanking the brooch and comb away, Glenna put them back.

"I willna disappear." She tried to sound a lot braver than she felt. The story of her aunt still haunted her. "Aunt Mary may hae run away! I often wonder."

"I think she did. Father told me that she wanted to marry a Campbell."

"A Campbell?"

"Can ye imagine that?" Glenna clutched her sister's hands. "Perhaps she got lost going to the Campbell lands, just as ye are doing right now. I dinna want ye to suffer her fate. I want ye to come back!"

"I will!" Brianna retrieved her possessions, carefully tying them in the curraichd. "I hae still to convince Father to let ye marry Alastair, hinny."

"But what will Father say when he finds out ye hae gone? He'll come after ye, move heaven and hell to catch up wi' ye. Ye'll be caught before ye get very far and a whipping will be yer only reward for being so braw!"

Brianna grinned. "Father will no' even realize I'm gone. That's where our being look-alike sisters will be to my advantage."

Brianna whispered what she planned, enlisting Glenna's aid, reminding her sister of how, when they were small children, they used to take great delight in tormenting their father by confusing him as to who was who with their masquerades. It had been an enchanting game. Now it could be employed to keep her escapade a secret from their father. Glenna could pretend to be Brianna. She had to.

"What?" Glenna was incredulous.

"It's very simple, hinny. Ye merely play a dual part. As yerself and me as well! That way Father will not even realize that I am gone. By the time he does find out I'll hae visited the Campbell hall and convinced Duncan Campbell of the wisdom of my proposal."

"Nae! We did that years ago. I could ne'er pretend to be you. Not now! He'd realize in an instant, the moment my knees started shaking. Ye canna go, Brie!"

"I *am* going. With or wi'out yer help I've made up my mind. Ye canna prevent it. Do ye ken? But I was hopin' ye'd remember that when I realized how important Alastair was to ye, I came to yer aid." It was a despicable thing, reminding her sister of how she had volunteered to marry The Campbell heir in her place, but Brianna was desperate. If Glenna did not agree, she would certainly be overtaken and brought back to the hall before attaining her goal.

"Aye, I couldna ever forget." Glenna did want to repay Brianna in some small measure for her self-sacrificial act.

"Ye might as well help me." By hook and by crook she somehow managed to convince Glenna of the perfection of her reasoning. "Ye can hae fun, hinny. Just be as bold as I am when ye're pretending to be me. I know ye can. Please. Will ye do it?"

Glenna nodded reluctantly, then suddenly threw her arms around her sister. Her tears splashed Brianna's face. "I'll do it. But take care, Brie. If anything were to happen to ye I'd never forgive myself."

"Nothing will happen! Ye'll see. Everything will be all right. And when I come back I'll talk wi' Father again about Alastair. I want us both to be happy, hinny, but the only way to get what ye want is to control yer own fate, I be thinking."

Bold talk. Forcing a self-confident smile, Brianna blew out the candle. "Now let's get some sleep. Before the sun comes up I'll need to be gone." Brianna was excited, but also a bit afraid of the magnitude of her act. Fumbling around in the dark with her precious bundle, she said a silent prayer that she would have no regrets for her decision.

PART II

THE RELUCTANT BRIDE

The Lochs of North Argyll
Summer—Autumn

> Had we never lov'd sae kindly,
> Had we never lov'd sae blindly,
> Never met, or never parted,
> We had ne'er been broken-hearted!
> —BURNS, *AE FOND KISS*

CHAPTER TWENTY-ONE

Duncan Campbell lounged drunkenly in his carved wooden chair by the roaring hearth fire, taking long gulps of his ale, idly watching his handsome dark-haired nephew. Something was wrong with the lad, but he couldn't quite figure out what it was. Since coming back from the Isle of Ulva, Ian was more subdued, less cocky. He seemed deep in contemplation for long periods of time, laughed seldomly.

"Did I not know better, I'd think The MacQuarie's sent back a changeling in yer place, Ian. Of a surety I would," he said at last. Ian's reflective mood was bothersome for he relied on the young man to amuse him.

"Perhaps they did, uncle, for I am not the same man who left this hall. Aye, I've changed." Strange how one wee lassie could work such havoc in his life, he thought, and yet she had. The very thought of her marrying Robbie caused a gnawing ache in his heart that he could not remedy no matter how hard he tried.

Squinting his eyes, Duncan tried to decipher Ian's meaning. "And I dinna like it! Hovering about the hall like an old woman. Och!" His mouth was tight as he said, "By Saint Michael, tell me what's wrong, mon. I canna read yer mind."

"All right. Since you asked me, uncle, I'll tell you." How

could he hand the woman he loved over to another man? It was a question which tortured him night and day as the Campbells made their preparations for the upcoming wedding. "I covet Robbie his bride!" There, at last he'd said what was on his mind.

"What!" Duncan bolted from his chair, trembling with ire. It was the last thing he'd ever expected to hear. *"What did ye say?"*

"You brought the subject up so I'll be truthful. If I thought there was any way I could convince you to let me take Brianna MacQuarie for my own I'd pose the question." Ian waited expectantly, but was warned of the answer before it was spoken when Duncan's black brows drew together in a scowl.

"Then let me warn ye to hold yer tongue! I'd as soon chop off my own right arm as to marry ye to that devil's spawn," Duncan thundered. In a show of contempt, Duncan threw his ale, cup and all, into the fire, watching as the flames sputtered.

"Devil's spawn?" It was an odd way to talk about a lass who was about to marry one of his kin.

Duncan realized his slip of the tongue and hastened to correct his mistake, cooling his temper. "Ye hae always been my favorite, though I hae never spoken so. I hae great ambitions for ye, laddie. There is no hill ye canna climb if ye use yer head."

"And if I told you I did not care about being a mighty man, only a happy one?" Strange how life seemed so empty without the red-haired lass. Ambition could not keep a man warm at night or give him comfort.

"I'd call ye the village fool!" Rage rumbled within Duncan. He could not tolerate any defiance to his plan. "Robbie will marry the lass and no' you. Get that through yer thick-boned head. I willna change my mind nor give to ye what has been promised to the younger lad."

"But why?" Ian ignored his uncle's raving and poured himself a dram of ale, sloshing it about in the tankard.

"Robbie has never even met her. She does not hold his heart. In fact, he has no care for marrying at all. I've talked with the laddie." Ian protested stubbornly, now that the subject had been broached. "But *I* have met her and I *do* want her. You speak of my aspirations and I will tell you she is just the kind of woman a man needs at his side. A brave lass who would do a man proud."

Duncan ground his teeth, damning the stubbornness of his nephew. "I willna gi' ye up to take on the MacQuarie name, I tell ye! They hae ever been our enemies."

"But perhaps they could be mighty allies now that our quarrel is ended." Taking a piece of charred wood out of the fire, Ian used it to sketch a hurried map of MacQuarie land. "The dun sits here atop the hill and could be used to give us warning."

"For the third time, nae! The MacQuarie lassie is to be *Robbie's* bride and no other. I will talk no more about it." Damn the strong-willed lad, Duncan thought. Well, he would have none of his prodding. Seeing a spider crawling across the stone floor he vented his anger on the hapless insect, grinding it beneath the heal of his *curan*. That was how he would crush The MacQuarie!

A troubled silence ensued. Ian stared at his uncle, watching the myriad of emotions that played upon the black-bearded face. Something was amiss here, but he could not say just what. In most matters a reasonable man, Duncan looked more like a snarling dog. One on the verge of going quite mad. But how did Brianna MacQuarie fit in all of this? Why, if his uncle hated the MacQuaries so, would he agree to marry Robbie into the clan, to let the lad take on the name? It was a troubling puzzlement but one which deserved contemplation.

"Something is wrong. Very, very wrong. I sense it." Ian was anxious to avoid the storm he sensed was brewing. He'd jested with Aulay that he feared Duncan was becoming an addled man, now he feared there was more to it than that. "Won't you confide in me, uncle?"

"It's none o' yer concern. I am the one who leads this clan!" Across the room blue eyes battled with eyes of like hue. Both men were strong willed, neither willing to budge. Something in Ian's expression angered Duncan. A fear that somehow his nephew might somehow sense the truth overcame his reason. He'd not let anyone rob him of his victory for the sake of a lassie's smile.

"I'm not questioning your authority, only wondering . . ." Ian queried sharply.

"Get out o' here!" roared the black-bearded Campbell laird. Realizing it was useless to pursue the matter at the moment, Ian did just that, passing through the doorway in a swearing huff.

"I ne'er thought I'd think it, much less say it, but it's shamed I am o' ye, Duncan," hissed a voice from the shadows. "I've hoped ye'd come to yer senses, to see that what yer doing is wrong." Cameron shook his head sadly as he entered the room.

"Ye heard?"

"Aye." He shook his head sadly. "How could I help but hear yer shouts?"

"Hmph. He may be my successor but I've no' given it up to him yet! Marry the MacQuarie lassie indeed. Well, I'll soon put an end to that."

"And are ye proud o' yerself? Now that Ian expresses interest in the girlie, it's more for shame. Ye'll be hurting so many people." Cameron sunk down wearily into the very same chair vacated by Duncan, putting his face in his hands.

"I'm only giving tit for tat. There's only one I hae my sights on bringing pain and ye know it." Folding his thick arms across his massive chest, Duncan stood as still as a stone statue.

"Why not marry Ian to The MacQuarie's lassie? Why not really give peace a chance. Think, Duncan. Think. There's a sense of calm over the countryside now that the warring has stopped. Yer people are happy, there's no more crying for their dead. Why no' gi' the lass to Ian. It isna too late."

"Because a MacQuarie isna fit to tie a Campbell's laces! I wouldna agree to any such marriage. *Nae,* Ian is a handsome and fearsome warrior who can be used to further my power. It will be a MacDonald, Cameron, MacLean or perhaps even a Gordon lassie for he."

"Then break off the marriage contract before it's too late. Please, Duncan, I've ne'er pleaded before, but dinna do it!"

"Ha! Our clans are battling for supremacy. I must stamp out their line. Loss of honor to The MacQuarie is of major importance. Ye know what I mean. After both the bride and groom hae given their consent and are bound, only the council of clans can annul the marriage and I'll ne'er consent to that. Aye, Brianna MacQuarie will be Robbie's bride." Throwing back his head, Duncan vented his evil laughter.

"Then there's naught I can say to dissuade ye. Och, I fear ye'll burn in hell for what ye plan."

"Or make the devil laugh."

"Even the devil must hae some scruples."

"Hold yer tongue! I am laird here. I willna listen to such words even from an old friend."

Cameron sighed, shaking his head. "Think, Duncan. Think. Ye canna marry the laddie to his own sister. Such an action will be the ruination of us all when he finds out the truth. Did ye no' think that it will go against ye when it's learned what ye hae done? Ye'll be a damned man in all eyes for perpetrating such a sin."

"I dinna care! This was just what I planned for eighteen years. The MacQuarie's two bairns marrying each other. There is not a man that can dissuade me from taking my revenge. Even God himself. When there is fruit of the misbegotten seed, when the bride is with child, then and only then will I reveal the truth and see the horror written on The MacQuarie's face. The ultimate revenge."

CHAPTER TWENTY-TWO

The sea voyage was far from the enticing adventure Brianna had supposed. The violently churning ocean soon turned her insides upside down. As the familiar shores of Ulva had fallen away, to be lost in the pale pink glow of dawn, she had felt an unnerving sense of wariness. Since she was a child she'd heard tales of mermaids and sea people; water horses and water bulls that enticed unwary travelers. *Nuckelavee. Glastig.* Were these creatures even now lying in wait to snatch the boat as it bounced on the waves? In consternation, she expressed her fears to Darach, the fisherman whose boat was taking her to Argyll.

"Dinna worry, Brianna. Water horses and water bulls live in the lochs and rivers, no' in the sea. I've been a fisherman since a boy and I've encountered nary a one." Darach puffed out his chest with pride as if to say it was fear of his prowess that kept them away. "Though I wouldna mind meeting up wi' a mermaid."

Crossing herself, Brianna looked over her shoulder from time to time. Though the fisherman assured her there were none around the boat, she watched the waves warily for any sign of such a beastie nonetheless. Fear only added to the misery she already felt. The unpleasant creatures were not her only reservation. She was instigating an act for which there might well be repercussions. Her father would be incensed if he found out what she had done. She knew naught of Duncan. For all she knew, she might well be walking straight into a beehive. And yet she could not turn back. Was Ian Campbell worth it? Aye, whispered a voice. He was the only man she wanted for her husband, the only man who stirred her blood. God willing, she would have her way.

Grasping the edge of the small *curach,* a boat constructed with wicker frame and covered with hides, Brianna reflected on her daring deed. Darach had not been as easy to persuade as she had supposed. His loyalty and affection for his chief had caused him to staunchly refuse her request at first. Only her threat to go all alone had softened his resolve. That and a steadfast bribe of a new sword had acted to change his mind. Brianna had convinced him of the favor he would be doing her father by acting as her guide and seeing to her safety. In the end he had grudgingly agreed, though not without ample warning.

Now, as the boat skimmed the rough waves, she found herself wishing halfheartedly that Darach had won the argument. Oh, she had been brave and fearless at home amid familiar surroundings. Now, she must fight her inner turmoil and bolster her courage.

Up and down, back and forth, the boat rocked unendingly. Brianna and the fisherman traveled until a dusting of powdery stars dotted the sky, fading into clouds of mist above the horizon. She looked for the familiar constellations and contented herself with counting stars. Lulled by the soft rhythm of the oars, soothed by the rise and dip of the blades as they slapped the waves, she drifted off into a fitful sleep. Her mind drifted from one fantasy to another, imagining the expression she would read on Ian Campbell's face when she walked brazenly into his uncle's hall. No shy, shrinking maiden she! She'd prove herself a worthy match.

Deep in her dreams she was conscious only of the motion of the boat and the sound of the water. Awakening for a moment, she could see the shadowed form of Darach as he bent and stretched at the oars. The moon was at its quarter, the black water glistened with the tiny dots that were reflections of the stars. The air was a penetrating damp cold, and she hugged herself to keep from shivering. Finally, complete exhaustion took control of her and she fell asleep again.

Brianna awoke just as the first beams of light tugged at the morning sky. The breathtaking mountain grandeur of Northern Argyll silhouetted the horizon, causing her to gasp audibly. "So beautiful!"

"Aye," Darach agreed. "And it's a paradise for salmon fishing. My father and I used to brave The Campbell's anger to fish these waters. And not once did we come up with empty nets." Darach grinned, his sun-toughened skin tugging into wrinkles. "Though we might hae doubled our catch had yer father not been so stubborn." In the true spirit of clan fairness, Lachlan MacQuarie insisted that all fishing lines and nets be of equal length to prevent any one fisherman from obtaining an unfair advantage in the waters.

Argyll's jagged coastline seemed to extend for miles, making the boat's landing harrowing as it swept ashore. Nonetheless, Darach artfully steered the tiny vessel up the coastline of a great sea loch and came at last to an area that facilitated a smooth beaching. Clutching her few possessions, Brianna climbed from the boat, fighting to get her sea legs under control. The cramped position had weakened her muscles somewhat. The Campbell's land was beautiful and colorful, its greenery covered with buds and flowers. Still, the journey to the castle would be a long and exhausting one, by foot over steep hills. That she wasn't certain of the exact location would be a further hindrance, though she was determined that if Ian could find her clan's castle she could find his.

As they climbed higher and higher, the changing colors of the sky lit up the variety of scenes below—valleys surrounded by mountains with rolling hills to the south.

FLAME ACROSS THE HIGHLANDS

The many flat and lonely brown bogs along the edge of the ocean were in stark contrast to the flower-covered hills she had seen earlier. It was rugged like her home, not completely good for farming. The fields near the mountains were stony, swampy, treeless, or bare.

Everywhere, shepherds could be seen driving their flocks of black-faced sheep along the moors, heading toward fresh pasture, others to market or fair. Peasants existed in miserable hovels built of wattle or some wickerwork strengthened with earth and clay, and roofed with heather, turf, rushes, or ferns. The huts were round, the windows small, and the smoke from the fire escaped through a hole in the roof. Her first impression of the Campbell lands as green and flower covered faded as she faced the reality surrounding her.

The long hours gradually lengthened as they traveled over the lonely landscape, hoping the shepherds had pointed them in the right direction. Sheep, goats, and small wild animals inhabited the area, roaming about freely. Whereas on Ulva horses had longer hair and were left outdoors even in the winter, here the horses were stabled. An English custom no doubt, she thought. Highlanders would never pamper their horses, she thought to herself, but strengthened them by exposing them to the weather.

They had made plans to camp along the way but found it unnecessary. Coming upon a small village, she discovered that like her clansmen, those from other clans were also very hospitable, even though they did not know who she was. To them, she was but a weary traveler who was offered hospitality at every door. Even fugitives from justice were safe from capture when visiting other clans. Although she knew it was Highland custom that strangers be given the best accommodation in the house and the best food obtainable, she hadn't expected such treatment here where many English customs were said to be recognized. Perhaps then, people were much the same wherever they lived.

She did find one difference in diet, however. The people in Ian's land were not hunters as were hers, and depended more upon domestic meat—lamb or beef—instead of venison. Indeed, they had also been offered milk, cheese, butter, oatmeal, and barley meal, prepared in various ways, and bannocks which seemed to be the staple diet. Herbs and wild fruits offered a pleasant variety to the diet.

It seemed the people were not as prosperous here as in her father's lands, and Brianna supposed it was this new idea of feudalism that was to blame. How glad she was that her father had been so staunchly against it. Possession of the land was the principal difference between the old and the new systems. After she was married, Brianna thought, she'd try to convince her husband to go back to the old ways of clan loyalty and mutual ownership of land. Highlanders needed to band together, not display the greed of the English.

She had never dreamed that Duncan's castle would be so difficult to find. Already they had been here for two days. This land was vast. Though Darach had been expert when it came to the sea, on land he was unsure of the route to be taken, even though the peasants had given directions. At last, just as Brianna thought she could not take another step, she saw the round tower standing tall against the deep blue sky. The Campbell stronghold. Dunstaffnage Castle. The ten-foot-thick outer wall was nearly indistinguishable from the black crag upon which it was situated. It hovered high above the earth, tangible proof of The Campbell's newly acquired power and strength. Had they known its location, they would have beached much further up the loch.

Brianna thought of all that she had heard about the castle. The peasants were proud of its history and had rambled on about it endlessly. Indeed, it had been the main topic of conversation. It was built on the site of a former home of Scottish kings who had moved their capital to Scone. It had been built for Alexander II's attack against the Norsemen when they held the Hebrides. A little over four years ago, Dunstaffnage had been captured in a bloody battle of fire and sword from the MacDougalls by Robert the Bruce. The self-crowned King Robert had appointed MacArthur, a distant relative of The Campbell's, as the constable and captain of Dunstaffnage. He had turned it over to Duncan for the strategic maneuverability of the land. Soon it would be Brianna's home.

They approached the castle over a natural causeway of barren rocks that was protected from the wind by trees. The castle was different than the MacQuarie dun. It was built upon a mound of dirt, with foundation beams and uprights of wood to hold the roof. Brianna had never seen a castle like this before. It had a foundation of stone but was built mainly of wood. Perhaps that accounted for the lack of forest land as they moved further inland. She seemed to have discovered yet another English custom put into practice here. How wrong they were to use building material that could be put to the torch. Her father's castle was nearly impregnable. She felt a bit smug to know that her clan was so much smarter than the Campbells, or any Lowlanders, for that matter.

Torches blazed along the ramparts. The Campbell banner was flying, indicating that Duncan was at home. The people had been so hospitable, she had no reason to think Duncan would be otherwise. The thought of a welcoming fire and the comfort within the castle's walls spurred her onward. So thinking, she motioned Darach to hurry. Before they had progressed very far, however, the roaring sound of thunder resounded in their ears.

"Is it going to rain?" she asked, looking skyward. Strange, but she saw not even one cloud in the sky. Not thunder then, but the sound of horses' hooves.

"Horsemen!" Darach's leathery face twisted in fear. Shakily, he pointed his finger. A large body of warriors advanced toward them from the south, sounding an alarm. With thumping heart, Brianna followed the line of his vision to see for herself.

"Campbells, I do believe. To welcome us?" She held that hope, but the ferocity with which the riders swept down upon them soon proved just the opposite. In mere moments they were surrounded.

"Who are ye and what is yer business?" Brianna raised her eyes to encounter a cruelly fascinating face that reminded her ominously of the horrid *fachan*, a one-eyed, one-legged, one-armed creature of folklore. Like that monster, this man was war-scarred and had only one black eye that stared at her from beneath thick brows; the other eye was covered by a patch. Holding one arm behind his back, he took a step forward and she suppressed a shudder as she scrutinized the man talking to her. He might have been handsome once, before the ravages of battle left its mark. His features were pleasant enough—a thick, gold shaggy beard, a nose as long as her thumb, and tawny hair that poked out beneath his conical helmet. "Why are ye trespassing on Duncan Campbell's lands?" the man questioned in a deep, booming voice. So much for hospitality, Brianna thought.

Mustering up her courage, she answered, "I've come to see the chief! He and I hae some important talk to initiate."

"This is The Campbell's land and ye are no' a Campbell," growled a second man, moving forward.

"Nonetheless, Duncan Campbell will be pleased to see me."

"Our laird allows no one access except wi' *his* approval."

Before Brianna could answer, she was forcibly captured, lifted none too gently to sit astride the man's stallion. The horses galloped up the rise of land toward the tower and though Brianna struggled and offered loud protest, her voice was lost in the rumble of the hooves. Her last thought, as the party of horsemen passed beneath the raised portcullis, was that instead of coming freely to Duncan's hall as she had planned, she was being taken to the Campbell stronghold with all the indignity of a prisoner.

CHAPTER TWENTY-THREE

Brianna was roughly ushered inside the Great Hall and pushed into a heap before a large carved chair. With her flaming hair tumbling wildly about her shoulders, falling into her eyes, she supposed she must look like some wild woman. Well, perhaps she was. Surely, her fury knew no bounds to be so ill treated. If this was any measure of Duncan Campbell's leadership, then she was not surprised the MacQuaries had scorned him for so long. Never would her father have so abused a woman. Only enemy warriors were so forcibly captured. And what of the poor fisherman? In the excitement she had lost sight of Darach but was fiercely determined to protect him. Venomously, she glared at her "hosts."

"Watch her, while I get Duncan," the one-eyed man ordered. Two of the others hurried to obey, hovering over her like a felled deer.

"Aye. Hurry to get yer chief and tell him that Brianna Nic Lachlan of the clan MacQuarie is awaiting." Did she perceive astonishment on the man's face before he hurried away? Well, so much the better. She'd soon have him taken to toll for such unwarranted behavior.

Dragging herself up from the floor, Brianna brushed at her gown and ran her fingers through her tousled hair.

Eyeing her captors, she snorted disdainfully as she squared her shoulders. They'd soon be begging her pardon. Affecting a haughty pose, she let her eyes roam freely about the room, critically assessing it. Her father always said that a man could tell much from another man's abode. What then was this man Duncan like?

Certainly, he seemed to have an affection for luxury. The interior of Dunstaffnage Castle was much grander than she had ever supposed. Just like in her father's hall, the walls were lined with benches, but these were covered in padded wool cushions with embroidered designs, not bare wood. The lofty hammer-beamed ceiling was hung with brightly colored banners, including those of scarlet and gold. The King's banner? Not surprising, since the King's own sister had married into the clan. Even the floor was lavishly decorated with curly sheepskin rugs. Huge tapestries depicting the Campbell bravery covered the walls, including several which very obviously spoke of victory over the MacQuaries. The sight of them angered her and were a reminder of years spent in turmoil.

The wooden walls were adorned with a gaudy display of shields and weapons—massive two-handed claymores as well as English broadswords, axes, spears, dirks, and long, tautly strung bows. Clearly the most important thing to Duncan Campbell was warfare, she thought with scorn. Although her father's castle also displayed some weaponry, it was nothing like this! Ah yes, she had heard about the Campbell laird's ambitions. In disgust at the whole idea she turned her gaze away. What a fool she was to come, to think for a moment that she could hold any sway over such a man.

"There was a fisherman with me," she declared to the tallest of the men guarding her. "What was his fate? I'd hae him treated kindly. He's done no wrong. Och, it was a churlish thing to sweep down upon us as ye did." Her eyes flickered accusingly.

"He's down below in the dungeon," the man answered

with a leering grin. "Which is where ye might well be if ye dinna hold yer tongue and mind yer ways." He gave her a not-so-gentle shove.

"If my father were here I'd hae ye boiled in oil," Brianna retorted loudly. "Ye touch me again . . ." She shrieked her anger as he called her bluff.

"Douglas, what is going on?" Ian's voice. "Who is this young woman I hear you are holding pris . . ." Ian's jaw dropped open in surprise as he entered the room and saw Brianna standing there. For just a moment he doubted his sanity.

"Ian!"

"Brianna? Is it really you?"

Without thinking, she flew to the haven of his arms, seeking his protection. He responded with affection, holding her close, stroking her hair. Raising his voice in anger, he bade the guards to leave.

"What are you doing here?" There were several weeks before the wedding. Why had she come so early? Dozens of thoughts raced through Ian's mind. "Where is your father?"

"I came alone to . . ." She raised her face to his, blushing furiously. He'd never said he wanted to marry her. Dare she tell him what she planned? "I came to see yer uncle," she blurted. "I canna go through wi' a wedding to a mon I've never seen. I thought ye . . ."

With a thud, the door behind them opened. "What is this?" A deep, rumbling voice boomed through the hall. Standing in the doorway was a man Brianna took for the very devil. Huge of girth, swarthy of skin, dark of hair and beard, he looked ominous.

"This is Brianna of clan MacQuarie," Ian said by way of introduction. "I fear she received a rude welcome from us."

"Lachlan's daughter?"

"Yes." Ian shook his head. "I don't know what got into Perth, uncle. If we are now fearful of women and seek to hold them prisoner then I say you go too far." Thrusting himself in front of Brianna, Ian guarded her protectively. "If we seek peace, then holding The MacQuarie's daughter seems a strange thing to do."

"Then what Perth told me was the truth! This is Lachlan MacQuarie's daughter. I thought he'd gone daft." Pushing Ian aside, he growled, "Let me take a good look at her." He did, his blue, squinting eyes scrutinizing her hotly. "She is reasonably fair. Bonnie. But then ye told me she was, Ian." There was no warmth in his tone of voice. Indeed, he sounded regretful, as if he'd hoped she'd be a hag, Brianna thought with surprise.

"It appears that Perth forgot to show her any courtesy. I believe we owe her an apology for such rough handling." Turning to Brianna, Ian said, "You have mine."

"Perth was merely carrying out my orders. A few of the serfs hae been showing disobedience, stealing cattle and sheep. Reivers of a sort. I told him to capture any unfamiliar travelers." Duncan Campbell bared his teeth in the semblance of a smile. "But then I don't believe this lassie looks to be very dangerous."

"You'd be surprised," Ian said beneath his breath. Brianna could have sworn she saw him wink at her. Somehow that gesture gave her hope. "She's very braw to come here all alone, I am thinking."

"I didn't come here alone. A fisherman came with me. I ask that ye set him free from yer dungeon."

"Done!" Nodding his head, Duncan gave the order, then turned to Brianna again. "Now, I hae a request of ye. That ye tell me just why ye hae come. Are ye then so anxious to marry young Robbie that ye could no' wait?"

"To the contrary. I came to bargain, to hae some say in my future." Brianna put her hands upon her hips. "I'll no' marry a mon I hae no' laid eyes on. Not when I hae my mind on someone else."

Duncan growled like a wounded bear. "Ye'd break the contract? Ye must be addled in yer wits, lass. But then I should expect such from a MacQuarie," he roared.

"Break my word? Nae. I agreed to marry a Campbell laddie and I will. It's only that I want to take my choice. It seems to be only fair. Ye sent a mon to woo me and he won my heart. I'm proposing that I take the same lad to husband." It was a bold, brazen suggestion, but one prompted by her heart.

"Brianna!" A surge of joy swept over Ian as he realized what she had said. So he'd found favor with the lass after all. She did want him. Perhaps upon hearing the request on the lassie's lips, his uncle would reconsider his request for such a happening. He looked expectantly toward Duncan only to have his hopes pricked by the expression written on the black-bearded face.

"Never!" He turned his anger on Ian. "I sent ye to do yer duty to me and this is how I'm rewarded! Betrayal. Ye couldna wait to get the lassie in yer bed. Ye young lusty dog!" Pouncing on Ian, he grabbed his shirt with both fists.

Removing Duncan's hands from his shirt front, Ian held his ground. "Easy, uncle, I'll not be manhandled." He faced his uncle calmly. "In answer to yer question, nae. I swear. I never touched her, though I can not lie and say I didn't want to. I've told you my feelings, uncle. I've spoken my mind." Ian's jaw tensed as he said, "In truth, you were playing with fire when you sent me to the MacQuarie Castle. A man and woman have no control upon their hearts."

"Please . . ." Brianna was horrified by Duncan's anger. What had she done? She'd never sought to make trouble here. "What difference does it make which of yer nephews I wed?"

"It makes a great deal of difference!" Duncan bit his lip to regain control, fearful lest he say more and give himself away. "The bann has been signed, the agreement made. Ye will marry Robbie Campbell and no other, make no mistake about that! Aye, and sooner than ye thought." With an outraged oath Duncan Campbell vented his anger, overturning a chair. "I'll hae no mere woman dictating to me, nor even my clansman. My mind is made up." He beckoned the guards forward. "Until that time it is my desire to make Lachlan MacQuarie's daughter comfortable as my *guest.*"

Guest, Brianna thought. By the blessed Saint Michael she'd just placed herself in the hands of a demented man, and an enemy. God help her, she'd made matters worse by coming here. She was to be Duncan Campbell's prisoner and no one would even know. By her own lips she had sworn Glenna to secrecy, had instigated a seemingly innocent masquerade for which she might very well pay dearly now.

CHAPTER TWENTY-FOUR

Glenna stared out the window, watching as the small hunting party led by her father left the castle. The number of guests for the betrothal festivities had depleted a goodly portion of the store of food, thus Lachlan MacQuarie and his men were of necessity out after more. It offered Glenna a reprieve, a haven from her father's piercing eyes, and seemingly just in time. Pretending to be Brianna was a far more difficult thing to manage than either she or Brie had ever thought it would be. Twice today, while pretending to be Brianna, she'd nearly muddled it, wilting under her father's frown when he had looked in her direction.

Aye, there is more to acting like Brie than just wearing men's clothes occasionally, she thought. It was the way her sister held her chin up, the toss of her hair, her jovial banter with the men, her laughter. This morning at breakfast Glenna had nearly given her identity away while masquerading as her sister. She had looked longingly at Alastair several times, then caught herself. And then when her father had invited her to join in the hunt she had said no far too quickly, flushing under his stare. Brianna would have said yes all too readily.

Only by pretending illness had she escaped questioning. Fleeing up the stairs, she hurriedly changed her clothes, then entered the hall again as Glenna. She had given out the story that Brianna was ill and had taken to her bed. Nae, but even that had nearly come to woe when the clan healer insisted he take a look at her twin. Playing a dual role was definitely not easy. Glenna had bounded into Brianna's bed, pulling the quilts up to her chin. Somehow she had been able to fool the *MacLay,* although she had suffered distress when *she* had been forced to drink one of his herbal concoctions. Disgusting! But it had saved the moment. How long could she pretend? How long would it be before someone questioned the fact that although the girls were very, very close, they never seemed to be together anymore?

"Oh, Brianna, hurry back, hinny. Please." If truth be known, she missed her. Brianna brought warmth with her smiles. Being with her was like basking in the sun. Without her it was as cold and desolate as winter. Indeed, she'd only been gone four days and already Glenna missed her. "Och, Brie, I wish ye well but hurry home!"

So far, the last four days had been hectic, thus it had been easy to pretend. Everyone in the castle had been recuperating from the guests and getting ready for the hunt; not even Orianna knew the truth. But what would she do tomorrow? And the tomorrow after that? Everyone knew that she and Brie were often together. How would she ever explain? She would have to think of something. But right now her concern was for Brie.

Would Brianna be successful in getting Duncan to change his mind about the betrothal? As for her own happiness, that was a different matter. Things had gone from bad to worse in a short span of time. Angered by her revelation of affection for Alastair, Lachlan MacQuarie had forbidden his daughter to see the bard. When they were together in the same room she had to act as if he wasn't there, and he in turn kept his eyes from making contact with hers. Even so, they were achingly aware of each other's presence nonetheless, and that in itself created heartache.

For the time being, the only time Glenna could be happy

was when she was alone in her bedchamber, succumbing to her dreams. Only in her fantasies did she dare give vent to her love. From the first moment her eyes were closed she envisioned Alastair, felt the stirring touch of his mouth, the fire of his hands on her body. Her dreams were so vivid, so feverish that she awakened trembling, half expecting to find his handsome face beside hers on the pillow. Instead, she always knew the disappointment of finding herself alone. Was there any hope? Brianna had insisted that there was, had promised to aid her when she returned. Until then, Glenna realized she would have to be content with only her fantasies. Aye, Alastair had spoken true when he said the world was a cruel place for lovers.

"Ah, Alastair. Alastair." Wrapping her arms around her waist, she laid her head against the cold stone and gave in to tears of frustration. Oh, how could her father be so stubborn? So hardhearted? How could he resign her to a loveless marriage when happiness was just within her reach? she lamented, burying her face in her hands. She was roused from her sadness by a soft tapping.

"Glenna! Open the door." Alastair's voice. Glenna hurried to comply, smiling at the sight of his handsome face.

"Father and the others hae left."

"I know. I saw." Pushing through the portal, he gathered her in his arms. "At least for a moment we can be together." He nuzzled her neck, breathing in the fragrance of her hair. "Och, Glenna. Ye'll never know how much I long for ye."

Glenna looked into the depths of his eyes and was lost. "Aye, to the contrary, perhaps I do." It was as though some strange malady possessed her, for she was giddy with love. Oh, to be his wife. Why must that be such an impossible dream? Why could it not be lovers who ruled the world?

Leaning her head against his shoulder she gave herself up to the touch of his fingers, his lips, whispering words of love and in return receiving them. Oh, how soft were his lips, she thought. A warm glow filled her body and she pressed herself against him, wishing to make this moment last forever. Feverishly, she clung to him, her breasts pressed against his chest. Their mouths met and caressed; she could feel their hearts beating as one.

"Glenna! Sweet, sweet, Glenna," he said at last, his voice thick with passion. His fingers swept down to cup one firm, budding breast, and then it seemed his hands were everywhere, touching her, setting her body ablaze. Then, just as suddenly, he pushed away. "Nae, I canna tumble ye like some common maid."

"I don't care. I only know I . . ."

"I am not a mon to take advantage." He took her hand, laying her fingers on his face. "No matter how desperate our love."

Alastair knew the consequences were Glenna to marry and not be able to offer proof to her husband of a maidenhead. Still, the beds in the middle of the room were tempting, even more so since Alastair shared the secret of Brianna's journey. Dear God, he wanted her so that he had nearly lost all reason. He wanted to be away from here, from the restrictions her father imposed. MacQuarie wasn't the only clan leader. There were others scattered throughout the land. He was a skilled bard. Surely there were other clan chiefs who would take him in. But no, he could not separate himself from his sweet lassie. It was just as difficult for her as for himself. She needed someone to depend on, particularly since Brianna had gone.

So thinking, he made an impassioned plea, tightening his grip on her hand. "We must hae patience. Together we will see this thing through. Yer father is a stubborn mon to be sure, but even he must see how much we need each other."

Glenna hung her head. "I dinna think he will be changing his mind."

Alastair thought the same, for Lachlan was a strong-willed chief, but he sought to bolster her spirits. Glenna reminded him of a newly birthed lamb, so soft and gentle. She needed him. "We'll wait. If yer sister would bear the mon a grandson perhaps all would change. Aye, then there would be a male heir." He laughed. "Or perhaps even twins!"

"Aye. Och, I do hope Brie can marry her Ian. I wish for her a great deal of happiness. And I wish for us the same." Her eyes misted but she smiled through her tears. "We can only be patient, Alastair. It is our only hope. Twins! Like Brianna and me!"

"Aye, bonnie wee boys!" He kissed her lightly on the cheek, then drew away. "In the meantime, hinny, I pledge my love to you."

"Father will change his mind, ye'll see. Brianna made me a promise." She wasn't sure she really believed that even Brianna could elicit a promise from Lachlan, but she wanted to soothe him. Didn't want him to lose all hope. The thought of Jeanne hovering around the hearth like a prowling cat, scorching Alastair with her heated gaze, was ever at the back of Glenna's mind. Men were said to be passionate creatures, goaded on by their lust. How long before Alastair gave in?

"Aye, Brianna will see that he changes his mind." His voice was choked with emotion. "I dinna know how much longer I can wait. I want ye so." With a rueful smile he kissed her one last time, then fearful of what might happen were he to stay, left as quickly as he had come.

Watching as his shadowed form flitted down the hall, Glenna was filled with thoughts of desperation. What if her father pledged her hand to someone else before Brianna returned? Could she face that moment if it came? She shuddered at the thought, missing Brianna all the more, wishing more than ever that her sister would hurry back. Brianna was her only hope.

CHAPTER TWENTY-FIVE

Fires blazed brightly in every room throughout the castle, yet even so Brianna felt cold. The very thought of her predicament sent a chill traveling up her spine, wondering just what Duncan Campbell was up to. What were his motives in holding her here? In truth, there seemed to be no purpose, for by his denial of her wish to marry Ian, he reaffirmed her contract with his younger nephew. She would be held to her word. Even so, he had acted troubled, as if he was apprehensive about the marriage negotiations because of her request. He did in fact seem as obsessed with the upcoming wedding as men usually were for a battle. Enough so to take the chance of angering her father by holding her against her will. It made no sense at all. He spoke in fact of hastening the wedding as if he foresaw trouble. Why did he see her coming here as such a threat? She found Duncan Campbell's behavior exceedingly strange. He was not at all as reasonable as her father!

Brianna sat on the edge of the soft feather bed in her chamber pondering her fate, reflecting on her time spent here. She'd been given a comfortable chamber on the second floor, had been treated with deference, yet she chafed at being anyone's prisoner. Aye, but she was as out of place as a hen among geese in the Campbell laird's hall. How then could she expect that any one of them would have a care as to her fate?

Though she was made comfortable, well fed, given pretty garments to wear, she felt ill at ease. Right from the first she had realized how different these clansmen were from her own. They dressed differently, the men covering their legs with trews, the women favoring a curraichd of linen over their heads and tonnags around their shoulders instead of arasaids. They talked the Scots' language, which was a blending of Gaelic and French instead of pure Gaelic, and they stared openly at her. Association with the English and the Lowlanders had made them different, though they shared a Celtic background with her own clan.

But Brianna was not totally unhappy. Quite the contrary. Something in Ian's expression, a determined tilt to his chin, gave her hope. He did still want her, his every look told her that. When she had proposed that she marry Ian and not the younger Campbell nephew, she had seen his wry smile. Nor had she been deaf to the arguments between Duncan Campbell and his nephew, all because of her. Ian had been adamant in his bantering. It was the one thing that made this entire episode worthwhile, just knowing he *did* care. Moving from the bed, putting her ear to the door, she could hear another heated conversation now, the timbre of the voices rumbling below in the hall.

"I ask you for the tenth time, marry the lassie to me!"

"And I tell ye for the tenth time, nae! Brianna Nic Lachlan is to be Robbie's bride."

"And will you hold her here until she agrees? Is that your plan? To hold the lassie prisoner until the wedding? Is it?"

Duncan's voice lowered to a whisper and Brianna strained her ears to hear his answer. Just what did he intend to do? For two days now she had been The Campbell's *guest*, given free access to all of the rooms but confined to the castle. Strange also was that despite his avowal that he meant for her to marry his younger nephew, she had not been introduced to her intended bridegroom. Was The

Campbell so sure then that she would find him unfavorable? And if so, why?

"Are you not afraid of what Lachlan MacQuarie will say and do?" Opening the door, Brianna crept slowly down the stairway, hoping to hear Duncan Campbell's answer. Oh, she had bluffed him unerringly, espousing threats that her father would show retribution for her being incarcerated behind the wood and stone walls. Had it worked? Or had it merely goaded him to hurry with his plan? Approaching the large room where Ian and Duncan haggled, she craned her neck.

"Good morrow!" A voice behind her startled her and she jumped. Turning around she found herself face to face with a tall, comely freckle-faced lad with auburn hair. His smile seemed to offer friendship. "Don't worry. I won't tell Duncan ye were eavesdroppin'."

"I wasna . . ." She shrugged her shoulders. "By *gorach*, I was."

"I've been known to do the same. It's a human trait, I suppose, to be curious. There's no harm done." He cocked his head. "I've ne'er seen ye before. Who are ye?"

She answered boldly. "Brianna Nic Lachlan of the clan MacQuarie!" As she spoke the young man turned quite pale.

"So ye are the one!"

"The *one?*" A prickly feeling traveled up her spine as if for just a moment she had the fey. "Who are ye?" she asked, somehow knowing what he would say.

"Robbie Campbell!"

"Rob! . . ." The man she was to marry. Certainly not homely, yet oh so *young!* There was not even the first fuzz of a beard on his face. He was not much more than a boy, she mused, eyeing him. Though she found him soothing to the eyes, he truly inspired no passion in her heart, though a stirring of deep liking pricked her. Taking a step back, she appraised him as he likewise scrutinized her. Och, he most certainly did not favor the Campbell clan, she thought. He must take after his mother's side then. The wide eyes were brown not blue, the hair a deep reddish brown not black, the face was thin not angular. Whereas Duncan's and Ian's noses were straight, Robbie Campbell's turned up at the tip, like hers, she thought with a smile. He was reed thin, his legs long, but somehow his frame gave the impression of strength. Most importantly, his face seemed to show character, a gentleness of spirit.

"Ye are a bonnie lassie, Brianna. Ye would do me honor to be my wife." He seemed to feel that was what he should say. Why then did he sound so sad?

"And ye would make any lassie proud but . . ." She read the truth in his eyes. "But yer heart is taken by somebody else!"

There was a long period of silence as if he was wrestling with his conscience before he answered, "Aye! A young lassie I meet when I can. She's a MacDonald." He shyly reached out to touch her arm as if to reassure her. "But it will come to naught, I promise."

"Because yer uncle has stubbornly insisted that ye marry *me*?"

"I wouldna put it quite that way." She'd flustered him, for he stood wringing his hands.

"But if ye had yer choice ye'd marry yer dearie. Answer truthfully, ye'll no' hurt my feelings." Brianna's smile prompted him to speak the truth.

"Aye." Thick brows shot up as he quickly tried to soothe her pride. "But I dinna mean to wound yer feelings. Now that I hae seen ye it doesna seem a quarrelsome prospect. And for my part, I would always treat ye kindly. I would ne'er be an unfaithful, unkind or careless husband."

"But ye would rather marry wi' yer lassie." Brianna laughed softly, hurrying to ease his mind. "Och, I am glad. Glad! For I find myself in the same predicament." Her voice lowered conspiratorily. "I too am in love wi' someone else."

A wide unabashed smile cut across the young man's face. "Ye are?"

Brianna nodded her head. There was no use denying it.

"That's why I came here." She looked at him from beneath her lashes. "And does yer lassie feel the same for ye?"

"She told me so. And yer laddie?"

"He's asked unsuccessfully for me, but yer uncle is just too stubborn." Putting her hands on her hips, she sniffed indignantly. "And it seems to me a terrible thing to make so many people unhappy."

"Aye, perhaps it does."

At last I have an ally, she thought hopefully. Surely, if Robbie didn't really want her it would make it that much easier to give argument for the marriage. At least she had a ray of hope. "So what should we do about it?"

Robbie Campbell didn't answer. Instead, his eyes were focused at a point behind her back. Slowly, Brianna turned around and was not at all surprised to find Duncan standing there. "What are ye doing here, Robbie? Ye should be out collecting the *cain*." Brianna knew this to be the rent, the first fruits of a *septs* portion of the land.

"I've finished." Taking off his flat bonnet, Robbie Campbell tugged at the deer bone that held the tuft of wild myrtle, the clan's badge, in place. Clearly, his uncle unnerved him. A twitch to the lad's jaw gave proof that he was trying to keep his emotions under control. Brianna was reminded of her father in the lad's manner, and that made her laugh to think so about a Campbell.

"Ye are finished?" The tone in Duncan's voice was stern.

"Aye, and it's glad I am, for at last I hae met a bonnie lassie." Robbie Campbell smiled at Brianna. "The Mac-Quarie did me proud."

Duncan grunted. "I suppose . . ." He did not seem to be pleased to find his nephew talking with his intended. Strange, Brianna thought. He'd been so insistent that they wed, she would have thought he would have been overjoyed to find they had gotten along so well on this, their first meeting. Instead, he seemed anxious to pull Robbie away from her.

"I came to refresh myself wi' a cup of ale. It's a wee mite hot outside, uncle."

He nudged and poked, guiding young Robbie toward the door. "Then come along!" Duncan's manner was stiff as he put his arm around the lad's shoulders. There was no warmth in his eyes for the young man, Brianna thought, no camaraderie shown as he led him back to the hall. Certainly, Duncan Campbell showed little affection for this nephew. How sharply that contrasted with her father and the way he treated his kin. In fact, she found herself feeling sorry for Robbie Campbell. Duncan looked at the young man with a stern countenance that seemed to border on dislike. Why? And why, if he was so anxious for her to marry his nephew, had he so quickly hustled the laddie away?

CHAPTER TWENTY-SIX

Inside the bailey of Dunstaffnage Castle was a noisy jumble of milling men and neighing horses. The hot, raging midday sun reflected upon slashing swords and upraised shields as the men of clan Campbell engaged themselves in mock battle, a procedure ordered by Duncan to keep them fit now that peace had been instilled. The clan had a definite formation in war which was often practiced. Duncan's structure of fighting included a leader for each twenty men. Leadership of the ranks was jealously guarded because if a man did not keep fit, he could lose his position. Thus Ian was determined to keep his fighting skills in shape. Besides, it did him good to get his mind off the turmoil that raged in his heart over the matter of Brianna.

Ian easily outmaneuvered two of the men in a furious wielding of his broadsword, leaving them winded and thoroughly shamed. "Gregor, you move as slowly as an old man! You need to practice your footwork. Menor, you thrust from the right side all the time, it makes you an easy target. Vary your aim," he chided, returning their confiscated swords, won in the skirmish. "Practice against each other and let me see what you have accomplished at the end of day."

Leaning against the stone wall of the bailey, Ian watched

the melee as he rested, but his mind was not on his fighting men. Duncan's stubbornness was troubling him. He could not understand why his uncle did not just send Brianna MacQuarie back to her own lands and wait in patience for the ceremony that was to come? Why was it that just the sight of the lass caused every muscle of Duncan's body to grow rigid? There were many questions that truly puzzled him about his uncle's behavior of late.

"Och, standing there like the village tinker, as if ye hae nothing to do. Shame on ye, Ian." Aulay approached with a grin, offering challenge, one that was quickly accepted.

"Have care!" Ian braced himself for a combat he knew would be hard fought. Aulay might be small but he was a most worthy opponent.

With the hilt of his sword gripped securely in one hand, Aulay tried to get the better of Ian, springing upward on his short legs as he lunged. In fighting, the first attack was always the fiercest. He found his thrust blocked.

"You will have to do better than that, Aulay lad. If I were a real enemy you would be in woe for it." Ian struck out, but his blow was also parried.

The sound of sword on sword rent the air as the two friends fought a furious game to show who was the better swordsman, a test of strength and of skill which both relished. Like two dancers, they moved back and forth, swaying in time to some unheard rhythm.

"Ye are in mean spirits today." Aulay gritted his teeth as the flat of the sword rapped him on the knuckles, a playful gesture that gave him warning that Ian was tiring of the sport and sought a quick win.

"Duncan annoys me. I canna understand him!" With the back of his hand, Ian wiped the beads of moisture away from his brow, then within the span of the blinking of an eye, returned to the game.

"Aye ye can. He is nearly as stubborn as ye are."

"Thrice so."

Ian was deadly with a sword, but Aulay's lightning-quick

agility was more than his match. At last, however, Ian knocked Aulay's sword to the ground to the tune of the little man's grumbling.

"Och, ye had the advantage. The sun was in my eyes."

"By my grandfather's sainted bones it was not!" Ian ran his hand over his stubbled chin and along the firm line of his jaw, his lips between a frown and a grin. A slight breeze stirred the tuft of fur club moss stuck in his bonnet. "But if you would like to try it again . . ."

Aulay threw up his hands in an exaggerated gesture of defeat. "Not I. You win! You win!" All of a sudden he grinned impishly. "So the fair Highland flower has come to seek ye as husband. Yer pride must be nigh to bustin'. So why yer vexation?" A devilish grin quirked Aulay's lips.

"How did ye know? About the lassie coming to have an exchange of husbands?" Ian's fingers clenched around his sword so tightly that they turned pale.

"It's all over the castle, from scullery to parapet. Yer cousin Caitlin has a chattering tongue, and she was in the Great Hall the day that Brianna was brought in. She was sitting in the corner, stitching when she heard. And wasted no time in spreading the story around. Aye, dear Caitlin. How very like her."

Ian grimaced in disgust. Of his three female cousins, daughters of Duncan, he liked Caitlin the least, for she was of a catty nature. "I'm sure she will expound on the truth as usual."

"She seems to hae taken a disliking to the MacQuarie lassie that goes beyond her clansmen's name. Jealousy perhaps." Bending down, he cross-laced his curans, which had come undone in the fracas. His voice hushed to a whisper. "Don't look now, but Perth is staring this way, and with such an evil expression that ye had best cross yerself!"

"Perth!" Ian spat the name with scorn. Perth had long been his adversary, circumventing his authority at every turn. "He is another who has aligned himself as the lassie's enemy."

"Enemy? I hae seen him staring at her from time to time with a far different look upon his face than that of a foe, but then I hae heard that he has an eye for bonnie women. And the MacQuarie lassie is certainly bonnie. Or hae ye not noticed," he teased.

"I've noticed as well ye know. Perth, as ugly a devil as he is, thinks there is no woman he canna try. Or then again, there could be far more to it. A man like that is not to be trusted. His allegiance is only to himself." Ian's deep scowl revealed his concern for Brianna. As he looked in Perth's direction and met his gaze, they fought a furious visual duel, as potent as with any weapon. "Aulay!" Ian put an insistent hand on his little friend's shoulder.

"What is it? I'll do anything ye ask, as ye know."

"I want you to help me keep an eye on Brianna, to keep her from that one's harm." Ian sensed danger with a warrior's instincts and was determined to avert it at all possible cost.

Shifting impatiently from one foot to the other, Brianna felt cooped up and fidgety as she gazed out the window of her chamber. She was impatient for something to happen. Now that she had discovered Robbie Campbell's love for someone else she felt optimistic. It seemed a good omen for her own frustrated love, a sign that somehow everything would work out just as it should. Robbie would woo his MacDonald lassie, and somehow she would find a way to marry Ian. That thought brought forth a warm feeling that was intensified as she watched the swordplay down below.

Unerringly, Brianna's gaze sought out Ian's tall, muscular frame as he stood talking to his small friend, and she pressed closer to the window ledge, leaning out for a better glimpse of him. He was such a magnificent sight, bare-chested, wearing only green and blue plaid trews. She stared longingly at his broad shoulders, the width of his chest, the hardness of his arms, remembering the feel of his strength wrapped around her. Her eyes slid over him, intent on the way the tight-fitting tartan trousers clung to his hips and thighs, revealing the perfection of his masculine body.

"He is quite a magnificent animal, isn't he?" A woman's voice startled Brianna and she turned around to see one of Duncan's daughters hovering in the doorway, the stocky one who resembled him so thoroughly that every time Brianna looked at her she could almost imagine a thick black beard. Caitlin was the young woman's name.

"What do ye mean?" Brianna feigned innocence. "I was just looking at the sky, feeling a bit lonely for my own land." Brazenly, the woman entered the room, affording Brianna no retreat.

"Fie if ye were!" Caitlin forced a smile. "Ye were looking down at the splendid manly form of my cousin. But I dinna blame ye. Ye are no' the first one who has fallen under his spell. Nor will ye be the last." Cold blue eyes scrutinized Brianna's apparel, for she had stubbornly changed into her own gown. "I had best get ye something to wear. That looks no better than a serf's garments."

Running her hand over the texture of the woolen cloth, Brianna winced but held her temper, saying as evenly as she could, "It suits me well." The gown she was wearing was made from cloth Glenna and Orianna had woven. She was proud to display it. "It is a special MacQuarie weave that I wear with honor. The rooms here at Dunstaffnage are chilly. Yer thinner cloth is not warm enough for my liking."

"Then I will find something more akin to yer frailty." Her eyes gleamed with contempt, belying her feigned courtesy. "But that must go. I wouldna want ye to shame my father before the clan and hae them say he is stingy."

Blood rose to Brianna's face, burning her skin. "And I tell ye this gown will do just fine!" Her cold brown eyes did battle with the other woman's blue ones, daring her to say another condescending word. "And as to yer father's being stingy, I would think it would be the least of his ills, he who holds a lassie against her will."

"Ye are my father's guest."

"Guest? Ha!" Brianna responded by throwing back her head and giving vent to unrestrained, scornful laughter that quickly sobered. "He willna let me leave, though I came here of my own free will."

"Everyone in the castle knows just *why* ye made yer journey. Is it any wonder my father holds ye here? A lassie of yer nature can be dangerous to the peace." Affecting the same swagger Brianna had noticed on the woman's sire, she walked around the room.

"A lassie of my nature. Just what do ye be meaning by that?" Brianna was getting angrier by the moment, for she heard poison and insinuation in the young woman's words.

"A brazen one to be sure." Insolently, the blue eyes looked Brianna up and down as if finding her wanting. "Who would seek a man who hasna asked for her." At Brianna's look of surprise she added, "It is common knowledge that ye came here with the purpose in mind of getting my cousin in yer bed as husband."

"Yer father has a chattering tongue to tell ye so." The very thought rankled Brianna's ire, but she somehow managed to keep the corners of her mouth turned upward. This lassie was trying to annoy her but she wouldn't allow such a thing. The answering smile was smug.

"Not my father but my cousin. I heard the story from his own lips of how ye burn so wi' passion for him that ye couldna stay away."

"*Ian* told ye?" Brianna was stung by that revelation.

"Och, how he loves to tell the story to all who will hear. Ye came to beg my father to let ye marry Ian, is that not so?" Brianna could not deny it. "Ah, how it puffs up my dear cousin's pride, to take poor Robbie's betrothed bride away from him. But then, there has always been competition between them."

"*Poor* Robbie doesna want me. 'Twill no' break his heart if we are not wed." Brianna remembered Robbie's confession of his liking for the MacDonald lass but held her tongue. Unlike Ian, she would prove that she could use discretion in what she said.

"Nevertheless, ye *hae* been promised to Robbie. My father is ever a fair mon and he willna hae Ian interfering. A bargain is a bargain." Even the way she emphasized certain words was amazingly like Duncan's. A singsong lilt.

"Yer father is ever a stubborn mon who will not listen. I've heard Ian discussing the matter with him. He would wed wi' me but yer father denies his request again and again." Brianna felt a surge of confidence push her irritation away as she remembered his emphatic words to Duncan. He'd spent the last few days quarreling. That had to count for something. "Why will yer father no' agree?"

"Because he wants peace, and he knows Ian too well to believe he means what he says. He would leave ye waiting at the altar just as he has done to several lassies before. It is, I am afraid, my cousin's favorite game. He would ne'er say the vows, for he treasures his sacred freedom."

"Men always do."

"But Ian all the more. 'Tis no wonder the way the lassies flock about him. My father knows Ian would be careless about the matter of marriage and then the peace *would* be broken. And my father wants the feuding to be ended, not begun again."

"Ian would no' leave me waiting." Or would he? Just what were his feelings for her? He had never told her that he loved her. Wanted her, yes, but wanting and loving were two different things. Suddenly, she was unsure of him, just as this woman had intended.

"Ye were no' the first woman who caught dear Ian's eye, nor will ye be the last. He moves from flower to flower with all the buzzing of a bee. Is it any wonder there are quite so many dark-haired and blue-eyed bairns about who mirror his face? If ye but look around ye will see." Placing her hand on Brianna's arm, Caitlin pretended sudden sympathy.

"Och, dear me, let us hope that is no' why ye are so anxious to wed Ian! Has he? . . . Is that why ye? . . ."

"Nae!" Brianna hurled the word. "He has ne'er touched me!"

"Then more the pity for there is none here that will believe. He has quite a reputation for the lassies as I'm sure ye must know. A smooth-talking laddie if ever there was one." Caitlin cocked a brow suggestively.

"Aye, he has a fine way of talking, but I don't see why . . ."

"Ian has intimated that he has put horns on Robbie. Aye, he laughed about it quite merrily. Said that he wooed ye quite successfully. Enough to bring ye here, panting after him. Now everyone here knows ye want to trade one groom for another, that ye make eyes at him whenever he passes yer way."

"Is that so!" Brianna was so angry that she choked out her words. "Well, I've changed my mind!" How could he? Love and longing were private things that he should never have talked openly about. That it was true only made matters far worse.

Brianna's throat constricted painfully, her heart lay like steel in her chest. Only her stubborn pride sustained her, gave her strength to stare straight back into those mocking blue eyes and order Duncan's daughter to leave. Caitlin did so in an outraged rustle of skirts. Even so, Brianna could not push the words from her mind. Ian had boasted about her coming here as if her love meant nothing to him. She had thought she was wrong about him, but she had been right all along. How utterly foolish she had been.

Going back to the window to gaze down at him, she saw that he *was* surrounded by a throng of giggling women. She could hear them espousing words of praise about his skill and bravery as if beating a man half his size was any great feat. Oh, how she wished now that the dwarf had won!

"I'm one among many, that is what I am. Just one of many flowers to that conceited ever-hovering, pollinating bee." Come to think of it, she had seen several small children with blue eyes, black curls and a facial profile that might name him their sire. With an outraged toss of her hair, she fled from the window and the visual reminder of her naiveté.

How could she have been such a simpleton? How could she have fallen so quickly for his smiling charm? Hadn't she known right from the first what a womanizing rogue he was? Now he had made her the laughing stock of all the Campbells by his jabbering. No wonder they had been snickering behind their hands at her. Lovesick, foolish, and overbold is how she must appear. And wasn't she? Just because he had wanted it, she had handed him her heart. Now he was dangling it for all his kin to see. A memento of another conquest and nothing else! It did not mean any more to him than the swords and *targes,* shields, hanging from Duncan Campbell's wall!

Groaning aloud, she felt the humiliation of it all, wishing with all her heart that she had stayed safely on Ulva with Glenna and had not been so impetuous as to come here. She, The MacQuarie's proud daughter, had been humbled most piteously by the enemy. But no longer. Ian had babbled about her love for him, but from this moment on she would show him that indeed, she *didn't* care. Before all his kinsmen she would prove his words to be false, and somehow she would make the pretense a reality.

CHAPTER TWENTY-SEVEN

In the next few days Brianna skillfully avoided not only Ian but Caitlin Campbell as well. She had no need of further heartache or any reminders of her stupidity in coming here to ask for Ian in place of Robbie. Let his clansmen twitter, let them smile and gossip, she would keep her head up and give them a taste of MacQuarie pride. Fie on them all! She hid her feelings beneath a haughty exterior, telling herself she didn't care when unfriendly eyes watched so intently as if to see what was in her heart. Ian Campbell was the last thought on her mind, or so she pretended for their benefit. And yet, just seeing Ian caused her pain, the pain of unfulfilled desire and shattered dreams. She had never known that the sight of a man could cause such great unhappiness.

Every morning she saw him, across the room at the morning meal, and in the evening when the clan gathered for their dinner feast. These were a few hours in which she was not spared the sweet agony of his presence. She was withdrawn and cool when they met on the stairs, what conversation they exchanged was nothing more than cold but polite words of greeting. It could not have been more obvious that she was avoiding him. But no matter how sternly she rebuked herself for feelings she did not want to have, she couldn't wipe him from her heart.

Of course there was a great deal to keep her occupied, and just as she had sought escape from her unhappiness at home by keeping busy, she did the same now.

Household tasks were fitted around the meal preparation, just as in her own clan, twice daily, morning and night. Here in Argyll beef and lamb were the mainstays of the diet, eaten in some form at every meal, as was milk, cheese, and butter. Grinding and baking were daily chores, for unleavened barley bread and bannocks needed to be eaten while hot or they would soon turn hard and stale. Flour was ground from a rotary hand quern, dough kneaded in a wooden trough and baked on long-handled iron plates among the embers of an open fire. The women also hung herbs to dry and gathered wild plants to supplement the diet.

Fionnghuala, Duncan's wife, was a big-boned, plump woman with graying brown hair whose beauty had long since faded. She soon made it clear that she considered Brianna to be an interloper and a nuisance and reminded her to keep her place by assigning Brianna the most unpleasant duties. Yet she finished every task without a word of complaint, trying to ignore the aching in her back.

Brianna was in fact more comfortable among the servants than among the women of the family. As she went about her chores she often felt the eyes of Caitlin upon her as if the ill-tempered, plain young woman held hopes that she would just vanish. Duncan's other two daughters, Cuini, a young woman of about thirteen summers, and Muireall, a sometimes smiling woman who was big with child, were more tolerant of her.

Even though the Campbells purchased a great deal of their cloth, spinning and weaving occupied several hours a day, as did the stitchery Ian had told Jeanne about. Brianna quickly gave up any notions of being able to master this agonizingly intricate task of thread and needle. Her fingers were stiff and clumsy on the delicate fabric, earning her reprimanding comments from the other women and the unwelcome sound of their laughter.

Like a wounded doe, Brianna began to spend more and more time alone. At least then she could think clearly and soothe her shattered emotions, hoping and praying that the next time she saw him across the room she could remain unaffected by the power of his presence.

When she was with the others, however, Brianna's pride lent her the strength of will to hide her feelings. She laughed gaily every chance she had, as if she had not a worry in the world. She hid the poignant loneliness that possessed her, leaning more and more toward Robbie like the haven in a storm. Somehow she felt an affinity with him. Brianna had always preferred the company of men and their interesting talk of hunting and fishing, and thus she credited the friendliness she felt for the young Campbell as being due to this. As to Ian, she made a great point of ignoring him. It made up a little for the humiliation of having so blatantly shown her feelings for him before all.

Brianna could sense Ian's piercing blue eyes upon her wherever she was and knew that he watched her. The sound of his low, husky laughter teased her ears. His smile haunted her at every turn, though she did not smile back. She was filled with an aching emptiness she could not explain. In these moments she wished for so many foolish things—that he loved her, that she could be his. Och, were only he not so handsome.

This evening she caught him gazing at her across the width of the dais and felt the familiar lurch in her heart. Determined to show him she really didn't care, she quickly turned her attentions to Robbie, seeking solace in his attentions.

"I've heard that the mountain grandeur of North Argyll is splendid. Would ye show it to me sometime? I promise I willna try to run away."

A shy smile was her answer. "Aye, I would like that. I will show ye our wild Highland peaks of Glencoe." Robbie was companionable. She would submit to him and comfort him with her woman's sweetness. He could make her happy. So thinking, she forced herself to smile, a grimace that was soon wiped from her face as several women sought to catch Ian's eye. The thought of him with any other woman brought out feelings that consumed her with misery.

But if Brianna suffered, so did Ian. He couldn't understand Brianna's coldness to him of late. Though he had sought over and over again to talk with her, she had succeeded in avoiding him. She had firmly put as much distance as possible between them and he didn't really understand why. Had she consigned herself to marrying Robbie? Were her feelings for him then really so shallow that she would give in to Duncan's stubbornness with his very first frown?

Her attitude angered and disappointed him. Here he was, risking his future, arguing with Duncan continually on her behalf, and she would not even grant him one glance. Worst of all was the way she had suddenly taken to fawning over Robbie as if they were already married. It made his blood boil. Not that he didn't like the lad, but it piqued him to see her show such sincere affection for the young man while all the time snubbing *him*. He found it intolerable and was determined that tonight he would find out the reason why.

"Ian, there is a fair coming to the village. Will ye take me?" A tall, willowy blonde sought his attention as she refilled his glass with wine.

"Perhaps. If I have time," he answered. For just a moment his eyes met Brianna's and held for a moment as he tried to tell her that the woman meant nothing to him, that his love was for her, but she looked away, laughing at one of Robbie's remarks.

So that was the way it was, he thought angrily. Well, two could well play the same strategy. Though he thought the young women at his side to be silly, prattling lassies that didn't interest him, he vented all his attentions on their behalf in a serious bid to make Brianna jealous, to make her care again. He would make her notice him.

Brianna did notice, and to her mortification she felt a tightness in her chest when she saw Ian's handsome dark-haired head bent near to the bonnie lass. She yearned for the magic of his touch, his kiss, though she did not show it. Just look at him, she thought. What Caitlin had told her was true, her smug smile reminded Brianna of all Ian's sins. Straining her ears, Brianna could hear nearly every word the yellow-haired lassie uttered.

Ian hardly heard a word. He was aware only that something was suddenly very, very wrong with Brianna. Even now her expression was like that of an effigy etched in stone. For someone who had come a long, long way because of love for him, she was suddenly acting as cold as a winter frost.

Well, she will talk with me come hell or high water, he thought, clenching his fingers tightly around the stem of his glass. He swirled the dark red wine about, staring at its murky depths. There were many things they needed to talk about.

"Yer frown is as deep as Loch Awe!" With a large wolfhound at his heels begging for scraps, Aulay sauntered up. Sizing up the situation, he knew in a moment what was wrong. "The lassie again."

"Aye. Women! I used to think I understood them until *she* came into my life."

"She's unpredictable. That's why ye like her!" Shooing the young blonde away, Aulay took a seat near his friend.

"Unpredictable and stubborn, to name only two of her flaws! She's a spoiled, willful lassie who is in great need of a spanking. Aye, a strong hand aimed at her well-shaped bahookie!"

"Are ye sure that is where ye want to place yer hand?" Aulay flashed Ian a devilish grin, reading his mind. All trace of a smile faded as he nudged Ian in the ribs, however. "Perth! The way he stares at the lassie is sure to set her afire one of these days."

Ian's head whipped around and he caught the leering man in the act. "He had best watch himself. One false move and I'll have his head. You know that I will." The ominous looking devil irritated Ian. Oh, how he unnerved him, staring at Brianna with his hostile ever-watching eye. Even from across the room he could feel his gaze on her, and the hair at the back of Ian's neck prickled. Brianna had to be warned to stay clear of the man.

Look at me, Brie! He willed her to turn her head and she did. His eyes lingered until he was certain he had caught her eye, knowing from the blush that stained her cheeks that she was aware of his perusal. Silently, his lips formed her name but she quickly turned away again. "By God, let her take care of herself!" he fumed. Why should he be her guardian angel? Ian convinced himself that he would be just as distant with Brianna as she was with him, but even so, he found a way to come to her side before she could move away. Ian appraised her coolly.

A shiver of pure physical awareness chased a strange sensation up and down Brianna's spine so that she knew he was there before she heard him say, "You have been as evasive as a ghostie, lass. Tell me what is wrong." The pressure of his hand against her arm caused her heart to flutter as wildly as a bird's wing.

"What should be wrong?" Her pulse began to beat at her neck and temple, and for a moment she feared he would sense how completely bedeviled she was by having him near. When he captured her hand, his fingers gripping her slender wrist, she quivered at his touch, but one look at Caitlin's grinning face caused her to pull her hand away. Too fresh in her mind was his boasting. It drove a painful wedge in her heart. Like a cornered fawn, she moved past him, bolting from the room, seeking the safety of the stairs.

Ian followed her through the door, up the winding steps

that led to a tower room. "Lassie?" He towered over her with a virility that was most unnerving to Brianna. She stiffened and took a step backward. For a moment the only sound was the hiss of the rushlight and the distant barking of the dogs, then he said, "You are trembling."

"'Tis chilly up here, that's all." A feeble excuse.

"I'll warm you." Quickly, before she could run away, he placed his hands on either side of her body, pinning her against the wall so she could not escape. His breath was warm upon her face, his voice husky in the darkness. "Brie! Brie! You have been so distant and I can't stand it. I hate seeing you with Robbie when you belong to me."

"Belong to ye, do I? I think not!"

"Aye, ye do."

Slowly, his hands slid up her sides, over her ribs, spreading out as they reached the swelling curves of her breasts. Slowly, he lowered his mouth and kissed her hungrily, as if he were starving for the taste of her lips. Such a potent kiss that it sent a series of quivering tremors through her blood. His mouth held hers captive as his fingers strayed to her breasts.

"Nae!" How she managed the protest she didn't know. Somehow, despite the beating of her heart, she found the strength to push against his shoulders. "Let me go!"

Ian looked into her eyes and what he saw there made him loosen his hold. With a disgruntled groan he moved away. "I don't understand you, Brianna MacQuarie. Not at all. What is it? Tell me."

"Ye are a scoundrel and a rogue!"

"What?"

In the stricken silence that followed they maintained a grotesque pose, staring at each other, their eyes locked unwaveringly. "Ye are an unfeeling mon, Ian Campbell, wi' no care to a lassie's feelings. It was cruel of ye to use me to bolster yer pride. I was a fool to come here, to think ye could tie yerself wi' one woman."

"But I do want just one . . . the right lass. You."

What a sweet-talking rogue! "Och, listen to ye. As if ye think I am some village fool." Her hair flowed from side to side like a rippling wave as she tossed her head. "Yer cousin told me what ye did, telling everyone who will listen that I came here to ask yer uncle to let ye wed wi' me. Can ye no' keep a secret?"

"Brianna. I didn't . . ."

"Well, let me tell ye that I hae changed my mind. Robbie is kind and loving. He'll make me a good husband. It's lucky I am that yer uncle said no to ye, I be thinking."

"You don't believe that."

"I do!" She lied to spite him. "A lassie wants a mon who is hers alone, not a mon who fancies every lassie he sees. I thought I was something special to ye, Ian. That's why I came. But in truth, I was just another lassie."

"Nae, you weren't. You were and are special, Brianna." He could see by her eyes that she didn't believe it. Damn Caitlin and her troublemaking. "Don't believe a word Caitlin says. She's a dried up, disappointed maiden who can not find a husband. She takes out her own disappointment by causing trouble wherever she goes."

"And have there not been many lassies in yer life?"

"Aye. But that was before I met you. You have spoiled me for any other woman, Brianna MacQuarie. You are the only one I want." She wanted to believe him but there was a little shred of doubt that he read in her eyes. "I will prove it to you, Brie." A smile teased the corner of his mouth. "When the priest says his vows it will be me at your side and not Robbie Campbell." So vowing, he turned on his heel and strode away, leaving a shaken but happy Brianna behind.

CHAPTER TWENTY-EIGHT

The sound of laughter echoed through the courtyard and Glenna joined in the merriment. It was washing day, a time she always thoroughly enjoyed. Tucking her long skirts up above her knees, she stepped into the huge low tub of water to join Jeanne. Her sister Orianna, Anne, and two other young women were in other tubs adjoining, all washing the laundry by trampling on it with their bare feet. Usually, the laundry was done inside in the bathhouse, but since it was such a lovely sunny day they had dragged the tubs outside.

"Where is Brianna?" Jeanne looked at Glenna askance, her lips curling up in a sarcastic smile. "Is she ill again?"

Glenna shook her head, averting the other young woman's eyes, realizing she could ne'er make that excuse again. "Nae. She's out riding. Ye ken? She hates washing day. Considers it drudgery."

Jeanne snorted in ire. "Och! I dinna ken why she doesna hae to do her part. She isna a Campbell just yet. It is her duty to join us."

"Yer jealousy is showing, if ye be asking me," Glenna retorted peevishly, quickly coming to her sister's defense. "She has a great deal to be doing before she leaves for Argyll with my father. I would think ye'd hae some empathy for her, no' be criticizing her."

"I do. It's just that for the last few days now she's seemingly as delicate as a rose, suffering from one malady or another. It seems strange, that's all I'm sayin'. And now ye tell us she's out for a morning ride. I warrant none of us hae seen her for longer than a minute, if for that long." Kicking at a submerged sodden shirt, Jeanne vented her frustrations. "Ha! Even her own father is getting suspicious. I heard him saying just this morning that he intends to sit on her if need be, just to hae the chance to speak wi' her."

"Aye?" Glenna tried to maintain her calm. Dear God, she was very close to muddling everything. Coward that she was, she'd been so nervous about pretending to be Brianna that she'd come very close to giving the deception away. If she did, and if Brianna was punished when she returned, she would never forgive herself. And perhaps she'd be punished as well for the deception. The thought made her so frightened that she slipped and nearly lost her balance. Only Jeanne's strong arm kept her from a bath in the warm water.

"Ye had best watch yer step, hinny!" the bold woman advised.

"I . . . I will." She concentrated on where she placed her feet, trampling the dirty garments furiously in her zest to get them clean.

Though Glenna joined in to sing a rousing song, and moved her feet and danced about just as playfully as the others, her heart was not in it. She had to think of what to do. If only Brianna were here. From the time they were just little girls Glenna had relied on her bolder twin for advice. Now she had to come up with a solution on her own. How was she going to placate their father before he carried out his threat?

Her tranquil mood broken, Glenna was silent, giving free reign to the thoughts stampeding about in her brain. First and foremost, she would have to conquer the fear she held for her father. Her trembling hands and stuttering were certain to give her away. Could she mimic Brianna's boldness? Could she pretend to be Brianna so fiercely that she could fool Lachlan? She had to try.

The lye soap made from wood ash stung Glenna's feet, thus she was the first from the tub. As she wrung out the garments and laid them to dry on the grass, she envisioned Brianna in her mind, the haughty way she always tilted her chin, her impish smile, the slight sway to her hips. Brianna had a way of looking directly in another's eyes when talking to them while Glenna usually looked in the direction of her toes. Brianna's voice was at a lower timbre while Glenna's seemed at a higher pitch. Brianna always met a problem head-on while Glenna did her utmost to avoid conflict.

All her life Glenna had admired her twin and yet if she were honest she would have to admit that she resented her just a wee mite too. It was like being someone else's shadow. No one had ever liked her as much as they did Brianna, with the exception of Alastair. Perhaps that was one reason why she loved him so. She always came first with her dear sweet bard. Brianna was too bold a lass, he had said, but she was just right.

That was not to say that she was mistreated, far from that. She knew her father loved her, it was just that he loved Brianna more. Brianna was so spirited, enjoyed the same activities their father did—hunting, riding, fishing—that it was no wonder they spent so much time in each other's company. Glenna, on the other hand, liked women's things —sewing, weaving, cooking—things a man had no use for. Thus, she never knew what to say to her father, and this made her overly shy in his presence. Tongue-tied. What could she talk with him about? She knew naught of hunting or weaponry, had not the jovial lilt to her words that Brianna did. In truth, all Glenna had thought about for the past weeks was Alastair, and she couldn't talk about him.

But wait! Perhaps she could. Brianna had laughingly told their father that she intended to pursue the matter of Alastair. She had fully intended to banter with him when she returned. Did Glenna dare do the same? Surely, it was the thing that truly mattered to her. The one desire of her heart. But could she put her feelings into words? Could she get up enough courage?

"Glenna! Glenna, what do ye think on the matter?"

"What?" Glenna looked up to see Jeanne looking at her.

"About that old woman who lives in the cottage on the hill." Her voice lowered and she crossed herself. "They say she's a witch!"

"A witch? Nae. She's just a lonely old woman who would do nobody harm." Glenna did not believe it, for the times she'd come across Riannon she'd been offered only kindness. "Fie on ye, Jeanne, ye should be ashamed of yerself for such gossip."

"Ha! Little ye know. She's been seen crossing Loch Tuath in an eggshell, a sure sign of a witch. And Jamie himself says he saw her transform herself into a hare."

"Foolishness. She is no' a bad woman."

"Perhaps she's a good witch," Jeanne relented, "but she's a witch just the same. Jamie says she gave him a potion to chase away his shyness." Jeanne grinned knowingly. "And believe me it worked."

"A potion?" Glenna pricked up her ears. Of course, therein lay the answer. She'd visit the woman and ask for her help. A potion to make her as brave as Brianna so that she would have the courage to confront her father on the matter of Alastair. Aye. It was the only way. Making her excuses to the others, she hurriedly left the courtyard.

CHAPTER TWENTY-NINE

Brianna lay in her soft feather bed watching the leaping fire tickle the stones in the hearth, mulling a dozen things over and over in her mind. True to his word, Ian had shown her a side to his nature she had not glimpsed before, his romantic side. Every look, every smile showed her that he cared deeply. It was a rapturous secret between them that no other shared, except dear Aulay, who often acted as their go-between for secret meetings and messages.

All her life Brianna had loved flowers. It was something she had confided to Aulay when talking about her Island of Ulva. Now her chamber was filled with them. Blossoms of all kinds, a gift from Ian as a token of his love. Heather. Scarlet pimpernel. Even sea lavender which was so rare in Scotland.

Nor had Ian given even a glance to any other woman. That thought brought forth a warm feeling. Closing her eyes, she snuggled against the pillow. For the first time in several days she drifted off in a deep, pleasant sleep, unaware that the door was slowly opening or that Ian stood at this moment gazing down at her.

She lay on her side, her head resting on one outflung arm, her flaming hair tumbling across her face and spilling like a living fire onto the pillow. Huddled up as she was, she looked almost childlike to him, and he was mesmerized by how truly lovely she was. The long sweep of her lashes against the curve of her cheek made her look vulnerable, and he vowed to protect her. His eyes moved tenderly over her form, moving from her toes to the top of her head, pausing for a moment as he studied the slightly tilted nose, the generous mouth that felt so soft against his own. The sight of her lying there, the rise and fall of her breathing stirring against the thin quilt, acted like an aphrodisiac. He remembered the way her breasts felt as they stroked his chest.

"Ah lass, how I do love you," he whispered, "but alas, 'tis hopeless that we will ever be together." Truly, Duncan had given him every reason to suspect that he would remain pigheaded and stubborn to the end. Should he tell her? Should he dash all her hopes? Breathing a heavy sigh, he bent down and touched the fiery hair where it grew near her temple in a gesture of loving.

Brianna awoke to the feel of a warm hand against her face, brushing back her hair. "Who?" She jerked upright, drawing the covers tightly over her breasts, all too aware of the thinness of her night shift. "Ohhhh."

It was Ian who knelt beside her bed, holding a finger up to his lips to warn her to keep silent. Brianna felt again that treacherous warmth of attraction she'd felt for him from the first time she had laid eyes on him.

"Ian?" She tried to adjust her vision to see him clearly in the fading firelight. "What are ye doing here?"

He looked like a man who was in need of sleep. There were hard lines around his mouth, furrows on his brow, the flesh beneath his eyes was shadowed with blue. Truly, he looked more like a prisoner than she. He had the look of a tortured man. "I just came to see you. I wanted to see you."

"Ye seem to be unhappy."

"No." How could he ever hope to make her understand? She was so very special to him, and yet by the laws of her clan and his, he must stand by and watch her marry someone else. It was tearing him in two, but he couldn't tell her that.

Brianna tried to pierce the unfathomable expression in his blue eyes. "The flowers, they are beautiful. Thank you."

"I wanted to give you something that was as bonnie as you." He lowered his hand and captured her slender shoulder. "I should not have come but I . . . I wanted to see you."

"Did you now."

"Fionnghuala says you purposely spoiled the *colcannon,* that you let it boil too long. She was in a dither."

"Not purposely, but it does serve her right for giving me all the unpleasant tasks. I never have been good at cooking or sewing."

Humor softened his features as he smiled down at her, then just as quickly he resumed his usual serious countenance. "You've created quite a stir, lassie, in more ways than one."

"Aye, all yer fine Campbells are angry that I willna eat out of their hands like a docile pony." She felt relaxed and contented being with him. There was an easy relationship between them as if those stormy earlier days had never existed.

"Duncan is incensed with you, with me, with the whole situation."

"Is he now?" Drawing her knees up to her chin, she pursed her lips. "Well, he isna the one who should be piqued, I'd be thinkin'." The corners of her mouth tugged into a smile.

Nodding his head, he caressed her with his eyes. How was he going to tell her? "Brianna, the last few days have been the happiest of my life. You have made me realize a great many things."

"Such as?" Her voice was soft, stroking him like a delicate hand, teasing him. Unwillingly, he felt desire stir and despite his resolve he weakened. He just could not escape her web of enchantment, could not take his eyes off her. She was quite a lassie. A bundle of beauty and bravery. "Why did ye come here tonight, Ian?"

Her gaze roved over his features—the thick, black Campbell hair, the blue eyes with their thick lashes. The sparkling firelight shadowed his hard, strong jawline and the hollows beneath his high cheekbones. It was his perfectly chiseled mouth, however, that drew her eye again and again as she found herself remembering the taste of his kiss.

"I came to tell you . . ." He stared grimly at the fire as if to take his mind off of her. He had come to say goodbye and to help her plan her escape, but suddenly he didn't want to say the words.

"It doesn't matter. All I know is that I'm happy that ye are here." On impulse she reached out and took his hand, smiling. She was completely unaware of how seductive such a gesture could be, for the contact of their hands was overpowering. Compulsively, his fingers closed around hers as he leaned down. He knew he had to kiss her, if for the last time.

Brianna opened her lips to him and was surprised at the strangely tender and wistful kiss he granted. Not at all like the impetuous demands he had made of her those times before. This kiss was from the heart. Gentle. So much so that she was deeply touched. Ian's arms closed around her, crushing her tight against the iron hardness of his body. Her blood screamed with wild delight as his mouth fused with her own. When he broke away he was smiling.

"Your reward, lass, for being so braw." He stroked her hair soothingly.

"*My* reward? I would hae deemed it yers, Ian Campbell." She laughed softly.

Tighter and tighter the band of his arms closed around her. The roaring of her own blood was deafening in her ears. She gave no resistance to his embrace. Indeed, knowing that Robbie Campbell did not want her was a balm to her conscience. Somehow, loving Ian did not seem a betrayal. This was what she wanted, not some wee bairn's arms.

Ian kissed her again. There was no ignoring the flicker of arousal which spread from their joined mouths to the core of her body. Thoughts of future heartache pressed against her soul, but she pushed them far from her mind. She reached for him, as if the only safety could be in his arms. Her touch was his undoing. As their eyes suddenly met they both knew what was to come.

Unfastening his shirt, slipping her night tunic from her shoulders, he drew her into his arms and pressed their naked chests together. The fire at the contact made Brianna gasp, finding the sensation of warm skin and prickly hair against her skin the most sensuous of pleasures.

"I will not give you up to him," he breathed. "Not now, when I know that in your heart you are mine!"

How could the hands of a fighting man be so tender, she wondered. She didn't protest when he removed his shirt and stretched himself the full length of the bed. The desire to run her hands over him made her tremble, yet she remained perfectly still. It seemed only right that the man she loved be the one to initiate her into the mysteries of lovemaking. The thought tugged at her mind that if he took her, if he planted his seed, Duncan would have to change his mind.

"Ye do want me, lass?" She'd been outraged so many times with him because of his desires, had accused him of being a rogue, that he hesitated in his kissing and caressing to study her expression. "Are you satisfied at last that I want no one but you?"

"Aye. I think I always knew, but I was just too foolish and too stubborn." His hot lips found her breasts and she trembled like a wild thing beneath him. He whispered words of love over and over again, and she sighed as sheer rapture spread through her body.

They rolled over and over on the soft bed, sinking in its warm feathered softness. But kissing didn't satisfy the blazing hunger that raged through Ian. He'd wanted her for too long. She was too tempting, too warm and responsive in his arms for him to gain complete control of his reason.

Pushing her onto her back, he slid his mouth sensuously down her neck, across her chest, to her breast, his teeth lightly grazing it.

A hot ache of desire coiled within her at the caress of his lips against the peak of her flesh. No matter what happened she would have this to remember, she told herself, bargaining with her shame.

"Do you want me, lass?" Taking her small hand, he gently pressed it down against the hardening of his manhood. Brianna tensed at such intimacy at first but then relaxed. "Don't be afraid of me. I would never hurt you."

His mouth fastened on hers with greedy passion, and with fierce longing she responded, eager to receive his body. If tomorrow her soul was damned for it, then so be it. At the moment she did not care. Her only rational thought was that Ian Campbell was making love to her, just as it was meant to be. Why had she fought him before? This was what she wanted, to feel this heady bliss.

Succumbing to the desire that raged within her, Brianna reached out to him. They were so close to mingling their bodies in the final vow of love, and would have, had a voice not cried out Ian's name.

"Who?"

He drew away. "Duncan."

She damned that man beneath her breath, watching as Ian hastily tugged at his clothes. With a hurried kiss he bid her goodbye, slipping out the door with a regretful sigh.

After he was gone, Brianna slid down in the soft bed, giving herself up to all her romantic fantasies concerning him. She had seen the soft glow of love in his eyes, and knew she couldn't be wrong. He did love her, as much as she wanted him, and that gave her the strength of will to win out against any odds. Nae, against Old Nick himself.

The fire in the hall had burned down to ash. It was chilly. All was quiet for it was well after midnight, that time when witches ruled. Only a torch lit the darkness, casting dancing shadows on Duncan Campbell's face, making the clan chief look like the devil himself. Nevertheless, he faced his uncle squarely, proceeding to enter into the same argument he'd instigated again and again since Brianna MacQuarie had been forcibly ensconced here. After tonight he knew he couldn't give up. He had been so close to claiming her.

"You can't hold her!" Love gave Ian courage. Remembering the fierce sweet kisses he'd shared with Brianna goaded him on. "It borders on insanity. Lachlan MacQuarie is not a man to be taken lightly as you well know. She's his favorite!"

"So much the better!" The rushes beneath Duncan's feet snapped and crackled as he shifted his bulky weight to stand erect.

"He'll come after you. The peace will be broken! Think, Duncan. Think!" He could see by the grim look on his uncle's face that he was getting nowhere. In frustration, Ian threw his hands in the air.

"I didna abduct her. She came to my hall willingly."

"By God, she came here in good faith to talk with you, and you react by keeping her here in the castle against her will. I'll be damned if I know why!" Ian was infused with incredulous anger.

"It is necessary. I will hold her here until the final preparations are made. I dinna want anything to happen to destroy the wedding plans." Duncan spoke with a calm finality that chilled Ian to the bone. He had been right when he'd told Aulay that something was wrong with Duncan. His obsession with this marriage endangered the good of the entire clan. What Ian could not understand was what drove Duncan. Not any admiration for the MacQuaries. What then?

"And you plan to hold a dirk to her throat to make certain she'll say the vows?" Ian said caustically.

"I'm hoping it willna come to that!" But the expression on Duncan's face warned he would not be crossed on the matter.

There seemed to be no reasoning with him and this

severely troubled Ian. He'd always admired his uncle's prowess in battle, his ambition, his determination to succeed. Since his uncle had taken over as chief of the sept he'd raised the Campbells from relative obscurity to a powerful force in Scotland, a clan that was at the King's right hand. Why then would he risk so much on this MacQuarie issue?

Was his uncle going mad? Ian carefully scrutinized Duncan's face. It was not unheard of. The strain of being a clan chief took a great toll on a man. It was a great responsibility to be a leader of so many people as well as pleasing the King. It had happened before. Now that the Campbells had been granted their charters there was the added burden of keeping them. No title to possession was worth anything without armed force to back it up. That had been proven at Bannockburn. It was in the interests of the chief to have as many followers as he could effectively muster. Why then was Duncan risking the goodwill of so many men? Could he so easily forget that if he caused a stir by breaching the Highland code of laws he would not only alienate the MacQuaries but their kinsmen as well. The MacGregors, the MacDonalds, the MacKinnons to name only a few. Truly, the situation did bear watching. And if he were really certain that Duncan's wits were addled, would he take over temporary leadership? It was his right as *toiseach*.

"Ian! Come, dinna be so glum. Drink wi' me." That seemed to be the answer to any argument, or so Duncan seemingly thought. Just as suddenly as he had scowled at Ian, Duncan now gave vent to smiles. Praising Ian for past victories. It was obvious he wanted to placate him. Gone was the tone of anger and in its place was a manipulative charm. "I hae great things in mind for ye. Ye were like my own son after Morgan died. Ye were! That is why I sent ye to Parliament at Sterling rather than going myself. To further yer power, lad. I think ye know that. In truth, ye remind me of him. I hae great affection for ye, lad."

"Then let me have some happiness," Ian answered bitterly. "I've earned it over the years."

"Och! Forget the lassie! She's no' for ye. A Gordon lassie or a Ross." He pushed Ian into the large, c rved wooden chair he usually sat in. "There lad, try it out! The MacQuaries are considered rebels. Oh, aye, they fought at Bannockburn but they were not as crafty as we Campbells. They and the MacDonalds began the Bruce's reign wi' rewards, but thereafter arrogantly resisted the Bruce's authority. A costly mistake. We, on the other hand, hae preserved our valor with cunning, playing on the gratitude of Robert the Bruce to found our mountain empire. Och, power. Ye'll soon learn there is nothing so stimulating to a mon as that." Ian started to get up but Duncan firmly held him down. "I intend to make ye my successor. Tomorrow night before all! Think on it, lad. Ye'll be tanist to one of the most powerful clans in the Highlands. And power must marry into a like powerful clan."

Earlier it would have seemed a logical choice, one Ian would have expected, yet now the declaration made Ian feel hollow. Empty inside. It was as if he were being bribed, trading his happiness to wear the laird's feathers in his bonnet. And what would be the cost of this prize? He knew very well. Aye, strange how at one time that had been his obsession, to be named as his uncle's heir. Now it seemed a curse. He would be named as tanist but Robbie would win the real prize, the woman Ian loved.

CHAPTER THIRTY

The hall was enshrouded in dusky torchlight, smoke from the hearth fires stung everyone's eyes as the Campbell clan gathered for the evening meal. And what a meal it was! Clearly, Duncan Campbell had something to celebrate. Platters were piled high with mutton, beef, English rabbit, and all manner of fowl. There were plates of oysters, bannocks, fruit, cheese, and even pastries. All to be washed down with tankards of ale and chalices of the finest wine.

Brianna watched as Dunstaffnage's servants hurried swiftly to and from the kitchen, their arms heavily laden with platters, bowls, and pitchers, thinking she would never get used to others doing the work for a few. Unlike in her father's hall, there was a distinct difference between those who served and those who ruled.

Looking around her, Brianna was once more stung by the contrasts between these people and her own. There was no laughter here, few smiles. Instead, an atmosphere of anxiety hovered about, a tense sense of anticipation. Even the bard's song was ponderous, a repetitive strumming with none of the lilt of Alastair's tunes. He warbled a history of the Campbell's progenitors, known as the race Diarmaid, who were for centuries a powerful influence in Argyll and who had originally settled the early Scottish kingdom of Dalriada.

"Ha," Brianna scoffed beneath her breath. They called themselves a race of Diarmaid, from a shadowy lord of Lochow into whose family a Gillespic Campbell had married, but the originator of the clan's good fortune was Sir Neil Campbell who had transferred his allegiance from John Balliol to his rival, Robert the Bruce, at just the right moment and profited thereafter with grants of lands and castles in the west. She'd even heard it said that the Campbells were of Norman or Saxon ancestry and had come into England with William the Conqueror. Now they paraded their noble lineage in song.

"There was none so fair as Diarmaid, no man could ever be as braw," the bard sang. It was a tragic tale of the handsome laddie with whom the wife of Fingal fell in love. In revenge, the song said, Fingal challenged Diarmaid to slay the wild boar that harried the village and then measure its carcass against the lie of its bristles with his bare feet. A bristle pierced Diarmaid's vulnerable spot on his heel, and Fingal heartlessly refused him a draught of his healing cup as Diarmaid lay dying.

Fingal? Ah, Brianna had heard other tales of him. Marauding Norsemen had been wary of landing their boats on Staffa because he had used the island as his base in warfare against the sea raiders so long ago. One of the caves on Staffa was named for the ancient hero. Alastair had composed many a song of him. *Alastair.* The name made her exceedingly wistful, for it reminded her of Glenna and home.

"Dinna look sad. Ye are much bonnier when ye smile." Robbie Campbell was seated to her left, and as he spoke he gently touched her hand.

"I was thinking of my sister."

"A sister? Och, how lucky ye are. I hae no liking for being the only child. 'Tis very lonely. But I hae my clan of course." He pushed his trencher closer to share his food with her, a custom she found most strange. English, she supposed. On Ulva they ate bread, here they used it as a plate. "Tell me all about yer family." His wide brown eyes offered her sympathy and understanding of her uneasiness.

"Morgana is the wee bairn, she's ten summers old; Orianna is four years older; and then there is Glenna, who looks the very image of me. And my father, chief of clan MacQuarie, a big bull of a mon. I love them all dearly."

Brianna felt comforted talking about her sisters and her father, relating humorous as well as sensitive stories. It was as if just the thought of them somehow brought them nearer. As she ate the highly spiced food, she told Robbie about her mother, and that poor woman's bout with insanity, and he seemed touched.

"Och, so sad."

"And your mother?"

"I didna even know her. I was taken from her arms shortly after my birth and fostered here wi' my uncle. I've been told my father was killed in battle, that my mother feared his enemies would try to take my life. For my own protection I was nurtured here." Picking up a leg of mutton, he toyed with it nervously. "And for that I am grateful to my uncle but . . ."

"But he isna always a gracious mon." She had noticed the curt manner in which Duncan talked to his nephew. She supposed he had never been as close with Duncan's daughters as she had been with her siblings.

"Aye." He laughed nervously. "I shouldna be sayin' this, but somehow it's as if I dinna belong here. As if I'm out of place. I try to please my uncle, I surely do. But somehow it seems a losing battle. He is always harsh wi' me, criticizes every little thing that I do. Indeed, I think my marrying you is the first thing that's caused him to smile."

His eyes mirrored a sadness as he looked at her, and Brianna was startled by the thought that even though she'd just met him there was something very familiar about his face, his expression. "Yer uncle, I beg to say, seems to be a very strange mon."

"A bit harsh perhaps. But very, very braw!" The way Robbie spoke, it was obvious that even though Duncan seemed to have little affection for him, he admired his uncle greatly. "But tell me what drew ye here. Surely, ye were not that anxious to wed wi' me."

"Nae. I hate to say it, but I came here with full intent of making your uncle change his mind." In a whispered voice, she told him the story of the voyage, her admonitions to her sister to take her place. It brought forth Robbie's laughter, a melodious, rippling sound.

"Poor lassie. She must be having quite a time. Being in two places at the same time must be difficult!"

Brianna joined in his mirth. "We did it all the time when we were small, just to be mischievous." Her smile sobered. "Aye, as a matter of fact it was Glenna and not myself who was to be yer bride at first. But she was in love with the bard, and I couldna stand by and see her cry. So I said I would take her place. How was I to know? . . ."

Her eyes were drawn to Ian, remembering in vivid detail the passion they had shared last night when their love had come so close to being consummated. One brief look at him set her blood to pounding as she relived the delight of holding him close. When he had held her in his arms, when he had pressed his hard, arousing body against hers, all thought of leaving here had vanished, dissolved in the heated torrent of their love. He had said he'd take her back to the MacQuarie hall if she wanted to go, but somehow she didn't want to leave. Not yet. Perhaps she still held hope of Duncan changing his mind.

Robbie caught sight of her stolen glance, the way her eyes caressed his cousin. "Ian? 'Tis *Ian* that ye love." Far from sounding piqued at the thought, Robbie's tone proclaimed his approval of such a match. "He is a fine mon."

"If a bit of a rogue."

"All bluff and bluster. In his heart he is most kind. He canna help it if the lassies all adore him."

"No, I suppose not. If only . . ." Brianna sighed, trying to concentrate on what was happening in the hall. Duncan had provided entertainment. Acrobats who performed wondrous tricks of skill, tumbling and balancing on each other's shoulders. Jugglers who tossed up brightly colored balls, spinning them with a steady hand. Not one dropped to the ground, much to her amazement. Oh, to tell Glenna of this game. Leaning back in her chair, she felt herself relaxing.

"Ye havena eaten much." Robbie pushed the trencher closer.

She didn't want to hurt his feelings so she forced herself to eat some of the heavily seasoned food, wondering how the Campbells could find it palatable. The portion that she took was a leg of rabbit, a small animal the English had introduced into Scotland several years ago. The meat had a yellowish cast which Robbie told her was from the saffron used as a dye. Somehow she choked the meat down, following each mouthful with the tangy, sweet red drink Robbie told her was French wine. That at least she favored.

A long time later, the long trestle tables were dismantled and pushed back against the wall. Duncan rose to his feet, putting his finger to his lips to gesture silence. The room quieted in an instant. Upon every face an upraised brow asked what was going to happen. That question was answered quickly as the Campbell laird addressed the gathering.

"There has been some concern avowed as to who is to succeed me. Though I'm no' anxious to become a ghostie, I've decided to address that issue now." He flashed a rare smile, enjoying the open-mouthed looks of surprise. All eyes were riveted his way. "From time to time I've mentioned Robbie, other moments I've given a nod to Ian and given thought to his becoming my tanist. It is, as ye know, a most serious duty. As tanist it will be his special duty to hold the clan lands in trust for you and your posterity. As clan chief, my successor will be called upon to determine all differences and disputes, to protect our followers, to lead this clan in times of war. I've made my choice and tonight I will make it formal. *Ian,* please stand up."

Nae, Brianna thought. Not now! She felt all hope for a future with Ian slipping away. It was Duncan's plan to placate Ian, she knew at once. If Ian was tanist, named officially, there was no way this side of heaven that he could agree to her father's terms for the marriage. He could not take on the MacQuarie name or allow any children he might have to be another clan's successor. All was lost! In a mood of hostile despair, she watched as Ian took his stand by the sacred stone of the Campbells, placing one foot upon the rock as custom decreed.

Had he known last night that he would be given such an honor? Had he? And yet he had not said a word. Instead, he had come to her room, initiated lovemaking and pretended that he cared for her. Suspicion poisoned her mind. Tears of angry frustration stung her eyes. No wonder he had run like a whipped hound when Duncan's voice had hailed him. So much for matters of the heart. Where honor and ambition were concerned a woman was naught. That was the way of men. Power was all they wanted. And now Ian had bartered his love for a tanist's crown.

Brianna watched silently as Ian was presented with a sword and a white wand as the Campbell bard recounted all his acts of bravery at Dumfries, the Forth of Clyde and many other battles. Ian Mac Niall was son of Niall who was son of Ian and on and on and on. There was no doubt that Ian came from noble lineage, nor that he was brave in his combat with other men, and for that she admired him. But she felt a sense of hopelessness too, for all the talk of fighting only proved that in reality there was a gulf as wide as Loch Tuath between them.

Ian, look at me. Let me know with yer eyes that ye still care for me, that yer uncle has not won after all. It was foolish of her to even make such a wish, she thought. The reality of the matter was that she had lost him, just as Duncan well knew.

Though she tried to hide it, tried to smile, Ian's seeming disregard for her throbbed painfully. Not once had he even glanced at her tonight, nor even exchanged more than polite salutations with her. Was he so afraid of his uncle then? Aye. Had being made tanist meant more to him than the love they had shared? If so, then she was extremely disappointed in him and angry with herself for being such a lovesick fool.

Ian Mac Niall can never be mine! she thought. Suddenly, the futility of her feelings for him came back to haunt her full measure. Now when she remembered last night, she was left with only humiliation. How quickly she had capitulated to his advances, like some besotted dairy maid. She had not even tried to hide her attraction to him. In truth, right from the first she had not even tried to be coy in espousing just why she had come to Duncan's castle. Ian knew her feelings. Had his been just as true, or was he the rogue she had first supposed him to be, thinking to take her virtue just to soothe his ego?

Her thoughts were tormenting. One instant she was appalled at herself and her boldness, the next she was overcome by a feeling of sharp disappointment that they had been interrupted before she had experienced fully what being a woman meant. Even now, the memory of the way he had caressed her and kissed her caused her body to long for the touch of his hands and mouth.

"What a fool ye are to love him, Brianna," she whispered to herself, "for he does not feel the same emotion in kind, I would wager." No indeed, she thought, watching him strut about the hall, so prideful at the honors being bestowed on him. He reminded her of a preening rooster. Sadly she was all too slowly learning the ways of men. Warfare was all they really cared about. Honor. Bravery. Did she really think he would give up his role as tanist for love of her? Of course not, though she would have given up the world for him.

"Lassie, what is wrong?" Robbie Campbell put a hand on

her shoulder, his wide eyes mirroring his concern for the tears that flooded her eyes.

"Wrong?" Brianna dashed the tears away with the back of her hand. "Just the smoke in my eyes, that is all. Dinna fash yerself, Robbie. It is nothing at all. Do ye ken?"

Nothing at all. That is what her love for Ian meant to him. The longer she watched the ceremony, the more she realized how quickly her own unhappiness loomed ahead. It was glaringly apparent. Even now, Ian did not deem to look at her. Had he heeded Duncan's threats? Was he fearful of losing his new prize? So much for his avowal of helping her.

Restless and unhappy, she rose from her chair, unwilling to think another moment about it. Oh, she would leave all right. But without his fine help. When the first light of dawn glowed on the horizon, she would be gone.

"So, ye are tanist, Ian. I'd say it's about time our uncle named ye so." Robbie pushed his way through the throng of revelers, maneuvering Ian to a far corner where they could be alone. "Congratulations!"

Ian stared hard at him, searching his face for any sign of jealousy, but there was none. By the large smile that cut its way across the freckled face, his sincere good wishes were not being feigned. Still Ian said, "I hope you are not disappointed."

"Disappointed? I've looked up to ye all my life and never doubted for a moment that it would be ye who would be named our uncle's successor. Ye are a fine mon, Ian. The best I've ever known. I only hope some day to be even half as fine a fighter as ye are."

"Ye will be, laddie. Ye will be." A twinge of guilt flashed through Ian as he looked into Robbie's unabashedly worshipful eyes and remembered the many times he'd come so close to making Brianna his own. In truth, it was Robbie who was the better man, for he doubted the boy would have come so close to wronging him had their *curans* been on the other's foot. Ian felt a sudden need to confess, before his conscience got the better of him. "Robbie . . . there is something I must tell you."

"That ye love Brianna MacQuarie wi' all yer heart. I already know."

"You know?" Ian looked at him, horrified. "Then you must think the very worst of me despite what you just said." He grasped Robbie by the shoulders. "I can not ask you to forgive me, only to understand. When I went to Ulva to act in your place I had it in mind to be honorable, but I saw this lovely lassie by the loch and I kissed her. I didn't know then who she was, I swear. Or perhaps I didn't want to know."

"And ye fell in love."

"Before I had the chance to arm myself against Cupid's bow. Aye, he is a devilish rogue and a very, very good shot! I can not tell you when I knew I loved her. It just happened." Ian shook his head sadly. "But that's not the worst of it. Perhaps I could excuse myself of any wrongdoing had it ended there, but it was only the beginning. I would have made her mine, Robbie. Not once, but several times, had she not pulled away. So, you see, the man you think so highly of is nothing but the lowest scoundrel."

"A mon canna help what is in his heart." Robbie was quick to forgive and this only made Ian feel worse.

"You forgive me too easily. I wanted your intended bride, Robbie. I still do, God help me. More than this honor I've coveted so long of being the Campbell's chief someday. You see, when all is said and done, and it is you who say the vows with her, 'tis you who will have been granted the greater prize. She is a bonnie, braw lassie."

"Aye, she is."

Ian sighed softly. "I wish you well."

Robbie put one hand on his hip, the twinkle in his eye replaced by one of anger. "Just like that! Ye'll gi' her up so easily? Shame on ye, Ian. That's not the mon I know so well."

"What else can I do?"

"There has to be something." Robbie made his own

confession. "I like Brianna, she's a comely lassie to be certain, but I dinna want to marry her, ye see."

"What?" The thought that Robbie would not want Brianna had never entered Ian's head. "She's a beauty! Any man would be proud to have her as wife."

"If he were not likewise in love!" As Ian met his gaze Robbie smiled again. "Aye. Ye see Cupid has an even stranger sense of humor than ye thought. I dinna argue the fact that the MacQuarie lassie is a fine companion. Lovely as ye say. But she doesna strike any chord in my heart. Nor does she hae any but friendly feelings toward me. She did in fact confide to me how very taken she is wi' you and I approved most heartily."

Hearing his words, Ian whooped with glee, sending all his clansmen's eyes his way. Cautiously, he lowered his voice. "Then surely there is something we can do to bring about a happy ending. For you, for me, and for the lassie I love. Don't you suppose?" Picking up two empty goblets, he filled them up. "To the future and to happiness for us all!" Now there was but one obstacle that stood in their paths. The most resilient of all. Duncan.

CHAPTER THIRTY-ONE

Drunken laughter awakened Brianna from a fitful sleep. The Campbells were celebrating Ian's thrust to power with ale, wine, and vainglorious boasts. She could hear feminine giggles as well and supposed that more than drinking was going on in the hall. Telling herself that she was disinterested in what was happening, she nonetheless tiptoed from her chamber and hovered just outside the large hall's door. It appeared that every member of the Campbell clan was assembled, each with a tankard, cup, or flagon in their hand. She could see Perth, Aulay, and the others, encircling Ian, men offering hearty congratulations. The women entwined themselves around him, and Brianna thought sourly that it would take little time for victory and pride to take her place in his affections.

Anger stung Brianna, though she told herself she didn't care. Ha! She didn't want him anyway. Overbold, leering laddie. She had been right about his true character the first day she had met him. Caitlin then was right after all. Duncan was doing her a favor in refusing to allow them to marry. Robbie was the better man. He was kind and gentle, considerate of her feelings. She would be better off with him.

"Nae." Brianna sighed. There was no use pretending. It was Ian who held her heart in his hands. She could not lie to herself. Perhaps he always would. No matter how logic told her to feel otherwise, she had no control over her emotions. She just wasn't drawn to Robbie in any way other than friendship. She liked the lad well enough, but she didn't love him. Just being near Ian, however, made her feel alive! Even so, it was hopeless and the sooner she came to terms with that the better it would be. She had to leave here. Escape, or risk the consequences of her attraction to Ian. For if she stayed she felt of a certainty she would succumb to her feelings for him and that she must not do.

Aye, she would get away from here and the temptation Ian Campbell posed. Darach had undoubtedly already left, but she'd find another fisherman and sail back to her clan. Her father would not even know what happened, nor would she tell him. She'd keep Duncan's vile nature a secret for the moment. She would not risk anger between the clans. Besides, he would undoubtedly place the blame rightly on her. No, instead she would merely take her place alongside Glenna and pretend she had never been gone. Ah, she would return to Duncan's hall, but with her father as protector. Then, after the formal betrothal had been pledged, she would marry Robbie. There was no other choice.

"Now!" she whispered. She had to act while the men were preoccupied with their ale guzzling. They would be too besotted to give any lassie a thought. So much the better. Perhaps Ian's rise to power could be beneficial.

Brianna made her way to the kitchen, thankful now that she had familiarized herself vaguely with the castle's interior. There she assembled what supplies she could for the journey, placing the larger foodstuffs in a large sack and the smaller in a fancily decorated sporran that she borrowed from a peg on the wall. It was dark, the hallway ill lighted, and she fumbled around, holding her breath once or twice when her gropings sent something falling to the floor. Gathering her courage, she stepped outside.

The moon was shrouded by dark clouds, her only guide was the light of the fading stars. Nevertheless, she plucked up her courage, looking back many times to make certain that she had not been seen leaving. If only she could put as much distance as possible between herself and Ian, she would get through her heartache somehow. At least her pride would be salvaged, she thought sadly. And perhaps happiness was only a dream after all.

Brianna stealthfully crept out of the castle, hiding in the shadows, conscious of every sound. That was why her ears perceived so readily the sound of footsteps behind her. Stopping in her tracks, she listened again. Her pursuer seemed to be playing a game. When she walked, he walked, when she halted, he did likewise. Trying to outsmart him, she dodged in and out amongst the barrels but seemingly all for naught. There, looming in the semidarkness, was a hulking figure, blocking her way of escape. Brianna recognized the man immediately as the one who had initiated her capture in the first place. The man she had heard called *Perth*.

Perth's features seemed to be carved in stone. He looked very strong and ominous as he stood there staring at her with his lone eye. Brianna was powerless against the storm of fear that shattered all her resolve like an eggshell. She spun around, intending to put as much distance as she could between herself and Duncan's henchman, but in a few swift strides he had caught up with her, his hand curving brutally around her arm, jerking her back to face him.

"Were you going somewhere tonight?" He smiled evilly and she thought how intensely she disliked this man.

Futilely, Brianna clawed at the imprisoning hand. "It was stuffy in my room and I thought to get some air." The lie tripped off her tongue despite her trembling.

His small, pebblelike eye narrowed, but after a long moment he released his hold on her, much to her relief. "Ye were going for a walk, is that what ye would hae me believe?"

"Aye!" she said cheerily. "A walk!" Clutching tightly to her sack, she took a few tentative steps backward. "And now

I'll be on my way. Back from where I came." She headed in the direction of the door. When he did not follow she was lulled with a false sense of security and retreated a few steps more. It was a mistake, just the move he wanted her to make, for with a snarl he was upon her, shoving her so hard that she tumbled to the ground. The impact with the hard earth jarred the sack loose and set the sporran around her waist to swaying, scattering objects on the ground.

Perth gave a bitter laugh. "So ye were just going for a stroll!" Bending down, he fingered the provisions with an oath, then stared hard at her. "And I call ye *liar*. Ye were leaving, make no mistake about it."

"Nae! Nae." She shook her head furiously.

"Lying slut!" His hand snaked out again, his fingers bruising where they pressed brutally against the fragile bones of her wrist.

"Don't ye be calling me names." Undaunted, she tried to wrest free of his grasp but he only squeezed harder, seemingly enjoying his torment of her. "Ye're a brute."

He laughed bitterly. "Ye canna insult me. I've been called worse."

"Ye remind me of a *fachan,* ye do. A large, savage, ugly beastie."

"And ye remind me of someone I knew. Someone as beautiful as ye are and just as deceiving." His eye was like a weasel's, hungry and ferocious. With a chilling laugh he moved closer. "Aye, ye are much like her, but it is no' a surprise since ye share her blood."

"What?" He thrust his face only a few inches from hers and Brianna knew suddenly that he meant to kiss her. "Nae! Ye leave me alone." In answer he laughed again, this time pinching her breast.

"Aye, I'll take ye back to the castle, but perhaps first I'll hae a bit of fun wi' ye. There are ways for a maiden to enjoy a man and still keep intact. Shall I show ye?"

"Ye must be mad!" Taking a deep breath she let it out in a scream.

Ian heard the shriek of outrage. In frightened curiosity he followed the sound. Seeing the two battling figures, he flung himself forward. At his intrusion Perth loosened his grasp and looked in Ian's direction as he asked, "What is going on?"

At that moment Ian's voice was the dearest sound in all the world to Brianna.

"She was trying to run away and I caught her red-handed. Ye know the orders we had from Duncan."

"Leave her be! I'll watch her. I doubt Duncan would approve of yer boorish pawing despite what he said." Brandishing a sword, Ian gave threatening warning. "Turn her loose."

"This is none of yer concern!"

"Ah, but it is. I make it so." Ian was not about to capitulate to this brute. He knew Perth too well to be frightened. Perth was a coward when faced by strength. Women and the helpless were who he preyed on.

"Ye may be tanist be ye are no' the chief yet."

"No, but I'm man enough to cut you down to size."

"Aye?"

Like an enraged bull, Perth sprang to his feet, challenging Ian to lay down his broadsword and meet him hand to hand. Ian accepted the dare. Grappling on the floor, the two men wrestled, Perth the burlier of the two, but Ian's lithe muscular grace giving him the edge.

It was a melee of cursing and shouting. Fisticuffs and kicking. First Ian would falter, then Perth would fail in his strategy. Ian's slyness and strength won out. He pummeled the taller man to near senselessness, stopping only when Duncan's guards, alerted to trouble by the noise and yells, came rushing to pull the two men apart.

"What is this all about?" Duncan came upon the scene with all the ferocity of a thundercloud. Looking from Ian to Perth and back again, he demanded an answer.

"Yer little MacQuarie lassie was trying to escape the hospitality ye've extended. I was merely trying to hold her in check when yer nephew appeared. He seems to hae a strange view of loyalty."

"Escape?" Duncan was as angry as Brianna had supposed. For an instant she thought he would strike her, but he maintained control. "Ye shouldna hae tried to run away. Ye are a guest here, lass."

"A prisoner, don't ye mean."

"Ye've been dealt gently with but from now on ye will get no such courtesy." He gesticulated to a man standing behind him. "From now on lock her in." He smiled beneficently at her. "It is my duty as yer future clan chief and kin-by-marriage to make certain ye dinna come to harm."

Brianna waited expectantly for Ian to come to her defense, to argue her enforced detainment, but only silence prevailed. So, that was the way of things, she thought. When it came to choosing between his laird and what was right he was a silent coward. Disappointment swelled within her. As Duncan Campbell led her back up the stairs, she rendered Ian a scalding look, more determined than ever that somehow, someway, she would get free without his help. And for the first time since she had initiated the masquerade idea with Glenna, she found herself hoping her sister would fail and that her father would indeed bring down his wrath upon Duncan's head.

CHAPTER THIRTY-TWO

The sweet scent of wild grass gave a breath of freshness to the air as Glenna trudged her way to Riannon's cottage. The path twisted round and round and passed across a burn, but she lifted her skirt and waded across without hesitation. She felt exhilarated by the walk and bolstered by the thought that what she was doing was right. It was the first time in all her life that she had been quite so bold or had initiated an act without first procuring Brianna's advice. She felt, however, that her sister would have agreed with her decision. As if to reaffirm that feeling, she had seen a cuckoo after breakfast, a good omen. Nonetheless, she crossed herself as the old woman's thatch-roofed cottage came into view. Taking a deep breath, Glenna knocked on the door.

"Eh?" A wizened old face poked through a small opening at the top of the door and Glenna's hands went cold. "What do ye want?"

Glenna couldn't find her voice, she just stood there staring as Riannon's dark-eyed stare assessed her. Those eyes drew her, lured her, yet in a calming manner, as if giving forth the feeling that all would be well.

"Is there a babe about to be born? Hae ye come for me?" Grinning her toothless smile, Riannon seemed the personification of evil, yet her voice was gentle and kind. "I'll get my pouch of herbs."

"No . . . no child." With trepidation she stared at the gray-haired old harridan, feeling a shiver convulse her spine. Was Jeanne right? Was this woman a witch? Would she be damned to eternal hell for even conversing with her? Suddenly, Glenna wanted to flee.

Shaking her head sadly, Riannon opened the door. "I know what ye are thinking. I know what has been said. But it isna true!"

"You're not a witch?"

"A witch?" The old woman laughed, revealing several missing teeth. "Nae, I'm a healer and midwife but any magic I might hae is good. Do ye ken? I dinna conspire wi' the devil! In fact, I fight against him every chance I get."

Glenna believed her, for there appeared to be nothing evil or sinister about Riannon. Quite to the contrary. If the people of the village were to be believed, the woman had done a lot of good and was a healer. "I'm sorry. I shouldna hae believed even for a moment." Succumbing to the old woman's invitation, she stepped inside the cottage. "I hae come to ask ye for a potion. One to make me bold and unafraid."

"A potion?" The thin lips curved up in a grin. "Tell me yer story, *nighean.*"

Glenna did, sparing no details. She talked about her love for Alastair, her hope that somehow she could convince her father to let her wed the handsome bard, her fright whenever her father grumbled at her. She spoke of Brianna and her journey to the lochs of Argyll. "I'm such a goose! I am as timid as a *feorag*, a squirrel. I hae not the courage to even fight for the mon I love. Och, how I wish I could be as braw as my sister. That's why I came."

"And ye think I can help ye?"

She sensed a deep loneliness about the old woman and was jolted by a feeling of pity. "I hoped that ye could."

Riannon was regarded as an object of fear, thus had been shown little kindness.

"I see . . ." The old woman motioned Glenna outside and there bent down and plucked some tiny berries and leaves on a vine. Wrapping the leaves inside a folded piece of wool, she formed a small bundle, then dipped it into a steaming pot of evil-smelling brew. Running her gnarled fingers over it, mumbling a few words, she held it forth. "Take this. It will aid ye in what ye must do."

When Glenna's fingers touched the talisman, a jolt of power seemed to surge through her. Such an eerie feeling. Was her mind playing tricks on her or was it real? "My thanks," was all she could manage to say. Reaching in the folds of her gown, she brought forth a spool of brightly colored wool thread to offer in return. "This is for you."

Riannon chuckled but seemed to welcome the gift. "Ye've a deep core of kindness, *nighean*. Aye, you'll win yer bard. On that ye hae my word."

That night, as Glenna sat beside her father at supper, the old woman's words reverberated in her mind. Glenna only knew that possession of the talisman gave her a feeling of confidence, even in the face of her father's frowns.

"Och, Brie, I hae been worried." Reaching over, Lachlan patted his daughter on the hand. "It's not like ye to be like a mole, hiding away in yer burrow. But now ye are back to yer spirited self and ye look bonnie."

"I feel very, very happy, though I fear I canna say same for poor Glenna." She clucked her tongue in sympathy.

"First one and then the other. I'll hae the MacLay gi' her a bit o' his potion. Eh?" He chuckled at the face she made. Glenna answered his laugh as she captured a piece of meat and lifted it to her lips.

The hall resounded with noise, laughter, chatter, and the barking of dogs as they begged for scraps. It was difficult to make oneself heard, yet even so, she knew she couldn't wait to ask her father the important question. Patting the small bundle tied at her waist she felt its power and blurted out, "I hae something I need to talk wi' ye about. Something I know will raise Glenna's spirits."

"What?" As a platter of meat was passed beneath his nose he speared it with his knife.

"Alastair!"

"Brianna!" He furled his brow.

"Ye canna be such a stubborn old goat!" Had she really said that?

"Old goat, am I?"

"Aye, but a sweet one. I wouldna like it said that Lachlan MacQuarie wouldna listen to reason, but that is the murmuring."

Lachlan turned his head from side to side very slowly, surveying his clansmen. "I am always a most fair mon! Ye know that, daughter!"

"Except where poor Glenna and the bard are concerned. Oh, why will ye no' gi' Alastair a fighting chance to win his lassie?"

"Brie!" His voice was gruff but this time Glenna didn't react in fear. "I've had my say. Ye know my thoughts on the matter."

"I do. I love ye wi' all my heart, Father, but in this ye are wrong! I know ye are. And that is all *I* will say."

The room crackled with tension. Folding his arms across his chest, Lachlan leaned back in his huge wooden chair with a husky growl. "Old goat, am I? Stubborn?" He pursed his lips in anger but Glenna did not squirm in her chair, nor regret her blunt words. She had spoken and that was that. When her father motioned Alastair forward, she knew she had set him to thinking, but what was he going to do?

Lachlan's sharp eyes focused on Alastair's face. "So, ye hae aspirations to wed wi' my daughter, eh, bard?" he asked coldly. When Alastair did not answer immediately, he banged the table with his fist, setting the tankards and wooden plates and bowls quivering. "Speak up!"

Alastair clenched his hands but did not flinch. "I love Glenna very, very much! And were she here I would say it again and again."

"Love! Och, a poem singer's dream. It doesna exist!" The clan chief stared at Alastair, daring him to say otherwise.

"In all humble respects I believe that it does. A magic too potent to understand." Alastair looked at Glenna out of the corner of his eye, caressing her with his gaze, then hastily looked away before it was noticed.

"Magic? Sorcery? And just how do ye define this magic of yers?"

"A deep caring! Two hearts that beat as one, two souls entwined for all eternity. I would do anything just to make Glenna happy." Alastair seemed to relax now that he had had his say.

"Would ye now. There is a spark of sincerity in what ye say. But I will put that to the test." Rising to his feet, Lachlan addressed the clan. "This young pup dares much. I hae decided to put him to the test and see if his bite matches his bark. Two days from now, when the sun is directly overhead, I will allow Alastair the bard to fight for my daughter's hand in marriage."

Glenna gasped, clutching her talisman, fearing to blink lest she wake up and find it just another dream.

"If the bard is able to best all opponents, I will agree to wed him to my daughter Glenna." A ripple of chatter moved over the assemblage like a tide. "But, if Alastair is brought to his knees he will be put out from our clan, banished to show his face no more." Lachlan seemed amused as he faced Alastair squarely. "What say ye, bard?" He seemed to expect the handsome young man to back down, to change his mind. Being banished was the harshest of penalties.

"I accept!"

"So be it." Lachlan nudged Glenna. "Do ye want to wager

on the outcome, Brie? Yer pony against my *garron?*" Somehow Glenna was able to nod her head. "Done!"

Dear God, Glenna thought, what have I done? Could she bear it if Alastair was sent away? She grasped the tiny bag of leaves fervently. Somehow she knew she had to believe. Alastair would win.

CHAPTER THIRTY-THREE

Ian floundered in his bed amidst the fragments of his sleep. Tossing restlessly, his mind churned as he met head-on the questions troubling his mind. He did not need the fey to sense that in some way Brianna was in terrible danger here. Duncan's resentment of the lass was apparent in every look he cast her way, but Ian had tried to justify his uncle's stubbornness because of the years of warfare between the clans. Then tonight, there had been something sinister in the way his uncle had glared at the girl. Hatred had glittered in his eyes like jewels. A madness that had chilled Ian to the very bone.

Why did Duncan feel the need to keep Brianna locked within the castle walls? Why had he panicked when he had learned of her near escape? What did he fear? Reprisals for holding her captive? Nae. Duncan held no fear of the MacQuaries, not really. In most of the battles throughout the years the Campbells had fared much better than the smaller clan. It was far more complicated than that. He seemed to have a foreboding that somehow Robbie would not be marrying the lass. Aye, that was it. Most of all, it seemed Duncan was loath to chance any halt to the wedding, though not for the reason he espoused. What was his motive then?

FLAME ACROSS THE HIGHLANDS

Sitting up, Ian braced his legs against the cold wooden floor, recalling to mind the conversation he'd had with his uncle a scant hour ago. Duncan had interrogated him about Ulva, its castle's defenses, the number of men that lived within its walls. Hardly a conversation to be held when they were on the brink of peace, Ian had thought.

"I did not take notice since my mission was one of peace," Ian had answered, throwing his uncle into a rage.

"Ye had an opportunity to be useful, to bring me back information about enemy country, and yet ye hae the effrontery to tell me ye *didna* take notice!"

"Was I sent to the MacQuarie castle to spy? You should have told me, uncle, and I would have been more alert. I thought our feuding with the MacQuaries had been settled. At least so you said."

"Nonetheless, I should hae thought any Highland warrior worth his salt would hae considered it his duty to learn all he could to help his own kin." Duncan screwed up his face, looking angry, fierce, and formidable. "Lachlan MacQuarie. Bah! I shall never forgive him. I shall be avenged. Aye, I shall!"

"By locking up his daughter?" Ian knew it would be a long time before he could forget the scene he had stumbled upon, Perth viciously assaulting Brianna. He had never liked the man and now he loathed him even more. But he would never dare touch her again.

"I did that for her own good. I wouldna want her to get lost or to come upon dishonorable men."

"Like Perth!"

"Hold yer tongue! Perth has always served me well. Och, indeed, he wears the scars of MacQuarie treachery." Duncan clenched his jaw as if to hold back his anger. Reaching out, he had patted Ian on the arm in a show of camaraderie. "But come, we shouldna be quarreling. What is done is done. Now ye are tanist, a justifiable honor I hae disposed." His upraised brow seemed to hint very strongly that Ian should show proper gratitude.

261

"And for that I thank you. I will serve you well, uncle, but as to Lachlan's daughter I think . . ."

"Shhhhh! My mind is made up. I hae decided that there is no need to wait for the joining of our clans. I hae sent to Iona for a priest."

"A priest?" A tight knot had formed in Ian's stomach at the thought of Brianna marrying. Though he had thought himself resigned to it, he could not block out the pain his uncle's statement fueled. All too soon the moment he had dreaded was to become a reality. "But The MacQuarie! He has the right to witness his favorite daughter wed." Ian felt the need to urge Duncan to caution. "You can't think to hold the ceremony without him."

"Nae. But I dinna plan to gi' him time to renege on his pledge, to involve the church in the matter. As soon as the priest arrives I'll bring The MacQuarie here to witness my deed!" Duncan's gruesome laugh exploded through the room. "Aye, if he doesna hurry here on his own when he realizes I hae his little treasure. Ah, I'll take great pleasure in his daughter marrying Robbie."

Now that Ian thought about it, his uncle's statement had sounded like a threat, as if there was something evil in what he planned. Why? How was the marriage between Brianna and Robbie going to be used to avenge Duncan? What harm was going to be done to Brianna? Ian knew he could not wait to find out. He would not take the risk of Brianna being hurt in this matter of Duncan's hatred. Though she had not admitted it, there was more than curiosity about Robbie that had brought her to Argyll. She had come because of him, because deny it or not she was just as much in love with him as he was with her. Aye, he knew that now. She had melted in his arms, would have given herself to him in love had not Duncan's robust intrusion spoiled everything. Now she needed him.

Ian dressed hurriedly in a shirt and breacon and slowly opened his chamber door. True to his word, Duncan had stationed a guard to prowl about in front of the room where

Brianna was housed. A faint gleam of torchlight glinted off the keys hung from the man's sporran, jingling as he walked back and forth. It would be a traitorous act to follow the urging of his heart, Ian thought. Even so, he knew there was no other choice. There were times when right must overpower wrong no matter what the price. True, Duncan was Ian's chief, for whom he had sworn loyalty, and his uncle, but kin or not, he was grievously unjust in what he was doing. So thinking, Ian grasped his sword, hoping with all his heart he would not have to use it to shed any blood.

Stealthfully, Ian approached the sentinel. Grasping the sword, using the handle as a club, he knocked the guard out cold. The man grunted, then slumped to the floor. Anxiously, Ian fumbled about for the key, tearing it free and unlocking the door.

"Brianna!" His voice was a harsh, whispered urgency.

"Mmmmm." She came only half-awake, disturbed by his hushed command, but opened her eyes wide as he shook her gently. "What do ye want?" Thinking him to have amorous intentions, she hissed, "Go away! Dinna touch me, Ian Campbell. Never again. I dinna want ye here upsetting my sleep."

"Not even if I've come to free you?"

"Free me?"

"Aye. A spirited little *kittiwake* such as you should ne'er be caged. Come, darlin'." With gentle fingers he grasped her hand and pulled her to her feet. "We've got to hurry before the goose egg I gifted the guard with is discovered. I don't know how long he'll be unconscious."

"Ye hit that mon, for me?" All the angry thoughts she'd had about him vanished to be replaced by a warm glow of love. "Why?"

Ian ruffled her already tousled hair. "We won't speak of it now, but I think you ken. Now, no more talk!"

By the light of a candle he helped her dress, his fingers lingering overlong on the soft swell of her breast as he fastened the folds of her tonnag together with a brooch. He looked down at the fiery red tresses illuminated by the glow of the flickering light and wrapped a strand around his fingers. A yearning surged through him. He wanted her so much that it was a painful longing. If only they could go away together, give free expression to the passion that sparked between them, he knew they could be happy. But that was a madman's wish. If his uncle didn't have both their heads, her father would. An impossible dream, that's what loving Brianna MacQuarie was. Even so, he allowed himself the luxury of holding her close, just for a moment, brushing his lips against her neck. Then, with a mumbled oath, he pulled away.

"Come!"

More than one unwary guard was the recipient of a painful crack to the head as Ian frantically sought Brianna's freedom, yet slowly but surely they worked their way across the inner bailey, hiding in the shadows. Ian clasped Brianna's hand so tightly that she winced. "I'll ne'er again call ye a rogue, Ian dear. In truth ye are more a saint."

"As I said, I just don't like to see a lassie held against her will." Ian felt a shiver convulse her slim frame and wrapped his arms around her, shielding her from the cool air with his plaid. An unpremeditated act but one that most definitely felt right. She belonged in his arms. "Duncan is a good clan chief on most accounts but something is seriously amiss here. I intend to take you back to your father's hall until I find out more about the situation."

She nuzzled her cheek against his chest. "I canna think of a more welcome companion." Hope kindled anew in her heart that perhaps all would turn out as it should after all. Perhaps when she told her father what had happened, he would listen to her request and exchange one groom for another. Duncan had transgressed, and she held onto the dream that when all was said and done, he would put his stubbornness aside in the interest of peace. "Brianna." Ian's mouth hovered only inches from her own and she wanted him to give in to the moment, but instead he shook his head. "We'll need horses. If we can make headway tonight there will be no way Duncan and the others can catch us." Holding her close, he led her to the stables and selected two horses he knew to be most noble steeds. "Have you ever ridden bareback?"

"Aye!"

"Then I won't take time to saddle these." Cupping his hands around her foot, he helped her mount then flung himself upon another horse's back. The dark shape of the huge outer gate loomed before them. "Push the ends of your hair inside your tonnag, lass, and keep your head down so there'll be no suspicion as to who you are," he ordered, guiding his horse toward the outer bailey gate. "Open up!" he yelled to the man atop the wall.

The creak of the portcullis was a welcome sound, though Brianna watched the iron grating ascend with anxiety. What would be Ian's punishment for aiding her, she wondered, knowing his betrayal of Duncan would not be taken lightly. The realization of what Ian had risked suddenly hit her full force. How could she let him make such a sacrifice? She had thought that being tanist meant the world to him, and yet now by his actions he was throwing the honor away. She couldn't let him do it!

"Ian, go back. I canna let ye go wi' me," she breathed, her voice blending with the wind.

"I know a shortcut that will lead you to the coast in half the time. I wouldn't let any lassie travel at night alone." He grinned. "Besides, call me a selfish man if you like, but I rather relish your company. You've come to mean a great deal to me, Brianna." It was as close to an admission of love as he intended to come. "Don't worry. I'll think of a way to make amends to Duncan, never fear. He needs me. I don't mean to boast, but I'm the best chieftain he has."

He proved his stubbornness on the matter, refusing to go back, following her through the gaping mouth of the gate and galloping across the glen. Sitting on her horse expertly and straight, Brianna felt a wild surge of excitement sweep through her. For the moment at least, she was free and with the man she loved. If they had only this time to be together she would cherish it.

They formed two silhouettes on the crest of the hill, riding against the wind, blending their bodies with the churning muscles of the horses beneath them. Brianna felt contented that all would be well until her eyes swept the dark gray horizon. Were those distant dots she saw on the hill what she thought them to be? Yes! Blessed Saint Michael, they were being followed!

"Ian! Horsemen!" she croaked, clutching the horse's mane with fingers that trembled. "Are they? . . ."

Ian looked over his shoulder, cursing loudly, answering her question. The cluster of distant riders were coming in their direction. There could be no other reason than pursuit. "They must have found the sentry sooner than I supposed. We've got to ride hard, Brie!"

Ride hard she did, until her legs ached and her hands were numb from holding on to the horse's mane. And all the while it seemed as if the sound of pursuing, pulsating horses' hooves was getting louder and louder. Had she had any wonder as to the horsemen's identity, the Campbell war cry of *"cruachan!"* left no doubt.

How Brianna longed for her own horse, for the Scots' *garrons* were bred for speed. Instead she made due, guiding the animal beneath her across the glen and down a steep hill. They had a head start that gave them a fair to middling chance of escape, she told herself. Looking over her shoulder, nonetheless, she cringed as she saw the riders steadily gaining. Her father had once told her there was no finer horseman than a Campbell. Now she had proof of that saying. Ha, but she would give them a race if that was what they wanted. In desperation, she nudged the flanks of her horse, determined to succeed. She might have if her mount had not stepped in a hole and stumbled. A scream tore from

Brianna's mouth as she felt the firm flesh beneath her plunge to the ground.

"Brianna!" Ian looked behind him and saw her fall. His heart lurched and pounded frantically as he hurried to the spot where her horse had gone down. It was like a terrible re-creation of that time in the forest, he thought, bending over her. "Brianna!" His voice was a soulful wail.

Reaching out, she clung to him, trying to still the black dots that danced in her head. "I'm all right! Just a bit shaken up!" She scurried to her feet, leaning on him for support.

"We'll both ride my horse and . . ."

"Nae!" The reality of the situation could not be denied. They could never escape now. "Listen to me, Ian. I willna hae ye sacrificing yerself to save me. Tell them I broke free of my room and ye were chasing after me. Say it! I willna deny it."

"I will not lie!"

"I will! Let Duncan think ye are a hero in capturing me. Then perhaps all willna be lost." Brianna hushed as the horsemen swiftly encircled them. Pushing at Ian's chest, she made a great show of fighting him. "Och, ye damned Campbell! Let me go! I willna go back."

"Aye, ye will!"

Brianna recognized that voice at once and damned the man. Perth. Like a cursed hound, he seemed to be always following in her tracks. "Ha! I should hae ken it would hae been yer horsemen following after me."

"I wondered if my instincts were right. They were. I know ye set her free, Ian. I watched and waited. This time I let her get past the gate, just so there would be no mistaking yer intent." At a nod of his head four men surrounded Ian, grappling him to the ground.

Striking out blindly, Brianna did her best to pull Perth's henchmen from Ian. She tried to claw at them. She kicked out, baring her shapely thighs in the tussle. "Nae! Nae! He was chasing after me to bring me back to the castle!" In anger she whirled around, her eyes darting fire at Perth.

His thin lips curled up in a snarl. "Ye are a liar. I willna doubt my own eyes. I saw what I saw. And now he will suffer for it."

"You blackhearted bastard!" Even in his defeated position, Ian's countenance blazed defiance. "I tell you to let the lassie go!"

"Go? She'll go nowhere but back to the castle. And as for you . . ."

"I am tanist! You have no right to overrule me." Struggling against the men who held him, Ian stared his adversary down.

"Tanist? Not when it is found out what ye hae done." Malice oozed from Perth's one eye, like a putrid wound. "Ye've brought yerself to this end. Ah, how I hae hated seeing ye get all the honors, glowing in all the glory when it's I who hae been Duncan's right-hand man all these years. I've wanted to bring ye down and now I hae." His voice lowered. "I've a claim to be Duncan's successor too. I'm his cousin, though he seems to enjoy putting it out of his mind."

"God help us if a man as cruel as you would ever take over as clan chief." Ian winced but did not cry out as Perth struck him. In the utmost show of disrespect he spat in his clansman's face. "Ye'll never wear the chief's feathers as long as I am alive."

"Then we'll hae to see to hurrying yer demise!" Giving Ian a shove, he commanded, "Take them away!"

CHAPTER THIRTY-FOUR

The dank stench of the dungeon assailed Ian's nostrils as he was shoved inside. "I swear, Perth, you will regret this! I will see that you pay," he swore, his eyes darting back and forth for any means of escape. There was none. He was being heavily guarded, like a mouse by three large cats, he thought wryly.

"By sending that dwarf to wreck vengeance? I'll swat him like a fly." As if to give an example, Perth clapped his hands. The air resounded with the slapping sound.

"You had better hide yourself when I am let out, Perth, for *I* will see that you pay!" In furious anger, Ian lashed out, only to be kicked back down into the dark hole. The clank of the door put an end to any other threats.

It was a tiny, cramped cell, more cellar than prison, with a stone and iron-barred trapdoor that could be locked from up above. Ian was familiar with the dungeon. There was no way of escape, of that he was certain. Even if he could crawl up the wall there was no way he could remove the stone from the hole. He was completely at his uncle's mercy, as was Brianna.

Duncan had been livid when Ian's duplicity had been revealed. He had vowed to keep him imprisoned until

Brianna was safely married, to use him as a pawn in whatever twisted game he was playing.

"Ye seem to hae a fondness for my elder nephew that hae driven ye to boldly cross me, girl," Duncan had said to Brianna. "Well, I make ye this bargain. If ye try to leave here again it will go hard on him, do ye ken? I will seek punishment on *him.*"

Brianna had gone quite pale. "I ken!"

"But if ye conduct yerself like a good little lassie and tell yer father that it was for love of yer groom that ye hurried here to accept my hospitality, then as soon as the marriage ceremony is finished and ye are *bedded* wi' yer husband, then I will set my traitorous nephew free."

"Then I will do as ye ask. Hae I any choice?" Brianna had looked at Ian then, love shining in her eyes. "Aye, I will marry Robbie but not for love. My heart belongs to you, Ian. Now and forever, my own dear love!"

"My own dear love," she had said. She was going to marry Robbie to save *him!* "Noooooooo!" The cry which tore from his throat was like that of a wounded animal. Sagging to the ground, he grasped his knees, hugging them with his arms as he had when he was a small boy and his mother had left him. Rocking back and forth, he sought to fight the demons that tore at his heart. Brianna belonged to him!

He didn't resent the boy. In this matter he was as much a pawn as they. But that didn't ease the pain. It would be that young boy who would glory in her body, that beardless lad who would be her husband, share her life, plant his seed. Why? What drove Duncan to such an end? What kind of man locked up his own kin? Why was he so insistent that Brianna MacQuarie marry Robbie? Was Robbie his own son? An illegitimate one perhaps? Or was there something else? Some dark secret? Questions he asked himself over and over, and of Aulay as well.

"I dinna ken, Ian, but I will find out what is going on. Yer uncle has a strange obsession with the laddie that I will soon find out." With a whispered promise through the cell opening to seek Duncan's sister out and find out about Robbie's relationship to his uncle, Aulay had left.

Ian seemed to lose track of time as he languished in the cell-like room. It was dismal, uncomfortable and humiliating. It was a disgusting hell hole. Walls of dirt infested with all kinds of vermin. Spiders, worms, and bugs of unknown origin. He thanked God for his plaid for it was long and thick enough to be a warm blanket to shield him from the damp cold.

"Brianna!" Her eyes haunted him, her voice seemed to whisper in his ear. "Och, I'm nearly as addled in my head as Duncan." Something sinister urged *him*. Something evil. Ian could not say what it was but he knew there was more to the matter than at first was visible.

"Ian!" It *was* Brianna's voice. He had not been imagining it. A circle of light appeared above his head as the grate was opened. He stood up, reaching up as if to caress the face he saw hovering above his head.

"Brie!"

"I begged Duncan to let me see ye one more time. Be . . . before the wedding." She stretched out her fingers and brushed his with the poignancy of a kiss. "To tell ye that I love ye."

His voice was choked with misery. "Don't marry Robbie, Brianna."

"I must!"

"Not for my sake. I don't care what Duncan has threatened to do to me. He would not kill his own nephew. Please!"

"Ian!" She whispered his name in a long, drawn-out sigh, wishing so desperately that she could be with him. More than anything in the world she wanted his arms around her, wanted his lips touching hers, but it was not to be. "I . . . I came to wish you happiness. I want that for ye, Ian."

"I'll never be happy now. Not without you!"

She forced a laugh. "Aye, ye will. Ye know very well that ye are a handsome laddie wi' all the lassies chasing after ye.

Ye'll soon forget me." Just the thought made her die a little but she forced herself to laugh again. "I know that ye will."

"Never!"

"I want ye to. I do! Duncan is sending Robbie and me away after the ceremony, to a castle farther south. And he told me that even though ye tried to help me ye still will be his heir. So there is no harm done."

"Harm? Indeed there has been. His stubborn obstinacy has created a great deal of unhappiness. For that I do not think I can ever forgive him." Standing on tiptoe he clasped her hand with urgency. "Something is amiss, Brianna. I don't know what, but even a fool could see that my uncle's obsession is not right." He threw back his head. "Och, if only I could get out of here."

Perth's face replaced Brianna's at the opening. "Get out? I wouldna be thinking it to be very soon. So sad that ye will miss the wedding, Ian, but then Duncan is being very careful just who he invites, ye see. Bad enough that the MacQuaries will be present!" he growled. "'Twas one of them that cost me my eye!"

"And I will cost you the other if you anger me any further. I swear it, Perth!"

"Ye'll no' be costing anybody anything!" There was a threat in his words that Ian understood all too well, though Brianna might not. Ian was at the mercy of a man who had no honor, no scruples. There was every possibility that it was at Perth's hands that he would die.

CHAPTER THIRTY-FIVE

Never had Glenna felt such fear as she did today! Alastair's combat was to be held in the same field where the games had been played for the betrothal feast. It was a level stretch of hard ground covered with a dusting of wild grass and surrounded by rocks upon which the spectators sat. Glenna's heart was in her throat as she watched the men file onto the field. Alastair was to have three adversaries—Jamie, Erskin, and a brawny young man from clan MacGregor she had never seen before.

Three opponents, she thought giddily. Where was the fairness in that? Surely, her father was a hard man. Alastair would be pushed beyond the endurance of a man who stroked a harp instead of wielding a sword. Surely, he would be overpowered. And yet it was a chance! Glenna clutched the talisman in her left hand. She would not even let herself contemplate what would happen if Alastair lost. She couldn't refrain from crying.

Voices rose in a cheer as Alastair and Jamie took their places, removing their plaids and throwing them on the earth. Just as the warriors in battle did, they would fight nearly naked, and Glenna blushed at the sight of Alastair's lithe but well-muscled body, remembering what Jeanne had said to her that day about tall men being well endowed.

Alastair chose the form of combat and chose, much to Glenna's horror, to fight with swords. The clansmen roared their approval but she felt panic grip her heart. She'd been certain it would be a barehanded fight, wrestling. Clearly, he would be in danger. The sword looked huge and cumbersome in his hand, an instrument capable of maiming or killing.

"Father! He knows naught of weaponry. Ye canna let him risk his life!" Running to her father, she gripped his arm.

"It was his choice." He cupped her chin in his hand and though there was stern resolve written on his face there was kindness also. "Yer bard said he was willing to die for ye. I hae taken him at his word."

There was no chance for argument. All Glenna could do was whisper a prayer. "Be safe, Alastair! Be safe, my dearie," she breathed as she watched him prepare for the battle. As if feeling the heat of her gaze, he turned and gave her a hesitant smile.

The eerie drone of the bagpipes silenced all talk as the two adversaries advanced, swords leveled. Like a grotesque dance, they bent and swayed. The air rang with the sound of blade on blade. It was a brutal fight. Glenna hung on tightly to her talisman, moving her hand back and forth as if to give Alastair aid.

The sun beat down full force as the two men lashed out at each other. Sweat ran into Alastair's eyes. Glenna could nearly feel his pain as the tip of Jamie's blade tore the flesh of his arm. Covering her mouth with her hand, she stifled her cry. Despite his torment, however, Alastair used his wits. He pressed in, driving Jamie back as he tried to maneuver him onto the rough ground and over the rocks. Alastair plied him on the right side, then on the left, moving with the grace of a mountain cat. Glenna blinked her eyes and in just that short span of time Alastair had Jamie on the ground, the blade of the sword pressed against his neck. The clansmen roared their excitement.

"Perhaps this willna be a rout after all," a young boy shouted out.

"Riannon's charm!" Glenna whispered, breathing a relieved sigh. There could be no doubt. It had given Alastair strength.

The MacGregor was a short, stocky lad who struck out at Alastair again and again. It appeared that there was a fierce power behind his sword, enough to send the bard to the ground. As the crowd gasped, he rolled away from another strike which was thrust into the soil just inches from his head.

"Blessed Saint Michael!"

Alastair pulled himself from the ground, keeping his eyes on his adversary's sword, feeling his head grow light as the blade whistled before him. He could feel his breath hammering inside his chest and knew that he was winded. His arm felt so heavy that it took great effort to lift it. One glance at Glenna, however, gave him a new surge of strength. For love of her he would win!

"Ye willna escape me so easily this time." Disappointed that his weapon had not drawn blood, Alastair's foe threw himself upon him. Locked together in combat, the two men rolled upon the ground as the clansmen rumbled their excitement.

"By God! I had no idea the mon could fight. He's been wasted." Lachlan's eyes held a new respect.

Freeing himself from the large man's grip, Alastair stood up. This time it was he who initiated the assault, diving for the MacGregor's legs. With a sudden burst of strength he tore the sword from his adversary's hand and hurled it away. Was the crashing in his ears from the onlookers or from his heart? He fought to catch his breath, certain that his lungs were so cramped there would be no room for any air, and yet there was to be one more battle. Could he fight on? Alastair saw Glenna's eyes upon him and felt the depth of her love strengthen the resolve of his abused body. He had to win!

Erskin strode onto the field, but this time Glenna felt no apprehension, certain Alastair would win. She leaned back against the large rock, relaxed but anxious for this matter to be at an end. This time, however, it was not as quick a battle.

The sound of sword on sword rent the air as Alastair and Erskin fought their furious battle, a test of strength, courage, and fortitude. Alastair's aching eyes seemed to imagine three men at one time hurtling toward him, lunging, striking. Shaking his head, he sought to clear his vision as Erskin poked out with the tip of his blade. Pain pierced Alastair's shoulder. The warmth of his own blood seeped in a rivulet from the fresh wound in his arm.

"Alastair!" He could hear Glenna's wail even from a distance. Clansmen were on their feet, awaiting his certain defeat, but he was equally determined that despite the blow he would win. He sang about the power of love, now he would prove it true.

Erskin was trying to maneuver him to the slope of the ground to gain advantage of footing, but Alastair would have none of that. Over and over again he remembered the tales of prowess and how the heroes of old had won their battles and he mimicked their daring. Bending his knees, he leaped up, startling his opponent with a loud shout. Grabbing Erskin by the arm he tore the sword from his hand. For just a moment the world seemed to move slowly, hang motionless. Hot agony clutched at him, sucking away his new-found strength. Alastair stumbled and fell to his knees as black dots danced before his eyes.

"Alastair!" Glenna's heart soared in wondrous flight, watching as her father walked across the field. The bagpipes droned again and she watched with fierce pride as Alastair was carried across the field to a place of honor at her father's side.

"As has been promised, Alastair the bard has won himself a very dear prize. The hand of my daughter, Glenna." Lachlan's voice was gruff and he looked disgruntled, but nonetheless he forced a smile as he looked in her direction.

His announcement was met with shouts and cheers for there was none among them who did not take pride in Alastair's win. Love had triumphed after all, just as the bards had always proclaimed. They had seen it with their own eyes today. A bard had bested three fierce swordsmen! It would be something to tell their children.

Glenna's eyes radiated pride as she approached her father. She started to speak but was shoved aside by one of her kinsmen. "A messenger from Black Duncan!" the man reported, pushing a tall, dark-haired man forward. "He says that Brianna is at Dunstaffnage Castle."

"Impossible! My daughter is here!"

"Talk wi' him yerself."

Glenna listened warily. Brianna was safe, a guest in the Campbell stronghold. Duncan was calling forth the MacQuaries to come for an *early* wedding.

"What treachery is this! I tell ye my daughter is *here*!" Shuddering with outrage, Lachlan grabbed the man by his shirt. "What trickery is being played here?"

Glenna pushed forward. "No trickery, Father. Brianna is no' here. She went to see The Campbell. 'Twas I who took her place. Just like when we were little. That's why . . ."

Lachlan's face turned bright red with anger as the pieces fell into place, Brianna's illness, the strange way his daughters had been acting. He liked it not at all. "I hae been deceived! By a wayward daughter and one wi' the charms of a wicked fairy." He waved his hands in the air, gesticulating wildly. *"An t' Arm breac dearg,"* he cried out. It was a war cry summoning the red-tartaned army, Lachlan's clan. "To Argyll!"

"To Argyll!" came the shout.

Glenna crossed herself, certain that what she and her sister had done would surely be their clan's ruin. Clutching her talisman, it was for Brianna she made a last wish.

CHAPTER THIRTY-SIX

Ravens, the ominous Celtic symbols of misfortune and death, rustled their black wings as they soared over the castle. Their caws seemed to issue a warning. A gruesome omen for a wedding day, Brianna thought.

"And yet there is nothing to be done," she sighed. Before the sun swept across the sky to give way to the moon, she would be Robbie's bride. The thought that Ian would be forever lost to her cut through her like a knife. A flood of tears hovered behind her eyelids, but remembering her MacQuarie pride, she fought to maintain her composure. "I will not go before these Campbells with red and swollen eyes. Fie, I will not!"

Looking at the sky through the open window, she vowed she wouldn't give in to despair and self-pity but would try to keep up her spirits. Robbie had a sweet nature, a gentleness about him that gave her assurance that she would not be an abused wife. Surely, she might have come to worse with an obstinate or brutal husband. Somehow she *would* forget Ian and try to be a good wife. Even so, her face paled and her hands grew cold as two young servant girls entered her chamber.

"We are to tend ye, mistress," the tallest one said,

showing Brianna more deference now that she had been named before all as a Campbell bride.

"Anything ye need, ask us freely," said the other.

They led her to the bathhouse where a tub of steaming water awaited. A pile of thick woolen towels were spread on an airer to warm before the fire. In a daze, Brianna stood still as they stripped her of her gown. How quickly the morning was flying by. Had her father received the message that on this day she was to wed? Was he even now on his way to Argyll to witness the ceremony? If by any means he was cheated of seeing his daughter bound in marriage, she knew there would be trouble. Her marriage was meant to avoid any bloodshed. There had been too much of that over the years.

Brianna sighed with pleasure as the pleasantly warm water surrounded her. She lay back as the women soaped her hair and tried to relax, but it was impossible. Even the soothing cocoon of water could not slow the pounding of her heart or make her forget the coil that was forming in her stomach. Over and over again she thought how it should be Ian she was marrying, not some gentle boy. Oh, how different her emotions would be *if* . . .

Before long two other servants arrived struggling under an armload of clothing in a veritable rainbow of colors. She was told that the Campbell chief desired that *she* choose her wedding gown.

So, she thought, I may not choose my groom, but I am to be given at least some consideration. Forcing a smile, determined to be amicable, she fondled each garment to scrutinize it with a discriminating eye. At least Duncan was not being stingy. Each piece of material was finely woven and artfully done. Some, of a much finer wool than came from MacQuarie looms, was artfully decorated with thread that Ian had called embroidery. She could nearly imagine in her mind's eye a woman's form bent to the task, sitting before a hearth fire. She had a difficult decision to make, but finally decided on a gown of pale yellow with threads of blue and green. A white *tonnag* pinned with an elaborately worked brass brooch of gold and red corral, a belt of leather and several pieces of brass intermixed giving the semblance of a chain, emphasized the trimness of her waist and completed her attire. As was the custom, she was barefoot.

"Oh, 'tis a fine sunny day, a perfect day to be wed."

"And ye have a fine looking laddie to wed."

The young women chattered and laughed with as much exuberance as if *they* were to be the brides. They combed and brushed her hair until it shone with a red fire, explaining that unmarried lassies bound their hair and wore a snood, but married lassies left their hair to hang free. As a symbol of her newly wedded state, therefore, Brianna's side hair was braided, her back hair left to flow down her back.

"Ye look bonnie, mistress!"

"As lovely as a fairy queen!"

Brianna stood unsmiling before the large, polished steel mirror, studying her reflection. Her father would say that her face was too pale, would be worried that she looked so thin. "Stand tall and proud, ye are a MacQuarie!" he would have said. Pinching her cheeks to bring a touch of color, squaring her shoulders, she prepared herself for the inevitable.

She walked hesitantly down the stairs to be greeted by a large throng of guests. Proudly, she moved toward the middle of the hall, feeling totally alone, ill at ease among these people. She would not let them cow her, she vowed. Holding her head high, she faced them boldly, like a clan chief's daughter.

"Kinswoman!" In an exaggerated gesture of affection, Duncan took Brianna's hands, pulled her to him and kissed her, first on one cheek then the other. "At last ye bring an old mon's dream to fruition. How anxious I am for the seeds to be sown in yer belly." He ignored her blush, motioning Robbie forward.

"Duncan! No! Ye canna!"

An old man Brianna had not met, but who she had seen constantly in Duncan's company, pushed his way through the throng, hissing insistently in the laird's ear. An angry roar from Duncan silenced him, but the mournful, tortured look on the man's face did not go unnoticed by Brianna. She looked at Duncan questioningly. He only shrugged his shoulders.

"Cameron has long been opposed to this match but I hae no' listened to him." Duncan laughed. "He is, I fear, becoming an addled old mon." Taking a large cup from the hands of a young male servant, he held it forth to Brianna. "Drink!"

The cup was adorned with a sprig of rosemary and colored ribbons and looked like some pagan offering. As she took a sip of the spiced wine, Brianna could not help but wonder if some ancient Celtic tribal bride had held such an object in her hand. Handing the cup to Robbie she smiled as he voiced aloud her thoughts. It seemed the cup had been handed down for generations, all the way from the first chief of the Campbell clan.

"And I will gi' it to my son when he weds," Robbie exclaimed, to be rewarded by a hearty slap on the back from Duncan. With a nod of his head, Duncan signaled it was time for the merrymaking. Rising to his feet he flung back his chair, leaped upon it, and raised aloft the bridal cup as a whirling, high-stepping, jubilant, laughing group of revelers gave vent to their joy.

Suddenly, the sharp toot of a trumpet interrupted the merriment. A huffing, puffing sentry bounded into the room, pointing in the direction of the north. "The *MacQuaries!* They are here! They've come by *biorlin,* across the loch. They are marching this way. Listen to the bagpipes!" The ominous hum sounded like a swarm of angry bees.

"My father!" Hurrying to the window, Brianna looked

out, lamenting the boldness that had brought her here. A fear gripped her heart that far from halting the warfare her willfulness had provoked an attack.

It was dark in the tiny dungeon. Only the glow of torchlight cast a faint flicker of light through the iron grate, illuminating the dismal prison. Ian was in a foul mood as he huddled in the folds of his plaid, trying to fend off the chill. Pulling the edges of his breacon tighter, he grumbled loudly, pausing only when a soft noise disturbed his solitude. The faint moan of faraway bagpipes cut through the stillness. Bagpipes! Ian held his breath, atuning his ears to the wail, cursing his uncle as he realized he was not imagining things. So the MacQuaries had come just as he had known they would. But this time Duncan could not place blame on anyone but himself! Were there a battle, the burden of the responsibility rested on the Campbell chief and not on a Macquarie.

Rising from the ground, Ian paced back and forth across the cubicle's hard earthen floor feeling like a trapped rodent! He had to get out! He had to do something to divert the disaster that he knew was going to ensue. Somehow! Someway!

Gripping the dirt walls, forcing a foothold, he tried to climb up the side of the hole he'd been flung into, only to slide back down each time he was within an arm's length of the top. His only reward was blistered and bleeding fingers.

Taking off the leather belt that held the sporran around his waist, he tried another approach, looping it through the bars of the iron grating. Again he failed, watching in abject frustration as the belt missed its mark again and again. It was as if the walls were closing in on him. Never had Ian felt so totally powerless in all his life.

"Like being gelded," he swore aloud. "Duncan knows well the way to torture me." The drone of bagpipes was getting louder, taunting Ian with his own helplessness. What was happening up there? Was Duncan going to anoint his longed-for marriage with blood? "Brianna!" Above all he wanted to make certain that she was safe.

A sound! What was it? The guard? Ian looked up expecting to see the familiar hulking form, but saw instead another face looking down at him. One as dear as his own visage. "Aulay!" The little man had returned. "Get me out of here!"

"Shhhhhhh! There are still two guards in the passageway. I'm so small that I was able to pass by them without their noticing my wee physique, but if ye are no' careful they'll be at my back."

"Can you get the key?"

"Nae. I think Duncan has it wi' him. He knows ye hae many friends within the castle. I fear I'm going to hae to dig ye out, loosen the dirt around the grate." The staccato noise above his head told Ian that Aulay was doing just that. Heeding the dwarf's words, Ian remained silent until his curiosity got the better of him. He had to ask.

"What's happening above? Tell me, mon. Are the MacQuaries going to instigate war?" Ian whispered as softly as he could. "Brianna, is she? . . ."

"Safe for the moment. Let us hope the MacQuaries hae it in mind to call off the wedding. Yer lassie is in peril, but not for her life. For her soul!"

"Ye found something out about Robbie on yer journey. What?" A chill swept over Ian as he had a premonition of what Aulay was going to say. Robbie was a changeling. One of the fairyfolk, exchanged for a human child.

"Aubra, Duncan's sister, has three children! Daughters all. She sent no male child to foster wi' her brother. Robbie is no' her son."

"Then whose? . . ." What lie had Duncan perpetrated on the clan and why? How did Brianna MacQuarie fit in the puzzle? Something sinister was being hatched but what? And why? And how? There was no time to find out now. Above all, the ceremony had to be stopped until Ian's questions were answered.

CHAPTER THIRTY-SEVEN

"The MacQuaries are outside the walls!" The tension in the room was taut as a bowstring. Every clansman's eye focused on the weapons hanging on the wall, poised, waiting for Duncan's nod.

Brianna's heart turned over in her breast. Hands clasped tight, she moved to the window and leaned over the stonework balustrade in an effort to identify the clansmen beyond a doubt, having but faint hope that it was other than her clan. The red-haired, broad shouldered man at the head of the small army left little doubt. Sunlight winked a glow from his sword, the red and green hue of the tartan beneath gnarled armor marked Lachlan as surely as any badge.

"Father!" Her eyes were imploring as she looked at the man who but a moment ago welcomed her as part of his family. "Please!"

Duncan paused for a long moment then broke into a smile. "I hae no need to quarrel. Perth! By the laws of hospitality, mon, invite the MacQuaries in for the ceremony." He patted Brianna on the shoulder. "In fact, they hae arrived just in time."

Perth followed his chief's bidding, opening the door to an angry swarm of MacQuaries. Lachlan moved ahead of the others, ignoring everyone else in the room as he jostled and shoved his way to Brianna's side. "Are ye all right? Are ye unharmed?" Her nod assured him that she was. Only then did he unleash his chiding tirade, his face turning purple with rage. "Ye must be daft, daughter!" Never before had he ever raised a hand to her, but he shook his fist now threateningly. "I should take the back of my hand to ye. Headstrong! Stubborn! Willful! All these things ye are, Brianna Nic Lachlan!"

Brianna recoiled in the face of his tongue lashing, knowing she deserved his censure and worse. She should never have come here! If it was possible, she had aged at least a year in just the past few days. She deserved his anger. There wasn't a thing he could say to her that she had not said to herself. It was true that a selfish, naive, bold young maiden had left Ulva to seek love and adventure, but now she knew the painful truth, that life often held disappointments and heartache beyond human control. Sometimes the greatest show of love was in giving up a loved one.

"I'm . . . I'm sorry, Father."

"Yer sister told me why ye had come. Och, I ne'er thought any seed of my manhood would go behind my back. Ye defied me! All for the sake of a lad." Folding his large arms across his chest, his expression softened as he asked, "And did ye get yer way?"

All the heartache she felt at that moment was mirrored in her face. "Nae! But I agreed to marry Robbie of the Campbell clan and I will hold to my word."

Having watched the fiery reunion between father and daughter from a distance, Duncan now stepped forward. "Yer lassie has been most amicable. She agreed there was no sense in delaying the ceremony since she was already within the bosom of my clan." There was an edge to Duncan's voice. Though the words were inoffensive there was a hostile tone to his voice. "It's glad I am that ye are here, Lachlan MacQuarie, or ye would hae *missed* seeing her joined forever to my nephew."

"Oh, would I now!" Lachlan stood nose to nose with his

old adversary. To Brianna's eyes they looked much like two hounds snarling over a bone as they sidestepped each other.

"Aye. But ye *are* here!" Duncan initiated peace by slapping Lachlan on the back. "And there is a wedding to put on."

Before anyone could offer any word of protest, Duncan took Brianna by the hand, hurrying her out to the stables as the mumbling throng followed close behind. It was Highland custom for bride and groom to ride pillion on the back of a strong gelding, thus Brianna mounted behind Robbie for the short ride to the castle chapel on the other side of the courtyard. On the back of the horse, in a leather pouch, was placed the marriage money, guarded by two strong Highlanders who walked on each side of the animal. A musical accompaniment of musicians playing harp, flute, and bagpipes proceeded.

Robbie's hands were gentle as he helped Brianna dismount. "I'll be good to ye, I promise I will," he said softly. "From this moment on we'll share our life. Try to be happy!"

Brianna forced a smile. "I will!" Entering the chapel, she stood tall and proud as she took the lighted candle the priest held forth. The holy man asked the standard questions as a matter of formality; if she was of age, if she swore that she and her betrothed were not within the forbidden degree of consanguinity, if her parents consented to the marriage, if the banns had been posted, and finally and most importantly of all, if she and her groom both gave free consent to the match.

"Then come forth, daughter, to be joined in this holiest of vows."

Brianna walked unsmilingly down the aisle, looking neither right nor left. Sobs choked in her throat, suffocating her, yet she somehow held them back so that none would hear. Oh, Ian! Ian! Clutching the folds of her gown, she somehow made it to that spot where Robbie and the priest awaited. There she knelt at her future husband's feet in a gesture of submission.

"Rise!"

Together they faced the priest and repeated their solemn vows. The priest sprinkled her with holy water and recited an intricate Mass. The ceremony unfolded so quickly that Brianna hardly remembered what she had said. Babbled words in a foreign tongue. And all the while she fought against crying, biting her lip so hard that it bled.

The joining of right hands concluded the transfer of a gift, Brianna's virginity for Robbie's protection and loyalty. Robbie then slipped onto three of his new wife's fingers, one after another, the blessed ring that signified marriage, a blessed circle of gold that would protect her from assault by demons.

The groom was the active party, bestowing not only the ring but also the customary gifts and presenting a charter of the marriage settlement along with thirteen coins as prescribed by Salic Law. The coins went eventually not to the bride but to the priest, the poor, or certain assistants, for the bride was not so much bought as invested with the mission of giving alms on behalf of the couple.

"With this ring I thee wed, with this gold I thee honor, and with this dowry I thee endow."

"A token of love and fidelity," the priest intoned. It was then the chapel doors were thrown open as the assembled guests looked on in surprise. Ian Campbell stood at the back, his face a mask of wretched misery. He had come too late! Duncan's snide grin told him so, even if the finality of the ceremony did not. It mattered little now just who Robbie was or to which family he belonged. Whoever he was, he was Brianna's husband now. All he could do was wish them well and say a final goodbye. Marriage was a bond that no man could break. Marriage was a sacrament, the most precious of all. All he could do was watch silently as the final phase of the ceremony was enacted. The groom was the recipient of the priest's kiss of peace. The groom then bent to transmit that kiss to his bride. Ian knew if he lived to be a hundred years old he would never face such devastating unhappiness as he did at that moment. It was as if a part of him had died. As his gaze met Brianna's, he read the same sadness in her eyes, such a poignant stare.

A blare of trumpets announced a different phase of the celebrating as the guests left the chapel. A show of generosity to those of lesser rank, including servants and villagers. Coins were thrown about in abundance. Brimming tankards of fiery whiskey were passed to all the guests.

"So . . . and did ye think to burst from my dungeon and carry off the bride?" Duncan's question was sarcastic, but he made no move to imprison Ian again. In truth, why should he? All had gone precisely as he had wanted.

"That was my intention. I would have, had the ceremony not been completed." Ian's eyes were hard as steel. "Who is Robbie? He is not your sister's lad. Aulay traveled north and gave inquiry."

"Ye will find out soon enough! But I warn ye. Nephew or not, I willna brook any more of yer defiance. The lassie is lost to ye. Accept that, Ian, and hae done wi' it." Turning his back, Duncan stalked off to join the revelers.

Ian pondered his uncle's words as he sat at the heavily laden trestle table. His uncle had sounded defiant, but not angry. What *was* to come? What was the truth that was to be revealed? He was anxious to know, hopeful that he had been wrong in fearing for Brianna. Perhaps his curiosity was the only thing that enabled him to get through the meal. He could not eat a bite, but was it any wonder? Even the fragrant, fruit-studded bannocks held no temptation for him.

After a dinner there was dancing, as a whirling, high-stepping jubilant, laughing throng of revelers gave vent to their joy. Brightly lit torches illuminated the steps of the dark, winding staircase that led to the bridal chamber. A chattering, drunken throng accompanied the newly married couple up the winding stairs and to their room.

The key element to the wedding was the blessing of the bedchamber and the bed to dispel any curse that might have compromised the couple's fertility and to wipe away any taint of female adultery. Robbie would never know how close his cousin had come to giving the priest concern. So many times he had nearly made Brianna his, and now he was torn between being thankful that he had not taken her virtue and disappointment that he had not been given at least one lovely memory to cherish.

As bride and groom took their places in bed under the watchful eyes of a circle of close relations, Ian nearly lost all self-control. Had he been a fool to come this far? What had he expected? For Brianna to throw herself into his arms, begging him to take her away? It was too late! What a wretched fool he was to stay and witness his own heart breaking!

"Ah, in this very bed will the seed be sown that will mend my heartache." Duncan looked on with a seemingly lecherous eye. He seemed to be waiting expectantly.

Once witnessed together in bed, the couple was to be left alone to consummate the marriage. The scene in the nuptial bed, which was a crucial element in marriage, symbolized what was at stake; power in and over private life. The Highland belief that honor, marriage, and a person's very being was for the sake of the clan. The betterment of all.

"But can I live with this? Can I?" Ian breathed, feeling an empty spot in that place where his heart had been.

The priest talked of death or annulment prior to the nuptial; the surviving party to the espousal was not free to remarry a brother, sister, or other relative of the other party. Relations by affinity were taboo to the fourth canonical degree and relations of consanguinity were taboo to the seventh degree.

"Have joy of each other . . ."

The guests started to leave, to give the newly wed couple time to be alone, but before the room emptied the chamber door was nearly unhinged. "By the love of God, I canna let ye do this, chief or no'. I canna! I canna! It is the greatest of evils." Cameron stood in the torchlight, his eyes shining with determination.

"By God, close yer mouth, old mon! Dinna speak words that will mean yer death." Duncan started forward with the intent of stopping Cameron from speaking, but Ian blocked his way. "Tell us, Cameron. Quickly. What evil?"

"The lassie and the laddie. Both from Lachlan MacQuarie's loins were born."

"What?" Ian had expected that something was wrong, but he'd never expected this. Surely the old man was mistaken. "It can't be."

"But it *is*." The silence was oppressive as the gaping crowd of people stared at Cameron in disbelief. "I was there. I saw it happen. Robbie is no Campbell. He is a MacQuarie. One of three children born. The lassie and laddie that were just wed can no' be allowed to bear a child, for they are related by the closest of bonds. They are brother and sister."

CHAPTER THIRTY-EIGHT

The torches' flickering flames illuminated the shocked faces of all the guests assembled in the bridal chamber. Silence reigned as Cameron's words were digested. The prattle of a senile old man or the truth?

"What are ye saying?" Lachlan MacQuerie stood as still as a statue, his voice a hissed shout. "Ye canna mean it."

"I do!" Cameron's eyes were sad as he looked toward Duncan.

"Speak and from this moment on any ties of friendship between us will be severed!" the Campbell chief growled.

Cameron drew back under the violence of the hostile blue-eyed stare, then shaking his gray-haired head, made the decision to put an end to what was begun. "I beg pardon and grieve. I held yer friendship as a precious thing, but I canna let ye endanger yer immortal soul or mine. 'Tis a grievous sin ye hae schemed to, Black Duncan, but now at last it will be at end."

Licking his lips, Cameron unfolded a tale both bizarre and demonic of what had gone on the night of Robbie's birth; of their entry into the castle after the battle, of witnessing the birth of a third bairn. "A male child."

All within the room gasped, and Brianna hurried to her father's side to take his hand, squeezing tightly. If what this man was saying was true then her mother's story had been true. She had not been delirious after all.

"A son for a son, that is what Duncan said, and yet I didna ken what he had in mind." The old man spoke of the old woman, of her stubborn refusal to part with the babe and the circumstances that led to her death.

"Ye so callously slew the midwife?" Lachlan's lower lip trembled his rage. "An old woman!"

"'Twas an accident but a blot on our souls nevertheless." Hanging his head, Cameron appeared to be a sincerely repentant man. "Wi'out her there was none to stop us from taking the child."

"Ye stole my son!"

"And Robbie!" Brianna was horrified. "Is my *brother?*"

"Aye! Upon my word he is. I hae no reason to lie to ye, lassie."

"But why, then? . . ." The answer was only too clear. "Blessed God!" Brianna was appalled. She had been used as an instrument of revenge to spite her father. Duncan had struck a foul blow and in so doing she had married and nearly bedded her own brother.

The shouting started then, everyone seemingly talking at once. Accusations. Denials. Anger. Louder and louder. It seemed everyone was shouting.

"Ye whoreson! Ye vile treacherous mon!" Lachlan flung his epithets at Duncan as everyone stared in stony silence. "Why? Why would ye do such a thing?"

"To seek reprisal, ye sneaking, back-stabbing bastard!" Duncan's eyes bulged in their sockets as he revealed his intent. "I took yer son awaiting this day and only a traitor's babbling tongue denied me." Baiting Lachlan, Duncan boldly boasted of the deed, heartlessly goading his adversary.

"Ye stole my infant son as reprisal for our feuding?"

"Nae! As well ye know, old mon. I did such a thing for vengeance's sake. For yer stabbing my son in the back and leaving him to lie all alone to shed his life's blood on the snow. 'Tis a thing I can never forgive, Lachlan MacQuarie. Anything that I hae done, ye rightly deserved."

"Killed yer son? I didna do such a thing unless it was in battle!" Lachlan hotly denied the charge.

"Ye struck him from behind by treachery and when I found him, he called out yer name. Over and over he whispered, *'MacQuarie! MacQuarie!'* Naming the one who so cruelly brought him down."

"'Tis a lie! No MacQuarie would strike down a man from behind. We are warriors, not assassins."

"I say ye are!"

Silence reigned once again, like the quiet before a devastating storm.

Brianna watched warily as her father and Duncan stared in angry fury at each other for a long time, knowing battle was inevitable. Blessed Saint Michael, the feud which all had thought over had now been rekindled.

"Father! Nae." She knew her words to be hopeless the moment she spoke. Her father was placed in an intolerable position. It was either fight or back down. She knew her father would choose to fight for his honor even though the MacQuaries were seriously outnumbered. Even so, she held on to his sword arm hoping to delay the inevitable.

"To arms! To arms!" Duncan Campbell dashed Brianna's hopes with his call to war. He laughed as his clansmen stripped every sword, shield, targe, and dirk from the wall.

The Campbells burst forth, pressing the MacQuaries back, but though Ian armed himself it was not for the reason Duncan supposed. Brandishing his sword, he fought against his uncle—not for him. Uppermost in his mind was Brianna. Above all, he would allow no harm to come to her.

What followed was a clashing and a slashing of swords, a bloody and violent melee. Hastening to join the battle, Robbie brandished a sword over his head, heeding the familiar cry, only to pull back. Which side should he fight for? He was in a quandary. Years of friendship and kinship had been cruelly obliterated by Duncan's revelation. He was a MacQuarie and not a Campbell as he had always believed. How then could he take arms against his own? Or for that matter, kill those who had nurtured him all these years at the fires of their hearths. In confusion he stepped back, drawn in two directions, and in that moment Brianna's heart went out to him.

"Robbie! Come stand beside me," she said gently, taking his hand to lead him to safety. Together they watched in prayerful silence as the battle exploded all around them like some ghastly dance.

Ian fought his way to Brianna, thrusting her against the wall to protect her with his sword. With a growl of warning, he wielded his broadsword. He would allow no one to come anywhere near her.

"Ian, ye are a traitor! Damned be ye, lad. Well, ye'll no hae yer lassie even now!" Bellowing an order that no MacQuarie was to be left alive, "including the lass," he surged toward Ian, his intent clearly written by his expression.

Two Campbells held the doorway but Ian was desperate to make an escape. It was the only chance he and Brianna had. "Brianna!"

"Nae!" She would not go and leave her father and newly found brother. If that meant her death then so be it. Stubbornly, she shook her head but her protestations were ignored. With determinedly strong hands he pushed her toward the corridor, his weapon darting this way and that to form a path. The tip of his blade shed Campbell blood, but he had no time to care for that. Only for Brianna.

"Ian!" Robbie thrust himself forward, making his decision to fight on the MacQuarie side. With a skill that belied his age and gentle temperament, he fought savagely, felling the two guards that blocked Ian's and Brianna's way. "Run for it, mon!"

"I willna leave! I willna leave, I say." Brianna was stubborn until a slicing sword engaged Ian's soft flesh. Realizing that her obstinacy might well mean his life, she capitulated to his urging. For the moment at least she would leave, but she would come back. Aye, with an army! She'd raise the MacDonalds, the MacGregors, the MacKinnons to avenge the wrong done today. It was her last thought as she turned to view the carnage, then followed Ian through the doorway.

CHAPTER THIRTY-NINE

Brianna and Ian ran for what seemed an eternity, looking behind them from time to time until they were certain there was no sign of pursuit. Coming to the stables, they quickly mounted two of the strongest looking horses and rode off, heading for the coast and freedom.

"We'll get a boat and sail to Ulva and alert the rest of the clan as to what has happened," she exclaimed, urging her horse to a frantic pace.

"Aye, but first we'll take a detour to a small stronghold of MacDonalds that I know about. Your father needs aid, lassie, if he's to last this day. Perhaps if Duncan realizes that it is not going to be a *rout*, that he will have to contend with others who will flock to the MacQuarie cause, he will cease the bloodshed."

"MacDonalds?" In Brianna's mind was Robbie's confession of his love for a MacDonald lassie.

He misunderstood the tone of her voice. "Don't sound so surprised. They are a branch of MacAlpin like your clan, with great reason to hold enmity toward Duncan. Dunstaffnage was once their home. I have little doubt but that this excuse to badger Duncan will be welcome." At her scowl he added, "'Tis a chance, lass."

Past the fertile fields of newly harvested rye and wheat

they rode with no pause for a rest. Ian swiveled in his saddle, looking over his shoulder at Brianna as she bravely and daringly kept up the pace he administered. She sat on her horse as expertly as any clan warrior, indeed looked as if she had been born on a horse. With her long red hair flying wildly behind her, she appeared to him much as the ancient Celtic goddess Epona must have looked ages ago. Pride for this woman he loved swept over him, and he vowed in that moment that they would never be parted again. She was *his* and it would always remain so until the day they both died.

Ian guided Brianna to the small remaining MacDonald stronghold on Argyll, a jumble of shattered and tumble-down stone walls. Scrambling down from her horse, seeking out the clan chief, she made an impassioned plea for aid. Once again, Ian felt admiration surge inside him. No noble warrior or titled English lady could have been more eloquent. In the end, she received the clan leader's pledge for help. The MacDonald war cry resounded in the air. Duncan would find a swarm of angry bees waiting to sting him.

Ian and Brianna rode all day, until their bodies ached for rest. So much had happened during the past hours that Brianna could scarcely believe it. Robbie Campbell was her brother! Even now she shook her head in amazement. Such a cruel hoax Duncan had played, pretending peace, proclaiming desire for a marriage to unite the clans, while all the time he planned a most heinous deed. She shuddered to think of the consequences, had she indeed consummated her marriage. Sweet Christ! Only the thought of Ian's love gave her the strength of mind to push such thoughts away. He had fought against his own clan for her! What greater proof of love was there than that?

"I love ye, Ian!" She shouted it out, feeling as if the burden of the world had been lifted from her shoulders. Never again would there be a barrier to their love. Never again!

"And I love you! Ah, that I could show you right now just how much, Brie! But I will. I will."

Once they were out to sea, sailing toward Ulva in a "borrowed" curach, he was true to his promise, holding her close, kissing and caressing her, despite his necessary attention to navigation. It was sweet teasing torture that was only ended once the small wicker-framed vessel was safely out to sea. Then and only then could their thoughts be turned to their mutual desire for one another.

Darkness brought a cold, heavy mist but Brianna and Ian did not care. Locked in each other's arms beneath Ian's heavy plaid, basking in the warmth of each other's bodies, they did not even notice the slight chill of the summer's eve.

"When I saw you standing by the bedside with Robbie, realized what was to come . . . You will never know how lost and helpless I felt, Brie," he whispered, compulsively tightening his fingers around her shoulders as if to reassure himself she was really there. "It was as if I died a little at that moment. I was miserable."

"As miserable as I was. I saw my life stretching out before me, a lonely existence without you." She closed her eyes to the pain that memory evoked.

"For me it was like the answer to a prayer when Cameron shouted out the truth! Forgive me, but I have never heard more welcome news." He tickled her ear with his tongue, sending shivers of fire up her spine. "Robbie's sister! Aye, I am glad, for it solves so many problems. At the same time it has given your father a son."

"A son!" She smiled as the importance of the new family member struck her. "Aye, not only I but Glenna will be benefited by that boon. Now perhaps Father *will* let her marry her Alastair. If . . ." Her smile faded as she remembered the fighting. "Oh, Ian, what if . . ." Her voice caught and she pressed her face into his shirt, wanting his comfort.

"We have to believe that all will be right. Your father is a fiercesome fighter. He will hold his own. I know Duncan. With the MacDonalds at the castle walls, he will soon have second thoughts about the merits of continuing the battle."

His voice held more confidence than he felt, but above all he didn't want her to worry. It was something that went far beyond her control or even his.

"I hope ye hae the sight!"

"We'll think of all the good things the day has brought. Your marriage to Robbie will be judged invalid. Now you can be mine. If you will have me. Rogue that I am." His eyes turned from bright blue to a darker, smokier hue, mirroring his desire. Brianna's heart hammered at the glitter of desire she saw.

"A brave and daring rogue who saved my life. Aye, I *will* have ye." Reaching out she clung to him as if she would never let him go.

"How long I've waited to hear you say it." His lips nuzzled against the side of her throat. He uttered a moan as her hands moved over the smoothly corded muscles of his shoulders. "Ah, how I love you to touch me." It seemed as if his breath was trapped somewhere between his throat and stomach. He couldn't say any more. The realization that she was finally to be his was a heady feeling that nearly made him dizzy as he brought his lips to hers. Such a potent kiss. As if he had never kissed her before.

In fact, Ian had the feeling that he was doing everything for the very first time as he made love to her. All memories of other women faded from his mind. Hers were the only arms he wanted around him, hers the only mouth he wanted to kiss, her softness the only reality in this hostile world of warring. She was the only woman he would ever love. Burying his face in the silky soft strands of her hair, he breathed in its fragrant scent and was lost to any other thought.

"Ian." Closing her eyes, Brianna awaited another kiss, her mouth opening to him like the soft petals of a flower as he caressed her lips with all the passionate hunger they both yearned for. Brianna loved the taste of him, the tender urgency of his mouth. Her lips opened to him for a seemingly endless onslaught of kisses. It was as if they were breathing one breath, living at that moment just for each other.

Desire that had been coiling within Brianna for so long, only to be unfulfilled, sparked to renewed fire, and she could feel his passion likewise building, searing her with its heat. They shared a joy of touching and caressing, arms against arms, legs touching legs, fingers entwining and wandering to explore.

Mutual hunger brought their lips back together time after time. She craved his kisses and returned them with trembling pleasure, exploring the inner softness of his mouth. The wickerwork and leather of the boat was hard against her back, yet at the moment she hardly noticed. All she was aware of was his tall, muscled length straining against hers.

"Brianna!" Desire writhed almost painfully within his loins. He had never wanted anything or anyone as much as he did her at this moment. It was like an unfulfilled dream just waiting to come true.

Pushing her tonnag aside, Ian's palm, firm and warm, slipped down the front of her gown, cupping the full curve of her breast. Lightly, he stroked until the peaks sprang to life under his touch, the once soft flesh now taut and aching. Then his hands were at her shoulder, tugging at the gown until her breasts were bare.

His breath caught in his throat as his blue eyes savored her. "Lovely!" And indeed she was, he thought, pausing to feast his eyes on the lush contours of her breasts. No longer forbidden fruit, he thought. Now she was *his*. Bending down, he worshipped her with his mouth, his lips traveling from one breast to the other in tender fascination. His tongue curled around the taut peaks, his teeth lightly grazing until she writhed beneath him. He savored the expressions that chased across her face, the wanting and the passion for him that were so clearly revealed.

A white mist hovered about the sky like the wisps of a bridal canopy. My bridal bed, Brianna thought, moving in sensuous fascination against him. Her hands crept around Ian's neck, her fingers tangling and tousling the thick waves of his black hair as she breathed a husky sigh. How wonderful it was to be loved!

The chilled air caressed Brianna's skin as Ian undressed her, slipping her gown over her head. She caught fire wherever he touched her, burning with an all-consuming need. She shivered in his arms and, fearing it was from the night air, he gathered her closer, covering her body even more tightly with his to keep out the chill. With tender concern he tugged at the plaid, giving her the largest portion, tucking it beneath the firm curve of her buttocks.

"I'm not cold!" she whispered. "It's just that I want you so." Now she knew how he had felt. If she had known then what she knew now, she would never have pushed him away.

"Brie!" A shudder racked through him as he pushed her away. Just for a moment. Quickly, he stripped away his own clothes and Brianna took her turn to appraise him. The image of broad, bronzed shoulders, wide chest, flat belly, and well-formed legs would forever be branded in her mind. Reaching out she touched him, her hands sliding over the hard smoothness of his shoulders, moving to the crisp hair of his chest. Ian had three scars and she lightly traced each one with her finger. "MacQuaries?"

"Nae. That is a reminder of my time at Bannockburn when we sent the English fleeing. I was little more than a boy then and gloried at war. Now I regret every time I wielded my sword if it caused your kindred pain."

"Then ye dinna believe Duncan's story, that a MacQuarie stabbed his son in the back?"

His fingers entwined themselves in her flaming hair, pulling her face closer. "I used to, but not anymore. I can see how an ocean of blood can be shed because of one misunderstanding. There's more to the laddie's death than we know. I sense it." His teeth nipped gently at her lip. "But come, let us put it out of our minds for the moment." He pulled her closer, rolling her over until they were lying side by side, and she felt a great pleasure in the warmth and power of the firmly muscled body straining so hungrily against hers.

He kissed her again, his knowing, seeking lips moving with tender urgency across hers, his tongue finding again the inner warmth and sweetness of her mouth. His large body covered hers with a blanket of warmth. Brianna felt the rasp of his chest hair against her breasts and answered his kiss with sweet, aching desire. But kisses weren't enough.

"Ian . . . love me," she breathed.

"In due time." His hands caressed her, warming her with their heat. They took sheer delight in the texture and pressure of each other's body. Sensuously, he undulated his hips between her legs, and every time their bodies caressed, each experienced a shock of raw desire that encompassed them in fiery, pulsating sensations. Then his hands were between their bodies, sliding down the velvety flesh of her belly, moving to that place between her thighs that ached for his entry. His gentle probing brought sweet fire, curling deep inside her with spirals of pulsating sensations. Then his hands left her, to be replaced by the hardness she had glimpsed before, entering her just a little then pausing.

"Tonight I make you my wife, Brie. To my heart, my mind, Robbie acted as *my* proxy. The ceremony today was ours. Do you feel the same?"

"Aye." Every inch of her tingled with an intense arousing awareness of his body.

Bending his head to kiss her again, he moved his body forward just as a wave rocked the boat. The surge of the water pushed him deep within her, fusing their bodies. There was only a brief moment of pain, but the other sensations pushed it away. Brianna was conscious only of the hard length of him creating unbearable sensations as he began to move within her. Capturing the firm flesh of her hips, he caressed her in the most intimate of embraces. His rhythmic plunges aroused a tingling fire, like nothing she had ever imagined. It was as if they were falling over the edge of a cliff together. Falling. Falling. Never quite hitting the ground. The rocking of the boat coincided with their own pulsations, and she arched herself up to him, fully expressing her love.

Ian groaned softly, the blood pounding thickly in his head. His hold on her hips tightened as the throbbing shaft of his maleness possessed her again and again, moving up and down with the waves. Instinctively, Brianna tightened her legs around him, certain she could never withstand the ecstasy that was engulfing her body. It was as if the night shattered into a thousand stars, bursting within her. Arching her hips, she rode the storm with him. As spasms overtook her she dug her nails into the skin of his back.

A sweet shaft of ecstasy shot through Ian and he closed his eyes, whispering her name. Even when the intensity of their passion was spent they still clung to each other, unable to let this magical moment end. They touched each other gently, wonderingly.

"Now you are truly my lassie! *My* wife. Och, and such a passionate one you are." He nibbled playfully at her ear.

"Am I now? And are ye not pleased?"

"Aye! But not surprised." Indeed, Ian was not surprised by the passion she expressed. Her lovemaking was as fiery as her hair. Indeed, she made love with all the same daring that she lived. She was a sensual woman who was more than his equal in passion, the perfect mate.

Brianna shivered again, but this time it was from the cold. A chilling fog was slowly engulfing the curach. She smiled as Ian massaged her body with slow, lingering movements, bringing warmth with his touch. It promised to arouse them to each other again, but he shook his head regretfully, pulling her gown over her head, helping her into her garments.

"Though I would like nothing better than to make sweet love to you forever, I had best look to where we are going." Tilting his head, he looked up at the sky. "Och, I do not like it at all. A dratted fog is rolling in. It will detain us. By my calculations, however, we are right on course." He kissed her lips gently, then hurriedly dressed himself. Bundling her in the warmth of his plaid, he held her close. "Try to sleep, Brianna. It's been a harrowing day and you must be near exhaustion."

She laughed. "Aye. Making love is strenuous, Ian dear. Ye should hae told me. But are ye sure ye want me to sleep?" She touched his lips in a smiling kiss, then pulled away.

"Nae!" His eyes roamed up and down her body, remembering the pleasure he had found there. "I do not want ye to, but ye must. And I must tend to navigating this wee ship if I am going to get you back to Ulva safely." An incredibly tender expression crossed his face. "You are the most precious thing in my life, Brie." Unexpectedly, he gathered her close against him, shuddering as their bodies embraced, but then he pulled away. "Now, do not tempt me. Close your eyes and when you awaken you'll be back at home. Our home if I have my way."

Though Brianna would have argued she gave in to his plea. The gentle sway of the curach rocked her, and sooner than she might have thought, she settled into a deep sleep, welcoming the warmth of Ian's arms as he at last gathered her close again.

CHAPTER FORTY

A cold spray of ocean mist splashed into Brianna's face, awakening her. She stirred, stretching her arms and legs in slow, easy motions. Feeling warmth against her flesh, she opened her eyes, remembering all that had happened. Not Robbie but *Ian* was with her. It had not been a dream after all! Ian was sitting beside her, his steady breathing rustling the strands of her hair. Her heart quickened as she turned her eyes in his direction.

"Good morrow!" Ian felt an aching tenderness. She looked so young, so vulnerable snuggled up against him. He felt a tightening inside. Just looking at her rekindled a fire deep within him.

Brianna flushed under the scrutiny of his eyes as the passion they had shared passed between them. "I thought perhaps I had been dreaming."

"Nae, it was real. You are here with me and I will never let you go!" Bending forward, grasping her shoulders, he kissed her long and lingeringly, running his hands through her hair, whispering that she was and always would be his treasure. When at last he broke away he was smiling. "I'm glad you are with me."

"So am I." Her hand found his and squeezed tightly.

"Where are we?" Sitting up, she stared out at the sea mist that engulfed them, a blinding swirl of white.

"I wish I knew. Somewhere off Mull, I believe." He tried to keep the tone of his voice calm for more than the fog concerned him. The wind was starting to blow, and though it would push out the fog, he didn't like it. A fiercesome storm was brewing. He could read it in the churning of the sea, smell it in the air. Instinctively, he gathered her into his arms as if to protect her from what was to come.

"Ian, what is it? I feel a tenseness in yer body that wasn't there last night. Ye are worried."

"There is going to be quite a gale. We'll have to brace ourselves, that's all." He stroked her hair again, remembering last night. Never had he realized that love could be like that, such a shattering ecstasy as to be almost pain. And then this morning it was a gentler emotion, such an overwhelming need to protect her that he would give up his own life for her. That is how he felt at this moment. No matter what happened to him he would protect Brianna.

"I hate storms! When I was a child my father told me that they were caused by huge sea beasties growling. And yet when I am in yer arms I hae no fear." Reaching up, she touched his cheek with her fingers. "I feel safe with ye, my love."

"Brie!" He cupped her face in his hand, kissing her soft open lips. Like a flower opening to sunshine, she moved her mouth upon his, feeling again the wondrous enchantment of the night before.

Lifting her arms, she encircled his neck and wound her fingers in his damp, dark hair, clinging to him, wanting him to love her again. "'Tis too bad that it is so chilled this morning, for I long so to be naked in yer arms."

"Oh?" Ian's hand reached out to caress her, sliding his fingers over the soft mounds of her breasts. Her body, pressed so tightly against his, drove him beyond all thought, all reason. "The cold should be no problem to those in love.

I'll show you." Lifting up his shirt and her gown, he caressed her bared flesh against his own. His hand moved over her body from shoulder to thigh, caressing the flat plain of her belly, then moved to cup her breast. "I can keep you warm. See?" The warm safety of his arms was a blissful haven from the storm.

"Aye." Oh how she loved the feel of her bare breasts against his chest. She arched against him in sensual pleasure. He had initiated a hunger in her that she had never even known existed, a desire for him that could only be appeased by blending with him as they had last night. Her whole world was Ian, now and forever more. She closed her eyes, sighing as he took her mouth in a hard, deep kiss. For a long time she relished being close to him, just being held by him.

"Oh, my darling lass. I love you so much!" he whispered huskily. The words trailed off as his mouth traced a pattern of fire on hers. Their lips caressed and clung, smiled against each other as they held each other tightly.

Ian's hand moved down her stomach and into the soft flesh between her thighs. Tremors shot through her in pulsating waves. She lifted her hips, seeking him. The whole world seemed to be rocking crazily, like an enormous wave crashing over her. Only the harsh recognition that it was indeed the sea and not her desire that was causing the tumult, brought her back to reality.

"By Saint Michael!" Ian sat up and looked around him, peering out at the ocean, straining his eyes for any sight of land. "The storm! Never have I seen one take shape so quickly." He damned himself for being taken unaware, for letting his attention wander from the boat for even a moment when he had known a storm was coming. But Brianna had been so tempting.

"Are the water beasties angry?"

"Angry and threatening. We're going to have to weather out the storm, Brianna. What ever happens, no matter what, hold on to the side of the boat. Do you hear me?"

"Aye!" Her heart lurched in her breast as she realized fully the danger they were in.

"Even if something should happen to me, do not let go. Do you understand? You will be safe as long as you stay inside. The *curach* is sturdy. It will float. Remember!"

Brianna nodded, holding on to Ian as tightly as she could, praying that the fearful gust of wind and turbulent waves would soon abate. Oh, how she suddenly wanted to be on land again. Never would Ulva and the MacQuarie side of Mull seem so dear.

The small boat rocked from side to side as the ocean pounded viciously against the stern. Ian looked nervously over his shoulder. "Dear merciful God," he whispered. Pulling away from her, he picked up the oars that lay in the bottom of the boat.

"What is it? Tell me, what is wrong?" Alarm rang through her, hurrying her heart, jangling her nerves, and stretching her courage to its limit. He confided in her, counting on her bravery. "The fear gnaws at me that we are off course and heading ashore. I have got to stabilize our course."

"Ashore?" The dark gray basalt rocks up ahead seemed to be drawing them, pulling them. Staffa! Brianna knew the danger of capsizing upon the jagged rocks. Staffa was an island to be avoided at all costs! She cursed her impetuous nature which had led them into this travail. It had been her idea to sail to Ulva. Now perhaps her daring would be the death of them both. "What can I do to help?"

"Just sit quiet!"

"I willna just sit by and be swallowed by the waves! Tell me, Ian." She crept cautiously toward him on hands and knees, intending to help him at the oars. A violent wave sent her sprawling, unbalancing the boat as she hit the side.

"Brianna!" On both sides of the boat the treacherous sea flung itself in massive crests, the spray whistling into the air. The rumble of the water was so loud it caused the boat to vibrate. "Are you all right?"

"Aye! Oh, Ian, what are we going to do?"

"Stay clear of the rocks," Ian shouted. "Perhaps I can steer the boat." The roar of another wave drowned out his words.

Suddenly, the boat capsized and Brianna was hurled into the air by a giant wave. A scream tore from her throat as she felt herself hit the water. She was engulfed in icy blackness. "Ian!" she cried silently. Blindly floundering about, she searched for him in the watery prison. No! This could not be happening. "Ian!" She choked out his name between mouthfuls of sea water. Where was he?

Taking a deep breath, she plunged into the water's depths, searching beneath the boat. There was no sign of Ian. Had the water beasties captured him? Was he even now being taken to their lair? In agonized fear for him she cried out his name. She wanted them to take her too. She couldn't live without him!

Frantically fighting the water, Brianna renewed her search, but he had vanished. He was *gone*. The burden of his fate was like a weight. She had cajoled him into bringing her here. He had stolen the boat just to get her back to her island. Now he had been devoured by the storm. "Ian!"

The watery prison seemed almost endless as she put one arm before the other, fighting for survival. Somehow she had to hope that Ian was struggling just as hard, that he was even now swimming for the shore. She didn't want to believe that death had been his fate. No! Oh, please let that be the answer. He was struggling toward the shore just as she was now.

She fought the strength of the ocean but as a large wave tugged her under, Brianna choked and swallowed some of the salty water. Oh, please! She had so much to live for. Blessed Saint Michael! Her life was still ahead of her. And Ian! She could not exist without him. Please, dear God!

As if in answer to her prayers, the flow of the water changed direction and rose to aid in her combat with the elements. She found herself drifting toward the shore. From childhood Brianna had known how to swim; it was something she always enjoyed, but that was in lochs and burns, not in such threatening water. Still, she knew if only she could reserve her strength and let the sea carry her to land she might survive. Trying to control her breathing, to relax despite her fear of the icy ocean, she determined that she would be the victor over the icy sea. She was strong. She was a MacQuarie! So thinking, when the next huge waves appeared she rode with them, and when they ceased she paddled in the direction of the land.

The ocean seemed to go on forever, the tall monoliths of Staffa were a large ominous speck in the distance. The longer she struggled the more hopeless the situation seemed. The icy water robbed her of her stamina. Her strength was wavering. She was weary. Despite her resolve she was just too tired to go on. Help me! Please. If there were any sea fairies to aid her, she needed them now. Opening her mouth she gurgled a plea for herself and for Ian.

A rock struck her foot and she realized that all was not lost. Not yet. Just a little further and she could make it. Somehow she had to find the courage and the physical prowess to stay alive! Fight. She must survive the waters. She would not give up.

Hands reached out for her, grabbing her, pulling her ashore. Ian? The salt water stung her eyes so she could not see. "Ian!" A hazy figure loomed in front of her. With a final effort she shook her head and squinted her eyes. Though half blind, she saw *her*. A witch! Dear merciful Saint Michael! A water hag!

Instinct told her to run. Run. Nimbly escaping the grasping hands, she sprang to her feet and sprinted across the rocks as fast as her weary legs would carry her. It was not fast enough. The hag had closed the distance and now was fast pulling at her hair. Screaming in outrage, Brianna pulled free of her grasp, fighting with all her waning strength. It was no use. With a shriek of despair she gave in to the darkness that swirled before her eyes and fell unconscious to the ground.

PART III

A LOVER'S TRYST

The Isle of Staffa

> But pleasures are like poppies spread:
> You seize the flow'r, its bloom is shed!
> Or like the snow-fall in a river,
> A moment white-then melts forever.
> —BURNS, *TAM O'SHANTER*

CHAPTER FORTY-ONE

A moaning wail whispered in the darkness, an eerie song as breathless as the wind. It echoed over and over. Haunting. Chilling. Brianna struggled to open her eyes. "Please. Help me," she murmured.

It was as if she were walking down a long, dark tunnel, groping about, struggling to come into the light. A figure waited for her at the tunnel's end and she reached out. Ian? She whispered his name over and over, needing him, wanting him, but the fiercesome mourning song was driving him away. That howling song!

Sea witches! They were singing! Brianna gasped raggedly for air, trying to scream. But no sound came. Her throat burned like fire. *"Glastig!"* she tried to say but her throat constricted, she was choking. Sea fairies! Singing their song. A frightening image hovered in her mind of the deceiving crones, part seductive woman, part goat.

She remembered seeing *her*. Run! Get away! Kicking and thrashing, she tried to move but was helpless. She was hot, burning up. The sea witch was trying to smother her, roast her alive. No!

The eerie song moaned again and Brianna put her hands over her ears in an attempt to block it out. The sea fairies always sang, trying to entice a human mate, luring them into the sea. *Ian!* "Nae, he is mine!" she croaked, tossing her head from side to side. Visions swirled through her mind— Ian lying on the rocks as a swarm of unearthly beings chanted over him.

Blindly, uncontrollably, she struck out like a wild thing at the figures. She would never see Ian again. They would hold him captive. "Please!" Opening her eyes to slits, she saw one of them bending over her.

"Sleep!" a voice said, touching her with fingers that were strangely gentle, like a soft summer breeze. Again warmth surrounded her but this time she didn't struggle. Unconsciously, she reached out, touching warm flesh, grasping tightly with her hands. "Ye will be all right!" It sounded like a promise. Again the whispering song. Despite her fear it lulled her to sleep.

When Brianna awoke she was lying on her back, swathed in soft wool plaid. Opening her eyes, she gasped as her gaze swept over the woman holding vigil by her side. A witch surely, and yet the pale face held a look of kindness. "Who? . . ."

"Hush. Ye must get back yer strength." The visage smiled with all the sweetness of an angel.

Brianna took a deep breath and slowly appraised the woman. The burnished brown hair was streaked with gray and hung wildly about her shoulders framing a strangely attractive face despite its thinness. Nearly pretty with a bold prominent nose and high cheekbones. A witch? There were tiny lines at the corner of the woman's eyes and mouth. She looked to be about twice Brianna's age and appeared to be thin despite her baggy dark blue gown.

"Where . . . where am I?" Brianna whispered, trying to focus her eyes in the dimly lighted room.

"My island!"

"Yer island?" Brianna shivered as her gaze roamed over her surroundings. Not a room at all but a yawning cavern of dark rock, lit only by torchlight.

"I pulled ye from the ocean and brought ye here to care for ye. Poor wee lassie! I couldna let the waters claim ye."

"Aye!" Brianna remembered everything clearly now. This then was the frightening woman who had fished her from the water, chased her and pulled at her hair. Was she to believe that she should have no fear of her? Quite the contrary, she felt apprehensive despite the woman's smile as she remembered being told of a mad "witch" who inhabited Staffa. Even fishermen were told to avoid that awesome stone-columned isle for fear of coming into the harridan's power. Now Brianna was in that fiercesome woman's company. As prisoner? "My throat . . . my chest."

"Ye swallowed part of the sea. I had to push it out of yer lungs." Opening a small leather bag, she drew forth a gnarled root, a mortar and pestle. "I'll fix ye something that will soothe the soreness of yer throat."

Brianna shook her head. She would have no part of any witch's potions. "Nae! My throat feels much better and I . . ." Pausing she listened. "That song!" Brianna shuddered. "It sounds like ghosts."

Throwing back her head, the woman cackled. "Not ghosties. Just the sea singing. It echoes through the caves like a chant. *An Uamh Ehinn*. The musical cave I call it. It soothes me, but then I've grown used to it." Rising to her feet, the woman walked slowly across the cave and poked about the embers of a fire. "Are ye cold?"

"Aye." Brianna tried to sit up, but the whirling inside her head caused her to lie back down. She was so dizzy, so weary. Tears stung her eyes as she remembered Ian! "Was there . . . a laddie wi' me?" The woman shook her head no. "No sign of him?" He was lost to her then. Such a devastating thought. To have had such happiness only to lose it. "Oh, Ian!" Why had she been saved and not Ian? The thought of being without him unleashed a flood of tears. Turning over on her side, she gave vent to her pain in great gulping sobs.

"Here, lassie, dinna cry." The woman tried to comfort Brianna but her torrent of weeping was uncontrollable.

"He is gone!" Mumbling through her tears, Brianna told her story of losing Ian in the storm. "I canna live wi'out him."

"Stop that!" Hunkering down, the woman reached out and shook Brianna by her shoulders. "Weeping will do no good. Believe me, I know. I hae cried an ocean full of tears but they canna soothe my pain."

"Yer pain?" Brianna wiped her eyes. There was something so tragic, so mournful in the woman's expression. She reminded Brianna of a lost soul. "Tell me."

Warily, the woman shook her head. "Nae! There are those who pose a danger to me. I canna tell ye."

"Are ye mourning someone? Ye seem so lonely." The sudden tensing of the woman's body, the look of utter despair mirrored in her eyes, answered Brianna's question. "Someone ye loved deeply?"

Fear etched the woman's face. "No one! I hae loved no one! No one, I say!" Rising quickly to her feet she flitted about the cavern like a cornered moth. "I shouldna hae brought ye here. Nae! Nae! Far better for me to be all alone. *Alone!*" Clutching her hands to her breasts, she gave forth a piercing wail then vanished through the mouth of the cave leaving Brianna all alone.

The waters swirling around Ian were freezing, debilitating. Trying to ignore his discomfort, he strained against the waves searching for Brianna. He had seen her go over the side, buffeted up by a huge handlike wave when the *curach* turned over in the water. Then it was as if she had just disappeared! Though he had gone below the surface of the ocean again and again he had not been able to find her. Even so, he had been determined not to give up! Brianna was his heart, his soul.

Taking a deep breath, Ian dove deep within the sea, stubborn in his resolve. He stayed under until his lungs were screaming for air, then surfaced. Treading water he continued his search, but at last he had to admit defeat. He was winded, his strength was giving out.

Keeping his head above water, Ian looked around him, taking note of the huge dark shape looming in front of him. It looked much like the massive trunks of a forest, bundled together, strange looking stone formations. Seemingly as tall as a castle. An island of sorts.

"An island!" he gasped. An island meant people and boats. He'd procure the aid of the fishermen who surely inhabited the land mass. Aye, he'd get help in finding Brianna.

How long he had been in the water, Ian did not know. He only knew his arms ached, his legs were numb, his breath was coming far too hard. He had to face the possibility that the icy water might very well be his grave. He was sinking beneath the surface but the memory of Brianna gave him new resolve. No! He would *not* give in to death. He would challenge the water. Aye. He would live to find Brianna! He would win! If he could only manage to survive, make the short distance to shore. That thought gave him renewed strength, and he struck out again, arm over arm, legs propelling his body through the water until something hard scraped his feet. He could feel solid ground beneath the water.

With a final surge of strength he fought his way through the last few feet of water and pulled himself up. Stumbling upon the shore, crawling across the slippery rocks, Ian fought for breath, then glanced in the direction of the ocean. The tide was coming in and if he wasn't careful he could be swept back out into the sea again.

"I can't stop now," he wheezed, scrambling over the slimy seaweed and jagged rocks. He had to find help, had to initiate a renewed search for Brianna. That thought drove him on to the point of total, unrelenting exhaustion. Black splotches danced before his eyes as he walked endlessly, but he refused to succumb to unconsciousness. He hadn't come this far to give up now. With determination he stayed on his feet, wandering about.

Rock. Nothing but rock. Huge basalt columns that rose up to the sky, crags, and caverns. There was no sign of life. No boats. No cottages. No vegetation. The longer he walked the more certain Ian was that there were no people. An uninhabited island. A never-ending acreage of nothingness. He was marooned with no visible way of getting off except throwing himself into the sea to swim endlessly. He had hoped . . .

Collapsing to the hard rocky ground, Ian realized he could not take another step. He was tired. So tired. Disappointment and disillusionment had taken a toll on his stamina, and he felt as feeble as a newborn lamb. With a deep sigh he ceased his struggle.

Surely, he must have lost his mind, for in the silence he seemed to hear music. He struggled with such an illogical thought. It was impossible. If he'd had the strength he might have laughed. Music! Eerie voices, muffled by the wind, groaning. Was it a portent of something evil?

Am I dead? Wearily he lifted his head. Surely, this was not heaven. Purgatory then? All the stories he'd heard of such things came back to haunt him. "No!" He urged himself to be calm. His head ached. The dead felt no pain.

He strained to hear the strange sound again to discern its direction. To the left? The right? Ahead of him or behind? He peered into the misty darkness hoping to see at least a silhouette, but could only see the dark water and gray swirling fog. Closing his eyes, he let the seductive darkness enfold him.

CHAPTER FORTY-TWO

Brianna sat upon the cold damp rocks gazing solemnly into the swirling waters. Hugging her arms around her knees, she breathed deeply of the sea air, remembering so vividly that night when Ian had held her in his arms and made love to her. How strange that the ocean should yield such happy memories and yet such tragedy as well.

The wind swirled around her, whipping thick strands of her flaming hair into her face. Reaching up, she brushed the silken threads away, not at all surprised to find her cheeks wet with a mixture of salt spray and tears. Brianna had spent the last few days in a haze of grief, haunted by tortured visions of that tragic moment when her happiness had been shattered upon the crest of a violent wave.

"Oh, Ian!" Never had she felt such overwhelming despair, an emptiness, as if a part of her soul had died.

Turning her face toward the sea, she watched as the foaming waves hit the stone cliffs with noisy fury. The expanse of water was an awesome reminder of her helplessness and her grief. Oh, how she wanted to get off this sullen, deserted island as soon as possible, to go back home, but she was trapped by the same waves that had so tumultuously brought her here. She was marooned with that strange woman who at times seemed more than a bit daft.

Apprehension for that woman gnawed at her, for she was not at all reassured that the woman was not a witch. Surely, there were times when she acted very strangely, murmuring to herself, showing a strange fear whenever Brianna asked her name, hiding within a dream-world shell of secrecy. It was unnerving and very puzzling. Yet, if not for this woman, Brianna knew she might well be dead. She had shared her cave, given Brianna food, and tried to soothe her grief with mumbled words of comfort. Even so, the woman made Brianna nervous, uneasy. There were times when she seemed a congenial companion, sympathetic, gentle, kind, but at other times her change of mood was frightening.

There were those in the islands far to the north who told of fairy-seal-women, beings who chose human husbands, came ashore, and then suddenly vanished. Was this woman one of them? It was said that they were very beautiful and surely the woman of the isle gave the impression that she must have been very lovely once. Brianna found herself watching, wondering if her new companion would suddenly doff her sealskin and plunge into the waves to be seen no more.

Had she? Where was she now? Brianna wondered. There were times when she hovered by Brianna's elbow and other times when she seemed to just vanish. But no, she had not disappeared after all. She could see her gathering driftwood for the fire, bending and stooping as if each little stick was a rare treasure. She was so self-reliant, not depending on anyone or anything for her comfort except her own skills, and yet Brianna was struck by how lonely it must be not to have a family. No clan! Who or what was she? And what had drawn her here? Was she a witch or fairie kin?

Brianna had tried to learn the story of what had brought the woman to Staffa, but all she had gotten for her efforts was silence. The woman refused to talk about herself, preferring instead to ask Brianna questions.

"I'm called Brianna," she had answered, "and I hae a

sister who is the mirror image of me. And a new-found brother."

Strange how despite her disquiet about the woman, Brianna had babbled so much about her childhood. The pranks she and her sister had played, the love they shared for their father. Brianna had noticed a smile trembling at the corners of the woman's mouth. When she had revealed her bold plan for winning the man that she loved, of extorting her sister's promise to take her place, then traveling to Argyll to speak with her lover's clan chief, the woman had actually laughed. It was only when she had mentioned the name *Campbell* that the woman had turned quite pale, as if that name held terror for her. But though Brianna had tried to find out why, it had been useless. She had seemed again to enter into her own private world and Brianna had wondered what thoughts tortured the poor soul.

Seeing the familiar form of the woman coming her way now, Brianna got to her feet and walked to meet her, granting her a semblance of friendship. "Here, let me hae a bit of that. It looks like a heavy load."

"Not so heavy, but a wee bit cumbersome." Thankfully, she gave up half of the pieces to Brianna. "There are some fine clams. I saw them. Just as soon as I hae started a fire I'll go get us a few. 'Twill be a welcome change from fish and seaweed, I would be thinking."

"Aye." Oh, what Brianna would not have given for a slice of venison. Fish, fish, fish, that's all she ate now, and yet she scolded herself for her ungratefulness. Without this woman she might well have gone hungry. "I'll give ye a hand gathering the clams. My father used to say I might hae been a fine fisherman were I not a lass."

"And indeed ye might hae been." The woman smiled sadly as if somehow Brianna's conversation brought to mind her own memories. Thoughtfully, she spread the pieces of driftwood on the rocks to dry. Brianna did the same.

"My father is such a fine, brave mon."

"Aye, my father was a fine mon too. Brave yet very, very kind to me and to my brother." Her eyes held a faraway look for just a moment as if remembering.

"Ye had a brother?"

The woman stiffened. "Aye. Once, but no longer." As if to put an end to the conversation, she hurried on ahead of Brianna, making her way to the cave. There she busied herself with stoking the small fire that kept them warm.

No, Brianna thought. I am not going to let her keep evading me this way. Her curiosity was much too fierce to pretend that she just didn't care about this woman's identity. If she was a witch or one of the fairy folk, if that was why she was so fiercely secretive, then Brianna wanted to know.

Coming up behind the woman, she laid a gentle hand on her shoulder. "Are ye angry wi' yer brother? Is that why ye look so sad? Or is that ye are afraid of something?"

"Afraid?"

The woman drew back, looking this way and that as if she wanted to run. Sensing her intent, Brianna blocked her way. "Please, don't run away. I won't hurt ye. I want to be yer friend."

"'Tis no such thing." Never had Brianna seen so much pain reflected in anyone's eyes as she did now. "Betrayal is all ye get for opening up yer heart."

"Did yer brother betray ye?"

Nervously, the woman brushed the hair from her face, shaking her head as if to clear it of unpleasant memories. "I canna remember all. Only that I can never return."

"To yer *clan?*"

"I can never go back to them, to my brother."

She was not a witch then. Brianna breathed a sigh of relief. She was just a poor daft woman who seemed to have been greatly wronged in some way. Driven from the bosom of her clan perhaps, but why? There were many reasons for being exiled—disobedience, going against the good of the clan, harm to another clan member. The system of clan justice was administered by a *brieve* who proportioned fines and imposed punishment for offenses. Had she been sentenced for a crime? What had this woman done?

"Why? Why can ye never go back?" As she pulled away, Brianna grasped her hand, holding her firmly. "Trust me. I will help ye if I can. I owe ye a debt of gratitude for pulling me out of the sea. I want to be yer friend."

Eyes like that of a wounded animal looked back at Brianna. "I dared to love . . ."

"To love? Who did ye love? Who has hurt ye?"

Burying her face in her hands, sinking to her knees, the woman mumbled piteously, "I canna remember all. My head aches when I try. All I know is that my heart is broken. The mon that I loved more than life itself is gone. Like yer love. Gone."

"I'm so sorry!" Reaching out, Brianna stroked the woman's head in a sympathetic gesture of comfort, trying to piece together what might have happened. Had she fallen in love with a man from a rival clan? Or a priest? Someone forbidden?

Wiping away her tears, the woman looked up. "Ye remind me of myself many years ago. Yer tears became my tears as I remembered." Her blue eyes widened as the woman put a hand to her throat. "Nae. It canna be. It canna be. Sweet merciful Jesus! *Morgan.*" A fit of trembling shook the woman from head to toe.

Brianna followed the line of the woman's vision, suddenly fearful of what she might see. A ghost? Stiffening her shoulders, she prepared herself for the most unearthly of sights. Even so, she was totally stunned by the visage that stood before her. If it was a ghost it was one whose presence she welcomed. Rising slowly to her feet she moved toward him, choking out his name. *"Ian!"*

CHAPTER FORTY-THREE

Ian's breath caught in his throat as he stared at Brianna. Had he gone mad? Was she *here?* He dared not blink for fear she might vanish into the misty haze that enshrouded the island. "Brie?" Realization that she was real was like an elixer, giving him renewed strength. He had cursed this barren isle and the fate that had brought him here, now he blessed it. "Brianna?"

She looked like a kelpie standing there in the early morning sunlight, her hair hanging down her back in glistening, flaming strands. Reverently, he worshipped her with his eyes, the slim curve of her neck, her profile with the haughty uptilt of her nose, the soft swell of her breasts as they strained against the finely woven woolen of her gown.

"Blessed Saint Michael, I thought ye were . . ." Brianna's throat went dry as she stared at him, mesmerized by the potency of his gaze. In his face she read her own longing and her heart gave a crazy leap as he moved toward her. Then he was sweeping her up in his arms in an embrace that crushed the breath from her, but she didn't care. For the moment nothing mattered except that somehow she was being given a second chance at happiness. Perhaps then Staffa was magical after all. It had given her back her love.

"When I saw you go over the side, when I couldn't find you I thought . . ." He buried his face in her hair, content for the moment just to hold her.

"I died a hundred times thinking . . ." She clung to him fiercely. Forgetting for a moment that they were not alone on the isle, she slipped her hands inside the neck of his shirt, shuddering at the warmth of his skin. She lifted her face for Ian's kiss but the rasping sound of indrawn breath behind her reminded Brianna of the other woman's presence.

"He isna my Morgan, though he is just as tall, just as dark of hair," she was whispering, a look of consternation still etched on her face. "Who is he?"

"Who is *she?*" Ian asked, eyeing the woman warily, in much the same manner Brianna had affected upon first seeing her. He allowed his eyes to drop to the slightly tattered garments, the hair spilling over the woman's shoulders in wild disarray. Quickly, he crossed himself.

"I know what ye are thinking, but she's *not*. She's just a poor tortured lassie who has faced some sort of tragedy." Pulling free of Ian's arms, Brianna hovered over Staffa's lady as if to give credence to her words. "She did in fact save my life and for that I am grateful."

Ian breathed a deep sigh. "Then if that is true, if I can thank her for finding you here, my love, then I am deeply grateful." He bowed gallantly. "Ian Mac Niall of the clan Campbell at your service."

"Campbell!" She gasped the name like an omen of evil, then taking to her heels, fled the cave as if she'd just come face to face with the very devil himself.

"Catch her, Ian! Don't let her go!" Brianna followed Ian in pursuit of the frightened woman, who led them a merry chase up and down over slippery rocks, across a small burn indented in the rock, past the singing cave. Only when she stumbled and fell was Ian able to catch up with her. Grabbing her by the leg, he fell to the ground, tangled in her arms and legs.

"Nae! Nae! Dinna kill me! Dinna kill me!" Her shrieks were pitiful, frightened cries. By her terror it was obvious that she really did think he meant her harm.

"Kill you? By Saint Michael, I swear that I will not, only cease your floundering, lass." Such a pathetic creature, he thought. Seemingly mad. Aye, daft she was. "I swear I will show you naught but kindness, for I owe you a debt of gratitude for the kindness you have shown my dear lassie."

"Ye willna hurt me?"

"Nae!" To prove his good intentions he loosened his hold on her. "There ye see. You have nothing to be afraid of."

Shakily, she got to her knees. "I . . . I thought for a moment that ye were the man I loved. I thought ye were *Morgan*. Ye look so like him."

"Morgan?" Ian had not taken heed of the name before, but now he did, in stunned amazement. "Morgan, did you say? I had a cousin of that name." A coincidence? Another named Morgan? Remembering her stark terror at the name Campbell, he doubted it. What then did this woman know of Duncan's son? His eyes blazed a question. "Who are you?"

"Just a woman who seeks peace and solitude," she answered evasively. Her eyes darted this way and that, nervously looking for a means of escape and finding none. "Please, let me be. I have not done harm to anyone."

"Not even Morgan?" He eyed her suspiciously.

"Least of all him. I loved him wi' all my heart. I died of grief when he was taken from me." Tears welled up in the woman's blue eyes. "I hae suffered much these years. Memories I seek to forget in my wandering."

"Ian, dinna torment her so. Canna ye not see she is enduring a broken heart, just as mine would hae been broken had I not found ye again." Brianna knelt down to the woman, putting her arm around the frail shoulders.

"She speaks of Morgan being taken away, Brianna. As if she knows something of his fate. He was of my blood. Therefore I have to know what happened the night he was killed, if she is privy to that information." He turned to the woman. "Are you? Do you know who struck him down so cruelly? He was foully murdered! Stabbed from behind. By whom? And why?"

"I dinna ken! I dinna ken!" Though she shouted it out, the look on her face nullified her words. She *did* know, but was terrified to speak of it.

"You do! Don't lie to me!"

"I dinna want to remember." Putting her hands to her ears she sought to block his questions out but Ian gently stripped her hands away.

"An ocean of blood has been shed because of that day. I have to know the truth." Ian's eyes compelled her to tell him. "Was it a *MacQuarie?*"

"MacQuarie?" She spoke the name softly, caressing it with her tongue. *"MacQuarie.* 'Tis a long time since I heard that name. It is dear to my ears." For just a moment she seemed to take refuge in a flight of fantasy, as if remembering long-ago days, a time when she had been happy. And all the while Brianna had a terrible premonition of what was to come. The woman's nose, the tilt of her chin looked alarmingly familiar. Just as she had been haunted by Robbie's visage in the back of her mind when first she'd laid eyes on him, so was she haunted now. Taking a deep breath, she called out softly, *"Mary!"* The woman reacted to the name, turning her head, tilting up her chin, but then looked away.

It had to be! There was no other explanation. Brianna's eyes met Ian's as they both came to the same conclusion. The pieces of a long-ago puzzle were slowly being fitted into place and this woman was the integral fragment. Brianna remembered all the stories she had heard about her aunt's disappearance so long ago and knew instinctively the identity of Staffa's mad woman. Blessed Saints! It was her father's sister.

"Are ye Mary of the clan MacQuarie?" Brianna asked gently, shaking the woman by the shoulders. "Please. If ye are then ye are my kin, for I too am of that clan. Are ye Mary, sister to Lachlan MacQuarie? Chief of the clan?"

This time the woman did not deny it. Slowly she nodded. "Aye!"

By all that was holy, Brianna thought, she had just been reunited with her aunt Mary. Mary MacQuarie was alive!

CHAPTER FORTY-FOUR

Mary's identity was confirmed by her own lips and by the stories she revealed to Brianna of earlier days when there had been less strife in the Highlands. Then she had been the young, lovely sister of the MacQuarie's clan chief, much sought after by all the young and handsome laddies. Her heart had been stolen, however, at first sight of Morgan Campbell's smile even though he was son of the laird who was boldly trying to usurp her brother's long-held lands.

"Ye look much like him," she sighed, staring unsmilingly at Ian. "Except around the eyes. His were more green than blue and they were deep set and often brooding. He was just a mite shorter and his hair was tightly curled. A bold, aggressive laddie." Crumpling up the end of her gown, she dabbed at the corners of her eyes. "I loved him more than words can ever say! There was a gentleness about him that he did not show to others. Only to me. We might hae been happy if not for *him.*" A dark cloud of anger passed before her eyes as she was reminded. "And all the while we thought *he* was our friend, that he would keep our secret. I can ne're forgive him for what he did."

"He? Who?"

As quickly as she had seemed to open up to them, she now withdrew into her silence again, rattling on and on about her childhood but making no more mention of Morgan or the man who had betrayed him. "At one time our father owned the whole of Mull as well as Ulva. Och, it was grand to hae no cares, just to while away the time in play like two wee brownies!" It was as if she could not dare let her mind go beyond the happy times. She seemingly chose now to forget those events that led up to that moment when she forever lost the man she loved. Brianna's woman's heart understood but Ian did not. He stubbornly insisted on pushing the matter, determined to find out the culprit.

"Tell me who killed my cousin!" Ian's gruff demanding voice at last got through the shroud that Mary had erected around herself. "Was it a *MacQuarie?*"

Brianna stiffened at his question. So, in spite of everything he had said, he still held a sliver of suspicion. Angrily, she frowned at him, holding her breath before Mary Mac-Quarie answered.

"Nae! No' a MacQuarie. It was a *Campbell!*"

"A Campbell?" There was a look of disbelief on Ian's face. "Nae. A mon would not kill one of his own."

"Hush, Ian, let her tell the story. Dinna goad her into saying what ye want just to soothe yer own family pride." Brianna patted Mary's hand. "Go on, hinny. How did yer Morgan die?"

"He was killed by a mon who was supposed to be his friend. And mine! But . . . I didn't know that he was but pretending. He didn't want me to be happy with my love because he wanted me for himself." She shuddered as she remembered. "He wanted to dishonor me. Wanted me to be his mistress, for he said no MacQuarie was good enough for a Campbell to wed. He told me after the deed was done. He said I was a bonnie lass and . . ."

It was as if a dam had burst, as if once beginning the story she could not cease. The entire story was revealed in a flood of tears. Mary revealed that she was in love with Morgan of clan Campbell just as he was with her, though a marriage between them had been hotly denied, by Lachlan and by

Duncan. The two young lovers had put their fate in the hands of he whom they had trusted, little realizing he was fanning the turmoil between the clans to get his own way. Traitorously, he had convinced Duncan Campbell to betroth his son to another clan's lassie. In desperation the two young lovers had planned to run away together, to set sail for Ireland and there live in exile.

In hushed tones Mary sobbed out the story, of how they had met clandestinely. It was a story of deep love and devotion, yet there was another story to tell as well, one of a more gruesome and malicious twist, of deceit, danger, and murder. Instead of finding her love waiting for her, she was met by their betrayer.

"When Morgan came, *he* revealed his evil nature to us both, and it was then . . ." She whimpered out the story as it passed vividly before her eyes. Brianna could visualize it too, could see the ominous shadow awaiting.

"You saw him kill Morgan?" Brianna asked, gently so as not to add to Mary's grief.

"Aye!" Teardrops ran in rivulets down her cheeks. She looked so desolate that Brianna's heart was squeezed with her pain. For a moment she considered putting an end to her aunt's agony by telling her to end the tale, but Mary continued talking without prompting.

Mary choked out the story of witnessing the man she loved struck down before her eyes. Her voice was shrill, her eyes wild as she said, "Morgan, hae care! He's drawn his sword! Och, dear God, he's stabbed him! The blood! It's everywhere. My darling's blood pouring over the ground. I must save him. Oh, God, my hands are covered with his blood."

Brianna put her arms around the distraught older woman, hugging her close. "It's all right, aunt Mary." No, it would never be all right. Had it been Ian so callously slain, she knew she would have been just as upset.

Mary pushed Brianna away with surprising strength, caught up now in the enfolding of her torturous nightmare.

Her eyes were wild. "He's coming after me! Staring with such a terrible grin splitting his face. I'll hae ye now, he says. He's pushing me down, holding the sword to my throat. But I canna! I willna!"

Mary was sobbing uncontrollably now but somehow Brianna sensed that what had been revealed today was healing to the poor woman's wounded soul. Softly she asked, "Did *he* harm you?"

"Aye! In the most brutal of ways. Tearing at my gown, battering my face, shaming me before my love as he lay dying." Mary closed her eyes that were awash with bitter tears. "As soon as I could I got to my feet and ran away. I . . . I brought help, but when I came back wi' a fisherman my Morgan was gone. God had taken him."

The shock of what had happened at first took away Mary's memory, and she had wandered about for a very long time. Then she had remembered bits and snatches of that terrible night, fearing the man who had done the deed, the man who had killed Morgan out of spiteful jealousy.

"My fault! I shouldna hae loved him so desperately. I shouldna hae teased him so to take me away wi' him. If I hadna he might still be alive." Mary closed her eyes, hugging herself as she rocked to and fro.

"Who was it? Who killed Morgan and treated you in such a despicable manner? Tell me I say!" Ian trembled his rage, his hands clenching and unclenching as he tried to maintain control of his temper. "Who?"

"His . . . his name was . . . was *Perth!*"

"Perth?" Ian and Brianna echoed the name at the same time. Perth, the treacherous cur who had been Brianna's tormentor in the Campbell hall.

"Perth killed Morgan and blamed the deed on Duncan's enemies. The MacQuaries. And we all believed him." Ian was incensed. "I should kill him for what he has done!"

Brianna sighed wearily. "It wouldna bring back the dead. It would just stain yer hands wi' blood. But if we ever get off this isle we'll see him brought to justice at one of the *moothills*. It was there, in a level circle surrounded by higher ground, that the brieve and his council held their meetings to administer justice. "Perth!" Brianna spat the name.

Ian spent his hatred in a sputter of cursing, then suddenly ceased his ranting as he became fully aware of the poor, pathetic woman who had herself been gravely wronged. "Why did ye not come home to yer kin?" he asked, bending down to lay a hand on the sobbing woman's head. "Yer clan?"

"Lachlan would no' hae taken me back. He said as much. Told me that if I disobeyed him I was no longer a member of the clan." Her tortured soul was in her eyes. "And I had been shamed. I couldna bear even thinking about it. I was no' myself. Immersed in my grief as I was, I wanted to be alone."

"But you should have named Morgan's killer and sought revenge. Men died who were blameless of the deed."

"I didna ken what Perth had said. All I knew was that I had no place to go and so I roamed the land. Perhaps I was trying to run away from what had happened in such a way."

Brianna's mind raced on, fitting together the pieces. So that was what had started all the bloodshed. A mistake! It had all been a ghastly misunderstanding. The oafish ogre Perth had maliciously murdered Morgan out of jealousy of Mary MacQuarie's love for him, then he had viciously raped her. Hatred seethed inside her for the man and the deeds he had perpetrated. Oh, how she wished she were standing before him right now. Her mind was swirling with the accusations she would hurl at him. And Duncan, how smug he had been in his hatred. What would he say when she and Ian told him the truth? Would he even believe them? Would Perth be able to lie himself out of his guilt?

"Ian."

He didn't seem to hear her, he was in a world of his own thoughts. "Dear God," Ian whispered. "It's all clear to me now. Morgan crying 'MacQuarie' was not naming his killer, but calling out to the woman he loved. He had been mumbling 'Mary.' Such a tragic tale. All the years of feuding, of hatred and killing have all been for naught. Perth! Perth was the culprit."

"But will Duncan believe us?" Brianna asked, taking his hand so that he could not ignore her.

"Nae. He is a stubborn old mon. He won't believe because he prefers to believe it was the MacQuaries. He will not want to be proven wrong. It will be too much for his conscience to bear."

Saddest of all was that even if he did believe, the truth wouldn't be able to bring back those who had died. MacQuaries had been killed. Campbells. The feud had been ignited and flamed. Nothing could change that, but perhaps some good could be built amidst its ashes.

"But if we could wrest a confession from Perth's own mouth . . ."

"Trick him?" Brianna's thoughts were merging with Ian's. Mary MacQuarie was the answer. But what would it do to the woman to put her face to face with the man who had so abused her? Was she strong enough?

"Aunt Mary?"

"Nae! I want no part of him. Ye canna ask . . ."

"But if this is not put to right there will be many others who will die if they have not already." Brianna trembled as she realized that she did not know her father's and newfound brother's fate. Were they already victims of this senseless feud? "Please . . ."

"I . . . I will try to be brave." Though her eyes held fear there was also hope within the deep blue depths. It seemed the revelation of all that had happened had turned Mary's mind to more lucid reasoning. "I will go. In memory of my own shattered love I will do all that I can to see that yer love survives and flourishes." In a gesture which touched Brianna's heart, Mary took first Ian's hand then Brianna's and joined them together.

"And oh how happy Father will be to see ye, Mary. When we get off the isle."

"If we get off this isle." Ian looked toward the east where a storm was brewing.

"I've got a boat hidden away in the cave where only I can find it. We must leave now."

Brave another storm? Brianna felt a flash of fear. She had nearly been parted permanently from Ian by those treacherous waters. Did she want to chance them again? Looking out at the sea, she knew the answer immediately. Aye! It was the only answer to happiness and peace for all in the Highlands. Plucking up her courage, she smiled at Ian.

"Perhaps there can still be a wedding after all. Our wedding." That was what she wanted more than anything in the world.

CHAPTER FORTY-FIVE

A torrent of rain fell from the heavens, drenching the inhabitants of the small fishing boat that bounced along the waves on its course for Ulva. Brianna huddled with Mary beneath Ian's plaid, shivering yet welcoming the downpour. The rain had chased away the furious wind. The journey had not been entirely comfortable, but at least it had not been as hazardous as she had first supposed, nowhere near the terrible gale that she and Ian had suffered previously.

"Never will the shores of Ulva seem so dear to me, Ian," she called out, competing with the roar of the waves splashing against the side of the boat as Ian wielded the oars. "I never want to go to sea again!"

"It will be as welcome a sight as heaven, I would wager." He said a silent prayer as the tall stone towers came into view. Oh, that she would have a happy homecoming, that her father and brothers would be there to greet her. Though they had not had much time to discuss it, Ian knew that Brianna was apprehensive as to the state of the MacQuarie hall. What had the death toll been from their violent sojourn in Argyll? He could only hope that the MacDonalds had arrived in time to put an end to the fighting, or if not that, then at least to balance it out. As the tiny boat headed for the shore he knew they would soon find out.

Soaking wet, but thankful to have reached land alive, Brianna, Ian, and Mary trudged through the mud up the hill toward the castle. The great portcullis slowly clanked open, giving entrance to the wide cavernlike opening. It was at that moment that Mary appeared on the brink of losing control of her sanity again.

"Nae! I shouldna hae come here! Too many memories! Too many. And what if my brother canna forgive me?" Her eyes darted from side to side like a trapped animal and for a moment it appeared that she might well flee. Only Ian's hand on her arm kept her from vanishing.

"The truth has to be told and you are the only one who can tell it. Many lives have been lost, Mary, but you can end this senseless quarrel. You must!" Gently but firmly nudging her forward, Ian was insistent.

"Pray God that Father is alive!" It was the first time Brianna had voiced her fears aloud to Mary. Somehow knowing that her niece was just as fearful, Mary turned from the one being comforted into the one giving consolation. Squaring her shoulders, taking a deep breath, it was Mary who led the way to the hall. Stepping inside the doorway, they headed for the roaring fire in the hearth, shivering as they sought to dry off.

"What hae we here? Two drenched hens and one soaking wet rooster!" Glenna gave a shriek of welcoming as the threesome turned around and she saw Brianna standing there. "Brie! Brie! I hae been so worried!" In a flurry of hugs and kisses she greeted her sister. In a moment her gown too was soaking wet but she blissfully ignored that fact. "Father said ye had run off with Ian and . . ."

"Father! Then, he is here?" Brianna breathed a sigh of relief.

"Aye! Bloodied, bruised, and broken, but all in one piece. Furious though at the thought of what The Campbell tried to do and . . ."

"Robbie! Is he?"

"Our new-found brother made quite a name for himself.

He may look as gentle as a lamb, but he proved himself a lion. Father is very, very proud of him. And now that Father has his beloved son, who he has named tanist, I would hae ye know, he has told me that Alastair and I . . . but who?" Suddenly noticing Mary, Glenna eyed her with avid curiosity.

Taking Mary by the hand, Brianna made the introduction in a proud exclamation. "Glenna, this is our aunt Mary. Aunt Mary, this is my twin."

"Aunt Mary?" Glenna was stunned. "I thought that . . ."

"As did we all, but now she has returned to us." Leading Mary over to a chair, Brianna prodded her aunt into telling the tale, a revelation which stunned Glenna. "So ye see we MacQuaries hae been blamed for something we didna do. A frightful misunderstanding caused by a brutal act! Mary has come back to put all to right. As much as can be done anyway."

"Father must be told quickly, for he is in the process of planning another attack on the Campbell stronghold." With an assertiveness that Brianna had never before witnessed, Glenna strode from the hall and returned with a bandaged Lachlan in tow. "We hae a visitor, Father," she said.

"Visitor?" His vision centered on Brianna. "Daughter!" he exclaimed, his voice tight with emotion as he gripped her against him in a stifling bearhug embrace. "Och, Brie! Brie! Where hae ye been, lass? Where?" As his gaze lit on Ian he stiffened. Pushing Brianna aside, he muttered gruffly, "So, ye thought to bring her back to me. It took ye a long enough time. I will make the assumption that ye did no' harm her in any way, for if ye hae . . ."

"Dinna get yer beard in a blaze, Father," Brianna teased, tweaking the fiercesome clan chief on the nose as only she dared, then kissing his grizzled cheek. "Ian saved my life. Ye should be grateful to him. But that is another story, we willna be telling *just* yet. Nor am I the visitor Glenna was talking about. Father, I've brought Mary home."

"Mary?" He blinked his eyes in disbelief as all the blood

drained from his face. "Nae, it canna be. My sister is dead!" He drew back from the woman standing by the hearth as if she were a ghost. "Away. Away, I say. For the love of God, leave me be and return to your . . ."

"This is no ghostie. Father, it *is* Mary! She come back to us. Shame on ye if ye hae no warmer greeting."

"Mary . . ." Lachlan took a tentative step forward, searching the woman's face, recognizing the blue eyes, the well-defined chin, the familiar planes of the face that time had lightly lined but not changed. "Och, it is! Mary!" Lachlan entwined his arms around his sister, kissing her on both cheeks with an exuberance that told very enthusiastically how much he welcomed her. Tears that were rarely allowed to show now ran unchecked down his leathery face, dampening his beard. "Mary, saints be praised, I never thought to see ye again this side of heaven!"

"Lachlan! I thought ye would no' want to see me." Clutching her brother, Mary wept her relief and joy. It was a tender scene that even brought tears to Ian's eyes. One more time the tragic tale was revealed, amidst sobbing and sniffling, then Mary stepped back, expecting her brother's scorn. "I loved Morgan, Lachlan. I dinna apologize that I was going to Ireland wi' him. He was my world. My life. I couldna give him up. I thought . . . If ye canna understand, if ye want me to leave, I will. I am used to being alone."

"Alone? Lachlan MacQuarie's sister? Dinna talk foolishness, Mary. If there was any punishment to be meted out ye hae suffered enough. I willna seek to add to yer woe. All is forgotten. Seeing ye again has brought the sun." Gathering her in his arms again he mumbled, "Welcome back."

Brianna heaved a sigh of relief. Her heart leaped with joy now that Mary was safe amongst her own clan once again. Sensing that there was much for Mary to say to her brother, she nodded to Glenna and Ian to follow her. "Come, sister dear, ye must tell us what has been happening while I hae been gone. There is something different about ye, I see. Hae ye lost yer shyness and timidity?"

"Aye, at first I thought 'twas the witch's charm, but now I realize it was the potency of my love for Alastair." They laughed gaily, like two little girls as they shuffled to the end of the room, leaving Lachlan and his sister alone.

Mary was heartily welcomed back into the bosom of the clan but there was little time for celebrating. Indeed, once Lachlan's gladness at having his sister return had mellowed it was replaced by a deep and all-abiding rage. The MacQuaries had been greatly wronged, he thundered. They had been accused unjustly of something they had no hand in at all. Murder! A dastardly blow from behind that no MacQuarie would issue.

"If Duncan Campbell was not such a stubborn old goat this ne'er would hae happened!" Pulling his claymore from the wall, he was determined to attack the Campbell hall to avenge the MacQuarie honor. It was his sister who had been wronged, brutally raped by a Campbell. "Now, this mon ye call Perth will pay with his life for that deed."

"So, ye want to spill more blood, is that it? And ye talk of Duncan being a stubborn old goat. Aye, it seems to me it takes two! Butting yer two heads together wi' no thought to common sense!" Brianna met her father's angry gaze unflinchingly. A myriad of thoughts whirled through her brain. Were the MacQuaries and Campbells then doomed to an unending turmoil of warfare? If so, then she and Ian had no chance for finding happiness.

"Hold yer tongue, daughter. I will not take such disrespectful talk even from you. Ye are careless in yer chattering."

She challenged him with an unwavering stare. "Not as careless in my talk as ye are in what ye plan." Putting her hand on his shoulder, she cautioned him to reason. "Ye'll strike a blow, then the Campbells will retaliate, then it will be our turn, over and over again wi' no end. Is that what ye want for the clan? Constant fighting with ne'er an end in sight?"

Lachlan fumbled with the folds of his breacan. "And just

what do ye propose? That we let the Campbells push our faces in the mud just for the sake of peace? That we swallow our pride and let them accuse us unfairly while the man who did the foulest deed laughs behind our backs? Nae!"

"I propose that we play Perth at his own game, for he thinks himself to be a clever mon. But what if he is out-tricked?" Her eyes met Ian's and he knew at once just what she had in mind. "Ye thought Mary was a ghostie when first ye laid eyes on her, did ye not? Perhaps he will think the same, for Perth knows not that Mary has returned to us alive. If we can take him by surprise then is there not a possibility that by his own words he will be damned?" Brianna's lips curled up in a smile as she revealed her plan.

CHAPTER FORTY-SIX

Three mounted figures bent over their horses, nearly swooning with fatigue as they neared the gates of Dunstaffnage in the wee hours of the morning. It had been a hasty journey, one in which they had first braved the ocean once more, then hurried posthaste to Argyll on horses borrowed from the MacDonalds' stable. The rhythmic pounding of the horses' hooves met with the pulsing of their heartbeats for it was a dangerous scheme they were daring, one which pivoted on Perth and his reaction when he came face to face with the woman he had so greatly wronged.

"Are you all right, lassies?" Ian asked, casting a worried glance in Mary's direction. A great deal had been heaped upon her slim shoulders the last few days. So much so that he was apprehensive lest she crack under the strain, like a fragile eggshell.

"Aye, but anxious for this to be over." Mary looked a bit pale, though dressed as she was in a new gown and arasaid, her hair combed and braided, she was a comely sight. The only evidence of the passing years was the gray streaking her hair and the tiny lines around her eyes and mouth.

"Soon it will be. Let us pray that all will be well." Certainly, they slipped through the postern gate without any trouble, Ian remembering that the grate was up for a few moments at dawn to allow for supplies to be taken into the castle. "Come! I know a secret way to Duncan's chambers where we will not have to brave the guards."

Abandoning their horses, Brianna and Mary clung to the shadows as they followed Ian through the courtyard, past the main gate, and up the narrow winding stairs. All three silhouetted figures slipped inside the largest chamber, closing the door tightly behind them.

"Who's there? Who dares enter my room without knocking?" Duncan was still abed, nursing a wounded leg. At the sound of intrusion he slid from the bed and hobbled about the room, coming face to face with his nephew. "So my wayward heir has returned, has he? Well, ye will soon find yerself keeping the rats company." He made for the door but Ian blocked his way.

"I do not want to harm you, uncle, merely to make you listen to reason."

"Reason? Ye lifted yer sword against yer own. Fie, yer blood ties seem to be wi' our enemies not wi' me! I ne'er thought ye'd let yer lust for a woman's twat turn ye against yer own." He was so engrossed in his tirade that he had not noticed Brianna or Mary until they stepped out of the shadows. Seeing the two women, he flushed an angry red. "Who? Ah, so ye've brought *her* and another one back here."

"We've come on a mission of peace."

"Ha! Peace, ye tell me?" He eyed his sword but Ian quickly plucked it up, handing it to Brianna. "So, ye take my sting away."

"For the moment. To insure you don't do anything we will both regret." Brandishing his own sword, Ian pushed his uncle back down on the bed. "I don't want to harm you, but I will if it is the only way. In the meantime I insist that you listen." Ian nodded to Mary. "You have blamed the MacQuaries for Morgan's death all these years, but I have brought an eyewitness to the deed. Mary, come forward."

"Who?" Duncan squinted his eyes but did not recognize her.

"Mary of clan MacQuarie. Lachlan MacQuarie's sister."

"Impossible! She is dead. The MacQuarie chief has said so himself." Glowering as he did at Ian, Duncan reminded Brianna of her father's snarling dogs. "What foolishness? Hae ye gone daft?"

"Take a closer look. She *is* Mary MacQuarie. She has come to tell you the truth about your son. Go on, Mary."

As Duncan wrung his hands in agitated helplessness, Mary enfolded the story yet again, giving every detail, shuddering as she revealed seeing Morgan struck down. "Dear God, I will never forget the sight of him lying there. My love, my life. But it was no MacQuarie who wielded the brutal blow, but Perth!"

"Perth? Perth?" Duncan snarled his rage. "Ye are a liar! Perth has ever been faithful to me and done my every bidding. He had no reason to kill Morgan. Ye flatter yerself, lassie, to pretend that he would do such a deed for love of ye," Duncan blasted.

"Not for love but through evil intent of the basest nature. But if ye dinna believe me, then let Perth tell ye himself."

"By Saint Michael, I will. He'll soon put end to yer foul lying! And then I'll see ye get the beating ye deserve!" Crouching down, he made as if to pounce on the poor woman but Ian wrestled him back down upon the bed. "'Tis a MacQuarie ploy and nothing more."

"If I have to tie you up, I'll make you see reason, uncle." Ian's threats held sway, for Duncan stopped his fuming. "Now, all I ask of you is that you keep silent and hide with me behind the panel in the hall while Mary here and Perth have a reunion of sorts. I am taking the chance that Perth's surprise, his first words to her, will prove his guilt. Agreed?"

Duncan grunted. "Agreed!"

"And do I have your word as a Campbell that you will see this through without turning on me?"

"Ye do!"

The planned mummery was carefully staged. Mary was dressed in a gown of purest white with long flowing sleeves. A garland of white henbane adorned her head. To make her look pale and unearthly, her face was powdered with flour from the kitchen. Balancing on a ledge outside the window, she prepared for her entrance as Duncan summoned Perth to the hall. Perth was quick to answer, though confused to find himself all alone. With a snort of annoyance he looked around. It was in that moment that Mary floated into the room on a gust of wind.

"Perth! Perth!" she called out in a choked whisper.

"Who the devil?"

"Dinna ye recognize me? 'Tis I, Mary. I've come back."

At first he didn't recognize her, then as she came closer he gasped. "It *is* ye!" His one eye glittered in the firelight, a reminder of her mark on him. "Mary! So, ye hae returned to me." In three quick strides he stood before her, reaching out to see if she was an apparition or real. "Let me look upon yer face. Are ye still as lovely?"

Mary carefully eluded him. "Ye dinna understand," she whispered, "I hae not come in flesh, ye murdering swine, but in spirit."

"In spirit? Then ye are . . ."

She howled in eerie laughter. "A ghost. I've come to haunt ye for what was done. For yer taking Morgan away from me. Ye murdered him and for that ye canna be forgiven. Hae ye anything to say about yer accursed deed? Are ye not remorseful?"

"Remorseful? Nae. I profited well by his death. That whining puppy was ever in my way. Now, get ye gone."

"Puppy! Dinna talk so about my son." Duncan stepped from behind the panel, trembling with rage. The silence seemed to stretch into eternity as they stood frozen in a tableau. Unmoving. Unspeaking. Slowly, Duncan was thawed by the knowledge that what Ian had revealed, what Perth had said himself, was the truth. Perth had brutally murdered Morgan and then quickly added perjury to his sins. "So 'tis true."

"Nae! I didna ken what I was saying! That she-devil tricked me. I wasna the one who killed Morgan, ye know that well."

It was no use denying it. The expression of guilt on his face was as potent as any witness. Duncan was rabid in his thirst for revenge. Ordering Perth to be taken down to the dungeon, he had him tortured until he cried out the story in a haze of pain, confirming the truth. But though Brianna had been anxious for Duncan to realize his mistake, she could not help but feel sorry for him. He was a truly repentant man who bore the tragedy of what had happened on his face. It seemed that he had aged in just a short span of time. Gone was his energy, his strength. It was as if the only thing that had driven him on was his hatred for the MacQuaries. Now that he no longer had reason to hate them, he seemed like a shriveled up old man. In truth, he seemed more ghost than human, a fact that was very tragic. Despite what he had done, she wished him no pain.

Duncan sat staring into space as Mary begged him to let Brianna and Ian wed. "I loved yer son but Morgan is gone. Perhaps, however, the love I shared with him can live again through Ian and Brianna. There can be peace among the two clans. A new beginning."

Duncan spouted no defiance, did not argue, and in fact nodded his head. Much to Brianna's surprise he grudgingly agreed. Perhaps it was his way of atoning for what had been done, Brianna thought. But whatever the reason it did not matter. Looking into Ian's face, darkly handsome and mysterious in the flickering firelight, she thrilled with passion as she realized that they were going to truly belong to each other at last.

"Oh, Ian, how I love you," she whispered, but her tender words were drowned by the deafening cheers of acclaim which Aulay led. Cries which echoed through the hall as the other Campbells welcomed Ian back. Somehow, as Brianna looked about the room, she knew that she had found a home.

CHAPTER FORTY-SEVEN

The day dawned bright and clear with hardly a trace of a cloud in the sky. A good omen for a wedding. And what a wedding it was. Not one but *two* brides, dressed in matching wedding gowns of pale blue, covered at the neck and waist with white and blue striped arasaids, walked slowly and regally to the altar of the MacQuarie chapel, following along Aulay's flower-strewn path. And not one groom, but two eagerly awaited the breathtaking beauties, both laddies attired in their very best breacans, Ian's of green and blue weave, Alastair's of red and black. For one hushed moment Ian's eyes met Brianna's and he smiled, knowing there was not a clansman present at that moment who would not have taken his place or Alastair's.

"You are beautiful," he breathed, bending to take her hand. Alastair was likewise softly praising Glenna's loveliness. Together, all four faced the priest who began his intonation of Latin words in a deep voice.

As the Mass progressed, Brianna felt peace and love in her heart, though a slight streak of mischief made her wonder what Alastair and Ian would do if she teasingly told them they had each married the wrong twin. It was a thought that made her smile as she repeated her vows, though in reality she would have no husband except her Campbell. The very thought of belonging to him misted her eyes with happy tears that were mirrored by Glenna's as she gazed in Alastair's direction.

Brianna felt the gold ring touch first one finger, then another, to rest on the third finger of her right hand, an unending symbol of eternity. She would belong to Ian forever, as well as to his clan. And by this marriage the decades of bloodshed between the rival families would be over. The clans too were bound by the marriage, though her father had insisted on restitution for all that the MacQuaries had suffered. The brieve had imposed a fine on Duncan, a *kimbot* was paid in cattle. Though it had taken a time for old wounds to heal, it was good to see her father and Duncan standing side by side with Robbie in between. Both seemingly approved of the ceremony that once and for all put end to the feud. As Brianna sank to her knees to receive the wine from the priest's brimming chalice, she could have even sworn the Campbell chief's mouth pulled up in a smile.

Then it was over, and before all assembled, Ian and Alastair kissed their brides. Brianna slid her arms around her husband's broad shoulders, relishing the ritual kiss, thrilling with passion to know that this handsome, daring man belonged to her at last.

"Come, my wife," he whispered, caressing her in such heated embrace before all assembled that she blushed. "It is time we tasted of each other again." He grinned as his eyes lit on Glenna and her bard. "All has turned out exactly as you planned. Are you sure you aren't a kelpie?"

"And if I am?" Her words were spoken into the firmness of his lips as he kissed her fervently, hungrily, with all the longing in his soul.

The wedding feast was a lively affair with ale by the barrel and an array of delicacies. Afterward, there was dancing as a whirling, high-stepping, jubilant clan enthusiastically gave thanks for the promise of peace. Aulay tumbled, juggled, and stood on his head to the delight of the crowd. Then, amidst jovial laughter and shouted congratulations, the newly wedded couples were escorted up the stairs to their nuptial beds, Ian and Brianna to one chamber, Glenna and Alastair to another.

"Seems this has been done before," Ian teased as Mary helped Brianna out of her gown and Robbie assisted him in flinging off his breacon. "Only this time you belong to me." There was such a fierce possessiveness in his tone that her breath caught in her throat.

Though nearly thirty pairs of eyes watched as they took their places in the large feather bed, they barely noticed, nor did they hear the drone of the priest as he gave the blessing to their conjugal union. They had eyes only for each other. And then at last they were alone.

"Brie! Brie! My lovely, lovely wife." Her hair, like a shimmering waterfall of flame, spilled onto his chest, and he entwined his fingers in the fiery strands as he kissed her long and hard, savoring the soft sweetness of her mouth. "I love you!" he murmured against her lips.

"Show me!" Her eyes were boldly challenging. "Though perhaps making love in a feather bed will not be as daring as our curach."

Ian's intense gaze clung to her as he beheld her naked beauty, and he ran his hand lovingly over the softness of her shoulder, down to the peaks of her full breasts. This was his bride, his mate forever and ever. With a quick, indrawn breath he drew her to his chest, molding his mouth to hers again in a sweetly scorching kiss. His hands stroked her body, gently igniting the searing flame she always felt at his touch.

A blazing fire consumed them both as their bodies met and caressed. With hands and lips and words they gave full vent to their love. Ian caught her in his arms and pulled her down, rolling with her until her slender form was beneath his. They were entwined in love, in flesh, in heart, and with their very souls. As he entered her softness she clung to him, lips parted, eyes closed as they reached a shattering culmination, much like the crashing of the waves against Staffa.

A long time later, Brianna pressed her head to his chest, contentedly knowing that there would be another time like this, and another, and another. "I love ye, Ian. Oh, I do! I only hope that Glenna is as blissfully happy right now as I am. If I hae my way there will soon be a son of yer seed."

Reverently, he bent down and kissed her stomach where his child might well have already been created from their love. "Or daughter," he breathed. "Or twins!"

"Och!" Brianna threw up her hands in mock horror. "I wouldna want to suffer what my father has endured. It would seem one child at a time would be quite enough." She smiled dreamily. "Though then there would be one for yer uncle and one for the MacQuarie chief. Ye can well imagine Father's pride at that." Touching his lips, she merged her smile with his. They lay in each other's arms, sated and happy, knowing that tomorrow awaited them with hope and the promise of deep, eternal love.

Author's Postscript

All "actors" in this work are fictitious, with the exception of historical personages mentioned. The clan leaders—Lachlan and Duncan—are blendings of the characteristics of certain Scottish Highland clan chiefs of the time period. The name *Lachlan* figures prominently in MacQuarie history; thus, I have taken that name for Brianna's father.

The clans MacQuarie and Campbell are very real and figured prominently in the history of Alba. The battle of Bannockburn occurred in 1314 and was a pivotal date in Scotland's history. The Campbells of Argyll were rewarded for their part in aiding Robert the Bruce by receipt of grants of land and guardianship of several castles, confiscated by the Scottish crown from other clans, including Dunstaffnage Castle. The clan MacQuarie is descended from the line of kings of Alba and though a small clan, held a place of honor as an ancient tribe in the councils of the Lords of the Isles. Thus conflict between the Campbells and MacQuaries, which I depict in this work, was very real.

For those wishing to know more about the Scottish Highlands or its clans, I list the following books which were most helpful to me:

FLAME ACROSS THE HIGHLANDS

Scottish Clans and Tartans, The Fabric of Scotland, Lorna Blackie
Scottish Clans and Tartans, Ian Grimble
Highland Clans and Tartans, R. W. Munro
A History of Scotland, J. D. Mackie
Scottish Lore and Folklore, Ronald MacDonald Douglas

About the Clans

For those who would like to know more about the two clans in *Flame Across the Highlands:*

MacQuarie of Ulva

Clan motto is *An t'Arm breac dearg,* which means "the red-tartaned army." The badge is a bent, mailed arm rising out of a crown and holding a dagger.

The clan is of ancient royal descent, traced by the *seanachies,* or Celtic genealogists to one of the branches of the great clan Alpin. The name derives from a Gaelic term of description *Guiaire,* meaning "noble." According to tradition, Guiaire was the second son of Gregor, son of Alpin, the famous king of Scots who fell in battle in 837. The MacQuarie chiefs had their seat in Ulva, an island off of Mull.

Most of the family papers were destroyed in a fire in 1688 thus early records are sparse. It is known that Cormac Mor, chief of the MacQuaries, aided Alexander II in his invasion of the western Highlands to free them of Norse rule. The first chief who survives in historical records is Iain of Ulva, who witnessed a charter of the Lord of the Isles in 1463 and died about ten years later. After the forfeiture of the Lords of the Isles, the clan acquired independence. They followed the MacLeans of Duart and supported a MacDonald in his effort to restore the Lordship of the Isles. This involved them in a disaster from which the MacQuaries never recovered, namely the loss of their chief and most of his clansmen at the battle of Inverkeithing in 1651.

There was still a chief on Ulva when Dr. Johnson and James Boswell visited Lachlan MacQuarie in 1773. He owned the island of Staffa with its famous Fingal's cave. The last known chief of clan MacQuarie, also a Lachlan, died in 1818.

From their clan territory the MacQuaries have spread themselves throughout the world, gaining distinction out of proportion to their numbers. Major-General Lachlan MacQuarie was Governor of New South Wales during the convict period, and under his government the colony prospered. He is recognized as one of Australia's founding fathers. He laid out the city of Sydney and returned home in 1821, leaving his name in commemoration in MacQuarie Island and other place names. This General MacQuarie repurchased much of the ancient patrimonial property in Scotland which had been sold to pay another Lachlan MacQuarie's creditors (the sixteenth and last chief in regular succession), and if not accepted as chief, was assuredly the first *ceanntigh* or cadet. He married Miss Baillie of Jarviswood; and his only son, Lachlan, by his second wife, daughter of Sir John Campbell of Airds, died without issue.

Campbell, Duke of Argyll

Clan motto is *Ne obliviscaris,* which means "forget not." The badge is a boar's head.

Known as the race of Diarmaid, and spoken of as being descendants of that handsome Ossianic hero with whom the wife of Fingal fell in love, the clan Campbell was for centuries a most powerful influence in Argyll and west Scotland. The clan was prominent in Dalriada, the earliest Scottish kingdom.

Sir Colin of Lochow, the progenitor of the Campbells of

Argyll, was knighted in 1280, and from him the chiefs of Argyll received the designation, MacCailean Mor, retained by the Dukes of Argyll till the present day. The support which Sir Colin Campbell and his two sons gave to Robert the Bruce was rewarded by a marriage with the King's sister, and the Campbells began their rise to supremacy in the Highlands. They assisted in the downfall of the Bruce's opponents. Five centuries later, the ninth Duke of Argyll wed Princess Louise, Queen Victoria's daughter.

The town of Inverary was founded in 1474 and has been the clan's headquarters ever since. From there, the rise to power of the Campbells continued. They helped the Crown destroy the mighty Lord of the Isles, took over MacDonald lands in Knapdale and Kintyre, then swallowed up the vast MacLean territories in Morvern and the Islands of Mull, Tiree and Coll. Their sixteenth-century persecution of other Highland clans like the MacGregors and the Donalds gave them a reputation for being unscrupulous. The seventh Earl (1576–1638) was involved with the Campbells of Cawdor in overthrowing the MacDonalds of Islay but ended his days in exile. In the seventeenth century the Campbells, however, picked the wrong side in the period's civil wars which resulted in the execution of two of their lords for treason.

The Campbells have helped safeguard Scotland's heritage. In 1899 the eighth Duke of Argyll gave the Abbey of Iona, the island off Mull and Ulva from which Saint Columba spread Christianity, to the nation. Its historic sites were put in the care of trustees and the abbey there has been completely restored. The clan is now said to have twelve and a half million worldwide. The present twelfth Duke of Argyll is also Hereditary Master of the Queen's Household in Scotland, Keeper of the Great Seal of Scotland, Keeper of Dunoon, Carrick, Dunstaffnage and Tarbert Castles, and Admiral of the Western Isles.